UNSPEAKABLE

Some secrets will haunt you.

D1484501

TONY
MARTURANO

a Different Angle

Published in the United Kingdom and the rest of the world by a
Different Angle 2015

Cambridge, UK

A catalogue record for this book is available from the
British Library

ISBN - 978-0-9540137-4-5

Printed and bound in the USA

Fear not the dark, but what it holds.

PROLOGUE

I blow on my cold fingers, but the mist of my breath does nothing to melt the numbness from them.

Ben, wrapped in his favourite woollen hat and scarf, seems oblivious to the winter wonderland that surrounds us; it has smothered the forest, painted the house and frozen the murky green waters of the lake.

It's our thirteenth birthday. One of the best things about celebrating here, at father's country home, is the skating. We can spend hours here, gliding on the ice and watching the trees blur by.

Ben calls to me from up ahead as he performs yet another pirouette on the ice. I don't know why he bothers showing off; we both know he gets more practise than me.

"Come on!" He shouts, waving and grinning me to him with a red-gloved hand.

I sigh and launch myself in his direction, squinting into the glare of the early morning sun and trying my best not to wobble as I glide up alongside him.

He clutches on to my arm to steady me and then asks with a grin, "What kept you so long?"

I just sniff and smile, petulantly.

"You okay?" He asks.

"I'm all right. I just can't feel my nose, that's all."

"Come on, let's go for a spin," he says, excitedly, as he offers me his hand.

I hesitate, knowing that if I accept his help I'll be condemning myself to endless mocking for the rest of the day.

"Come on!" He prompts.

I reluctantly accept the offer and extend my right hand to him, secretly enjoying the feel of his warm glove around my frozen fingers.

"Hold on," he warns.

Then, we're picking up speed, gliding across the ice to the far side of the lake.

The wind chill nips at my nose and stings my eyes as I allow myself to be transported by his momentum, but I find it increasingly difficult to keep up.

I start to wobble as the strain on my arm intensifies.

"Ben…"

…I try to hold on…

"Ben!"

I stumble…

"BEN!"

Then, I'm falling. My arms flail, clumsily, as I try to steady myself, but I can't, gravity is heavy on my body and it eventually brings me down onto my backside with a loud thump.

The shock of the impact drills through me like a jackhammer and I'm momentarily paralysed by it. My rear hurts although it's partially numbed by the freezing wet patch that is seeping through the denim of my jeans.

Up ahead, Ben skids gracefully to a halt.

He is laughing!

I want to swear at him. But, the more I see how stupid I must look, sat here on the ice, the more I manage to share his amusement. Before long, I'm laughing with him.

Our laughter echoes around the lake, bouncing off the surrounding forest, the house, and I wonder if our parents are awake yet.

Then, I hear it.

No, I don't hear it but I sense it, travelling through the ice and my body like an electrical current. I look down and around me but see nothing, I can only feel it; sharp sonar tugs pull at my being.

Something is wrong.

I hear a loud splitting sound.

The ice is cracking!

My twin brother is doubled over in fits of laughter.

I yell at him, "Ben!"

He looks up, but it's too late; I watch as his expression changes from amused laughter to incredulous horror as the ice protests and crackles before suddenly giving way beneath his feet.

He disappears right in front of me.

"NO!" I shout, instinctively.

I'm paralysed. My limbs are frozen but not from the cold, from the terror of what I just witnessed.

Did that just happen? Did my twin brother just fall through the ice?

Yes! Get over there! GO! NOW!

I scramble to my feet but slip.

I try again.

"Ben!"

I can hear his icy gargled screams, but I can't see his face, just red-gloved hands waving at me from the hole in the ice.

"I'm coming, Ben! I'm coming!" I scream through gritted teeth as the cold air bites into my vocal cords.

I move into a kneeling position and then, carefully and as quickly as I can, I scramble to my feet.

My heart pounds, the adrenaline pumps, and a cold sweat breaks out on my forehead.

Please God, please let him be okay until I get there, please.

I lunge forward, but the movement is too sudden and I find myself swaying back and forth, side to side, waving my hands to steady myself, but I can't!

"NO!" I cry as I topple forward and the ice reaches up to smash me in the chin.

The pain shoots through me like a bullet, my vision blurs and I can taste blood. I don't know where it's coming from and I don't care.

"BEN!" I gargle through the coppery taste as the icicles of tears leak from my eyes. "BEN!"

I'm fewer than five feet away and determined to get to him, but my feet keep slipping and sliding on the glassy surface.

I'm crying, trembling with angry exasperation as I drag myself across the ice. I dig with and snap fingernails as I inch my way painfully forward, smearing a trail of blood behind me.

Seconds seem like hours, but I eventually reach the well to see Ben's pallid face; it's a blurry mask of horror beneath the surface.

I plunge both hands into the freeze.

"GRAB MY HANDS!" I scream in a hoarse voice, "GRAB

THEM!"

I yearn to feel my fingers connect with any part of my brother's body, but the inches between us are growing. Ben's outstretched hands sink deeper and deeper as his facial expression changes from horror to bewilderment.

"NO! BEN NO! GRAB MY HANDS! GRAB THEM!"

But it's too late.

His boyish face slowly dissolves into a white blur until all that remains are his eyes, his beautiful blue eyes that are now lifelessly watching me from the watery gloom.

"NOOOOOOO!"

1 THE AWAKENING

Rupert Harrison awoke from his nightmare with a start, and was instantly comforted by the warm rays of the early morning sun. It streamed into the lavishly furnished bedroom, through large picture windows, and bathed everything in a soothing amber glow.

"Oh God," he whispered through shallow breaths, "Oh God."

"Are you okay?"

He looked up to see Ashley standing in the bathroom doorway. Her red hair, still shower wet, cascaded over her milky white shoulders.

Dressed in her underwear, she was looking down at him with a frown of concern.

Rupert scanned her slender figure. It was as if he were seeing it for the first time; her painted toenails, her long, athletic legs, her flat stomach and, most deliciously, the way she filled her bra. He found comfort in her vision, and sighed deeply, running his hand through his hair, as if the act would shrug off the dregs of his nightmare.

'I think so," he croaked, with a dry throat.

'You were dreaming again," Ashley said, handing him a bottle of water as she sat on the bed, beside him.

Rupert gratefully accepted the drink, broke the seal, and drank with great thirst.

"Same dream?" She asked, touching his face, like a worried mother would her fevered child.

'Yes,' he answered, enjoying her touch and breathing in her perfume. She smelt good and, despite his recent ordeal, he found himself instantly aroused.

He pulled her close.

"Are you sure you want to do this?"

"Oh absolutely," he responded, breathing deeply, enjoying the intoxicating scent of her shampoo.

"I mean go back to Kenning Hall," she said, making a space between them. "You've started having these nightmares ever since you decided to go back there to celebrate your birthday."

"Well, I guess it's to be expected, don't you?"

"Of course, but the fact that it's having this effect on you means that what happened there is still on your mind."

"It was my home, Ashley. It's bound to be on my mind. It's been almost two decades. It's time to go back."

"I appreciate that. But I think you may find it helpful to talk this through with Peter, first."

"No," he replied, sharply. Then, taking her hand, added, 'I know what I'd find helpful." He said, mischievously.

"Oh no you don't," she said, putting both her hands on his chest. "I've just showered, and already have my makeup on."

"So?" he asked, building a road of kisses up her arm, to her neck.

She turned her face, and allowed him to kiss it gently. Then whispered, seductively, "Wasn't last night enough for you, big boy?"

"You know I can't get enough of you."

He wanted to make love to her. He needed her closeness right now.

"Give me one good reason why I should."

He paused his kissing. Pondered over the question for a few seconds, then said, "Well, I could cite any number of reasons, but the fact that you love me has got to trump them all."

"Oh, yes, that is a compelling reason," she said with a wry smile, sliding her hand down his chest, under the sheet and between his legs. She smiled satisfactorily, when she found he was indeed ready for her.

He moaned with pleasure, as he felt her hand around him, and focused his kissing attentions on her cleavage.

"You like that?" She whispered, seductively.

"Yes," he breathed.

"Good. Because you won't be getting much of it while we're away," she said, pulling her hand out from under the sheets, and standing up.

"What?" He wailed in bewilderment, as he watched her gorgeous legs disappear inside a pair of jeans. "What did I do?"

"You know what you did," she said, in mock discontent.

He sat up. "Um, no, I can't say I do."

Ashley admired his lean, hair-speckled torso.

At the age of thirty-two, Rupert maintained the body of a twenty-year-old and, despite his strong stubble clad jaw, his wavy blonde hair gave him irresistible boyish looks.

Nevertheless, she resisted the urge to jump into bed with him, and pulled on a white T-shirt, smothering her breasts, much to his disappointment.

"You just had to invite her, didn't you?"

"Oh, not that again," he groaned. "Ash, Elisabeth is my cousin. We've been close since we were kids. What was I supposed to do?"

"Oh I don't know," she replied flippantly, as she buttoned up a denim shirt. "Maybe show a bit of loyalty."

"Come off it, Ash. You know I'm loyal."

"Not when it comes to her, you're not."

"Stop being silly. You know I love you. But I love her too. She's all that is left of my close family. She's practically my sister."

Ashley said nothing, and he found it difficult to establish whether she was genuinely upset or just trying to make a point.

In one move, he threw back the covers, and walked over to her. "I'm sorry," he said, slipping his arms around her waist. "You know the last thing I want to do is upset you, but you know how close we are. I can't help it if you two don't get along. You know there's nothing in the world that would please me more."

His ever-effective reasoning tone worked its magic; she disarmed.

Ashley shook her head. "No, I'm the one who should apologise. It's your birthday. Of course, your cousin should be there. I'm sorry. I'm just being selfish. It's just, you know how she disapproves of me, of us! She always has a way of making me feel like some wretched character out of a Jane Austen novel, like I don't belong. I just have no idea how the hell I'm going to get through a whole weekend with her."

"With a lot of saintly patience and murderous restraint," he offered, with an encouraging smile. Then, pulling a puppy face, he looked into her deep blue eyes. "Come on, baby.

After all, it is my birthday."

"Not yet it isn't," she said, petulantly, with a faint smile.

"No, but it will be soon," he grinned.

Sulkily, she said, "Sometimes, I wish I never applied for that job."

"No, you don't. Because then you would never have met me."

"Exactly."

"And you would have never experienced good sex," he winked.

She laughed, "That's modest."

"Yet true."

"But subjective."

They smiled, as they held each other.

"Come on, Ash. It will be okay, I promise," he said with a beaming smile and a jerk of the head, as if to say, *come with me, all will be well.*

She looked into his dark brown eyes. She loved this man very much. The problem was, he also happened to be her boss.

And it was this particular detail that his cousin, Elisabeth, found most unpalatable. In her mind, it was beneath Rupert to be seen fraternising with the staff.

No matter how hard she had worked to earn the position of Senior Fiction Editor at his publishing house, people would always think she had screwed her way to the top, but that simply wasn't true. But who would believe that? Certainly not his precious cousin.

"Hello? Where have you disappeared to?" he asked.

She looked down between his legs, shrugged and smiled, "Nowhere. Just didn't realise how cold it was in here."

With that, she walked off into the bathroom, to finish getting ready, leaving her handsome boyfriend standing there, naked.

"Yeah, funny. Very funny," he said.

2 THE ARRIVAL

It was a spectacularly sunny October day. The air was autumn fresh and the countryside a vibrant canvas of greens, auburn and reds.

They had spent most of the two-hour journey, southwest from the city, competing in car-karaoke; who could hold the best notes, and make the best impersonation of well-known artists and their songs. Ashley definitely had the edge although Rupert refused to concede.

It was 2:01 pm when the Lexus reached the heart of the New Forest.

Much to Ashley's delight, they had passed a whole Noah's Arc of living creatures; horses, deer, foxes and even an owl.

Also of interest was the smattering of gated driveways, discreetly set back from the road. They led through trees to some of the most impressive mansions Ashley had ever seen.

It wasn't lost on her that owning a home here was a privilege exclusive to the seriously rich and wealthy.

Rupert steered the Lexus off the main road and onto the gravel track, where they passed a sign that read, *'Kenning Hall - Private Property'*.

Kenning Hall was bought in the '30s by Henry Harrison, Rupert's grandfather. It was one of his early acquisitions after founding the Harrison Printing Company that spawned the Harrison Publishing empire; a multimillion pound publishing house that Rupert inherited, along with the rest of his father's estate.

The ten bedroom mansion, a country home to the Harrisons for many years, was set a mile back from the main road, amidst trees. The only access was via the gravel drive they were travelling on, which was guarded by imposing oak trees.

Neither Rupert nor any other member of his family had returned to Kenning Hall since the tragic event of his thirteenth birthday, yet nor could they bring themselves to sell the place. Instead, Rupert appointed an administrator to care for and maintain the property, until he was ready to go back.

That day had come.

Ashley gasped with all the magical wonder of a child as they rocked down the road, through pools of filtered sunlight.

Rupert looked across, and smiled.

He loved this about her. She appreciated the simpler things in life and, therefore, was often happy. Unlike his ex-wife, who not only possessed a voracious appetite for the expensive, but appeared, nonetheless, to be in a perpetual state of discontent.

"How long now, Rupert?" Ashley asked, excitedly.

"Well," he said, peering through the windscreen, "you should be able to see it any time…."

"…there it is!" she squealed, pointing at a blur of white through the foliage of the trees, and promptly buzzed down her window, flooding the car with the fresh scent of the forest.

"Yes, that looks like it," he agreed, trying hard to adopt Ashley's excitement, but finding it extremely difficult.

It felt as if a cement ball had suddenly settled in the pit of his stomach.

When they weren't by the lake, Rupert and his fraternal twin would escape into the woods that shrouded Kenning Hall. Tree climbing, insect hunting, den creating, and hide and seeking were just some of the activities the brothers shared during their stay here.

Thus, the musky smell of moss, tree bark and leaves was imprinted onto Rupert's memories, and it never failed to dredge them from the ocean bed of history to the surface of his mind.

The car emerged from the gloom of the trees, into the sunlit circular forecourt of the mansion, and pulled up alongside a giant fountain.

Inside, stood a pair of gargoyles, ominously overlooking the machine, as if it were an intruder.

Ashley gazed up, at the twin stone weather worn sculptures of the fountain. They bore down on her with cracked eyes and mouths open in a silent screech, that she imagined once spurted water. The floor of the stone basin was dry and covered with twigs, dead leaves and dirt.

"The source was a natural well, but it dried up years ago," Rupert offered, as he surveyed the rest of the area with his eyes.

The gravelled forecourt was immaculate, the hedging trimmed, and the ivy, that smothered the stonework of the building, kept in check.

Nothing had changed, yet Rupert felt like a stranger. After all these years, the house, that had been his family's favourite holiday retreat, seemed alien to him.

"Come on, let's explore!" Ashley said, excitedly, unintentionally reminiscent of Rupert's young self.

She didn't notice his reluctant smile, for she had already left the car.

Rupert took a deep breath, slowly pulled on the door handle, and stepped out of the car into a chilling breeze, that brought with it that familiar scent, and a whole flurry of memories. The last time he had stepped out of a car and onto this forecourt, Ben had been with him.

"Scary, aren't they?" Ashley said, interrupting his thoughts and reaching up to caress one of the statues.

"You'll get used to them, after a while," Rupert said.

He looked up at the house, to an arched window that overlooked the fountain. He and his brother had spent many hours standing on the landing and scaring each other, with stories of how these massive creatures took flight in the dead of night, and hunted humans.

"Can we go inside?" Ashley asked.

"Of course."

They climbed the five stone steps leading to the large front door, which was a masterpiece of wooden artistry; ornate swirling patterns carved into dark wood and bound by black bars of steel. The head of a lion hung heavily against it, as a door knocker.

Rupert unlocked the door and, not for the first time today, Ashley gasped, "Oh my…" This was all new to her. It was like the set of a period drama.

Directly ahead, was a large glass coffee table, with ornate golden legs. It was flanked by two leather upholstered armchairs, crowned by a low-hanging chandelier, and overlooked by a large balcony, reached by a gleaming wooden staircases. To their left, a doorway led into the study, to their right, a heavy oak door opened to the lounge.

The smell of wood polish and lavender hung heavily in the air, as their footsteps echoed on the marble floor.

Rupert's heart was thumping. Nothing had changed.

Clarence, the administrator, had taken his brief literally, and ensured the building's meticulous preservation, as was. So much so, that Rupert half expected his mother to call to him, from the kitchen.

"Rupert?"

A small pressure on his shoulder brought Ashley's blue eyes and button nose into focus.

"Are you okay?" She asked, tenderly.

He smiled, and nodded.

She took his hand, "Come on; show me what our bedroom looks like."

"Now you're talking," he said, breaking into a grin.

They climbed the stairs, passing gold-framed paintings of the countryside and portraits of the men and women of the Harrison dynasty.

The first floor was a long corridor of doors. The walls were made of mahogany, adorned by more canvases. Overhead, hung a row of small gold-plated chandeliers. They ran the length of the corridor, to a small window that did its best to banish the gloom.

Ashley paused to take everything in, and, as she did so, she unconsciously leant on the balustrade, overlooking the entrance hall, and suddenly jumped back, when she felt it give slightly.

Rupert smiled, fondly, "That banister has been wobbly since Ben shoved me up against it."

Ashley pulled a face.

"Boys being boys," Rupert said. "Don't worry. It's safe, but I probably should ask Clarence to have it seen to."

Ashley scanned the row of doors that disappeared into shadows. "Which one's ours?" she asked.

"This one here," Rupert said, pointing to the door in front of them. "Would you like to do the honours?"

Ashley's face lit up with excitement.

She placed her hand on the door handle, and lingered there for a few seconds, as she imagined all kinds of romantic images of the room beyond.

That's when she noticed it.

The painting hung to the right of the door. It was similar to the others, in that it was framed in elaborate gold, but here the similarity ended. Even to Ashley's untrained eye, the different brush strokes were obvious, the colours more vibrant and modern.

The painting was of a dark green lake, as seen through balcony doors. In the foreground, a winding footpath led to a patio of stone and shrubbery. On the still lake, sailed a group of ducks, beyond them, a wall of trees shared their reflection with a cloudless blue sky. On the footpath, a young man, with short blonde hair, was laughing and waving at the painter. Behind him, his doppelganger, sat, with his back to the world.

Ashley was mesmerised; the canvass was magical.

"My mother's," Rupert said.

"Really? It's beautiful," Ashley replied, breathlessly.

"Yes, one of her best ones."

"One of?"

"Yes, my mother often painted during the summer holidays. It relaxed her."

"She was very talented," Ashley said, unable to take her eyes off the scene. "So, who's this cute little thing waving at her?"

"That would be me," Rupert said, with a smile and a tinge of embarrassment.

"You look adorable, and your hair! I take it this other guy is Ben," Ashley said.

"Yes, it's my brother, having yet another one of his sulks."

"What about?"

"Oh I don't know, probably something insignificant."

"So, were you two identical twins?"

"Almost, but for the colour of our eyes."

"Really? Is that possible?"

"Well, it must have been, because most of the time that was the only way people could tell us apart; me with the hazel brown eyes, and Ben with his baby blues. Anyway, did you want to look inside?"

"Of course," she smiled, and opened the door.

They stepped into a large room with subtle light blue wallpaper, four-poster bed and more of Miriam Harrison's paintings, all accentuated by the golden rays of the afternoon sun that spilt in through large balcony doors.

Ashley moved across the parquet floor, to the opposite side of the room. Then, with one grandiose move, pulled open the double doors and caught her breath; the scene that greeted her could have been a photo of the painting she had just been admiring. This is where Miriam Harrison must have sat to create her masterpiece, it was all here: the lake, the woods, the sky and even the ducks!

"Is the room to your satisfaction, Madam?" Rupert asked, admiring the glow of the sun in her fiery red hair.

Ashley stepped out onto the balcony and uttered, "It's beautiful, Rupert. It's so pretty!"

"I'm glad you approve." He joined her on the balcony, and slipped his hands around her waist.

They watched in silence, as birds fluttered to and from trees, the ducks bathed in the water, and a chilled breeze kissed their faces.

Minutes passed, then the silence was broken by Ashley who said, "It's difficult to think that something so terrible could have happened somewhere so beautiful…." The words just fell out of her mouth, and she could have kicked herself.

She turned to him, "Oh God, Rupert. I don't know why I even said that. I am so sorry…"

"It's okay, Ash," he reassured her. "There's no point in skirting around it. This is where my brother died. I was there, and even I can't believe it." His eyes glistened as he reminisced. "We had so many happy times here."

"I am so sorry, baby," Ashley apologised, stroking his hand.

He planted a kiss in her hair.

"Of all the years, that was the one where I refused to come here. I wanted to celebrate with my friends, back in the city, but Ben, as usual, got his way." He sighed. "I can't help but wonder just how different things would have turned out, had I not given in."

Ashley looked him in the eyes, then gently cupped his face in her hands, "No Rupert. Don't talk like that. It wasn't your fault."

He smiled at her. "My parents thought it was."

"Rupert... you don't know that..."

"I do. They told me," he said, flatly, swallowing the lump in his throat.

The pain was clear in his watery eyes.

"Oh God, baby," she said, unable to find words comforting enough.

He continued, "My mother hardly spoke to me after that day. In fact, we were never the same again, right until she took her life. And my father," he paused, as if choking on the words, "well, he banned me from ever coming back here. Kenning Hall had become a shrine to Ben, and I wasn't welcome anymore."

Ashley said nothing.

She knew that no words could take away his pain. All she could do was hold him close. They remained that way for a few minutes, neither of them willing to break the silence, until Rupert said, "Nothing has changed, though. Perhaps my teenage perspective has, but apart from that, everything else seems the same."

"I love you," Ashley said.

He looked into her eyes. "Are you sure?"

"I'm sure," she said with conviction.

"Willing to prove it to me?" he asked with a cheeky grin.

She replied by kissing him full on the mouth. He responded by pulling her into him and running his fingers through her hair. Then, with all the grace of a black and white classic, he scooped her off her feet and carried her back, into the warmth of the bedroom, where he laid her on the bed.

They kissed again, but this time their passion was hungrier. She unzipped and pushed off his fleece as he unbuttoned and let her shirt fall open, pausing momentarily to admire the tightness of the white T-shirt over her breasts. She took the opportunity to unzip and unbuckle him, revealing the pleasure trail of hair that started from his navel, and disappeared down, into his jeans.

The sight excited her, as it had many times before, and the naughty smile on her face spurred him to action.

He pulled off his T-shirt in one masculine move.

This overwhelmed her, and she responded in kind by yanking off her T-shirt and pulling him down on top of her, where they kissed hungrily until he broke off to nip her neck. The action tickled and tingled her extremities at the same time.

She ran her fingers through his hair, as his face disappeared into the valley of her breasts, where he continued to sow kisses before pausing to nip at her nipples.

They were protruding through the delicate fabric of her bra.

They both giggled at this discovery.

She wanted him. She wanted him now.

They laughed as obstinate jeans refused to be removed.

But their laughter was cut short when the bedroom door swung open and slammed loudly against a nearby dresser, sending a white vase, with a subtle flowery motif, flying then smashing to the floor.

They both jumped up like naughty teenagers that had just been caught.

"What the hell…?" Rupert breathed as he stared at the door.

Ashley pushed herself up against the head rest, hurriedly and self-consciously covering herself with her shirt.

"Hello?" Rupert called out to the door without moving.

"Rupert…" Ashley prompted, pushing him off her and urging him to investigate.

"Is it the others?" She whispered although she didn't know why.

"Probably James, playing one of his pranks," Rupert said, sliding off the bed, buttoning and zipping himself up as he went.

He looked back at Ashley, her beautiful cleavage now covered once more by the shirt she was still clasping.

He made a dramatic forlorn face.

Ashley rolled her eyes and nodded him towards the door.

He sighed and, with a reluctant smile, turned once more.

He shivered when he reached the door as an icy gust of wind blew at him from the corridor, making him wonder if they'd left the front door open.

"Hello?" He called out as he stepped into the hallway and looked over the balustrade.

"Ash?" he called over his shoulder.

No answer.

"Ashley?" he called again.

"What's the matter?" she replied in a loud whisper as she appeared in the doorway, buttoning her shirt over her bra.

"Did we leave the front door open when we came in?"

She thought about the question. "I don't think so," she offered, hugging herself as the icy cold breeze danced around her, and played with the strands of hair in front of her eyes.

She followed his gaze to see the door was wide open.

"Weird. It's hardly a wind…."

"…Shhh!" he interrupted. "Can you hear that?"

"Hear what?" she asked, still rubbing her arms. The house's temperature had plummeted. It was suddenly very cold.

"That hissing sound," he said.

Both paused as they listened.

Silence but for the call of a wood pigeon.

"I can't hear anything…." Ashley began, but Rupert was already moving towards the stairs. "Rupert…" she said, suddenly unhappy with the idea of being left in the gloomy, cold corridor.

But Rupert was gone, descending the staircase slowly, but with purpose, listening carefully as he went.

Ashley looked down the dark corridor and then back at her man as he rapidly moved away from her.

She glanced down the hallway once more and then said very quickly, "Wait for me!"

The hissing sound seemed to be coming from outside. And its pitch was changing, from a high fizz to a low chopping hum.

Rupert reached the front door and looked out at the forecourt, the Lexus was where he had left it and it was alone. Nobody had arrived, but something was different.

And it was as he was contemplating this that he noticed it

and audibly gasped.

"Rupert?" Ashley caught up with him "What is…?" She stopped in midsentence, for she too could not believe her eyes.

Their attention was drawn to the fountain. In particular, to the mouths of the gargoyles from which powerful jets of crystal clear water was now spurting. It rapidly filled the concrete basin, resuscitating the desiccated leaves that had lain dormant all this time and bobbing them about the surface.

"I thought you said the source had dried up," Ashley said.

"It had." Rupert responded, incredulously. "I can't believe it."

"It must be you, Rupert. Coming back to the house after all this time, you brought it back to life," Ashley said, brightly.

Rupert said nothing. He was still in awe of the spectacle before him.

The fountain had stopped running water shortly after Ben's death and he had never known it to run since, until now.

Ashley put her arm around him. "It's a welcome home, baby." She smiled, affectionately.

"Yes, I guess so," was all he could say.

"Oh, who was at the door by the way?"

"Nobody," he answered distractedly.

"What do you mean nobody?" she laughed.

He turned to her. "I mean nobody."

"So, who opened all the windows?"

Rupert looked up, turned around; every single window this side of the house was indeed wide open. That's when the world darkened as the sun disappeared behind a black cloud.

3 THE GUESTS

It was dusk when the black Range Rover Sport drove onto the Kenning Hall forecourt.

Elisabeth Harrison, Rupert's 53-year-old cousin, immaculately dressed in a black designer trouser suit, left the vehicle and checked her outfit for creases. She scowled, when she discovered a seatbelt indentation down the front, and tried to brush it out with her hand, but to no avail. It was while she was doing this that she noticed the cascading water of the fountain.

I thought this thing had stopped running.

She pondered this for a few moments. Then, reached into the car and pulled out her mink coat. She wrapped it around herself with a big smile, as if cloaked by the very money it took to buy it.

Yes, it was real fur and yes, that is why she loved it so.

Elisabeth was not an animal rights believer. She had been invited to many such fundraising events, but attended none. She believed society was governed by a natural pecking order. In her opinion, animals belonged at the bottom and not where bleeding heart animal lovers campaigned them to be.

Her green eyes surveyed the building.

It had been a very long time since she had been here. A lot of memories. Many of which came flooding back, as her attention lingered on the arched window. Even now, after all these years, the darkness lurked behind the glass like an evil stalker, biding its time. She remembered how, as a child, she avoided looking directly at that window for fear of discovering a pair of eyes glaring back at her. Much to her surprise, those feelings were still present.

The slamming sound of the car door broke her thoughts and she hurried up the steps to the entrance.

"Come on, Adam!" she shouted when she reached the front door.

Officially, Adam Lewis had been dating Elisabeth Harrison for nearly a year now.

They had met at a charity ball, where not even the tyrannical millionaire shareholder of Harrison Publishing had managed to resist the thirty-year-old in his tuxedo. He had a lean six-foot frame, wavy strawberry blonde hair, big blue eyes, and a strong jawline wrapped in a manicured beard; everything Elisabeth's ego required.

Adam had learned much about the Harrison dynasty, including details of the tragedy that had befallen it, here at this very place.

However, it wasn't death that unsettled him but something much more important; Rupert Harrison, Elisabeth's cousin. He was a multi-millionaire, and the majority shareholder of one of the most successful publishing houses in the world. Adam had met him but a few times in the past year. Each meeting was more nerve-wracking than the last. It wasn't just because the man was, albeit indirectly, his boss, but more because he was Elisabeth's closest family member; a family that he planned to marry into very soon.

It was not lost on Adam that Elisabeth doted on her younger cousin and that the two were more like siblings than relatives. It was for this reason that he wanted to make a good impression, and this was the best opportunity to do so.

Nobody was going to get in the way of that, Adam thought as he watched the blue Ford Explorer make its way onto the forecourt, and come to a standstill behind the Range Rover.

He had met the driver, James Howard, Rupert's closest mentor and corporate lawyer, multiple times before. They worked in the same building, and, regardless of Adam's intimate relationship with Elisabeth, the lawyer had made it pretty obvious that he trusted him only as far as he could throw him. It was clear that he'd already written him off as another of Elisabeth's opportunistic toyboys.

Adam resented the presumption.

He watched the pot-bellied sixty something-year-old man, in the unflattering grey sweatsuit, get out of the car, and unload his bags, and vowed to convert him to his way of thinking.

James Howard hooked the overnight bags over his shoulder and, as he did so, he watched Adam put an arm around Elisabeth She promptly shrug it off as they entered the building.

James looked up at the building; it had been a long time. So many memories.

Eventually, he turned to his partner to find that she had left the car, and was now reaching up to feel the stone gargoyles of the fountain.

"Isabella?"

No answer.

"Isabella?"

He walked over to her and placed a hand on her shoulder.

"Isabella.

She spun to face him.

"Wow, sorry, I didn't mean to startle you," he said, looking into her pale face, "but I called you and you didn't answer. Are you okay?"

After a few lingering moments, she said, "I'm fine," zipped up her coat, and added, "Just cold."

The tone of her voice was flat, her accent Polish.

James smiled, "Then we best get you inside."

Born in London, and after spending most of her childhood there, Isabella Meltza returned to Poland with her parents and the Meltza Globetrotting Fairground. This is how she lived and worked for the next twenty years, until her father's business failed and they settled into a house near Warsaw. However, Isabella's home was London and, after a painful separation from her parents, she moved back home to train and earn her living as a counsellor.

Eleven months ago, as James struggled to cut the umbilical cord of an eighteen-year marriage, his secretary suggested he meet with Isabella and, after much encouragement, he did.

Isabella opened his eyes and helped him see the end of his marriage did not mean the end of his life, but that it was, in fact, a new beginning.

In fact, it wasn't long after James checked out of therapy that he began to see more of Isabella. Nothing serious. Just the odd show, the occasional meal.

She had managed to avoid the other people in James' life, until now.

She looked at the building as if it were a great wall she was about to scale.

"Are you sure you're okay?" James asked.

"Yes," she replied, sweeping a curl of black hair from her blue eyes.

He placed a gentle, reassuring hand on her arm. "Don't worry about this lot. They may be rich, but they're lovely people." He paused and then added with mock seriousness, "Well, all but Elisabeth, she's a bitch."

They laughed.

"Come on," he said, looking up at low-hanging rain clouds, "looks like the weather is turning again."

Inside the house, Elisabeth had called to her cousin, but the only reply was the hollow clicking of her heels on the hard floor.

"Where do you think they are?" Adam asked.

"How am I supposed to know?" Elisabeth snapped. "She's probably taken him around the back for a quickie. That's her speciality you know, quickies."

"Really?" Adam asked. He had heard this story before.

"Don't be glib, Adam. It doesn't suit you."

"For God's sake, Elisabeth, lighten up…"

"Lighten up?" she echoed in an angry whisper. Then, moving closer to him, she added, "How do you expect me to lighten up when I've agreed to spend a weekend with some gold digging slut who's attached herself to my cousin like a parasite, and a throwback hippie who's idea of a fun day is probably a sale at Oxfam?"

"I don't think they're as bad as you're making them out to be," Adam said.

"Yes, well you wouldn't," Elisabeth retorted, dismissively.

"So where are our hosts?" James asked, somewhat breathlessly, as he struggled through the door with his bags and ample paunch.

"Your guess is as good as mine," Elisabeth threw back.

"They've probably gone for a walk," Adam offered.

"Not by that lake, I hope."

"Why, what's wrong with lake?" Isabella asked as she marvelled at the interior of the building.

Elisabeth's eyes widened with interest. "You mean you don't know? James hasn't told you?" She asked with a wry smile.

"No, I haven't had the chance yet," James said with a glare.

"Tell me what?" Isabella asked, half-heartedly, for the ornate balustrade and the red-carpeted stairs mesmerized her. The place looked so regal.

"Well, umm... "James fumbled with words.

"Well?" Elisabeth prompted him, smiling mischievously. She relished his discomfort and could not wait for Isabella to find out that someone had actually died here. She was bound to freak out.

James knew this. "I'll tell you later," he said not taking his eyes off Elisabeth's smirking face.

"Oh well, if you aren't going to tell her then we may as well go see if we can find my..." Elisabeth cut her words short and her face creased into a big smile, "Rupert!"

"Hello everyone," he said as he entered the front door, closely followed by Ashley. "I'm sorry. We went for a walk and completely lost track of time."

"So we gathered," Elisabeth said, embracing and kissing her cousin on both cheeks.

"How are you?" Rupert asked, looking her up and down.

"Oh fine, considering the journey."

"Was it not a comfortable one?"

"Yes, it was but..."

"I think what Elisabeth is trying to say is that she couldn't wait to get here." Adam interrupted, extending a hand. "Good to see you again, Sir."

"Sir? Adam. Only a few years older than you! Call me Rupert. And thanks for taking the time to come over."

"Wouldn't have missed it for the world, Sir... Rupert!"

"Sir Rupert? For crying out loud, man, you'll be calling him lord next," James mocked, as he hugged Ashley and said loudly, for Elisabeth's sake, "Can I just say, you look fabulous today, Ashley. If you don't mind me saying so."

"Oh thank you. No, I don't mind at all," Ashley said, putting on a very posh voice.

They laughed.

Elisabeth rolled her eyes.

"So, where did you go? I was thinking of taking a stroll

with Isabella later," James said.

"Oh, you must… I'm Ashley, by the way," she said with a big smile, and touching Isabella affectionately on the arm. "We walked the whole mile through the woods to the next estate. I can't believe it's all part of the same property."

"It's good to meet you," Rupert joined in.

He moved to embrace her but Isabella pulled away, abruptly, as ice cold tentacles shot up her arms and stabbed her brain. Daylight turned to night and she felt as if the room was going to implode on her.

James was fast off the mark and rushed to catch her fall as Rupert, dumbfounded, just watched the woman as she was helped to a nearby chair.

Ashley rushed to assist.

For what must have been the tenth time already, Elisabeth rolled her eyes.

"Isabella, are you alright?" Ashley asked, her voice laden with concern.

After a few moments and what sounded like panting, she replied, "Yes, I think so. I'm sorry. I get these silly things all the time. I will be okay in a minute," she said.

"Are you sure?" James asked.

"Yes. Honestly, I'm sorry."

James looked at Rupert; "Well, you always did have this effect on women."

The comment worked to dispel some of the tension in the air.

They all laughed.

It was then that Ashley gasped. "Isabella, you're bleeding."

Indeed, Isabella's nose had spontaneously begun to bleed. The blood was dribbling over her lips, down her chin and onto her anorak.

"Oh God," Elisabeth groaned under her breath.

"Come on, let's get a cold compress on that," Ashley offered, helping the woman out of the chair.

"Oh, I'm sorry to be such a nuisance." Isabella apologised.

"Don't be silly, it's no problem. I get these all the time. Admittedly, it's after a few rounds with him." She exchanged comforting glances with Rupert and James, who watched as

Ashley led the Isabella away, towards to the kitchen.

No sooner were they out of earshot and Elisabeth perked up, "Well that's just perfect."

"I'm sorry about that," James said.

Rupert smiled. "Why are you apologising? It's not your fault. I just hope she's okay."

"Pretty smooth, Rupert, bringing women to their knees just by the shake of a hand," said Adam.

"He's a very handsome man," Elisabeth replied, putting her arm around his waist. "Unfortunately, he doesn't set his sights very high."

This was an obvious dig at Ashley that Rupert ignored and said instead, "I'm a very happy man, Elisabeth."

"Yes, but…"

"…he's a very happy man, Elisabeth," James reiterated. Rupert smiled.

It's going to be a long weekend.

"Come on, I'll show you to your rooms," he said.

4 RUMOURS

Kenning Hall's first guests for two decades spent the next few hours unpacking, exploring and settling into their respective rooms.

It was 7:03 pm when Rupert and James found themselves sharing a drink in the study.

It was a large traditional wood-panelled room, with one entire wall made of books; an eclectic collection of soft and hardbacks of all sizes. Some in pristine condition, others dog-eared and tired. Most were Harrison imprints.

Rupert's grandfather began the collection when his publishing house printed its first book. The tradition was passed down to his son, but ended that fateful day, many years before, leaving a lonely gap in two of the long shelves.

A sad metaphor of the hearts of those left behind.

A large open fireplace sat at the opposite side of the room, surrounded by a couch and a pair of armchairs.

There was a massive square window that almost ran from floor to ceiling. An imposing oak desk sat in front of it.

The desk was clutter free but for a blotter, two cradled fountain pens and a lamp which was on, creating a tawny smog of the cigar smoke that was rapidly filling the room.

Rupert pushed open a section of the window and dusk's fresh air hurried in like a whirlwind of chambermaids eager to purify the contamination.

"You know, if Ashley catches me smoking this thing, I'm a dead man," Rupert said with a smile.

"It's okay, I'll confess to coercing you into keeping this old fart company."

They were sitting in two of the leather upholstered armchairs that guarded the front of the desk.

"*Oliva Serie V Melanio Figurado* and single malt whiskey, Rupert? Your intimate knowledge of my most treasured vices is frightening."

"If there's one thing I learned from my father, it's that the cigar is one of man's finest pleasures and, as such, only the finest will do," he said with a silky, dreamy voice, and then promptly had a coughing fit.

James laughed. "Indeed," he said, knowingly.

Rupert quickly stubbed the cigar out in the nearest ashtray, causing James to wince until it was replaced with an affectionate smile.

"Thanks, Rupert."

"Don't mention it," the younger man said, swiping at the air in front of him, still spluttering, and then taking a swig from his glass. "It's my way of saying thank you."

"For what?"

"Well, just for being there. You've always been there for father and, most importantly, for me when I needed it the most. I know things are different in the city, that we tend to talk work most of the time, but I just want you to remember that, for me, you're part of the family."

James smiled, warmly, at the young man.

Rupert had travelled such a long, difficult and often lonely road, and James was immensely proud of what he had become. The fact that he may have somehow been instrumental in this was a bonus.

The reality was, James had played a significant and positive role in Rupert's journey to adulthood. Ever since that tragic day, the young man had struggled not only with the burden of his loss, but with the grief he believed his failure to save his brother had caused their parents.

"So what's with your best-kept secret, Isabella? Why haven't I met her before?" Rupert asked.

"Oh, you know. It's still early days. We've been more like companions for the past year. It's only recently that we've started to spend more time with each other, so I thought it was time she met you all. By all, of course, I mean you."

"It's mine and everybody else's privilege. She's lovely, and it's good to see you moving on."

"What about you and Ashley?"

Rupert nodded, thoughtfully, "Yes, things are good."

"Just good?"

"What else do you want me to say?"

"Do I hear wedding bells?"

Rupert shuffled in his seat "Um, no, can't say we've discussed anything like that yet. She won't even move in with me, so I don't think there's much chance of me walking her down the aisle just yet. Besides, I've already been through one of those and you know how that ended. I'm in no particular hurry to rush into another."

"That was over two years ago."

"Just under, actually," Rupert corrected.

"Whatever. I'm wondering if you're enjoying this whole *most eligible bachelor* thing way too much. Has it occurred to you that Ashley may not be interested in just playing house with you? Maybe she's expecting more of a commitment."

Rupert lifted an eyebrow. "I'm sorry, doctor, could you say that again?"

James continued, "Ashley's right for you, son. I've never seen you this content."

"Really? Is it that obvious?" Rupert asked with a grin.

"Elisabeth seems to think that I've not been myself since the divorce."

"That's because your ex happened to be her best friend."

Rupert nodded, pensively, before taking another drink from his glass.

James took advantage of the moment.

"Rupert, there's something we need to talk about. I wanted to wait until after your birthday but, hell, you'd only give me a roasting for not telling you sooner so I'm mentioning it now."

Rupert shifted in his chair. "What's up?"

"I spoke to Jonathan today, and he shared something with me that I think you should be aware of."

"Go on."

"Someone's been showing a lot of interest in Harrison stock."

Rupert cocked his head, "Interest?"

"They've been buying unusually large chunks of shares."

"Someone? You sound dramatically cryptic, James."

"We don't know who. All we know is that they've hired Dillon, Harris & Norris to transact on their behalf."

Rupert frowned.

Dillon, Harris & Norris were a partnership of notoriously ruthless stockbrokers, with a rumoured reputation for market manipulation.

"Yes. That's why I thought you should know," James added. "I've scheduled a meeting with Jonathan and the rest of the team first thing Monday so we can discuss. Just as a precaution. Of course, you and Elisabeth are still majority shareholders."

"Does Elisabeth know about this?"

"Not yet."

"Okay. Let's not say anything to her just now. You know how she can get, and nothing may come of it."

"Whatever you think's best," James nodded.

There was a pause as an owl signalled the onset of night.

"So, what do you know about this Adam character?" James asked.

Rupert pondered for a few seconds then shrugged, "Not

much, actually. Seems a pretty decent guy, though, he's put up with Elisabeth for the best part of a year so all due credit to him." Rupert raised his drink as if to toast that fact. "Why?"

"No particular reason, just wondering," James replied, casually.

"Right," Rupert said, knowingly, and then added, "You don't like him?"

"I don't even know him. Nobody really knows him."

"Well, I get the impression that Elisabeth has got to know him very well," Rupert said with a smile.

"Yes, about as well as a praying mantis," James said, dismissively.

Rupert smiled. "Ashley seems to like him. They've been working together for a few months now and she thinks he's doing really well. And if Elisabeth has her way, he'll be promoted to executive status pretty soon."

"What?"

Rupert laughed, "Don't worry, your job's safe."

But James wasn't smiling.

Rupert noticed this. "What's going on?" He asked.

"Oh, nothing. Just, with all of this funny business with the shares. Introducing strangers into the company doesn't seem wise."

"James, we're a multinational. We hire people all the time."

"You know what I mean. Introduce them into the inner circle. Allow them to get close."

"He's hardly a stranger," Rupert defended.

"To the company he is. I mean, the guy didn't even have any editorial experience, did he? Yet he's managed somehow to get onto Ashley's team. I just don't think it's wise to job create for people just because they happen to be banging your cousin."

Rupert was taken aback. "Wow, that's a bit strong, isn't it? For your information, Adam happens to be more than qualified to be working with Ash. He has a lot of journalistic experience, along with a bunch of honours in media studies or something of that ilk. Ash checked out his CV and his references, and she was pretty impressed, hence why she hired him. You know her. You know how she feels about Elisabeth. She's hardly going to do my cousin any favours. She hired Adam on merit."

James realised he may have overreached. "You're right. I'm sorry. I was out of line."

Rupert nodded. "I know you're only doing what you've always done; you're looking out for us, and I appreciate it, although I get the distinct impression that there's more to this. Is there?"

They were interrupted by a knock on the door, it opened and Adam stepped in.

"I've been told to come and get you for supper," he said with a smile.

"Thanks, Adam," Rupert said, standing up. He then slapped a hand on James' shoulder, "Come on, old grizzles," he said loudly causing Adam to laugh unnecessarily loud.

James pulled a fake grin which he lost as soon as he crossed eyes with Adam, killing the man's laughter, instantly.

5 THE SUPPER

During her house exploration, Ashley had discovered a collection of records; one of them was a compilation of thirties classics. It was playing on an old record player in the dining room that was situated at the back of the house, with an enviable daytime view of the lake.

The dulcet tones of Billie Holiday blended beautifully with the opulent red and gold colours of the dining room, recreating an era far gone, but forever revered.

Ashley and Isabella had tastefully laid the dining table with gold rimmed china, red candles and gleaming silverware that they found neatly stacked away in various kitchen cupboards.

Dinner was Spaghetti a la Bolognese, courtesy of Isabella, who may have been of Polish descent, but appeared to have all the skills of a Mediterranean chef.

Initially, Elisabeth turned her nose up at the food, but then managed to devour her whole plate and even wipe it clean with a bread roll.

Clarence, Kenning Hall's administrator, had ensured that the wine cellar was well stocked. This meant that the alcohol flowed abundantly and thus adequately loosened tongues.

True to the radio forecast earlier in the day, the weather had changed, and a northerly gale, with light rain, tapped on the window as if eager to join in the evening's events.

The guests of Kenning Hall were oblivious to this since most were well passed sobriety, and deeply immersed in a series of diverse topics that ranged, from politics to reincarnation.

It turned out that Isabella was quite an authority on the latter, having spent a lot of time sitting in the corner of a tent while her mother read Tarot cards and peered into a crystal ball for a living.

The profession was nothing but an elaborate illusion, but it fired little Isabella's imagination. She used what she had learned to intrigue her dinner partners with stories of fortune telling and psychic reading. Even Rupert, a disbeliever, found her stories fascinating.

"So, Isabella, what you're saying is that we're all just bits of energy piloting the shells that are our bodies, and that when we die, we leave said shell and float off to find another. And that can belong to any animal, like a dog or cat?"

"Something like that, yes," Isabella smiled.

"So, when someone sees a ghost, what they are seeing is just this energy?" Adam asked.

"Yes," Isabella nodded.

"Well, how come some people see them and others don't?" That was Elisabeth's petulant contribution.

Isabella shrugged. "I don't know. Some of us are able to tune into this energy and others aren't. It's a bit like tuning into a television."

"And that's your scientific answer, is it?"

"Elisabeth, I'm not a scientist. This is just my belief," Isabella replied, patiently.

"So what about poltergeists?" Ashley asked more solemnly than she had intended, just as a gale whistled around the building.

They all looked at each other for a few seconds and then, like a bunch of silly schoolchildren, exploded into fits of laughter.

Rupert mimicked her ominous tone, *"Oooh, what about poltergeists?"* and then added through chuckles, "Bloody hell, babe, you'll have us wetting ourselves!"

Ashley laughed. "Sorry, it sounded worse than it was supposed to."

"Yeah, well, let me just warn you, if you carry on like that, I'm sleeping with you two tonight!" James said.

More laughter.

"So… what about them, Isabella?" Rupert prompted.

"Well, we all know that poltergeist is German for *noisy spirit*. I believe that a poltergeist is a frustrated spirit or energy, unable to leave this life and move on to the next."

"But haven't we just finished saying that ghosts are just harmless energy?" It was Adam speaking.

"Yes, but I believe that, in this case, the mother and child principle applies."

"Mother and child?"

"Yes. You've all heard about it; child is stuck under motor vehicle, mother lifts the vehicle and saves her child."

"Oh please," Elisabeth sneered.

"There are many documented cases proving this theory," Isabella continued.

"How does this relate to poltergeists?"

"Well, as I say, a poltergeist is a frustrated spirit. Just like the mother defies nature so does it. Such is the energy generated by its anger, its rage that it's able to interact with our physical world."

"But why? Why would it want to?"

Isabella shrugged, "I don't know. Myth tells us that these entities cannot move on because they have been wronged by something or someone, but I really don't know. I haven't personally experienced this. Like the rest of you, I've only heard stories."

"What kind of stories?" Rupert asked.

"Ghost stories. People or houses plagued by poltergeist who have been known to scratch, speak or physically touch people."

There was storyteller seriousness to Isabella's words. It had captivated the attention of the diners, whilst riling the elements outside; rain spat at the windows, and a wailing cold draught crashed the dinner party by forcing itself through the gap under the door.

"In one case a married couple had been happily living in their home for over ten years when, suddenly, they started to hear unidentifiable scratching sounds from the ceiling and walls. Objects would disappear then reappear days later in different parts of the house. They'd hear whispers and, most frightening, they had a constant feeling of being watched. Eventually, believing the house had something to do with the haunting, the couple moved, but the manifestations continued until, one day, they end as abruptly as they start.

Later they learn that on that same day, the wife had invited the next door neighbour and her three-year-old son to the home. The little boy, while he play, he knock over and smashed a vase. That's when she realise that it was since she had bought that vase that the trouble had begun. It seemed that by bringing the vase home, the woman had somehow invited the entity, which had attached itself to the object, into her house."

A loud scratching sound made everybody around the table physically jump in their seats; the needle had slipped on the record player.

They gawked at each other and then, once again, burst into fits of laughter.

"That's it! No more wine for you," James said, removing the glass from in front of Isabella, to everybody else's amusement.

And so the night moved on with more supernatural tales and more laughter.

It was nearly 01:00 am when they finally retired to their

respective rooms.

Rupert was beyond tipsy, and was lying back on the bed as Ashley unbuttoned his shirt. His hair was tousled, where she had run her hands through it moments before, and he had a smile on his face as she planted kisses on his navel. He murmured his appreciation and looked down at her. Their eyes met, and she held his gaze. She was smiling.

"What?" he asked.

"Nothing," she said, resting her face on his belly and enjoying how it rose and fell with each breath he took.

"I'm just so proud of you."

Rupert grinned. "What makes you say that?"

"I don't know. Just the way you were with everybody tonight," she sighed, "the way everyone relaxes around you. All that stuff about ghosts, it couldn't have been easy. Even Isabella seemed to take a shine to you and, despite your cousin's constant put-downs, seemed to enjoy herself tonight."

Rupert nodded his head, "Ah, well, I would like to take the credit for that, but I think the wine played a crucial part."

There was silence between them as the wind howled at the balcony windows.

Rupert played with Ashley's hair and marvelled at how it shone, crimson, in the lamplight. She closed her eyes, enjoying his touch and listening to him breathing. The sound was mesmerising.

"It's amazing," she said, distantly.

"What is?"

"To think that over a year ago, you didn't even know I existed and now..." she trailed off.

"And now?"

"And now I'm incredibly happy. I just wish my father could have met you."

"So do I, Ash. And if he was anything like you, then I know he'd be an amazing man."

"He was."

"What do you remember about him?"

There was a pause as if Ashley, eyes still closed, were searching her memory for images of her father.

"Blackberry jam."

"Blackberry jam?"

"He used to take me blackberry picking. Of course, we'd spend the first half hour or so eating the blackberries. By the time I got home, I'd be one big black stain. My mum would throw a fit. She hated us doing stuff together because she knew that my dad didn't care about how I looked, he was much more interested in making sure I was happy. I was devastated when he died, we were so close."

"How old were you?"

"Twelve, I couldn't get over it."

"What about your mother?"

Ashley paused and then said, flatly, "We just didn't get along. I don't really remember much about her. Just certain things, fragments. It's strange, it's like she existed, but she's just like some shadow lurking in my past."

"Both of my parents featured heavily in my life. At least they did before Ben died."

There was sadness in Rupert's voice.

Then there was silence but for the howling wind that appeared to be getting worse.

"Tell me more about your parents, Ash, you hardly ever talk about them," Rupert said.

She took a few seconds. "Well, after my father died, my mother just faded away," she said.

"Faded?"

She looked up at him and said, solemnly, "I love you."

He smiled. "Are you sure?"

"I'm sure," she replied, earnestly.

"Feel like showing me just how much?" There was a mischievous twinkle in his eyes.

She looked down and noticed that he had not been immune to her closeness.

She giggled. "That's what I love about you; always ready for action."

She kissed her way up his chest until their mouths met. Then, without breaking the lingering kiss for longer than was necessary, she manoeuvred herself until she was in a sitting position on top of him. He was still clothed from the waist down, and she enjoyed feeling the encased hardness beneath her.

He smiled a sleepy smile at her as she teased by rubbing her rear on him, gently feeling for that mound of pleasure. Rupert took his cue and pushed both of her dress straps onto her shoulders, and was delighted to discover that she was not wearing a bra.

Ashley leant back allowing the dress to slide further, aided by his fingers that were now tracing their way, delicately, down from her slender neck all the way down to her now exposed breasts. He lingered on her nipples, running circles around them with his finger and then promptly replacing it with his mouth. He kissed and nipped them gently making her gasp.

Ashley enjoyed the sensation for a few more seconds before she pulled back abruptly, but only to unbutton and unzip him as fast as she could. Then, their eyes met once again and they kissed, hungrily, greedily each yearning to unleash the passion that had been suppressed since their earlier encounter.

When they emerged for air, he took a few more seconds to enjoy her breasts, running his hands over them, down to her slender waist and then under her skirt where he searched the mounds of velvet red fabric. It felt delicious to the touch as did her skin.

Then, once inside, he pushed the soft material up her thighs, gently enough to tickle her in the process. Then, with one lightning movement, he tugged at her underwear, ripping the dainty fabric with ease.

Ashley was as surprised as she was turned on by the action. The underwear had been a Victoria's Secret gift from one of his many trips to America, and they were her favourites, but she had no time to consider this for his finger was probing the evidence between her thighs that she had enjoyed the action.

She squirmed from the feeling of his fingers at the entrance to her sensual world, and sucked in gasps of air as he ventured deeper. His touch was as exquisite as her arousal that was amplified by the love she felt for this man. It fed her compulsion to feel him inside her.

She lifted herself slightly so that she could take control, but he had already had the initiative and, within seconds, had freed himself and was pulling her back down onto him, invoking a small whimper of pleasure, as if she had only just discovered his size.

Ashley searched Rupert's chest with her hands, then took both of his arms and pushed them onto the pillow above his head.

She was going to take it from here.

Rupert offered no resistance. Instead, he closed his eyes and smiled as Ashley absorbed all of him into her as deeply as she could, breathing with delirious pleasure as she did so. Then she moved, slowly at first, savouring every delicious stroke, and she enjoyed this for a while until it was his turn, and, in one move, he flipped them over so that she was now on her back and him between her legs.

There, he pushed deep once more, as her hands, low on his back, urged him forward, deeper and faster.

They both revelled in the intoxication of the act which rapidly reached its climax, amplified by the fact that they were finally able to satisfy that which had been denied erstwhile.

6 MONDAY

Monday morning arrived too soon with the sound of pelting rain against balcony doors.

It was 07:30, and Ashley, already dressed in a grey suit and white blouse, was applying the final touches of her makeup in the hallway mirror.

She smiled to herself; it had been a good weekend.

The sun had shone brightly on Sunday, in complete contrast to the day before. The wind had been cold but, dressed warmly, they had toured the estate.

They came across an excavation area near the lake. Rupert explained that the deep holes, that had been covered over with planks of wood and cordoned off by yellow barriers, would house the foundations of a giant gazebo. It was being built in memory of his twin brother.

It had been Clarence's suggestion, and one Rupert believed was fitting, considering that the brothers had spent a lot of happy times there.

It was a poignant moment for those present, made light by Rupert who recounted, in dramatic detail, tales of his childhood mischievousness.

Later, they had picnicked near a fallen tree in the woods behind the house, much to Elisabeth's displeasure, for she did not take well to lunching with wood lice, crows and even a pair of grey squirrels!

In the afternoon, they played competitive tennis, boys against girls; of course, the girls had thrashed the boys but nothing new there.

Then, they had set off on their way home, during which Rupert had resurrected the ever so familiar subject of her moving in with him. This had become a ritual between them, especially after they had spent the day with each other. He would highlight how right it all felt and how it made perfect sense that they live together.

But Ashley had always resisted the idea.

She wasn't keen on moving in with her boss, at least, not as his girlfriend, mistress, lover or whatever the hell she was to him.

Even if her whole apartment could fit three times into his penthouse.

She had worked hard to make a career for herself and, as much as she didn't believe in living her life for others, she didn't want people to undervalue her achievements by attributing her career progression to the fact that she was sleeping with the C.E.O.

And, every time she thought about their relationship in this way, it made her cringe. Not just because it portrayed her as yet another cliché, but it undermined what she and Rupert actually had together.

And what they had was good. No, it wasn't good, it was *excellent* and, most importantly, it was real.

On the other hand....

She loved Rupert. She loved him very much. Truth be told, she did want to move in with him because she enjoyed being with him, she adored sharing his bed and she relished waking up next to him.

"I spend most of my time at your place anyway," she blurted.

He just shrugged as if to say, *"Right, so what's the problem?"*

Realising she was making his case for him, "No, what no, that isn't what I meant."

He just smiled, smugly.

She shook her head and narrowed her eyebrows.

"You tricked me."

"I didn't say a word," he said, beaming and feigning concentration on the road ahead.

Then, "Come on, Ash, what do you have to lose? It's not like I'm asking you to sell up your flat or anything. Just come and spend more time with me, and if you feel, although it's highly unlikely, that it isn't working then you can move back to yours. I promise I won't say a word," he said, and then added a few seconds later, "at least not until the following week, because then…"

"…OK."

"…I think I could probably make a case…"

"Okay," she repeated.

"What? Did you just say okay?"

"Yes, I did, stop pestering me."

"Seriously?"

She nodded with a big smile, "Yes, seriously."

She added that she'd only move in if he actually managed to get them home in one piece. By that, she meant that he needed to stop looking at her and keep his eyes on the road.

And that's how Ashley found herself in Rupert's penthouse first thing Monday morning.

He had left early for the office as he had a series of meetings he needed to prepare for and, since he'd taken the weekend off, he now needed to make up the time.

When Ashley offered to wake early so they could ride in together he insisted that she do no such thing. He liked the idea of going into work knowing she was at home, sleeping in his bed.

That was three hours ago.

The time was now 08:25, and she was running late. This was made worse by the fact that she had forgotten to pick up her vanity case, containing most of her beauty accessories, when they visited her apartment last night. She had left the *damn* thing by the front door!

Thankfully, she had some makeup in her bag, and it was this that she was now applying in the hallway mirror, where the light was best.

The entrance lobby was actually a spacious antechamber to the penthouse; a semi-circular room with doors leading off in various directions. The room was flooded with light thanks to a large overhead glass dome that offered a breathtaking, observatory-like view of the stars on a clear night.

Magical.

But on a clear night.

Today it was just dark clouds and drumming rain.

She finished applying her makeup, took in a deep breath and paused in contemplation.

What have I done? I've actually moved in with him.

And it was a move that made both emotional and financial sense, and it made her feel giddy inside, giddy and immensely happy.

She watched her own smiling reflection, as if corroborating the thought she'd just had, and that's when she noticed it, hanging on the wall behind her.

Miriam Harrison's painting.

Rupert had wrapped it in the first thing he could find, a tablecloth, and had somehow managed to smuggle it out of Kenning Hall without her noticing.

Ashley was thrilled.

She knew how much it must have meant to him and went on to promise that it would take pride of place in her flat.

But Rupert had a better idea.

"Consider it a moving in present. We'll give it pride of place in *our* apartment instead."

Then, he took her by the hand and led her to the entrance lobby, where the walls were already adorned with three other paintings, perfectly illuminated by picture lights.

In the centre, hung a large print of Monet's *Japanese Footbridge over Water Lilies*.

He replaced the painting with his mother's.

Then, they both stood back to admire it.

"It's beautiful," Ashley breathed.

Rupert turned to face her and said, "You're beautiful."

They kissed.

That was last night.

This morning, Ashley was admiring her gift, and she loved it. It held the same enchantment here in the apartment as it had the day she had first seen it at Kenning Hall.

She traced her finger over the face of the grinning boy that was young Rupert, and lingered a moment on the hunched shoulders of his twin brother. She wondered what Ben would look like if he was still alive today. Would he have grown up as handsome as his brother?

I suppose we'll never know.

That's when she heard it. The thud was so loud, it sounded as if the front door had been kicked in.

She whirled around to see that the door was tightly shut but that the mirror she had just been using, on the opposite side of the room, was now face down on the floor.

"Jesus…" she breathed, holding her hand to her chest as her heart thumped furiously behind her rib cage.

After a few seconds, she slowly and cautiously approached the stricken object, as if it might jump up and start biting her ankles.

She looked up at the picture hook; it was still intact as was that on the back of the frame. She pulled on them both; they didn't budge.

Really….?

She crouched down and slowly lifted the heavy frame. She expected to hear the sound of broken glass but was amazed to find there was no damage. The mirror wasn't even cracked.

She stared at her perplexed reflection as if expecting an explanation from it.

She examined the floor; sure enough there was a small indentation in the wood.

She cursed. Then, slowly, she picked the mirror up and attempted to rehang it, but struggled to get the picture hook to engage. As she did so, the reflection of Miriam Harrison's painting slipped in and out of view.

Eventually, the hook clicked in.

She grunted with satisfaction, stepped back to make sure it was hanging straight and promptly screamed; Ben was watching her from the other side of the room.

She spun around to find the painting as it should be; Rupert's smiling face and Ben's sulking stance with his back to her.

But she could have sworn that he'd turned around, that she had seen the reflection of his steely blue eyes. They were watching, glaring at her.

That's impossible. It's a painting!

She gingerly turned and checked the painting's reflection once more.

Normal.

That's what you get for going to work without caffeine.
She checked the painting and its reflection several more times before eventually grabbing her work satchel and hurrying out of the apartment, pulling the door shut behind her.

7 HERON HEIGHTS

The rain fell lightly as a taxi pulled up outside the Heron Heights building.

Rachel Harper, a twenty-six year old with a clean complexion, and mousy brown hair tied into a ponytail, reluctantly stepped out of the vehicle. She squinted up into the falling rain at the impressive ten storey apartment building.

Built during the thirties, Heron Heights was the brainchild of a local competition winner, and it reflected the architect's passion for the gothic.

The building was made of black stone. Each of the ten floors was separated by broad ornate ledges and large picture windows. They ran in a symmetrical fashion until they reached the penthouse, where the ledge bore the weight of horned gargoyles dribbling rainwater onto the streets below, as if vomiting on their potential prey. Above them, two fairy tale towers erupted from the roof like phalluses towards the gloomy sky.

Heron Heights' dark, elaborate and ornamental design effused a medieval presence in stark contrast to the other modern buildings around it.

However, its decadent appearance was exactly that. The inside of the building had been luxuriously refurbished throughout with state of the art security, a laundrette, personal gym, and a whole acre of private gardens packed with trees, flowers and a fish pond.

Heron Heights was just a stone's throw from fashionable West London's Notting Hill, and that's why the monthly rent was way beyond the means of most average folk. Indeed, the tenants of Heron Heights tended to be leading actors, foreign dignitaries or wealthy business people, looking for short-term accommodation in the heart of London.

The taxi drove away, leaving Rachel to struggle with her handbag, a holdall and a suitcase as she made her way towards the security gate.

She pressed the one button, labelled *All Visitors Must Report to Security* and peered into the CCTV camera mounted in the recess of the wall.

A few seconds later, a tinny voice boomed out of the speaker.

"Hello. How can I help you?"

"Hello, yes, I'm here to see Jason Tyler. He's expecting me," she spoke loudly with a subtle northern accent over the drumming rain.

"And you are?"

"Rachel Harper."

There was a pause then, "I'm sorry, Mr Tyler isn't in at the moment."

Rachel thought for a second. "Are you sure he isn't here? He was supposed to meet me over an hour ago at the train station," she said, masking her irritation. The rain, that felt more like a cold shower, had plastered her fringe to her scalp and was slowly dribbling down her neck and into her bra.

"Sorry, Miss. His card isn't in his apartment."

"Well look, has he left a message or something? He knew I was arriving today."

Didn't he?

"I am sorry, Miss. I've checked, there are no messages and I can't let you in without someone's say so."

Rachel sniffed. Her coat wasn't waterproof and it was getting rain heavy. She'd been travelling since the crack of dawn, she was cold, hungry and feeling emotional.

It was bad enough that Jason hadn't met her at the train station as promised, but now she was stuck here, in the middle of London without a clue. She had no idea where she was or where to go until he got back.

"Did you forget your key?"

Rachel looked up and rainwater dribbled off her nose.

A tall woman stood behind the gate, she was holding an enormous crimson umbrella with a white motif and the word *Harrison* emblazoned on it.

"Not exactly, I just got here. My boyfriend was supposed to come and pick me up from the station but," she shrugged, "I don't know where he is."

"Why don't you wait for him inside?"

"I can't."

"Why not?"

"Because the doorman won't let me in without somebody's say so."

Ashley glanced at the suitcase and the sodden holdall. She swiped her key card; the gate clicked open, "Come in," she said, quickly.

Rachel's face lit up. "Are you sure?"

"Go wait for him in the lobby? I'm sure he'll be back soon."

"Oh thank you so much," Rachel said, gratefully, forcing a smile.

A Mercedes pulled up as Ashley punched the button on the intercom. Seconds later, there was a reply, "Yes, Miss Marshall."

"Paul, would you be kind enough to send someone out here to help with some bags, please?"

There was a moment's hesitation and then, "Of course, Miss Marshall, right away."

"My name's Ashley," she said, moving in close to the girl so they could share her umbrella.

"I'm Rachel. Thank you so much for this," she said, lifting up her bags, as if to say *my hands are full otherwise I'd shake your hand.*

Actually, given how she was feeling, she probably would have used them to hug the woman.

Nodding at the luggage, Ashley said, "Are you moving in?"

"Yes, with my boyfriend. Or at least, I thought I was." Rachel laughed, nervously, as she started to wonder what exactly had happened to him.

"Don't worry. Men have a habit of coming back, eventually." Ashley said, glancing behind her as a young man in a blue uniform hunched against the rain and ran towards them. "Sorry about Paul. He's new and a bit over zealous," she added, furtively. "Well, I've got to go. I'm already late for work. See you around, Rachel. Welcome to the neighbourhood."

"Thank you. Thank you very much."

With that, Ashley took the keys from the car park attendant, climbed into her Mercedes, and pulled away as the young man gathered Rachel's belongings and escorted her into the building.

8 HARRISON PUBLISHING

It was 09:45 when Ashley drove down Uxbridge Road, West of London City centre, where the Harrison Publishing building towered over her car with mirrored windows that reflected the rest of the city, as well as the multi-storey car park that flanked it.

Ashley pulled up at the entrance barrier and greeted the security guard. The gate lifted and she drove up the ramp and spiralled forward in search of a parking space. She reached the fourth floor before she found one and reversed into it.

She retrieved a bundle of manuscripts from the passenger seat. Then, as the occasional trumpet of car horns drifted up from the stream of traffic on the street below, she hurried into the neighbouring building.

The Harrison Publishing reception lobby was well lit with terracotta marble floors and walls to match. Hanging on them were modern pastel paintings in silver frames. The front desk was made of oak and gleamed. Behind it, were two receptionists wearing headsets and seemingly talking to themselves. Behind them, a wall-size sign with gold lettering welcomed visitors to Harrison Publishing.

Ashley smiled at the two girls and walked over to the lift which she rode to the fifth floor. There, her footsteps clicked down the corridor until she reached a door, labelled '*Meeting Room 4'*.

She opened it to find a group of people sat behind a blue and grey table, laden with breakfast snacks and pump flasks of hot beverages.

"Good morning, gang. Sorry I'm late," she said, rushing into a free chair, dropping her bag and the manuscripts on the floor beside her.

She breathed a loud sigh of relief as she gathered her

thoughts. Then, noticing the look on the faces around the table, said, "Bloody hell, it may be Monday morning, but those faces are going to turn that milk sour."

"I don't know why you don't just come in with Mr Harrison," said Sam; a petite girl in her twenties with black shoulder-length hair and tiny glasses resting on a small nose.

She poured a cup of black coffee and slid it in front of her boss.

"Don't you start, Sam, I get that lecture from him all the time," Ashley replied.

"Well, it does make sense," the girl added.

Ashley pulled a face at her and then looked around the table. They were all present; Fiction Editorial. They, and a small selection of interns, were responsible for sifting through hundreds of manuscripts each week. They separated the good from the dire, the inspiring from the sleep inducing, to achieve the shortlist that would make it onto this year's publishing list.

"Okay, so let's get started," Ashley said, taking the bundle of manuscripts from the floor and unravelling them on the table in front of her.

She picked up the first one. "I read through this, Chris. I didn't mind it, but it didn't exactly grab me. What did you think?" She looked across the table at a young man, who held her gaze until his lips creased into a smile.

Ashley shook her head, knowingly, "Chris, why do I get the feeling that you were testing me? You thought the same, didn't you?"

"I just needed a second opinion."

"Well, you've got it. Too contrived; this bloke needs to add subtlety to his vocabulary. A lot of potential but I don't think it's for us. What do you say?"

Chris shrugged his shoulders in approval.

"Great. Do you know if he has had it independently assessed?"

"I don't think he has."

"Okay, suggest an editor will you."

"No problem."

"So, what else do we have?"

"There's Martha Blazer-Smith." It was Sam speaking again.

"Blazer-Smith," Ashley mused, "Why does that sound familiar?"

"We rejected it last week."

"So why…" Ashley began but stopped when she realised exactly why the manuscript had returned.

In her opinion, Martha Blazer-Smith's manuscript was quite simply awful. It was a poorly written sex book. It lacked any imagination or talent, should have been and was rejected upon receipt. However, Martha Blazer-Smith was a close friend of Elisabeth's, and for some reason Rupert's cousin thought she could simply bypass her department, the entire selection process, and force the manuscript into print. This was not going to happen, not while Ashley still worked there.

She took a deep breath and said, "Didn't we all agree last week that this thing wasn't good enough to line a cat's litter tray?"

"We did," it was Geoff, a thirty-year-old Cambridge grad with wiry blond hair, "but she came down personally this morning and insisted we reconsider."

"She asked if it was worth my job not to include it," added Sam.

"Really?"

Ashley exchanged glances with Adam, who shrugged apologetically, and then there was silence in the room, as the hum of the London city drifted to them through a tiny slit in the window.

Ashley resolved not to give way to the tide of rage that was threatening to drown her. Instead, she straightened in her chair and said, "I'm sorry she said that to you, Sam."

Now if you would all excuse me, I think I'm going to go hunt down the bitch and rip her head off!

"Let's forget her and talk about Jackie Harris. What's the latest with legal, Sam?"

The awkward silence continued and this was beginning to grate more than Elisabeth's meddling.

"Now what?" She asked, masking her irritation.

"Well," Sam began, "we got word this morning that legal

are not going to pass it after all."

"What? Why?"

"They don't think it's," she made speech marks with her fingers, "suitable," she added, "They feel it isn't the kind of thing Harrison should be associated with."

"Says who?" Ashley asked, incredulously.

"We're just Indians, Ash." This contribution was from Paul, the youngest team. He'd initially joined as an intern, but made such an impression on Ashley with a series of editorial initiatives, that she decided to offer him a permanent placement.

"Yes, and I bet I know exactly which chief is responsible for this," Ashley retorted.

"So what now?" asked Paul.

"Now we get on with the rest of these," she said, putting her hand on the pile of paper in front of her, "and then we put the world to rights," she added with an evil smile.

"Uh oh, I feel a bad moon rising," Paul said, blowing air out of his mouth.

"Anyone would have thought I was a violent person," Ashley said, thumbing through pages.

The others responded by feigning interest in their own written material.

"Hey!" Ashley complained, her eyes narrowing and a grin spreading across her face. She grabbed a croissant from the basket in front of her, ripped it apart in a dramatic action and devoured part of it. "Come on then, let's get on. Who's up next?"

Sam read from the notes in front of her, "William Barber and Tales from a Tomb."

"Ah," Ashley said, knowingly, picking up the manuscript. "This light-hearted fable."

"Um, boy buries mother alive, isn't it?"

"Yep, I quite liked it, actually. I thought it was quite creepy," said Adam.

"I agree," said Geoff. "Although, you could say, it was a bit samey," he added, sardonically.

Paul laughed. "Yes. I guess there isn't really anywhere else to go when the story revolves around the fact that he buried his mum in a hole in the garden, and then spent the rest of the book agonising over it."

"Oh come on, there was a bit more to it than that," Adam defended.

"Yes, a bit more waffle. Reminded me of Stephen King," Geoff threw back.

"You wish! Sam?" Ashley asked.

"I think it was quite good."

"I need more than quite good, Sam."

"It's much better than a lot of the crap out there."

"Yep, that's really insightful. Is it for us?"

"I should hope so. He called enough times to make sure we were looking at it. You know, just to remind us he was still there," Adam said with a grin.

"I see. I think we should put this one to a vote."

They did, and it was two for and two against; Ashley's vote was the decider.

She picked up the manuscript and then looked at each member of the team. "Well, I guess I have to be a bit of a coward here and blame you lot really. Well, as usual, a bit like any jury, we have to be unanimous in our decisions. I don't feel that is the case here. Some of you obviously *like* this manuscript, but you don't love it and, although I thought it wasn't a bad read, I don't believe that we can afford the risk with the current budget. That's why I think we should turn it down."

There was an audible groan from some, while others smiled smugly.

Ashley sighed and dropped William Barber's manuscript to the floor beside her, and they moved on to the next item on the agenda.

It was 11:07 am before Ashley managed to get to her office.

It was a small room, scantily furnished, but with everything she needed to do her job; a personal computer, a couple of filing cabinets, some plants and a window that overlooked the small courtyard, popular at summertime lunch breaks.

She switched on the computer and tried to make some order of the mess that was her desk. She stacked manuscripts in a pile on the corner and sorted through a heap of post, instinctively separating the junk mail from the genuine correspondence as Marie, her assistant, walked in carrying a cup of coffee.

"Oh, you're a saint, Marie."

"I know," the woman said, shrugging her shoulders as if she couldn't help it.

Marie Pennington was a plump middle-aged woman who kept up to date with fashion, and wore her prematurely white hair in an immaculate bun on top of her head. She was an original Pitman typist, who hung her reading glasses on a chain around her neck as if to prove it.

With grey eyes and a shadow of a double chin, Marie could quite easily pass as the tyrannical head teacher, but was a warm-hearted woman who worked hard and had become somewhat of a surrogate mother to Ashley, who cared for her very deeply.

Glancing at the door to ensure nobody was listening, Marie said in a hushed voice, "So, how was the weekend?"

Ashley stopped her tidying and grinned, "It was fab. Would have been better if it was just the two of us."

"I see. Did they get in the way?"

"Oh no, the others were fine. It was just Elisabeth."

Marie rolled her eyes, "I don't know what that woman's problem is."

"She's evil. I think that pretty much sums it up. You won't believe what she did this morning."

"Oh yes I would," Marie said, knowingly.

"Oh, of course, it stands to reason that I am the last person to know about affairs that relate direct to my office."

"You're not the first and you won't be the last. The question is; what are you going to do about it?

"I'm going to sort it out," she said, her eyes flashing with determination.

Marie smiled proudly as Ashley read the first paragraph of a letter from a recruitment agency, offering accounting staff at a fraction of the cost of other agencies.

"Well, here is a bit of news I'm sure you haven't heard about," she looked up, "Rupert asked me to move in with him *again*."

Marie's eyes narrowed, "What makes you think I don't know about it?"

Ashley cocked her head in disbelief.

"Only kidding. So when are you moving?"

"I'm not," Ashley said, dismissively, as she sliced through another envelope with her mail opener. She didn't give Marie her eyes.

Seconds went by.

"Yes, I'm still here, staring at you," Marie said.

Ashley, couldn't keep up the pretence any longer and looked up. When she did so, she was smiling.

Marie cottoned on immediately.

"Really?" She breathed.

"Last night," Ashley confessed.

"Oh, that's wonderful!" Marie squealed.

She'd been an avid Harrison/Marshall campaigner for some time now.

"Oh it'll be wedding bells next," Marie said excitedly.

"OK. Easy. I'm in no hurry for that just yet," Ashley said turning to her computer with wide eyes, as if her secretary had suggested she run around the car park, naked.

"Good gracious, girl, why ever not?"

She clicked keys on her keyboard.

"Ashley," Marie prompted.

"Yes?" She looked up.

Marie sighed impatiently like a mother who had just discovered that her child had spilt ink over her favourite sofa.

"I don't know, I just don't think it would work. It's too soon."

Marie let out a short laugh. "Why on earth would you say such a thing? Have you any idea how many women in this building would be grateful just to share the man's bathwater."

Ashley laughed.

Marie moved closer to her. "Ashley, sweetheart, why do you insist on denying yourself something you so richly deserve? The man is obviously smitten with you. He is gorgeous looking and, just one other minor detail, he's loaded! Why on earth would you turn him down if he asked?"

"I haven't turned him down, Marie. He hasn't even asked. I'm just," she stuttered, "I'm just not ready for something like that. I need more time."

"Yes well, I wouldn't take too long if I were you. That queue of women is growing by the day and if you aren't careful, one of them might just pip you to the post," Marie said, almost huffily, then she turned and left the room.

Ashley smiled after her.

Marie was right. Rupert's so called *'Most Eligible Batchelor'* status shot up the moment he became C.E.O. at Harrison, and the national press ran a series of features on him.

She was lucky.

At least she felt lucky but, this had nothing to do with Rupert's Bachelor status, his looks or his wealth and everything to do with how he treated her. She'd never met a man with such a kind heart. He was sensitive yet strong, fair but firm, and he made her feel safe.

But marriage?

She logged into her email and watched as her inbox counted up, and she allowed herself to fantasise about what exactly her wedding day would be like. She thought about the dress, the flowers, the love, and the thought brought a smile to her face. *Mrs Rupert Harrison.*

She felt her cheeks flush and scolded herself. She had work to do and this was madness.

That's when she felt eyes on her.

Someone was in her doorway.

"I'm ready, I'm ready," she said without looking up. "I just need to send a quick email and I'm all yours." Then she glanced at the clock on her computer and frowned, "anyway, you are early… " she did not finish her sentence for when she looked up, she saw that the doorway was empty.

Perplexed, she left her seat, walked over to the doorway and looked out. The Fiction Editorial office was empty; most of her team were at lunch.

Marie was at her desk. She was busy pecking at her

keyboard and peering into her computer monitor, through her spectacles that were now perched on the end of her nose.

"Marie…?"

The secretary looked up from what she was doing, "What do you need?"

"Were you just in my doorway"?

Marie frowned, "Um no, should I have been?"

Ashley didn't reply, she was busy surveying the rest of the office and rubbing her naked arms, as if to reassure the hairs that had risen there.

"Is everything okay?" Marie asked, inquisitively.

Silence

"Ashley?"

"Yes, thank you," she managed eventually and turned back to her office when…

"Ash?"

The voice startled her. She turned to see Romance Editor, Julie Emerson, looking at her. "Wow, jumpy."

"Were you just standing in my doorway?"

Julie looked at her curiously, then at Marie and then back at her again, "Um, no, I just stepped off the lift. Are you okay?"

"I just asked her that, but I don't think even she knows," Marie chimed in and then casually returned to what she was doing.

Ashley shrugged, "you know, I could have sworn someone was just standing in my doorway. I thought it was you."

"Well, it wasn't me. Maybe it was my spirit leaving my body because I died of starvation!"

Ashley looked at her and forced a smile. "I just need to get my coat."

Lunch was a Caesar salad complemented by a gigantic portion of Julie's zany wit, which never failed to lift Ashley's spirits.

The topic of conversation was Julie's latest date, who was everything but the man of her dreams. Ashley laughed so much she cried, washing away the unsettling feeling that had haunted her just minutes before.

9 PLEASURE

Jason Tyler hurried into the entrance lobby of Heron Heights and was irked to find his girlfriend sharing a laugh with the building's handyman, Tomas Kellerman.

With grey eyes, short blonde hair and towering six point four feet, Tomas looked every bit the stereotypical German, but the similarities ended there.

Tomas' parents were German, but he was born and bred in the East End of London, and had an authentic Cockney accent to prove it.

After leaving school, Tomas worked for a large firm of painters and decorators before applying for, and winning, an apprenticeship opening as Assistant Maintenance Manager at Heron Heights.

He was promoted to manager a year ago when his boss retired due to ill health. Maintenance Manager at Heron Heights was a well-paid job and one he was very good at.

At least he thought so.

Jason Tyler, on the other hand, was a twenty-eight-year-old who loathed his job as a computer programmer for a London software house where his office was a cubicle and his name a number. He dreamt of getting 'paroled' out of that place and working as a freelancer, but never had the guts to do so. Living in London was expensive and starting your own business from scratch, even more so.

That was until six months ago when an acquaintance introduced Jason to a particular group of investors, who were very happy to invest in his venture for very little in return.

Now, he could afford to move out of his shitty flat in North London and into Heron Heights, of all places, for a fraction of the work.

Now, he could spend much more time in the gym, chiselling the perfect physique to showcase for the opposite sex at various parties and clubs around the city.

And with short black hair, a white smile, killer hazel green eyes and a self-assured demeanour, Jason Tyler had no trouble attracting the girls, and he knew it.

But this wasn't enough.

Despite his achievements, despite his new-found success, Jason often felt unhappy, unfulfilled.

No sooner had he conquered one thing, he was ready to move onto another, and thus he seldom stopped to appreciate anything.

He certainly disliked Tomas, although even he didn't know why.

Maybe it was the way he lorded around the building like he'd personally designed it, or the way he chatted to any female that came in his direction, or maybe it was just because of the way he towered over Jason who was just five foot, three in stature.

Whatever it was, it really annoyed him to see the handyman, of all people, chatting up his girlfriend. That's why he bounded over to them as fast as he could.

Rachel saw him coming and, before he could say a word, sprung up from her seat and threw her arms around him, "Oh My God! Jay, where have you been?"

Her embrace diluted his displeasure, "I've been looking for you," he responded, forcing a smile.

"What do you mean?" She asked, breaking the embrace and looking into his eyes.

"I've waited at Kings Cross for over an hour. I thought you were arriving on the ten o' clock train."

She frowned, "Um, no baby. It was the nine o' clock, remember? You said you wanted me to get the earlier train, because you had a meeting later in the day. One you couldn't be late for. I emailed you the details."

"No, the email said ten," he snapped and then, noticing that Tomas was still listening to everything they were saying, he asked, "Haven't you got any work to do?"

"I was working," Tomas replied. "I was takin' care of the young lady," he said with a big smile.

Rachel returned the smile and said, "Thanks, Tom. It's been fun."

He stood up and winked at her, almost as if he was trying to wind Jason up some more, "All in a day's work, ma'am," he said, putting his hand to his forehead and tipping a fictitious hat in her direction.

"Yeah, I bet," Jason mumbled as he slipped an arm around Rachel and steered her away, over to the front desk.

Paul, the security guard, stood up, "Yes, Mr Tyler?"

Jason nodded at Rachel's bags. "Have these brought up to my apartment."

"Yes sir," Paul said.

He waited for Jason to turn his back and then pulled a face, much to Tomas' amusement. Then he looked at his sidekick, "You heard the man; he wants the bags brought up to this apartment."

The boy huffed. "Do I have to take them? I was the one who fetched them from outside."

"And you're the one who'll be fetchin' his P45 if you don't get on with it, pronto, and with less lip."

With that, the boy ambled off and grabbed the bags.

"Want a hand?" Tomas asked.

"Yeah, cheers mate," the boy grinned.

Paul shook his head, sat back down at his desk and feigned interest in the bank of monitors in front of him.

Meanwhile, in the elevator, Jason was locked in a passionate kiss with Rachel. At least it appeared that way. The kiss, initiated by Jason, was more intense than passionate, almost as if he was proving a point.

Marking his goods.

Eventually, they both emerged for air.

"I missed you," Rachel said, keeping her arms around his waist.

"I've missed you too," he replied, breaking the embrace.

Rachel pouted, "I was really sad to get off the train and not find you there to meet me," she said.

Jason, who was busy looking at himself in the mirror that adorned the walls of the lift's cabin, said, "I'm sorry about that, crossed wires again. Anyway, you're here now and that's all that matters."

"Yes," she said excitedly. "I can't wait to see the flat!"

"Apartment," Jason corrected.

"Whatever. I'm just so happy to be here. I've already met one of the neighbours."

"Oh yeah, who?"

"Umm, Ashley I think she said her name was."

"Oh, her. She doesn't live here. She's just banging the millionaire guy who owns the penthouse."

"Wow really? Now, why can't I find someone like that?" She teased.

Jason looked at her.

"I'm just kidding," she said, cheerily. "You know I wouldn't swap you for anybody."

"You sure?" he asked, suspiciously.

She paused in mock pondering. "Umm, well now that you ask…." she laughed and ran her fingers through his short, wet hair, which renewed the fresh scent of his styling gel.

Jason ignored the act of affection and turned to face the door, feigning grumpiness.

Rachel loved to tease him. She knew he hated her making any comments about other men. Even admiring someone else could often put him into a mood for hours. Although she found it hard to completely understand this insecurity in a man who was clearly popular with the opposite sex. Yes, she'd seen the way girls looked at him, and then her, in that judgemental kind of way that girls do so well.

A bell sounded, the doors opened, and they stepped out into a dimly lit corridor.

The walls were cream, with the occasional gold stencilled flower that rose up to a white ornate ceiling, where a symmetrical line of gold spotlights subtly illuminated the hallway, and a collection of black and white wall prints of London in the thirties.

At apartment 7, the door's keyhole was a gold plated key card slot that flashed green in response to Jason's card swipe. Rachel noticed this, and thought it was cool to have something like that in an apartment building.

Equally cool was when Jason closed the door behind them, and dropped his key card into a wall-mounted cradle and the lights came on.

"Ooh, very flash… Jay, this place is gorgeous," Rachel breathed, taking in the hallway where the floor was a chequered flag of tiles and the walls were white.

They walked into the lounge, where the furniture was dark

mango wood, with black leather sofas faced by a glass coffee table.

Rachel was beaming. "Are we really going to be living here?" she asked, incredulously.

"Where else?" he asked with a smile.

"Wow," she breathed. "This place must cost a fortune, and I love it!" she said, bounding up to him and jumping into his arms.

"I'm so proud of you," she said, planting a kiss on his nose.

"You haven't seen this yet," he said, regaining his balance and then promptly setting her down.

He led her, by the hand, across the room to a large set of balcony doors and pushed them apart.

Instantly, they were assaulted by an icy cold gale spitting freezing rain at them.

Rachel flinched, but if Jason noticed he didn't show it. He pulled her out onto the balcony, causing her to gasp, but not from the cold but the London view that, although misty, was literally breathtaking. Beneath them, the whole building was surrounded by green lawn, flower beds, trees, garden benches, and a pond. It was secured by high metal railings.

It was their own private island in the middle of the city.

"Do you like it?" Jason asked.

Rachel was breathless, both from the cold and the spectacle before her, "I love it," she said.

"That's good, because I would have hated you to come all the way down here and be disappointed."

She turned to him as the wind tossed her hair about her face and said, "I could never be disappointed as long as I have you."

"Really? Sure you wouldn't rather be with Tommy boy?"

Rachel laughed, "Tom was just being friendly."

"Yes, well Tom likes to get friendly with all the new girls," he said, folding his arms around her.

"Really? And there's me thinking that I was special."

They held each other for a short while as the rain seeped through their clothes.

"I love you," she said, kissing him full on the lips.

"That was nice."

"You think so?"

"I know so," he said gazing straight into her eyes.

"Wait until you see what else I have in mind," she said, pulling the shirt out of his suit trousers and rubbing cold hands over his belly.

He shrieked as she laughed. But he retaliated by lifting her sweater.

"NO!" she screamed through giggles.

"Ah ah, my turn now!"

"NO! PLEASE!" she squealed, but Jason was having none of it, and proceeded to rub cold hands over her breasts, where he felt her nipples had had a reaction, although he wasn't sure to what. Nonetheless, he lingered over the pertness, gently teasing them.

She looked him in the eyes.

"You getting cold out here?" he asked, winking at her.

"A bit," she replied with a big grin and realising that she was trembling.

"I've got just the thing," he said, taking her by the hand once more, and leading her inside.

He pushed the balcony doors shut behind them, leaving the rain to drum at the glass in protestation, and kissed her again. "Your nose is cold," he said.

She laughed, "I know!"

"Best we get you out of those wet clothes then."

He pulled off her sodden jumper.

"I agree," she said, sliding off his jacket and untying his tie, as he unhooked her bra and freed her firm breasts.

The sight of them exciting him.

She shivered, but he wasn't sure if this was from the cold or the anticipation of what was to come.

"Come with me," he said.

He led her into the bedroom and through to the en-suite bathroom, of grey marble and chrome accessories. It was a large room with a bath, separate shower cubicle and a luxuriously wide granite basin.

He ran the shower and both of them, now naked, stepped inside where the hot water burrowed deliciously into their skin.

After warming through, they took it in turns to soap each other, paying particularly lingering attention when lathering those sensitive areas.

The steam in the cubicle accumulated rapidly, as did the blood to Jason's loins where, Rachel's slow, delicate and deliberate strokes, had worked up a cloud of foam around an impressive erection.

The sight of it turned her on, for it had been weeks since she had enjoyed the touch of her man, and she was yearning for him.

She trailed her lips like the water over his skin, down his chest, to his navel, until she was on her knees, and placed her lips where her hands had been massaging moments earlier. This made him lean back against the tiles, onto the balls of his feet, and turn his face into the cascading warmth.

She responded to this, by teasing his tip with her tongue, enjoying the building anticipation as her hands pawed his belly and his chest.

This continued for several minutes until he could resist no more.

He scooped her up with muscular, strong arms until her face was facing his and then he kissed her on the lips, his passion as hungry as her desire to feel him inside her.

Then, almost as if he had read her thoughts, he spun her around so she was facing away from him and her breasts were pressed onto the cubicle glass.

The movement was so fast, it actually snatched the breath from her lips.

Then, he grabbed her wrists with his right hand and pushed them high above her head. He held them there in a vice-like grip, whilst his left hand slid over her left breast, then down to her flat stomach and then between her legs There, his finger teased for a few seconds before disappearing inside, making her gasp.

Seconds washed by as he tickled and teased, invoking and enjoying her gasps and moans of pleasure, which in turn made his hand move faster and hungrier until, suddenly, he pushed a knee between her legs, pried them apart, and pushed his way deep inside her.

The event was so deep and sudden, it made her cry out in an intoxicating concoction of surprise, pleasure and pain.

He nipped, or more precisely, bit the back of her neck, she reacted by squeaking, which fuelled his excitement, causing him to thrust deeper, fully and faster, each movement accompanied by a grunt of intense satisfaction.

She turned to try and kiss him but found his left hand on her face, smearing her cheek against the glass.

He licked, kissed and bit as he continued to thunder inside her. The act fast, angry, ravenous.

It was both beautiful, exciting and painful for Rachel as she sucked in gasps of air and water.

"Take it! Take it all!" he hissed through clenched teeth as he pounded her.

Both the act and the awkwardness of Rachel's position was actually hurting. She tried to tell him, but the words came out as a drowned gargle.

"Ja...Ja...son..." she was silenced as he pushed her face harder and harder into the glass, reducing the rest of her protestations to a gagged murmur, as he exploded inside her in a raw and tempestuous climax.

10 CATS

It was a few minutes after 2 pm when Ashley summoned the lift that would take her to the ninth floor, and the legal department, where she had a meeting with senior lawyers.

The Harrison Publishing legal team included some of the best brains in the industry. It was their job to ensure that none of Harrison Publishing's authors, editors or publishers infringed the copyright of, or libelled, any organisation and or citizen in any of its books and or magazines.

They were despised by most, if not all, of the department editors. They had the ultimate power to edit anything before it was printed, and often did so, in order to protect the company's interests and, of course, it from lawsuits.

Ashley already knew what this meeting was about. Not that she had actually been told. The meeting was scheduled under the guise of a publishing schedule review, but she knew better, and she was ready for them.

A bell sounded and the lift doors slid open; Ashley's heart sank.

Elisabeth Harrison, dressed in a white designer suit, was already waiting inside. The millionaire flashed Ashley her trademark raptor smile. "Good afternoon, Ashley."

Ashley drew in a long breath and stepped inside, "Good afternoon, Elisabeth," she said, promptly finding abnormal interest in the level indicator.

The doors closed and the lift ascended, beeping on its way, as Elisabeth checked her hair and makeup in the wall mirror. "So, come across any potential best sellers today?" she asked, seemingly distracted.

"Some. Otherwise, it was the usual dross. You know, people deluding themselves that they have talent."

"I agree. Unfortunately, some of those people, like stray dogs, end up working here."

"You'd be right. Just as well there are others who work really hard to keep profits up and your dividends high."

"Oh, I didn't realise they all worked gratis."

"They work."

"Yes," Elisabeth began, admiring her cropped black hair. She had recently had it fashioned into a severe fringe and shoulder-length cut that, along with her green eyes and thick eye makeup, made her the embodiment of Cleopatra.

At least she thought so.

"Some are destined to lead, while others are intended to serve," she said, like a scene straight out of Dynasty, turning from the mirror and locking eyes with Ashley, whilst wearing her best supercilious grin.

It was right then, at that very moment, that Ashley could have slapped her face. Just lifted her hand as high as it would go, bring it down and across with such force, that would knock the bitch silly.

Instead, she returned the smile, "You're right. The board of Harrison, of which you are a member, pays me, my staff, one of which happens to be your boyfriend, our exorbitant salaries, because they need the best people to sift through and edit the crap from the marketable, and that is what we will do. Hence why any trashy novels by bed hopping has-beens, with pretentious names, will be consistently rejected, regardless of how many times they land on my desk."

Dramatically, a bell sounded and the elevator doors opened.

Ashley moved to exit, but Elisabeth blocked the door with her arm, "You know, when push comes to shove, you're just another employee," she said with narrowed eyes.

Ashley looked at Elisabeth's arm as if it were a thing from outer space, and not part of her body, and it was this contempt that made Elisabeth's blood boil.

Regardless, slowly, she removed the blockade.

Ashley stepped out of the lift, leaving Elisabeth to contemplate how exactly she was going to get that hick bitch out of her cousin's life, once and for all.

And, as the doors closed, she smiled an evil smile.

11 AFTER

An hour had passed since their encounter in the shower.

Rachel, dressed in one of Jason's shirts, lay on the bed, and for the first time since arriving, noticed that the bedroom was so big it could probably fit the flat she'd just surrendered, twice.

The décor followed the same masculine, minimalistic theme as the rest of Jason's apartment; white-washed walls, a large built in wardrobe with mirrored doors, solid dark wood bedside cabinets, and chrome fixtures and fittings. Even the king size bed was made of matching dark wood, speckled with silver studs.

Across the room, a large picture window framed an angry grey sky.

Rachel smiled. She couldn't help it. This was her new home. This luxurious pad in the city of London was where she now lived with her boyfriend.

Her boyfriend.

That sounded so good.

Finally, after years of aimless searching, she had found her place in the world, and walking out on her parent's family home ten or so years ago, suddenly didn't feel like the worst mistake of her life.

And it was all thanks to him.

She watched Jason return from the hallway. He was naked but for a pair of black boxers, and carrying two mugs of tea.

He placed Rachel's on the bedside cabinet, kissed her long and lingeringly on the mouth, then looked into her eyes.

"That was nice," he said with a grin.

By the look on his face, Rachel knew he was referring to what happened in the shower and not the kiss.

She didn't reply.

A few seconds went by.

"Are you okay?" he asked, taking a seat on the other side the bed and then leaning against the headboard, cradling his mug in his hands.

"I'm okay. Just surprised," she said without turning to him.

"Surprised?"

"By how you were in there. You've never been like that before."

"You didn't like it?"

Rachel could still feel a stinging sensation between her thighs, and had noticed red marks on her wrists. "Not particularly," she said.

"I thought you enjoyed making love."

"I do, but you weren't making love."

"What was I doing then?"

"You weren't making love."

He frowned, "You seemed to enjoy it at the time," he said, slurping his tea.

"Not that rough, Jay," she forced a smile. "I have marks on my wrists too", she said, thrusting her hands at him. And sure enough, both wrists were visibly red and would most likely bruise.

He shrugged, then kissed her wrists. "I'm sorry," he said, "I got carried away." And then added with a grin, "It's been a long time. I promise I'll be gentler next time," he winked.

He pecked her on the cheek. "Now, drink up before your tea gets cold."

Rachel felt the bed lift as he got up and padded over to the walk in wardrobe. She watched him pull out a white shirt and slip into it.

"What are you doing?"

"Getting dressed."

"What for?"

"I need to get back to work."

"What?" Rachel sat up. "What do you mean you have to get back to work?"

He turned to her, while buttoning his shirt, as if she had asked a silly question.

"What about me?"

"I'm sure you'll manage to amuse yourself for the rest of the afternoon."

"Jay, I don't want to be here on my own."

"Well, I'm sorry, babe, I really can't get out of it."

"But you're your own boss now; you should be able to do whatever you like. Besides, I thought you just worked from home."

He laughed, "In theory. But I still have clients to meet. You'll be okay. Take a look around. Go explore. Notting Hill is just minutes away. I'd have thought you'd love a mooch around there."

"Yeah, I would, but not on my own. I wouldn't even know how to get there."

"You'll be okay. Just ask at the desk downstairs, they'll point you in the right direction. You'll have fun."

"Well, I'll be the judge of that," she snapped, irritated by his apathy.

The least he could have done was taken the day off, and she

was about to tell him so, but then thought about it; did she really want to start their first day together with an argument?

So she took few seconds to consider; she'd made the best of much worse situations before.

But this wasn't just about being abandoned to her own devices for the afternoon. This was more about her surrendering her independence to be here. She'd given up her everything. Her own place, her job, and what few friends she had, to be with him, and it was terrifying. Especially, to someone who learned the importance of being independent the moment she took on her own paper round.

Yet here she was.

For love.

And it freaked her out.

It's not like she could call her parents; she had spurned them as soon as she was old enough to do so, and had learned to cope on her own ever since. The experience had been as heartbreaking as it was character building.

There weren't many days that she didn't regret severing her family ties, but her relationship with her mother was nothing but a diet of arguments about school, work and chores.

Nothing was ever good enough for Mrs Harper. No matter how hard Rachel tried, it seemed she could never meet her mother's exacting standards and thus complete anything to her satisfaction.

And this is something that affected Rachel. At least it did until she reached her teens and began to develop a personality of her own. It was then that the rebellion began, arguments turned into full on screaming matches, and things only got worse.

Barely a day went by when Mr Harper wasn't forced to choose between the devil and the deep blue sea; the wrath of his wife or the happiness of his daughter.

The wife won almost every time.

This left Rachel feeling victimised, alone, and angry, very angry, for she took every decision her father made as a personal betrayal, and each of her mother's victories as yet another reason for later retribution.

Things came to a head one day when all of Rachel's

frustrations boiled over and, in the heat of an argument, she actually punched her mother. The impact propelled Mrs Harper backward, sending her sprawling onto the kitchen floor, under a shower of water and dog food.

Rachel knew there'd be no coming back from that, so she packed her bags and left her childhood home.

She was barely out of school.

The good thing was, she had a strong work ethic. Her paper round, and the weekends she spent mucking out stables at a nearby farm, meant she had savings.

She used some of the money to buy a bus ticket to the Northwest of England, a town just outside Manchester.

There, one of her best social media friends, who happened to be a few years older than her, shared a flat with her boyfriend.

She gratefully accepted a place on the couch.

A few years later, after a stint of live-in jobs for a chain of restaurants, as well as several temp jobs, she managed to put herself through an evening course in finance and computer science. They weren't the most exciting academic achievements, but ones she knew would be essential for a decent career progression.

Thus, it wasn't long before she was offered, and accepted, a position in the accounts department of a technology company, specialising in the design of key card entry systems.

And that's where she met Jason.

His company had been commissioned to design and develop a bespoke sales order management system that interfaced with the existing finance software.

Rachel was seconded by the in-house project manager to work on the implementation team. Specifically, she was made responsible for testing the new interface. This was new territory for her; she'd never been involved this kind of project before, but then she never had been one to shy away from a challenge either.

The first thing she noticed about Jason was how handsome he looked in his pinstriped navy blue suit. It fitted him perfectly. He was obviously a man who took pride in his appearance, as he was well groomed with a short haircut, freshly shaven faced and even manicured nails.

The other notable feature was his stature; he wasn't particularly tall, but he was certainly well formed. She noticed this each and every time he took off his jacket to reveal figure hugging shirts that highlighted well-defined biceps, and the pectoral bulge across his chest.

He projected a professional demeanour at all times. Although he did pepper their interactions with the occasional compliment; nothing too cheesy or anything that could be interpreted as a pickup line, but more casual observations about her perfume, the way she'd typeset her testing log, her hair, and, of course, the way she was able to identify particular bugs in the most obscure places of his code. She was also one of the few who understood his sense of humour, which was as dry as it was witty.

One afternoon, whilst making coffee, Rachel overheard two of the office girls talking about some guy from the South.

"You're a lucky bitch, Rachel," one of them had said.

"What did I do?"

"You get to talk to him nearly every day."

It was then that she realised that they were talking about Jason.

"I hadn't really noticed," she said.

But she had.

Not that anybody knew.

He certainly didn't.

But in the two months since her regular interaction with him, Rachel had suddenly come to love the job that, up until then, she'd written off as an uninspiring means to an end.

Now, she looked forward to each and every day, where there would be a chance to either correspond or see him.

She particularly treasured the moments where he'd visit her desk in a subtle breeze of aftershave that she'd surreptitiously breathe in. Or, her personal favourite, when he'd point to an area on her computer screen and leant forward, sometimes brushing against her.

Indeed, the anticipation of any potential contact with him electrified her, to the point where it would literally give her goose pimples.

And yes, although she'd never confess to it, there were times when she'd angle the position of her chair just so, in order to make contact inevitable.

Ironically, despite this, it took Rachel some time to translate these *small triumphs* into the fact that she'd fallen for Jason, much harder than the control freak in her would like.

However, her boss was just weeks from signing off the project. After that, Jason's work there would be done, and she'd most likely never see him again.

The thought of this distressed her.

Her best friend's advice was to bite the bullet and declare her undying love. And yes, it had been delivered in exactly that melodramatic fashion which actually annoyed Rachel at the time, because it seemed like her friend was not taking her romantic predicament seriously.

What she didn't realise, was that she didn't need the advice. The very thing that threatened to tear them apart also offered the opportunity to spend serious quality time with the man of her dreams.

The project was just weeks from sign off. There were many last minute tweaks that needed to be written, tasks performed, and tests completed before the system could go live, and be deemed fit for purpose.

To this end, it made sense for Jason to spend the last week of the project 'on site'.

Not literally, of course. He asked Rachel if she could recommend a decent hotel nearby, as his boss had suggested he stay for the rest of the week.

It was all Rachel could do not to squeal and clap her hands with excitement. Not that she was prone to such over girly practises.

Instead, she managed a casual smile and, with equal casualness, revealed the name of the nearest Marriott hotel.

Inside, her heart pounded, her temperature rose and beads of perspiration prickled her forehead.

"Are you okay?" he asked her.

"Yes, I'm all right," she said, much more quickly than she'd intended. "Why do you ask?"

He was watching her. "I don't know. Your face looks flushed."

"Yes," she croaked. "I was just thinking that. It's hot in here. Do you feel that?"

He shook his head, "Not really."

"I still think we should get maintenance onto that. So, anyway, yes, the Marriott, it's probably the best place, you could actually walk to it from here."

"Thanks... that sounds good."

"And of course, if you need someone to take care of you...."

...his eyebrows lifted.

"...I mean as in show you around. Maybe check out some of the pubs or restaurants, I'd be happy to."

"Thanks. That's sweet of you," he said and then, much to Rachel's disappointment, he stopped short of making a date. Instead, he changed the subject, and started asking if she had managed to validate the test data he had imported earlier in the day.

She shook her head, and heard herself say that she'd been tied up with some time sensitive work for her boss, but that she'd get onto it first thing Monday.

It was Friday.

The rest of his words may as well have been spoken from the bottom of the ocean for all the clarity in which Rachel received them. Her disappointment had her thinking about nothing else other than, he must not be into her, otherwise he would have jumped at the opportunity to go to dinner and maybe even spend the evening.

She'd failed.

It didn't matter how much she'd styled her hair, perfected her makeup, added brand new items to her wardrobe, he hadn't truly noticed her.

At least not as a potential partner.

Or so she thought. When she finally shifted her focus from middle distance, those beautiful hazel eyes were looking at her once more.

"Are you sure you're okay?" He asked.

"Yes, I'm fine," she said, masking the tone in her voice.

He was still looking at her.

"What?" she asked.

He smiled, disarmingly, "Well, you didn't answer my question."

"Which one? About the data, no, as I said, I didn't get the...."

"...No Rachel, not about the data, about tonight."

"Tonight?"

"Yeah, I asked if you were free so I could take you up on your offer to show me the sights. I figured that dinner is the least I could do, given how well you've taken care of me since I've been here."

He was still smiling, and it was a beautiful smile.

It was clearly infectious because Rachel started grinning.

"I would absolutely love to," she declared.

And that's how, an hour later, they found themselves in a busy bistro. One of those relatively small places situated off the main thoroughfare, but always busy because of their excellent reputation.

It was Rachel's favourite place, made of red brick and decorated with a subtle Mediterranean influence, featuring heavy wooden tables and chairs, with rustic pots, pans, and even a bicycle, hanging from the wall.

Rachel loved the place; each time she visited was another opportunity to savour good food and imagine she was in a different European city.

Tonight, she was on a romantic dinner date in one of the many *ristorantes* of the one of the many *vias* of Roma.

She looked across the table at the man she had been idolising all this time. He looked particularly handsome, since he was sporting an unusually dishevelled look; his tie was loosened, his hair ruffled, and his sleeves were rolled up like he had serious business with the crusty bread and oil dip in front of him.

Rachel relished the relaxed imperfection.

They ordered alcoholic beverages with their food, both eager to consign the working week to history and welcome the weekend.

It helped.

Before long, they were talking about anything and everything but the office, and it was so liberating to be able to speak about subjects other than numbers, credits, debits and surcharges.

Instead, they shared details of childhood, previous dates, first kisses, life ambitions, favourite movies, and actors, including which they'd actually bed.

If the sexual preference and type questionnaire was obvious, neither of them chose to admit it.

Later, once they'd both calmed slightly from the initial excitement of discovering intimate details about each other, the conversation strayed to their professional roles. However it was only a temporary reflection to share the fact that neither actually liked their job, but both viewed it as a necessary evil.

Jason went one step further and criticised the organisation for which he had been working for over five years. He described it as a corporate pimp that charged extortionate fees but whored out staff for a fraction of that. He went on to share his dream of starting up his own freelance business, with a few subcontractors to help out with the bigger projects. He was sanguine enough to concede that such an enterprise would require a considerable amount of funding and that, so far, his pitches had fallen on deaf ears.

Rachel was sympathetic since she was equally miserable. She'd taken her job because she needed the money and the security that a regular salary afforded, otherwise the position was dull, and had only become interesting when he arrived there.

The last part just fell out of her mouth, right after she'd drained another vodka and Coke.

It was too late to take the words back, or mask them as anything other than what they meant.

Their eyes locked on each other for a very long time, and it was obvious.

Less than an hour later they were in his hotel room, on his bed and he was inside her. He gently cupped her face with his hands and brushed her lips with his, while she urged him deeper, eager to satisfy the aching hunger she had endured each and every time they had been in each other's proximity, until now.

Yet he shared no such haste, and appeared eager only to pleasure her with each lingering, gentle yet probing thrust of his thighs.

They made love, because that's exactly how it felt, two more times before morning, and each time felt like the first, differing only in its intensity, not of the act, but of her love for him. The love that engulfed her like a billowing curtain of silk, each and every time she clung to and dissolved into his body, as if to absorb each and every cell of him.

Six months, hundreds if not thousands of text messages, numerous video chats, telephone calls and long weekends later. Jason brought her tea one morning, sat on the bed next to her and said, "I've got something to ask you."

Rachel's stomach lurched. Instantly, her mind raced through a myriad of potential subjects, some she had actually flirted with and others she hadn't even allowed to enter her mind.

Jason must have noticed the look on her face. He smiled, "Don't look so worried," he said, and then added, "I want you to move in with me. I want you to move down south and into the new apartment with me."

Rachel was struck dumb; this wasn't a scenario she had considered.

Jason went on to explain that, thanks to his new investors, the business he formed just three months earlier was doing extremely well. So well in fact that he had secured a lease on an apartment in one of London's most sought-after properties, Heron Heights, and he wanted Rachel to move in with him.

"Rachel?"

Jason was looking down at her; he was dressed in a blue suit and with his freshly gelled hair was looking every bit as handsome as he first day she'd met him. "That's the third time I called you, what were you thinking about?"

She shook her head, "Nothing important."

"I'm going to be late," he said, fiddling with the cuffs of

his shirt.

"Why don't you take me with you?" she asked, getting up from the bed and moving into the living room in search of the bags that had been dumped there, most ungraciously, by the so-called porter.

She pulled out her favourite pair of stonewashed jeans.

Jason followed her out, just in time to see her slip out of his shirt. She had a beautiful body and her breasts, oh how he loved her breasts…

"…Because it would be boring for you," he said, feeling compelled to move over to her and touch them, and he did.

"I don't mind. I'd like to see you in action, so to speak." She smiled as he circled her right nipple with his finger.

"Yeah, well, I do. You've just got here. You should take some time to get settled in." He could feel himself getting aroused once more. "Hmm," he said, appreciatively. "I can still remember how you felt in the shower," he whispered in her ear and then proceeded to kiss it.

But she twisted away from him, "Yeah, well keep remembering. I'm trying to get dressed," she said more petulantly than she intended, and then pulled on white panties.

He groaned.

"You'd better go. You're going to be late," she said, strapping her breasts into a matching white bra and then returning to the bedroom.

He looked at his watch. Considered going after her but instead he called out, "Okay. I'll see you later then."

Rachel didn't reply. She couldn't decide how she was feeling.

She felt pride that Jason's new venture was doing well, ecstatic about sharing a gorgeous apartment with him, yet also somewhat miffed that he hadn't made an effort to be at home with her today.

What's wrong with you?

She was behaving like a petulant brat. After all, she was used to and perfectly fine with her own company.

She enjoyed it.

In fact, instead of being annoyed, she should be pleased that her boyfriend (she loved that word) wasn't there to smother her on her first day, but instead gave her the space to unpack, settle in, and maybe even do some laundry.

Suddenly, she felt foolish, and rushed out of the bedroom just as the front door slammed shut, toppling a paperback book from its perch and sending it crashing to the floor with a loud thud.

She picked it up and turned it over in her hands. As she did so, a business card fell out and to the floor.

She retrieved it and read:

Night & Day Professional Services
B1, Heron Heights
London

Apartment B1, she resolved, must be in the same building although, as far as she'd noticed, all of the apartments were numbered, and none prefixed with a letter.

There was no telephone number on the card. No clue as to the nature of the business, but Rachel couldn't help but think how perfect it would be if she could land herself a job here, in this very building.

She finished dressing.

12 LIBEL

Martin Barren was a spindly man, in his early forties, with a gaunt face and bright ferret eyes showcased behind small square spectacles. He had a traditional cockney accent that stereotypically would, on first impression, place him as a market stall owner or London cabbie. It was this very assumption that often gave Martin an edge over his adversaries for, despite appearances, Martin knew the law, and he possessed a razor sharp mind to practice it.

He sat in a leather chair, at the head of the large frosted-glass boardroom table that dominated the rectangular room that was nothing like the clone-like meeting room boxes on the lower floors. Here, the décor had been contemplated over days, and not someone's coffee break.

This power room is where Martin held court.

The lawyer, and the two paralegals he'd asked to sit in on the meeting, stood up when Ashley entered the room.

Martin smiled a fox-like smile, "Ashley, good to see you. Please sit down."

The young men sitting opposite her smiled a greeting. They had never met Ashley before. Rumour had it; she was *banging* the Chief Executive, or at least that's the conversation they were having on their way here.

Both were eager to see just exactly how Martin was going to handle this particular cross-examination.

"Nice to see that chivalry isn't dead after all," Ashley said with a smile.

"I trained em' well," Martin replied. "How's your day?"

"Busy."

"Oh, I know that feeling," Martin said, opening a manila folder on the desk in front of him, "Obviously, I won't keep you any longer than necessary. I've just got a few things I'd like to clarify with you."

Ashley nodded, knowing exactly what was coming next. "Happy to oblige," she said with a smile.

"Well, of course, as you've probably guessed, this manuscript by," he made an action of consulting the text before him…

"Jackie Harris," Ashley offered, leaning back in her chair and placing her arms on the armrests.

"Yeah, Miss Harris." He looked, smiled then leant back in his chair, "Ashley, the Met are… how shall I put it…"

"…Pissed off?"

He smiled. "Yeah, pissed off about this manuscript."

"I'm sure they are."

"Apparently, they're worried it may contain text that libels them."

Ashley snorted. "Oh please, Martin. We both know this book is not libellous. She hasn't written anything that hasn't been printed in the press already, a hundred times over."

Martin cleared his throat. "Well, Ash, can I call you that?"

She nodded her acceptance, but was irked, because she was already feeling handled. She knew Martin, if not personally then by reputation, this isn't how he would typically *clarify a few things*.

He was a shark. An ambusher.

Of course, this could be part of his strategy.

"I don't know exactly what this manuscript's about. I haven't had a chance to read it. Apparently, they haven't either. I was told you refused access to it. Is that right?"

"It is."

"And why's that?"

"Because, I'm not obliged to. I'm not an agent, Martin. I don't undertake the dissemination of work, especially not without the author's permission. Besides, the manuscript isn't even finished yet. I've only seen a few excerpts."

"Right," Martin said, calmly, while maintaining eye contact and gently tapping the folder.

A few seconds drifted by, then, "Ashley, I can't stress how important it is that we resolve this. Ya' see, they've threatened to sue if that manuscript so much as circulates between offices, forget it seeing the light of day."

"Jackie Harris is no longer employed by the Metropolitan Police."

"No, she isn't. But it doesn't mean that they won't fight tooth and nail to protect their reputation."

Ashley laughed. "Reputation? You are joking, right? You do know what they put that woman through, don't you?"

"What they did is irrelev…"

"…Some of her so-called colleagues raped her and then left her for dead."

"Not according to the jury…"

"…The jury failed to reach a conclusion because some of those cowards were afraid to testify against their own. The same cowards who held that woman down and then took it in turns with her."

The two paralegals visibly shifted in their seats.

Ashley's eyes were blazing with revulsion, as she pictured every sickening detail described to her by Jackie. That kind of detail, that kind of pain can only be described by someone who experienced it first-hand. Somebody so broken by such an ordeal that she was now unable to face the world, get another job, or any semblance of a life back.

"Ashley," Martin cleared his throat and leant forward. "Ash, it's not for this company to get involved in the personal vendettas of the general public. Jackie Harris had her shot in court and it was too bad that she…"

"…Too bad?"

"Yes, Ash, too bad," Martin asserted with jaw muscles flexing.

He was obviously suppressing an outburst, which Ashley had learned, he was prone to. He had once suffered a nervous breakdown because of the way he mishandled his stress.

Allegedly.

There was a very awkward silence.

Martin sighed and shifted in his chair. "Look, we're both on the same side here…"

"Yes Martin, we are. And please don't bother with the 'what is best for the company' speech as I am liable to puke all over your shiny table. I believe I am doing what's best for the company. My job is to select manuscripts that are commercially viable, and I think Jackie Harris has written such a manuscript."

"I thought you said that she hadn't written it yet and that you'd only seen excerpts."

Ashley's eyes flashed with rage, "Martin, I'm not one of your fucking witnesses," she seethed.

The paralegals glanced at each other.

If Martin was surprised by the woman's attack, he didn't show it but said, calmly, "I didn't say you were. I'm just trying to establish the facts."

"The facts are as I have explained them to you."

"And I appreciate your candour. So I'll afford you the same courtesy: I haven't got the foggiest what's in this manuscript and, quite frankly, I don't give a shit. But I think there's a good chance that, if published, it's going to libel the London Metropolitan Police and, if it does, the proverbial will well and truly hit the fan, and if that happens, there's going to be casualties."

Ashley let out a short laugh. "You're threatening me now, Martin, is that it?"

"No, I'm just giving you counsel, that's my job here."

"Well save it. We both know you have so-called jurisdiction over editorial, but let me give you some advice; I'm no rolling over on this one. I'll fight it until I am physically incapable *or* fired."

"It may just come to that," Martin retorted, dismissively.

Ashley's eyes narrowed; "Fuck you," she spat. Then, glancing at the paralegals, who were shrinking back in their seats, and then back at Martin, she said, "We're done here."

She stood and left the room.

Martin took a few seconds to contemplate what had just happened and then, in one swift action, he sent the manila folder skittering down the table.

This isn't over. He thought. *Not by a long shot.*

13 VOICES

It was late afternoon by the time Rachel finished unpacking and sorting through her belongings.

She hung her clean clothes in the gargantuan walk-in wardrobe, next to Jason's, then sorted her laundry into a neat pile on the floor. But she was baffled to discover that there wasn't a washing machine in the kitchen, nor anywhere else in the apartment.

It was only as she stood, hands-on hips, in the doorway that she spotted the fire plan. It listed, in meticulous detail, the whole building's floor plan; apartments, stairwells, lifts and emergency exits. It also showed there was both a gym and a laundrette in the basement of the building.

Very American.

It was as she moved to scoop up her clothes from the

kitchen floor, that she heard a deep thud above her head. She looked up and listened carefully.

Nothing.

Then, just as she was about the resume her task, she heard it again.

Thud! Thud! Thud! Thud!

She looked up and listened, as the sound travelled from one side of the ceiling to the other; heavy footsteps.

It sounded like two people chasing each other across the apartment; from the kitchen to the dining room.

She followed the sound to where it stopped, somewhere near the balcony, and that's when she heard them; voices, drifting to her from a slit in the balcony doors.

Curious about her new neighbours, Rachel approached the doors and put her face to the tiny opening, where a powerful jet of cold wind blew in her face, fanning her hair behind her.

She listened hard to the muffled, indiscernible voices that came to her like a bad long distance telephone call. Two people, one voice slightly louder than the other. They were apparently standing out on the balcony, but the gale was making it hard to pick up exactly what was being said.

She widened the slit in the door so she could fit through it, allowing the bustling sound of London city to rush in as she stepped out.

She looked up to the overhead balcony, turning her head like a satellite dish in her attempt to tune into the words, but they remained indiscernible although, from their tone, it was clear that the neighbours were having a serious argument about something. Whatever it was, Rachel could not tell.

She remained that way for several minutes until, eventually, frustrated and cold, she returned to the apartment, sliding the doors firmly shut behind her.

Not bad. My first day here and I've already witnessed a domestic.

She returned to the kitchen to retrieve her laundry pile, but as she did so, she noticed the *Night & Day* business card on the side.

She picked it up, considered her next move for a few seconds, and then made her way to the bathroom, where she styled her hair and applied makeup.

The laundry could wait.

Yes, there was a slim chance that showing up at this place, unannounced, asking for a job, was unlikely to come to anything, but it was worth a try.

What's the worst that can happen?

Besides, it's not as if she hadn't been in this situation before.

She knew when she left the family home, that if she never wanted to return, she'd have to find work and work hard. And whilst she may have started out as a proud girl, she soon learned that if you don't ask you don't get.

When she discussed moving to London, and in with Jason, they had agreed he would line up some suitable interviews for her but Jason had changed his mind recently. He told her that, since the business was doing so well, she no longer needed to work.

But that conversation didn't really come to any conclusion. Rachel knew that, as enticing as the offer was, the idea of being imprisoned in the apartment all day, playing housewife, and having to rely on Jason for handouts, every time she needed to buy something, was not in her nature.

Anyway, the point was moot until she actually found a job, so she resolved not to mention anything further about the subject until she did.

With that, she made her way to the front door making sure to grab the key card from its cradle on her way out.

14 HOME

6:30 pm.

Ashley had spent the afternoon in meetings and teleconferences, but every time there was a lull in her schedule, her mind went back to her argument with Martin.

She was still smarting from it.

Although she knew why, as much as she didn't want to admit it to herself. This wasn't just about the Jackie Harris book. This was because she had allowed her emotions to get the better of her, and the meeting to get out of hand.

This was unlike her.

In fact, now that she stopped to think about it, she'd been off her game all day, and she couldn't work out why.

It all started when she woke up in Rupert's apartment and was forced to get ready without her stuff. Then there was that creepy business with the mirror, getting into work late, her confrontation with Elisabeth and then this.

She knew that if this had been any other day, she would have handled things differently, instead of letting that dick rattle her.

And this was just the beginning.

There was no doubt in her mind that this whole situation would get much worse before there was any chance of it getting better. Ultimately, if the commercial decision was made not to publish, there would be nothing she could do about it.

I'm just a cog in this machine.

Perhaps, but she meant every word of what she said in that meeting room; she wouldn't give up on this book, at least not without a fight. She had promised Jackie. She had promised not to fail her where everybody else already had, and she intended not to.

The very same people who had sworn to uphold the law had victimised and hurt one of their own, and then attempted to cover it up. This was something they should have paid for yet never did, and the public had the right to know that.

The hands on her shoulders startled her.

"Wow, bad day?" Rupert asked.

"You could say that," she said with a weary smile.

It had been an exhausting day.

He put a reassuring hand on her arm. "Can I offer you a lift?"

"I have my car."

"Oh good. You can give me a lift then," he said with a grin.

They stepped onto the elevator, and neither said anything until the doors had closed behind them.

"So, do you want to tell me about it?" Rupert asked, without taking his eyes off the floor indicator.

"Not really," Ashley said, glumly, knowing where this was going.

"Was it your meeting with Martin?"

And there it is.

Ashley looked at him and shook her head. "I might have known he'd come crying to you."

"Well, I do happen to be the boss around here."

"So, he thought he would get you to have a word, is that it?"

"He just filled me in."

"And?"

He cocked his head, weighing up his response. "What do you expect me to say?"

Ashley rolled her eyes.

"… No, hang on a minute. This isn't the first time and it won't be the last, but we're talking about a story that dominated the front pages for weeks. There have been something like half a dozen documentaries dissecting every angle of the event, and subsequent trial."

"So? You should be thanking me. You can't buy that kind of publicity."

Rupert looked at her. "Things are just starting to get back to normal for The Met. They're not going to take kindly to us publishing a book about what happened there."

The bell sounded and the door slid open.

Rupert swiped them out of the building, and they made their way towards the multi-storey car park.

The air was autumnal crisp and smelt of burning coal.

Laughter drew Rupert's attention across the road. A group of people were wrestling with a giant inflatable Casper the ghost that was threatening to snap its tether to the office building, and take off to the skies.

"I love Halloween," he said. "The sights, the sounds, the atmosphere. We used to trick or treat every year when we were children."

"So, that's your master plan?" Ashley asked, "Small talk me into submission."

"Is it working?"

She threw him a look, pressed the elevator button for the car park and said, "You know, I really don't understand what the problem is, exactly. Is it the fact that it's the police? Is it a testosterone thing? What's everybody so afraid of? This is, after all, the perfect book, commercially. It, in your own words, has had something like six documentaries made about it, extensive media coverage. It has public interest stamped all over it and it exposes that whole institutional thing that's become so popular of late. What exactly is the problem?"

"Ash, come on."

"What?"

"You know what. You're doing that whole passive aggressive thing."

"Am I?"

"You know you are. I can tell from your nose."

"My nose?" She instinctively put her hand to it. "What's wrong with my nose? I thought you said you liked my pixie nose."

"I do. Especially the way it wrinkles every time something annoys you."

"It does?"

Now it was his turn to throw her a knowing look.

The elevator doors opened and they stepped in. Again, as if somebody was listening to their conversation, they waited for the chime and the doors to close before they spoke. It was Rupert again.

"You're asking why we feel so strongly about this. Why we're not chomping at the bit to publish this book. Have you asked yourself why you are?"

"I told you. Because I think…"

"…Come on, Ash, it's me you're talking to. What is it about this book? Is it genuinely good or is there something else?"

"So now you've taken to analysing my motives?"

"I'm just trying to understand why you're courting trouble."

"Courting trouble?" She echoed, angrily. "I thought I was doing my job."

"I don't believe you," he said, flatly.

She watched him for a long time then said, "That's your prerogative."

The bell chimed, the door opened and a cold gale puffed at them.

Ashley walked into it, her hair swishing angrily from side to side as she went.

Rupert hurried after her, "I just want to know, Ash."

"I've already told you," she threw back, her voice, bouncing off concrete columns and echoing loudly around the car park.

Rupert caught her arm and spun her around. "Hang on a minute."

She was facing him now, their eyes met and he saw something in hers, something that he couldn't quite decipher; sadness, empathy?

"Talk to me," he prompted.

Seconds ticked by as the warmth from his eyes began to chip at her stoical stance.

"I hate it when you do that," she said, eventually.

"Do what?"

"Do that. Act like you know me. Like you can read my mind."

"That's because I can," he said, teasingly.

She didn't respond to the grin on his face, and instead suddenly said, "I knew moving in with you was a bad idea."

Then, she turned, and walked toward her car.

The words had an edge to them, a sharp edge that began to sting.

Rupert hurried after her.

"Hey!"

She ignored him.

"Hey!" He yelled, forcibly.

But she didn't stop.

"Hey!" He yelled. He caught up with her, just as she reached her car and spun her around to face him once more.

A car horn blared angrily from the street below as if to

protest against the action.

"Don't do that," he said, now irritated.

"Do what?" She asked, petulantly.

"Walk away from me when I'm trying to have a conversation with you, and bring our relationship into this argument. It's not cool and it's beneath you. If you want to have a professional disagreement with me, then do so, but don't drag us into it."

His eyes were burning, and she could see that she had irked him.

Perversely, that pleased her. It was like a small victory, although why she was treating him like an enemy combatant she did not know.

"Is that what this is about?"

She looked at him.

"Are you freaking out because you've finally agreed to move in with me?" He asked, incredulously.

She sneered. "So now it's amateur psychology?"

"Or you could just tell me that I'm wrong."

She thought about this for a few seconds as a wave of rage swept over her.

"The…there you go again!" She stuttered, "Acting like you bloody well know me."

"Then just tell me I'm wrong."

She said nothing, for she was suddenly overwhelmed by a fluttering sensation in her belly, and in her heart. It made her feel giddy.

She turned away from him and found an unusual fascination with the slit of London by night that, like a modern canvas, could be seen through the gap between the parapet of this level and the next.

"Are you using this as an excuse to sabotage us, Ash?" Rupert pressed.

Tears pricked her eyes and she wanted to speak, but she couldn't.

"Ash?"

He was holding both her arms now, and she could feel his eyes on her. His big brown eyes, that she dare not look into because she knew that she would not be able to lie.

He was right.

Rupert continued, "You know this, us, it means everything to me and you know that I've been ready to commit for some time now, but if you're going to try and wreck this before it's even started then let's…"

"…I don't want that," she whispered quickly, and finally looked at him.

There were tears sliding down her cheeks and she was trembling.

He slid his hands up from her arms to cradle her face, and slowly wiped the tears with his thumbs.

"Then, what do you want?" he asked.

"I don't want to get hurt," she whispered, the words barely audible above the din of London and the gale that was funnelling through the building.

In fact, the pixie nose that he loved so much had turned red from the cold, and he bent his head to kiss and nuzzle it, tenderly.

"Me neither. But I'm willing to give it a try, but only if you are."

She nodded like a blubbering schoolgirl and he pulled her to his chest with a big smile.

"You know, next time it'd be easier if you just say you love me, okay?"

He felt her muffled chuckle against him, and it felt good.

Eventually, she emerged from his embrace, sniffing and forcing a laugh.

"I must look a mess," she said.

"Well, I wasn't going to mention it…"

…She play thumped him while fishing a tissue from her bag.

"I'm not giving up on this book," she said, dabbing her eyes. "I can't and I don't want to, Rupert. I gave her my word. And, before you ask, it isn't just about that. I'm not naïve. I know this is a business. In fact, it's because this is a business that I feel this strongly about it. It's an excellent book, and I believe that it makes commercial sense for us."

"Are you sure that's all it is?"

She hesitated and then nodded, "Yes, I'm sure. I mean, I'd

be lying if I said I didn't want to stick it to these people too, of course I do, but that's because they're a bunch of institutional bullies, and they need to be held accountable. Oh, and before you say it, I know I can't do that at the expense of the company."

"Good. I'm glad you said that," he said, stepping in closer and framing her face with his hands once more, "because if you want to get this book published, you'll need to make sure it gets passed by Martin."

There was seriousness in his tone. Ashley was under no illusion that if it came to supporting her or safeguarding the family business, she'd lose.

And she was sanguine about that.

She put her arms around him and squeezed him tightly as she considered this.

He smelt good and his embrace was warm, strong and exactly what she needed.

They remained that way for a while until he said, "Shall we go home?"

"Yes," she nodded, emerging from the embrace. "As long as we can stop by mine first, because there's no way I'm having another morning like this one."

"Why? What happened?"

"Oh, you don't want to know. Let's just say, it started strangely and then went downhill from there. You can drive," she said, holding up her car keys.

Within minutes, Rupert was steering the Mercedes out of the car park and home.

15 NIGHT & DAY

It took Rachel a couple of elevator rides to work out that apartment B1 did not exist or, more precisely, it wasn't any of the luxury apartments situated on one of the ten floors that made up Heron Heights, but that the "B" in B1 actually stood for *Basement.*

That's how she now found herself walking down a long, dimly lit corridor passing, to her right; a lonely looking, but well equipped gym, and to her left; a mini laundrette, equally deserted.

Beyond these, the gloom of the corridor appeared to thicken like dirty dishwater, it was as if the building's designers did not care about the riff raff who dared to venture into this uncharted part of the building, and Rachel found herself wondering if she should.

The walls here were coarse and appeared unfinished, as if skimmed by an unenthusiastic plasterer and then abandoned.

At the end of the corridor, she found three doors. The one directly ahead was marked *Private,* the one to her left *Storage.* The other seemed to have lost its plaque, the discoloured glue outline now the only clue to its existence.

Is this it?

She leaned forward and listened carefully for noises beyond the door; nothing, just the distant hum of electricity and the whirring sound of a boiler.

Suddenly, a muffled door slam ricocheted down the corridor to her, making her jump. She spun to track the sound's origin; the laundrette, but there was nothing there.

She waited, and listened carefully for any other clues as to whether or not she was alone down there, but none came.

Eventually, she turned back to the door in front of her, but not before a final glance back down the corridor; nothing.

This place, this dungeon, was giving her the creeps. She wondered if she wanted, or could even work in a place like this, and considered retracing her steps back towards the light.

But then she had a word with herself. A job here would be perfect. No commuting, no nothing.

Get a grip!

Another slam scraped its fingernails down her spine, and she snapped her head back to the corridor.

Now, she was scared.

A few seconds later, an insect silhouette of an unhealthily

thin woman appeared in the corridor. She was wearing an apron and her thin wispy hair hung, untidily, around her shoulders. She coughed a rattling smoker's cough, as if to make her presence known.

Someone's housekeeper?

The figure stopped suddenly and looked down the corridor, and although she could barely discern the woman's features, Rachel could feel eyes on her.

Without even thinking, she knocked on the door.

No reply.

She glanced down the corridor; Spindolina was still watching her.

Way too creepy!

She tried the doorknob; it was unlocked. She entered the room and quickly closed the door behind her.

The room was steeped in shadows. The only light was stingily provided by a dirt spattered strip of window that ran the length of the opposite wall.

The spacious yet cluttered place was in no way similar to the world above. It was more like the land that time forgot. It reminded Rachel of the set of a dated American detective series. It featured battered wooden desks laden with documents, old typewriters and general antiquated office paraphernalia, smothered in a layers of dust.

The wooden desk in front of her had seen better days, but it actually carried what appeared to be a modern day computer monitor, and desk lamp that contributed little to lifting the gloom.

Behind it, sat a woman with curly black hair. She wore a large headset like a hairband. She had her back to Rachel and appeared to be looking out of the slither of glass above her head, and the bland grey sky beyond it.

She was talking on the phone in a subtle northern accent, that Rachel placed somewhere in Yorkshire.

"...I am afraid she isn't in right now, but may I take a message?"

Rachel advanced into the room and noticed a bank of filing cabinets lined up on one side, and yet another pair of desks. It seemed that a whole team of people worked out of this place although none but one appeared to be on duty right now.

"…It would be my pleasure," the woman continued, "I shall ask her to contact you the moment she returns to her apartment. Thank you so much for calling. Goodbye."

The woman swivelled on her chair, scribbled something on her pad and then looked up.

If Rachel's presence surprised her, she didn't show it. Instead, in a business-like manner, she asked, "May I help you?"

The woman was in her late fifties, although her demeanour exuded ten times that. She had a well-worn complexion and a pair of owl-like eyes that sat behind thick lenses.

"Oh yes. I'm sorry to trouble you, but I'm looking for the manager," Rachel said.

"You've found her. What can I do for you?"

"Oh hello, I'm Rachel Harper. You don't know me, but I've just moved into one of the apartments upstairs and just stopped by on the chance that you may have an opening."

"Are you from Manchester?"

Rachel was temporarily speechless, for she didn't even know she had a Mancunian accent.

"It's okay, love. I can tell you probably weren't born there, but it seems you lived there long enough to pick up an inflection."

"Wow," Rachel said with a big smile. "That's incredible."

"Yes, for my next party trick, I'll make my husband disappear. Oh, no, I've already done that."

"That's really impressive."

"No, I've just been working here too long. So, you're looking for a job, are you?"

"Yes."

"Here?"

"I was hoping you might need some help."

An antiquated buzzing sound, like an old alarm clock, interrupted their conversation.

The woman turned to what looked like a giant mixer desk of switches and slides. A red light, labelled *Line one,* in black, felt tip scrawl was flashing.

"Oh be a love and grab us some coffee, it's over there," she said, pointing to the coffee machine on one of the desks across the room, before spinning on her chair and pressing a switch, "Douglas Residence, how may I help?"

Pause.

Then, "I am sorry Mr Douglas is not available right now. May I take a message?"

The coffee machine was a big, cumbersome brown thing that, like everything else so far, appeared to have been manufactured a couple of decades ago. She poured filtered coffee into blue mugs with black painted ducks.

Okay, so it is a bit grim and stuck in some kind of time warp, but I can help with that. And she seems down to earth.

Rachel returned to the switchboard desk, where the woman was still talking on the phone, and noticed that the computer wasn't switched on. In fact, it looked like it wasn't even plugged in.

"…okay. I will make sure he gets the message. Thank you for calling. Goodbye."

Rachel handed the woman the mug. "Ooh, thanks love."

"I wasn't sure if you took it with sugar or not," Rachel said, looking over at the coffee machine.

"Oh, I am afraid I do, got a bit of a sweet tooth. As you can well see," she added, patting a relatively slim tummy. Rachel returned to the coffee machine table and grabbed the bowl of sugar cubes, along with some milk capsules, and handed them to the woman.

"Thanks," she said, plopping six cubes into her mug and three capsules of milk.

Rachel made a conscious effort not to flinch since she appeared to put on weight just at the thought of anything sugary.

"Please, sit down," the woman said, "I'm Lilly by the way." Rachel shook her hand and then sat down. "So, what makes you want to work at night and day, Melissa?"

"Umm, actually it's Rachel."

"Oh Rachel, I'm sorry, love. Not very good with names," she smiled, "that's why I have to write everything down."

"I have got to be honest with you, Lilly, I don't really know much about what you do here. As I said, I just dropped by on the chance that you might be looking for help."

"I see. Do you have any secretarial experience? You know, typing, talking on the phone."

"Oh absolutely. One of my first jobs was as a call centre customer service representative for a couple of mobile phone and utility companies. I did this for a couple of years before going into the leisure trade. So, I have a lot of experience talking to and dealing with customers, both on the phone and in person. There was also a lot of general administrative work. You know, booking rooms, typing up letters, organising meetings, etc. I also put myself through college to get a business degree which eventually landed me a role in the finance department of a major security firm in Manchester.

Rachel smiled, "That's how I met Jason. He was one of the programmers subcontracted to do some work there."

"Wow, I heard those boys earn a lot of money."

"Well, he did okay. He's now started his own business and that's doing really well."

"But what about you? You seem to have moved a lot. What about your family?"

"Well, my parents are from Cambridge but, we kind of lost touch quite a few years ago."

"Oh, I see."

Rachel waited for some kind of maternal judgement, at least in Lilly's eyes, but there was none. Instead, she asked, "So why Manchester?"

Rachel shrugged. "Well, a friend of mine lived there, and it was a good change of scenery."

"So, then you met Jason and decided to move to London?"

"Yes." She laughed, embarrassed. "Yes, I know, following a boy. Doesn't sound very sensible does it?"

"Oh no, I admire your sense of adventure." Lilly smiled, taking a gulp of her coffee.

"I've known Jay quite a while. The distance was starting to take its toll, and he was keen for me to make the move down here to be with him."

"Good decision?"

Rachel laughed, nervously. "I hope so. I only got here this morning."

"Really?"

"Yes."

"So where are you staying?"

"Here; apartment seven."

"Really? Apartment seven. "

"Yes."

"Well, fancy that. Your boyfriend must really be earning the big bucks to afford a place here."

Rachel shrugged, "It certainly seems so. I was just as surprised when I arrived. I actually thought the cab had dropped me off at the wrong address, but I absolutely love this building. It's amazing."

Lilly nodded proudly as if she had personally designed it.

"Do you know much about its history?"

"Absolutely. It was actually something we were tested on when I first started working here many, many moons ago. It was part of the sales patter. The owners believed it imperative that we girls be familiar with the building's history, so that we could share that knowledge with potential tenants.

It was built way back in the thirties, and was one of London's most unusual gems, attracting a lot of publicity because of its rather ostentatious design and, of course, the amount of money that was spent both on acquiring the land, and then building on it.

Heron Heights has ten floors and, as you will have noticed, is almost hexagonal in shape. Now, it has multiple spacious apartments but, back then, they were a series of hotel rooms.

The inside was fitted with the most opulent décor; velvet curtains, oak panelling, brass light fixtures and satin sheets in the double rooms. It became the talk of the city and the place to stay for anybody who was anybody.

In its prime, it even gave places like The Ritz a run for its money.

Some of the most powerful men and women from around the world chose to stay here, when visiting London. In fact, deals that have made many of today's conglomerates were forged in this very building. Historic events, and product launches have all taken place at here.

Then, over time, the business evolved. From a five star place to stay to more of a home from home. With some guests booking extended stays.

That's when demand for a different kind of front desk service was born.

Enter me.

Within weeks, what was the old laundry room was refitted with desks, kitted out with typewriters and wired up to a then very sophisticated telephone system. This enabled guests to hand out a direct dial telephone number to what was effectively their very own personal secretary.

Visiting dignitaries and businessmen, no longer had to worry about office space or secretarial staff. From this room, we took care of all of that for them.

We answered, relayed and replied to hundreds of messages from around the globe. We'd type letters, even prepare presentations and forward these on behalf of our clients.

It was an exclusive and innovative service offered by Heron Heights, and it went from strength to strength.

Unfortunately, to use one of today's vernaculars, we became victims of our own success. Bookings soared, as did staying times, which meant that some guests would monopolise some rooms for months, often booking multiple rooms to accommodate families travelling with them. This meant that other regulars were forced to seek alternative accommodation.

Before long, Heron Heights began to lose many of its core guests to rival hotels that were now providing similar services.

So, the owners were forced to diversify; they laid off most of the staff and converted the hotel into a luxury apartment building, and long term bookings were welcomed.

Fortunately, there was still some need for secretarial and administrative services, but demand was nowhere near the same as back then ..."

Lilly paused here. Her eyes roamed around the room and the empty desks, as if looking for the people who once sat there. "...I lost most of my girls. We were downsized from a ten-strong team to four and were given the responsibility of taking care of the actual building's administrative services."

Lilly sighed. "Over time, demand diminished further, and, with the advent of mobile phones, I had to lose another two of my girls, which left Keri and me. The service has been retained by a handful of tenants but, of course, wealth brings with it the prestige of agents and personal secretaries. Our subscriber list is just a shadow of what it used to be."

There was sorrow in Lilly's eyes, and it touched Rachel. "So, where's Keri?" She asked.

Lilly looked at her somewhat perplexed and then she said, "Of course, you wouldn't know about this as you're not from around these parts.

Keri was an aspiring actress. She went to classes here in London. She was also a fan of the musicals and watched as many shows as she could afford. And that's when she got involved with him."

"Him?"

"Daniel Morris."

Rachel shook her head.

"You don't know him? He's been in a few BBC programs, rough piece of work, really fancies himself. Anyway, he befriended Keri and got her involved in all sorts of stuff. Not that she'd ever admit it to me. All I knew, is a number of times she'd turn up for work looking more than worse for wear. Sometimes, she'd just burst into floods of tears, but when I'd ask her about it, she'd tell me she couldn't say. Then, suddenly, one day, she didn't show up for work at all. Didn't leave a note for anyone, nothing. She just vanished. Of course, the police questioned that nasty piece of work. He claimed he hadn't seen her in weeks. That was a year ago. To this day, the police still haven't found her."

"That's terrible," Rachel whispered.

"Aye. I'm sorry, love. Me and my big mouth. It hasn't exactly been a secret around here. It was all anybody could talk about for months but, of course, like most things, she's faded from everybody's mind, but not mine."

"I'm very sorry to hear it, Lilly."

Rachel felt awkward and wondered if she should lean over

and hug the woman, but she decided against it.

"I loved that girl as if she were my own. Needless to say, I was over the moon when that so and so got his just deserts a few months later. He was arrested, for possession I think."

"It all seems so very sad. You've been through a lot. It must have been terrible for you."

"Aye," Lilly nodded. "It wasn't easy. But you have to move on, don't you. I learned a long time ago that there's no point dwelling in the past."

The irony of that statement, when compared to the state of the room, was not lost on Rachel.

However, after mentally castigating herself, she asked, "So, how have you coped on your own?"

She was genuinely interested, but also keen to establish whether or not there was any chance of her getting a job here.

"Well," Lilly began, tapping the computer monitor, "At first, I tried this. The sales pitch was that it would allow me to man this place, singlehandedly, twenty four hours a day, seven days a week with little or no input from me. The reality; three thousand pounds and three days of training later, I'm none the wiser. All that touching and clicking is beyond me. Give me a pen and paper any day."

Rachel smiled. "So, what did you do?"

"Well, I had a few girls in, but none were really up to it. You see, they were particularly young girls, not unlike yourself, and didn't seem to have much actual secretarial experience."

"Well, I have had a lot of that," Rachel said, quickly.

"And of course, the night shifts didn't help."

"Night shift?"

"Yes, this is a twenty four hour service, hence the name. I've had to put in most of the hours and hire temps for when I'm not here, but that's working out expensive."

"Oh." Rachel uttered.

"I know. It didn't appeal to them either. Unfortunately, it is a prerequisite for the job." Lilly said, meeting Rachel's eyes as if she were reading the girl's thoughts.

Rachel hesitated. Yes, she liked the idea of this job and yes, it actually sounded exciting, since she might even get to speak with some of the celebrities, but night shifts? It must get lonely, and maybe even scary.

She said, "It's just; I came down here to be with Jay and…"

Lilly smiled, knowingly. "That's okay love, I understand…"

"…Oh no…"Rachel blurted out. "It doesn't mean I don't want the job, just it isn't exactly what I had in mind." She paused a second and then asked, "How often will I be required to work nights?"

Lilly thought about this. "It's up to you, really. I appreciate you will want to spend time with your boyfriend. And I will try my best to work around you."

"How about every other night to start with?"

Lilly smiled. "That sounds reasonable."

"And would Jay be allowed to visit me?"

Lilly wrinkled her nose as she pondered the idea. "Well, I would expect something like that to be against company policy."

Rachel's shoulders slumped.

"But, as we don't particularly have a company policy with regards to visiting boyfriends, then I would say that would be fine…"

"Great!" Rachel exclaimed with a big grin

"…on the understanding that it would not in any way interfere with your work because if it does, I will have to reconsider. Is that clear?" Lilly's eyebrows lifted, in an expression that reminded Rachel of her old school teacher.

"Clear. So," she shrugged her shoulders, "Have I got the job?"

"Just as soon as you have learned how to use this," Lilly said, nodding at the switchboard.

"Really?"

"If you want it."

"That's brilliant! Thank you, Lilly!"

"Don't thank me yet. You haven't heard about the pay."

Rachel paused, Lilly winked at her, and then added with a big smile, "It isn't that bad."

"So, when do I start?"

"Tomorrow okay for you?"

"No problem," Rachel said, although she would have liked to have settled in and had a look around the area before getting stuck into her new post.

"Perfect. Of course, because of the kind of tenants we have here, I am going to need some references for the past three years, you'll also need to sign a non-disclosure agreement, and I will have to run a check with the police, if that's okay?"

"Oh, of course," Rachel replied. "So, who exactly do you have living here anyway?"

Lilly smiled mischievously, "Pull that chair little closer, love, and I will fill you in."

She explained how the antiquity that was the switchboard worked, how to plug in the headset, and how to answer and release calls. She also made Rachel write down a list detailing all the room numbers and their inhabitants.

Lilly already had a list, but she wanted to be sure that Rachel made and was aware of her own.

She went on to say that all of the tenants took their privacy very seriously. It was very important that Rachel not divulge or discuss anything she learned from *Night & Day* with anybody, especially members of the press. Her contract would reflect this.

Then, in the next breath, the woman was dishing out the dirt about each and every one of the celebrity tenants, covering each floor, room by room.

Rachel listened with incredulous wonder. She'd actually heard of some of the people Lilly was talking about. It was beyond her imagination that she would actually be living in the very same building.

The storytelling continued into the evening after more coffee and several biscuits.

Before long, Rachel found herself viewing Lilly not as her boss, but as a dear long lost aunt.

16 THE INVITE

Later that evening, Rachel was changing into one of the few dresses she owned; a black maxi dress. And while she'd choose jeans over a dress any day, she did love how sexy this one made her feel.

Rachel had planned on an exploratory shopping mission after her so-called interview, but she'd been unable to extricate herself from Lilly's chat happy stories.

Not that she had tried very hard. She was having fun, and would often remind herself that this would be her new job, and she couldn't wait to get started.

Of course, this meant that when she finally returned to the apartment it was to a bare fridge, but for a couple of bottles of mineral water, half a bottle of milk, three eggs and a very sad lemon.

Luckily, Jason had returned sooner that she had expected and had brought with him a bunch of flowers, a box of chocolates and a dinner invite. When Rachel asked where he was taking her, he told her it was a secret, but that she should dress in her poshest frock.

"I think it's going to work out. I think I'm going to like it here," Rachel said, raising her voice so Jason could hear her from the bathroom.

"I did say you would. You just need to give yourself time to settle in," he replied.

"I was thinking of having a chat with the neighbours. See if they have any vacancies," Rachel said quickly and waited for a reaction, as she sat in front of the mirror and began to touch up her makeup.

Jason came out of the bathroom and sauntered over to the walk in wardrobe. Rachel could see his reflection in the mirror, and she momentarily stopped what she was doing, to admire his sculpted body and his shower wet hair.

She loved him.

Okay, so he had been off earlier, certainly not as considerate as she would have liked, but she knew he could be very sweet when he wanted to be. She also loved his intelligence and admired the fact that he, not unlike her, had endured hardship, and had worked very hard to get what he wanted from life. He was tenacious. Focused. Everything she admired in a man, and, most importantly, he was hers.

Yes, he did have an edge, especially on a bad day, but it was this same edge that she found attractive. That, as well as the fact that he had the most perfectly formed rear, she thought, as he slid into a pair of briefs which he filled nicely.

He then turned to her and asked, "What did you say?"

She smiled. "I was going to see if I can get a job."

"What?"

"I know you weren't that keen, but I think…"

"…Wait, wait, wait," Jason interrupted, as he pulled on a Ralph Lauren shirt. "You went to look for a job?"

"Well, I found a card in one of your books."

"I don't read books."

"What do you mean, you don't read books? You've got a shelf full of them."

"They were gifts."

"Well, whatever," Rachel continued, "anyway, I lied, I'm not going to look for a job; I've found one!" She said, excitedly. "Right here in the building. Working for the answer service downstairs. I start tomorrow."

He stepped into a pair of black trousers and paused.

"Rach, we talked about this."

"I know we did, and you said how you felt about it, but I didn't get a chance to tell you how I really felt. You know me, Jay, while the idea of being a kept woman sounds appealing, it isn't who I am. You know I like my independence."

She decided against telling him about the shifts. Now wasn't the time. She just wanted to go out and enjoy the evening.

"But why would you want to work there of all places? This is London. There's loads of opportunity out there."

"Because it seems really interesting."

He observed her for a long time then, "You're mental, you are," he said.

"I know. But that's why you love me, right?"

He tucked his shirt into his trousers, buttoned them up,

stood behind her and watched her reflection in the mirror.

"What?" she asked.

He put his hands on her shoulders and smiled one of his boyish smiles. "You look good," he said, earnestly.

Rachel grinned. "Why thank you, kind sir. It's really sweet of you to notice."

She felt a warm feeling inside. It was the first nice thing he had said to her since she had arrived here.

"I love you," he said, bending down to kiss her full on the mouth.

And things just kept getting better.

When the kiss was over, she laughed, noticing a pink sheen to his lips, "You're wearing my lipstick now."

"Does it suit me?" he asked, pouting and pulling faces at the mirror, sending her into a fit of giggles.

"Umm, no, not your colour," she said, dabbing his lips with a tissue. "So, where are you taking me tonight?"

"Well, I thought we would go across to the West End. You know, have something to eat and catch a show."

Rachel beamed with excitement. She'd never been to a London theatre before, but had wanted to for years.

"You ready?"

"Am I ready? I'm already out the door," she said, standing up.

They stepped out of the brightness of the apartment into the dimly lit corridor. Rachel looked up; the recessed lighting was casting pools of light on the carpet yet, unlike earlier, they seemed somewhat inadequate, as if too weary to continue performing the task for which they were installed.

She spotted a man with a long coat at the end of the corridor, next to the elevators, and called out to him, "Excuse me! Could you please hold the lift for us?"

She turned to Jason, who was just pulling the front door shut.

"Hurry, he's holding the door for us."

She took his hand and hurried him down the corridor.

"Who is?" He asked.

She followed his gaze; the lift doors were closed.

"Oh, thanks a lot."

Jason pressed the arrowed button to summon the lift. Then, noticing her frown, he asked, "What's up?"

"Well, there was a man here just a few seconds ago. I asked him to hold the lift, but now he's gone."

"I didn't see anyone."

"He was standing right here."

"Are you sure?"

She looked at him, hands on hips, "Of course I'm sure," she said, mildly irritated.

"Well, I can't see how," he nodded at the floor indicator, "the lift's still down in the lobby."

Rachel looked up; it was.

"Can't be. He was just here …"

Jason laughed and made a display of shaking his head. "And we haven't even started drinking yet," he said, jabbing the button again as if doing so might speed the thing up.

At night, the Heron Heights lobby was a futuristic spectacle of glass, metal and light.

The lift shaft was the main feature. It stood, like a Roman statue, in the centre and was encased in a glass cubicle with four gleaming metal struts, bejewelled by hundreds of LED lights that disappeared high into the ceiling, like a runway to heaven.

A trio of men stood to the far side of the room. Next to them, a silenced flat screen monitor beamed images of a Sky News segment about racing cars. It featured close-ups of a grinning driver in a red jumpsuit.

Nearby, seated on one of the chocolate leather divans, two smartly dressed women were deep in conversation.

When they stepped out of the elevator, Rachel took a moment to admire her surroundings. The place looked completely different by night, and it was stunning.

When she noticed she was being watched by a series of close circuit cameras, she waved, making one of the reception desk security guards smile. He then went back to flick switches with an air of utmost importance.

Rachel broke into an excited squeal when she spotted a couple walk through the revolving doors, and she actually recognised one of them.

"So you found him then?" Ashley asked.

"Yes I did, thank you," Rachel replied, linking Jason's arm. "Jason, this is Ashley...."

"...Marshall. I think I've seen you around."

"Likewise," Jason nodded with a smile.

"Wow, you mean you both live in the same building and haven't ever spoken to each other?"

Ashley leaned in and in a lowered voice said, "The people who live here tend to keep themselves to themselves, Rachel." Then she wiggled her nose, implying that most of the tenants were snobs.

"Oh, I don't know. You were nice enough this morning when I was stuck out there all on my lonesome, under the driving, *freezing* rain," Rachel replied.

She was obviously teasing Jason.

Both women smiled, conspiratorially.

Jason pulled a face and said slowly and deliberately, "It's a pleasure to meet you."

"And you. This is Rupert," Ashley said.

"Pleasure," Rupert said with a big smile and shaking both their hands.

"So, are you on your way out?" Ashley asked.

"Yes, going over to the West End to have something to eat," Rachel beamed with excitement.

"Are you not dressing up for the occasion?" Ashley asked. Rachel must have looked mortified because she quickly added, "as in Halloween costume."

"Oh no, we're not going to that kind of event," Jason said.

"Well, good luck out there, because the ghosts and ghouls are already on the rampage, and there's no knowing if you'll make it back alive."

It was Rupert's contribution,

Ashley looked at him.

"What?"

They laughed.

"Why don't you join us?" Rachel offered.

"Oh, no, that's sweet of you, but after the day I've had, I'm just going to vegetate in the bath while he orders pizza."

"Really?" Rupert asked.

"Yes, really…"

The sound of crying drew their attention to the entrance where a man with wavy black hair, wearing a quilted jacket, stepped through the revolving door. He was holding the hand of a little boy, who looked about five years of age, with blonde hair and teary grey eyes. He was obviously unhappy about something.

Behind them, a wafer thin blonde, carrying two shoulder bags followed them inside.

A smile spread over Jason's face; "It's Darren."

"He was just on TV," Rachel uttered.

"Yes, he's superb," Jason replied.

"You think so?" Rupert asked.

"Oh yeah," Jason said, not taking his eyes off the man who nodded at the duty guard and hurried over to the elevator. "I reckon he's without a doubt the new Lewis Hamilton."

"Uh oh, here we go," Ashley said, rolling her eyes as the two men launched into a discussion about Darren Stanton's talents as a racing car driver.

"They actually live on the floor below Rupert," Ashley said.

"Do they? Wow, what are they like?"

"Oh, they seem okay. You don't really see much of them…"

"…Don't tell me, they keep themselves to themselves."

"You learn fast."

"I guess it's easy to get like that when you have loads of money."

Ashley smiled at Rachel's candour, "Some do, yes. So, how are you settling in?"

"Oh great, it's absolutely brilliant. I love the apartment, and this," she added looking around the lobby, "it's just beautiful. It's really beyond anything I could have imagined."

There was a genuine wonder in Rachel's expression and Ashley related to this.

"The only downside is that I don't know anybody here. Oh, except you of course."

"Don't worry, you'll soon settle in. In fact, we're hosting a dinner party next Saturday, nothing fancy, just a few people. Why don't you come along?"

"Really? That sounds awesome! But I wouldn't want to impose."

"Don't be silly, you wouldn't be. Please say yes. Rupert's friends and cousin are coming and it's going to be so dull. It would be nice to have a couple of people there that I actually like," Ashley grinned.

"You know I can hear you, right?" Rupert said, interrupting his conversation.

Ashley kissed him on the arm.

"What do you think, Jay? Ashley's invited us over for dinner next Saturday."

Jason forced a smile, "Yep, that would be cool." he said.

"Great. Say, around eight?"

"That would be lovely. Thanks ever so much. Oh, what number are you at?" Rachel asked.

"Well," for some reason, unknown even to her, Ashley hesitated, then said, "*We* are in the penthouse."

"The penthouse?" Rachel made a show of dropping her jaw.

"I know. Please don't judge us," Ashley said, affably.

"We're in seven," Rachel said. "Wow, the penthouse. So I suppose you'll never overhear your neighbours having a domestic."

Ashley leant in closer, "Tell me more."

"Well, our neighbours who live one floor up? They were really going for it this afternoon. It started with them chasing each other around the room, and then it ended with them having a row right next to the balcony. For a second I thought he was going to throw her off."

The men stopped chatting and looked at her.

"What?" Rachel asked.

Ashley smiled, "You must be mistaken, Rachel. It couldn't have been apartment eight."

"Oh no, it definitely was eight, that's the apartment above us, right?" She asked Jason, who nodded, "because I heard them talking or should I say screaming at each other."

"Did you actually hear what they were saying?" Ashley

asked.

"Not really, although it's not that I didn't try."

Rachel bit her lip. She realised she was fast turning into Lilly, and she'd only just got there.

"Rachel it wasn't eight," Jason interjected.

She frowned, "I'm telling you it was. I heard them *above us*. That's eight, isn't it?"

"You're right, that is eight, Rachel." It was Rupert speaking now. "But you couldn't have heard anyone because that apartment is empty, has been so for weeks now."

Rachel stared, incredulously, as a nearby wall light flickered, then died.

17 X-HILERATION

The house in Chelsea, London was in complete darkness but for the street light that flooded in through large windows.

The shag pile was clean and the surfaces gleamed in the six bedroom home that employed no less than three maids daily to ensure that every doorknob was wiped, every piece of furniture polished, every flagstone floor cleaned and disinfected.

Elisabeth sat in the oversized armchair, gazing at the wriggling shadows created by the rainwater, as it dribbled down the glass of the patio doors.

The tumbler in her hand was nearly empty, as was the vodka bottle standing on the nearby coffee table.

She didn't feel guilty; she hadn't touched alcohol since leaving the clinic, for the third time, three hundred and ninety one days ago. But she needed it tonight for tonight was the night, tonight was the night she'd finally driven Adam away. Tonight was the last time he'd storm out of her home and her life, in anger.

She knew it.

She could feel it.

She was alone again.

She had pushed him too far.

Something else to add to that ever-growing list of self-loathing, but she couldn't help it. It was an addiction, worse than the one she'd been battling with ever since she could remember. The one that was drowning her misery at that very moment. Her reliable, dependable companion who never left her side and always numbed her pain.

Except for tonight.

Tonight there was an ache in her heart, one that she hadn't felt before. One that she had foolishly allowed to grow stronger over the last year. Ever since she had decided to publicly acknowledge Adam as her boyfriend, her man, her other companion. The one that accepted where others shunned, who understood when others didn't, who loved where others daren't. The lover who made her hot by night and burn for more by day. The one thing that gave her courage to face her fading beauty, whilst keeping her anchored to her youth.

But she had ruined it all.

Why did she always have to test him? Why did she always have to push against the boundaries of his love for her? Had he not done enough? Had he not constantly and consistently proved himself worthy, and deserving of that elusive thing she secretly yearned for, but never publicly revealed - love?

The answer was yes.

So why did she laugh in his face tonight, after he had fallen to one knee and proposed to her? Why did she humiliate him so callously?

Admittedly, she did uncharacteristically wait for him to finish, before erupting into guffaws of laughter. In fact, she had waited most impatiently for him to pour out his heart and extol all the reasons why they were good together. She listened to him drone on about how she meant everything to him, and how he wanted nothing more than to spend the rest of his life with her.

But she couldn't help herself.

She couldn't stop herself mocking his vomit inducing

sentimentalism, and accusing him of only wanting to get hitched to her for her money.

She had been hateful even when, with glistening, incredulous eyes and trembling voice, he had looked at her and uttered, "How can you be so cruel to me, Elisabeth? I love you."

She had just shrugged, indifferently.

Shortly after, Adam grabbed his car keys and ran from the house, chased by the sound of her hollow laughter.

That was over two hours ago.

Now, she was alone, but for her other two companions; vodka and misery.

She had done it again.

But it was Adam's fault, he shouldn't have been weak. He shouldn't have walked out on her, he should have weathered her spiteful ways as he usually did, but instead, he chose to abandon her to the mercy of her worst enemy, herself.

She poured more vodka and drank with thirst, wincing as the alcohol burned its way down her throat.

Why was she even upset?

She knew this was coming, ever since she met him at that charity ball, but not last year, the year before. That's when she spotted him in that tuxedo. That's when she noticed how, for most of the night, a conveyer belt of females made their move on him, yet he only had eyes for her.

Not that he was perfect. He had unusually large ears for a start, but he had a magnetic personality, she could tell that just from the demeanour of the conversationalists that flocked to him like bees to honey. There was no doubt he was an agreeable companion, with a perpetual smile and the ability to regale those around him, to the point of causing them to regularly burst into annoyingly loud laughter.

Yet still, despite his audience, from time to time, she'd spot him looking through his gathering and watching her with those keen eyes of his.

At first she was affronted. How dare the younger man even look at her with such arrogant intent? She would never allow herself to be the mature conquest of any male, no matter how funny he might be, or how attractive he may look in a tuxedo.

She refused to become a statistic, and would not become the rich bitch of record, a drunkard's story to be told to his friends or anyone else he'd care to brag to.

Oh fuck it! What do I have to lose? It's not like I'm going to see him again. Just use him and kick him out. It's not as if you're ever going to get married to him. It's not like you're ever going to get married to any man.

Ever!

So she gave him what he wanted and took her own physical gratification in return.

In her house.

On her terms.

And it was surprisingly enjoyable.

Very much so.

That was two years ago.

In the first year, she'd made it clear that it was just an arrangement. A bargain that suited them both. Something that could not and would not be shared with anybody else. In return, she'd keep him close, close enough for convenience, but not too close to compromise her in any way.

He, was working for a small publishing outfit she'd never heard of at the time. She, was a major shareholder of a major publishing house.

He could do better, and it just so happened that there was an opening in Fiction Editorial, and nobody would actually question a candidate if he was suggested by their Chief Executive Officer.

So, she spoke to Rupert.

Adam started shortly after.

Like their relationship, she didn't expect Adam to last, but he did. Apparently, going from strength to strength, charming and impressing everybody he came into contact with.

His resilience became her aphrodisiac, his strength her rock, his desire her addiction. There was something about that man that made Elisabeth want more, from life.

That's when she decided to publicly acknowledge him as her partner. Not that he had ever pressured her to do so. In fact, he told her that he'd much prefer they keep their relationship secret, at least for as long as he was working for

Ashley.

Which, of course, prompted Elisabeth to make the announcement that very day.

Her eyes filled with tears, as a bitter sadness burrowed deep into her stomach. The hurt she was feeling burnt like grazed skin.

She looked at the fluorescent dials of her Cartier watch; a gift from Adam, and swore.

He was out there somewhere right now. Probably with some whore. Maybe he hadn't even bothered to get a room. Maybe he was doing her right now in the backseat of his car.

She was shivering, not from the cold but from the rage that had been growing like a beast inside. It fed on her wondering, anticipating, envisioning all kinds of scenarios, all sorts of sexual encounters, all kind of filthy sluts touching, feeling, and enjoying her man. The first man she had had actually allowed herself to trust since the disasters of her past.

He'd regret this, though. He'd regret not trying harder. She'd show him. She'd show him soon enough. In fact, she was going to show him right now.

She wiped the tears from her eyes, smudging her mascara, and slipped into her shoes.

Then, she left the house, climbed behind the wheel of her car and drove off at great speed towards Soho.

Soho, deep in the heart of London, had grown far from its origins as a sex district.

It used to be a dirty and dingy place, lit only by the colourful characters that stalked its pavements. Those dressed in fishnet tights and skirts that barely covered their modesty, the night prowlers who searched for tomorrow's breakfast in alleyways and the backseats of cars.

Today, much of the insalubrious area is gentrified. It is a bustling multicultural district, with both business and residential buildings, as well as upmarket restaurants, specialised food stores, and entertainment venues, such as the Palace Theatre, which is home to some of London's most popular West End shows.

Peppered in between the above, are still some of the

original albeit more discreet sex shop retailers. Behind them, hidden in back streets, away from the everyday hustle and bustle of new London, remain some of the original entertainment venues whose fixtures and fittings may well have been modernised, but whose remit continues to cater for the varied predilection of man.

Tonight, the rain soaked streets had been invaded by a legion of ghosts, ghouls, monsters and demons who stalked the area in search of a fun time or sexual encounter, whichever came first.

Elisabeth knew she was close to her destination because she could hear the pounding bassline, faint yet clear as a beacon.

She slowed the car, as it passed various alleyways, until she drew level with one featuring a giant red neon '*X*', for '*X- hilaration*'.

It was hammered high onto the wall of a red brick building that looked more like a factory than a nightclub.

The sign winked at her, enticingly.

She smiled.

A loud slam on her door startled her.

"Sorry, sorry."

A middle-aged man in a makeshift office worker zombie costume held up his hands apologetically. Then, he turned to punch his friend, who continued to play fight him while their companion looked on, laughing.

They all disappeared down the alleyway, toward the X.

They were everywhere.

A whole new breed of Soho scavenger, the worst; the middle class. The wretched that worked from nine to five, five days a week to fund their mediocre existence, and to afford the occasional night of revelry.

And now, the 31st October gave them an excuse to dress up in their ridiculous costumes, terrorise the neighbourhood and each other. Halloween was indeed about the lifting of the veil separating the living from the dead, but it wasn't supernatural, it was metaphorical.

A loud, angry claxon made her jerk once more.

Instinctively, she looked in her rearview mirror and squinted into the glare of the headlights. She wanted to give whoever the driver was the finger, but instead pulled the car over, onto double yellow lines, and killed the engine.

She stepped out and almost lost her balance as the fresh air met the alcohol in her system. She waited a few seconds for the sensation to pass by holding onto the car. Then, without locking it, she followed a man with an axe in his head, and woman with peeling skin into the alley.

Her reflection in a café window reminded her just how conspicuous she looked in her tight pencil skirt and stiletto heels, but she didn't care.

She looked good.

Albeit cold.

And now a faint mist had descended which she knew played havoc with her hair. So, she resumed her journey to the club's entrance, carefully picking her way through the cobblestoned pavement to avoid catching a heel, or worse, snapping one.

As she approached, the music percussion gradually grew in intensity and could be felt underfoot, and it was putting her in a mood; a mood for dancing.

However, it was as she joined the queue of horror characters that she noticed something else through the corner of her eye. Somebody watching her.

She swayed to a stop almost causing those following to crash into her.

It looked like the shadow of a man. He was standing, legs astride, black coat hanging behind him, about fifteen feet further down the alley.

Elisabeth gawped as revellers, eager to get inside, shoved passed her.

She took a step forward, out of the line of ghouls, ghosts and zombies, and squinted through the dim light of the overhead neon sign, that had tinged the whole scene crimson.

He was still watching her; short hair, jawline, coat and boots.

"What are you staring at?" she called out, drunkenly, slightly unnerved.

There was no reply. The figure did not move, did not speak, nor shift; it just watched.

"Hey! I'm talking to you."

Nothing, just a cold breeze blowing in her face as the mist continued to shift and fill the alley.

She waved a dismissive hand at the shadow, and turned to barge her way back in line where she smelt alcohol on the breath of a werewolf and the cheap deodorant of superman.

It was so bad she felt momentarily nauseous.

At the door, something compelled her to look back once more, but there was nothing there, just mist.

So, she forced a sultry smile at both of the bouncers, whose eyes, she felt, followed her backside through the doors, until it descended a gloomy stairwell to a tiny kiosk window.

She tossed a note inside and didn't wait for change.

At the foot of the stairs, she pushed on double blue doors that opened to reveal red brick archways, lit by ultraviolet light, that highlighted graffiti scrawled all over the walls and ceiling.

To the side, was a long bar staffed by a group of topless young men and bra wearing women.

She looked over her shoulder for the alleyway stranger, but he wasn't there. Oddly, she felt a tinge of disappointment, yet she had no idea why.

Still, it was nothing that couldn't be cured with alcohol.

She pushed her way towards the bar.

A few shots later and she felt much better. She turned to see a large space, lit intermittently by flashing colour and laser lights. They licked over a sea of undulating bodies that ebbed and flowed with the colossal sound of the pulsating beat.

She stared as the whole place started to float eerily in front of her face, made worse by the sweaty aftershave aroma of her neighbour.

It made her want to wretch.

She steadied herself against the bar.

As she did so, a barstool was conveniently vacated and she instantly set about mounting it, but this was no mean feat in an ankle length, figure hugging pencil skirt and heels.

Bloody thing makes me feel like a geisha woman!

Then, much to her surprise, it was actually sweaty aftershave man who was, somewhat appropriately, wearing a cape and a fanged smile, who lifted her with strong arms onto a barstool perch.

She smiled gratitude, but it disappeared the instant he turned his back on her to resume his conversation.

The atmosphere was exhilarating.

There was so much potential around her; the place was teeming with males, most of which, she was confident, were seeking a mate, just like her.

She was determined.

She was going to show Adam that he was not the be-all and end-all of men, and that she could, and would, have anybody she wanted, whenever she wanted them.

And it hadn't been but five minutes, before the slinky outline of her legs reeled in the first two would-be candidates, or boys as she saw them. They couldn't have been long out of puberty.

They made a show of looking over her body and smiling at her. She made a show of smiling back, but she got bored very quickly.

It was flattering, but she wasn't interested.

Adam may have been a few, alright, many years her junior, but he was different, he was much more mature than many men his age and certainly more mature than this motley duo.

It was as they approached her, and began to spout pathetic chat up diatribe, that she slid down from her perch and walked off, through the throng, towards the ladies, where, of course, there was a queue.

What was it with these places? It's bad enough having to share a bloody toilet with the world and its crotch but being forced to stand in line for it is fucking ridiculous!

Nonetheless, Elisabeth waited as patiently as she could, which was no more than two minutes, and then, much to her displeasure, she noticed that she wasn't standing in line at all! She had merely joined a clump of bimbos who could find no other place to converse, but in front of the convenience!

What is wrong with you fucking people?

The alcohol was mixing nicely in her stomach now, and the result of this fermentation was coursing through her veins, feeding her already intoxicated brain, where it continued to make her feel deliciously giddy.

With that, she shoved her way through the clutch of females, or prostitutes as her mind had dubbed them, to angry protestations, and made her way inside.

The room, stylised in blacks, greys and more urban graffiti, was heaving with girls reapplying makeup in front of drab stained basins, rearranging clothing and generally chit chatting about the evening's events.

She paused to watch two girls, one of them with a pin through her eyebrow and a shaved head, tongue the other against the hand dryer.

She smiled, as she searched for a free cubicle, whilst considering the idea of a lesbian encounter, but dismissed it when she concluded that she enjoyed men too much.

If only they weren't such bastards.

"Come on," *she* chanted as she waited for a cubicle vacancy. Ideally, one furthest from these classless bitches, where she would have the opportunity to throw up in private, because she certainly had no intention of doing so in front of them.

But all of the doors remained firmly shut until, suddenly, one was relinquished, somewhat hastily, by a girl with spiky gelled hair, pink horns and a miserable face, made worse by lumpy smudged mascara.

She rushed out with her head bowed and a quivering bottom lip.

Elisabeth watched her scarper through the crowd, and was still half watching her when she pushed on the cubicle door, only to find that it was still occupied by a red-faced devil.

He was sitting on the toilet with a joint dangling from his lips while manoeuvring, with both hands, the backside of the scraggly blonde girl who was straddling him.

Elisabeth watched as the angel's wings fluttered up and down in tandem with the bouncing motion of her body.

The devil paused momentarily to see who had opened the door. Satisfied it wasn't who he expected it to be, he continued with the business in hand, soliciting more squeals of pleasure from his sexual companion.

Elisabeth apologised and then instantly felt foolish for

doing so.

She turned away from the cubicle, awkwardly closing the door behind her.

It was then that, for the second time that evening, she felt eyes on her and her head snapped up; there he was, across the room, like a preacher among his disciples.

He was standing in the doorway, unmoving, in that same stoic way, oblivious to the girls pushing by him.

Elisabeth's first reaction was to avert her gaze, but she couldn't. She felt drawn to him just as she had outside. This, despite the fact that his face was obscured by the black hood of his coat.

She could just about discern a stubbly jaw, and, occasionally, as she angled her head, his eyes! They were piercing blue, almost violet, and they were observing her, fixing her to the spot, burning deep into her soul.

Her heart was pounding now, in synchrony with the thumping music, as a low-lying fog escaped the dance floor and slithered along the floor like a knot of snakes.

The mere presence of this man, and the danger that he exuded, made her stomach flutter, her blood pulsate, and elicited a delectable tingling between her legs.

She closed her eyes as she was enveloped by the massive bassline and raw guitar of Depeche Mode's 'Barrel of a Gun'. It crawled over her body and under her skirt as the walls leant in to kiss her, making her instinctively close her eyes.

When she reopened them, he was close, so close she could smell him; fresh, like a frosty winter's morning, and now she could see his face, strange yet uncannily familiar...

Rupert?

His skin was tight, translucent, vibrant, and free from impurities. His nose was broad and proportioned, his lips full and kissable.

He was looking at her...

Oh God, save me from those eyes.

...Deep blue eyes, almost violet, beautiful, drinkable. They caressed her face, explored her body, while leeching her energy, causing her to sway.

She swallowed hard with a dry throat, "Rupert, what are

you doing here?" she croaked.

She drank in his face. He was beautiful yet surreal, recognisable yet featureless, like a blurred being from a dream, a beautiful, beautiful dream.

Rupert? Is that you?

It had to be him, and this pleased her, it pleased her immensely.

Then, as if he had read her mind, his lips curled up in what would have ordinarily been construed as a smile, but Elisabeth knew it to be more, much more; it was a promise, a promise of inconceivable pleasure.

The rhythm oozed and the drumbeat burrowed as the volume increased. The metallic rock accentuated her senses, as his cool hand touched her face and instantly constricted her breath to short, rasping spasms. His fingers traced their way over her lips, and down to the back of her neck, eliciting small hairs, like soldiers, to attention.

His blue eyes shimmered in the neon ultraviolet light, and his steely gaze bore deep into her as his face drew closer…

Closer…

… his lips offering to quench her lustful thirst.

"Oh my God, Rupert, please…"

She stilled her breath, as her heart continued to drum rhythmically in her ears. She closed her eyes once more in anticipation of the moment, as the music's gravelled vocals drew to a seductive crescendo; they scratched through her extremities and electrified her senses, as everyone else in the room dissolved to shadows.

Kiss me!

And that is when they caught her; strong fingers closed around her wrist, spun her on the spot and tugged her so fast forward she nearly lost her balance.

Elisabeth Harrison was yanked, unceremoniously, into a cubicle and thrown up against the plywood wall, causing it to protest against its rusty metal restraints.

The door was still ajar giving onlookers a side view of the action.

For her, the action was violent but delicious.

He was in front of her now.

Her eyes were closed once more, but she could sense his proximity, and she breathed him in, that same fresh morning scent, deliriously intoxicating her nostrils.

She dared to open her eyes to see that she was now penned in by two strong arms. They leant against the wall, on either side of her.

He was watching her again, and it was all she could do to not look away, for all her nervous extremities were on fire. She couldn't bear it.

He was smiling again. That same smile, like he knew what she was thinking, had learned of her arousal for him, and enjoyed tormenting her with tantric anticipation.

His lips hovered enticingly close. Just inches away.

OH YES! Kiss me, Rupert. Kiss me!

After all these years of yearning, all of these years of anticipating this forbidden moment, she was finally going to have the only man she had ever wanted but was never allowed.

The start of a new track whispered, "*It's time to burn*" and then a pounding percussion of house music faded in, shaking the wooden partition and jangling Elisabeth's desires.

The stranger tilted his head slightly, studying her, as a dog would as it tries to understand the fluttering of an insect. And then, in one lightning movement, his hand shot out and delicately caressed her face as he pressed his body close to hers. Then he began to rhythmically, almost in sync with the music, push himself against her.

She moaned with excitement as she could feel him.

She reached down to touch, but his hands grabbed both of her arms and pushed them up, over her head.

Oh yes, be rough with me, please be rough with me, I want all of you.

But Elisabeth would have no choice in the matter. It took the stranger seconds to reach down and tug roughly at the hem of her skirt, which he then yanked upward, over her face, encasing both her arms and transforming her into a human chrysalis.

Through the haze of the thin fabric, the only thing she could discern were dancing shadows of humanoid outlines projected on the dingy walls all around her.

No Rupert! No! Not like this, I want to see you.

Her mind spoke the words, not her mouth, as a hand grabbed her thigh in a grip that made her squeal. Then, she felt her left leg being lifted onto a strong arm as something pulled at her panties.

Seconds later, she felt his freezing cold body pressing against hers, and then he was inside. Not small but large, not gentle but as rough as a mounting stallion, burning his way so deep that the pain fractures shot through her, like an aching tooth.

She screamed, but her voice was muffled inside the cloth, and drowned by the pulsating rhythm that accompanied each and every one of the probing thrusts that were violating her.

"No, Rupert, not like this! Not with you!", but he wouldn't stop, he continued to pound her as if she were not a human being, but an animal to be inseminated.

Then she saw them, through the haze of the Lycra, the very eyes that had seduced her, those beautiful blue eyes had metamorphosed into ugly black cavities.

"NOOOOOOOO!"

She battled to free herself from the cocoon, but the powerful arms kept her in place as he pushed deeper and faster, deeper and faster until he suddenly shuddered inside her; the climax as quiet as it was painful.

Then, abruptly, he withdrew as a sword would from a wound, leaving her standing there, body shaking and face sweating in the impromptu, claustrophobic cloth sack.

And then he was gone, the presence dissipated like mist in the moonlight.

In her inebriated, nauseous state, it would have been easy for her to think that she had dreamt the encounter, but the grazing on her thighs, pain between her legs, told her that her ordeal had indeed been real.

Slowly, Elisabeth Harrison allowed her violated body to slide down the cubicle wall, until her naked buttocks hit the cold tiles with a thump.

There, with breathing that was quick and shallow, she sat, unmoving, inside her cocoon, as the door to the cubicle slowly closed, as if leaving her alone to weep with some dignity while contemplating the darkness that had been planted inside her.

Across the city, Adam opened the front door to find the house in total darkness.

He called Elisabeth's name, but she didn't reply.

He dropped a bouquet of flowers on the coffee table and turned on the table lamp, revealing a handwritten card, *"I'll always be here for you, Elisabeth. If and when you decide to see it. Love Adam x."*

He was very sorry about tonight, but he wanted to try again. He needed to try again, for both their sakes.

18 ALONE?

It felt as if she had been asleep just minutes when three loud raps at the front door echoed down the hallway, reached over the bed and jolted Ashley awake.

She bolted upright.

There, bleary eyed and in the still of the room, she waited for a few seconds to make sure she hadn't been dreaming.

Nothing, but the sound of Rupert's heavy breathing.

She looked over; he had his back to her and seemed to be sleeping soundly.

Seconds ticked by until she finally allowed herself to fall back onto the pillow.

BANG!

She bolted upright once more.

Somebody was at the front door.

She glanced at the red digits of the clock; it was 03:03 am.

"Rupert?" she called softly.

No answer.

"Rupert!"

But the only reply was a mumble about how he loved her. She considered yelling at him, but by the time she'd roused him from his sleep, she would have already dealt with whatever emergency this must be.

She rolled her eyes and climbed out of the bed and instantly regretted it, when a freeze enveloped her.

She snatched up her dressing gown from the nearby chair, pulled it tight around her and then padded out into the hallway, where her bare feet slapped loudly on the floor.

BANG!

The hammering was so loud, it shook the doorframe.

BANG!

"Oh my God. Alright, alright…Who is it?" she demanded as she reached the door.

Silence, just the low drone of the city nightlife outside.

"Hello?"

Still nothing.

She slowly approached the door.

"Hello?"

Silence.

"Hello?" She called, louder this time, in the hope that it would actually wake Rupert, as she was finding the whole *knockdown ginger* routine unnerving.

Seconds ticked by.

She neared the door and then, carefully, and somewhat reluctantly placed her eye to the spy hole.

The hall outside was in total darkness, which she knew meant nobody could be there.

The hall lights were motion activated. They'd stay on for as long as they detected movement. If they were off, it meant that there was nobody out there.

Or was there?

She considered opening the door, and even looked at the handle, but decided against it. Unlike horror film heroines, she had no interest in exposing herself to whoever may be out there.

She looked back down the hall, towards the bedroom. She wanted to wake Rupert and maybe, just as a precaution, ring security.

It was as she was deliberating this that she replaced her eye to the spy hole and shrieked in horror when she found one piercing blue eye staring back at her.

She jumped back from the door, skidded on the bare floor and fell, backwards with a heavy thud.

She yelped as pain fractures splintered up her body.

"Rupert…" she whimpered.

BANG!

The sound was so loud it echoed around the entrance lobby, and rattled in her brain.

BANG!

"Rupert!"

BANG!

Flakes of plaster filled the air as sound shockwaves vibrated through the floor.

"RUPERT!"

BANG! BANG! RATTLE!

Louder…

"…Rupert!"

BANG! BANG! BANG!

….the coat stand shook, the vase on nearby table toppled and someone was shaking the doorknob!

"…Rupert!"

BANG! BANG! BANG!

"RUPERT!"

The door whined, splintered and then smashed open, slamming against the wall…

…Ashley screamed, and then awoke with a start, gasping and sweating.

Oh God.

It took her a few seconds to register the security of Rupert's bed.

She breathed deeply as relief washed over her, like the sunshine streaming in through the bedroom window.

She pushed the hair from her eyes.

Just a dream, Ash. It was just a dream.

Perhaps, but she hadn't experienced anything as terrifying since her teens.

Then she realised...*sunshine!*

After days of miserable weather, it was wonderful to finally see some sun, even if it did little to thaw the chill that had settled in her bones.

She rolled over to cuddle Rupert but, much to her disappointment, his side of the bed was empty. In his place was a folded sheet of paper.

She promptly unfolded and read:

> *Good morning, gorgeous; I've gone to fetch breakfast.*
> *I called Marie and told her that you were going to be <u>very</u>*
> *late in this morning.*
> *I love you.*

The note was signed with lots of kisses and a smiley face.

Ashley grinned, and surveyed the tastefully furnished room, as if seeing it for the first time.

She wondered if the furniture had been Rupert's personal choice or if he'd hired an interior designer. She made a mental note to ask as she considered exactly what life might be like as Mrs Harrison.

She allowed herself a few minutes to daydream that beautiful dream in an effort to banish all remnants of her nightmare, and then she slid her naked body out from under the covers and shivered.

It was freezing in the room, and this invoked immediate goose bumps all over her skin.

She hurried into the bathroom, turned on the shower, waited for the water to run hot, and then stepped underneath it.

She welcomed the feeling of hot water on her body and closed her eyes as it burned into her muscles, driving out the cold that had settled in there.

It took a few minutes for the water to melt away the eeriness of her nightmare, only for these to be replaced by thoughts of Jackie Harris and her book.

There was no doubt that the book was somewhat explosive, but could it actually spell trouble for Harrison? She doubted it, the company had published much more incendiary material, including a series of controversial autobiographies from well-known human rights abusers.

On the other hand, she could have the project taken away from her, since she wasn't supposed to be dealing with it in the first place.

She worked in fiction.

The Jackie Harris book was autobiographical. The only reason she was involved was because Jackie had approached her directly, and refused to deal with anyone else.

Jackie had also promised to deliver the complete manuscript over a week ago, but so far she hadn't seen anything.

She made a mental note to contact her at some point today. Maybe have lunch. In fact, lunch was best. Jackie was a jittery creature and Ashley had noticed, during their previous encounters, at her best when she actually had something to focus on.

The slamming of the front door startled her as a cold draught swept in, bringing with it the scent of Rupert's aftershave.

He was back.

She poured shampoo into her hand and then massaged it into her scalp as the steam that had filled the room shifted when the bathroom door opened and a shadow appeared on its threshold.

It stood for several seconds, watching her naked outline through the glass of the walk-in cubicle.

A minute or so washed by before she opened her eyes and was startled to notice Rupert's outline standing there.

She squinted through the foam and the blur of the misted glass. "Rupert?"

He did not reply.

"Rupert, you pervert!" she called out to him. "Why don't you go and do something useful, like putting the kettle on."

She heard him chuckle.

"And close the door behind you; it's freezing!"

He disappeared but did not shut the door, and he was going to pay dearly for that.

She finished washing, stepped out of the shower, and dried

herself with a bath towel, before moving over to the steamed up mirror and rubbing a patch clear until her reflection was revealed.

She gasped; dark shadows circled puffy eyes. She still looked drained, if not haunted.

Great. Now I'm coming down with something.

She fixed the towel around herself and brushed her teeth. When she was done, she left the bathroom and walked back into the bedroom where she slipped into panties. Then, instead of pulling on her own clothes, she plucked out one of Rupert's shirts.

Wearing his shirts made her feel good. Closer to him. She especially loved them when they had been worn, and smelt of him, along with remnants of his aftershave.

She left the bedroom and made her way up the short corridor towards the entrance lobby, then the kitchen.

The penthouse was deathly silent, the only sound was that of her bare feet slapping on the parquet flooring, which, of course, reminded her of her dream. Outside, the muffled hum of London rush hour was in full swing.

"Hey you…" she began as she entered the kitchen, but did not finish the sentence for it was empty. The cooker and coffee pot were cold, the black marble surfaces gleamed, and the room was quiet until the fridge sprang to life, making her jump.

She shook her head and then headed across the hallway to the dining room; glass pendant chandelier hung still, glass table clean but no sign of Rupert.

"Rupert?" She called, aloud.

No reply.

She looked back into the entrance lobby, as the clouds shifted overhead, and a strobe of sunlight flickered through the vast domed ceiling. It resurrected an army of shadows, and sent them marching across the walls and paintings as if inspiring the subjects to life.

"Rupert?"

The shrill of the telephone, mounted on the nearby wall, startled her. She instinctively snatched it from its cradle. "Hello," she said, testily.

"Hey you. I'm on my way back and I just wanted to call ahead, check if you were awake and if you needed anything."

A roller coaster sickness gripped Ashley's stomach, and the hairs on the back of her neck began to prickle.

"Rupert?"

"Yes baby, it's me."

Blood pumped behind Ashley's ears and her eyes widened, as she scanned the room and the doors that led off to darkness.

Suddenly, the air chilled once more and the goose pimples returned to her legs and arms. It was as if the air conditioning had been turned to high.

"R...Rupert...Where are you?" she croaked for her mouth was dry.

"I'm just walking out of the bakers. The pastries are still oven warm. Did you want me to pick something else up for you?"

There was silence as Ashley backed up against the wall, gripping the handset tightly as if her very life depended on it.

Another cloud smothered the sun, plunging the place into a duskish hue.

Ashley's eyes darted over to the dining room door, where she thought she'd just seen a shadow.

Oh, God, Rupert, help me.

Her whole body began to tremble as the realisation sunk in and fear, like a rat, scuttled up her spine.

"Ash?" the voice on the phone called, but she could not respond, for horror had frozen her tongue; someone was in the apartment and whoever it was, it wasn't Rupert.

19 NOISES

Rachel awoke to an excellent mood.

She'd spent a fantastic evening with Jason. It was everything she'd hoped for, and more.

They had been whisked away from Heron Heights in a limousine, for a whistle-stop tour of London by night. It included crossing the River Thames, over Westminster Bridge, with the giant wheel that was the London Eye on one side and the Palace of Westminster, Britain's Parliament, on the other.

Rachel was awestruck; these were places she had seen many times on TV and in movies, but never in person.

The best, and most hilarious part, was when Jason encouraged her to attempt sunroof selfies with the iconic tower of Big Ben in the background.

They laughed a lot and she was reminded why she loved him so.

Then, it was off to see one of her favourite musicals, and to have dinner in a small restaurant, just off Covent Garden.

It was well after eleven when they left the restaurant, yet the city was still wide awake, buzzing with the sights, sounds and smells of a bustling metropolis.

Rachel very much enjoyed Manchester's nightlife, but she soon discovered that it wasn't a patch on London. There was something about *The Old Smoke* that lifted her spirits, as if she'd come back home to an old school friend, the crazy one, forever spontaneous and always up for a good time.

She felt invigorated, inspired, happy and deliriously in love.

Jason had been very affectionate; they'd kissed and held hands the whole time they walked among the crowds.

The streets were alive with people of all different nationalities and colours. From green ghouls to red demons, white ghosts and blood oozing zombies. All kinds of folk who used Halloween as an opportunity to express jaw-dropping makeup creativity, many to movie standard.

Rachel was enraptured.

Jason suggested that they go to a club, but she reluctantly

declined.

She had work the next day.

There was only so much excitement a girl could handle in one night. Besides, now that they lived together, they had all the time in the world to go out and do the things they enjoyed, whenever they wanted.

"Speaking of which," Jason reminded her with that inimitable smile.

It was well after 01:00 am before they returned to the apartment.

They'd both had quite a bit to drink, and were schoolchild-giggly as they undressed each other and climbed into bed, to make love.

Because that was exactly what they did.

Jason was how she remembered him; attentive, sensual and considerate this time. The only point he hadn't been was when she had taken control by climbing onto him and regulating the pace, until they both climaxed in an explosion of shudders.

Rachel smiled at the memory.

She had been in London but one day and she'd already fallen in love with the place. That, and the fact that she felt like she'd become some kind of socialite.

It was a show last night, drinks with some of Jason's business contacts tonight, and then they also had the dinner invite to Ashley and Rupert's penthouse!

She was very much looking forward to that because she liked them. They were, after all, the only two people she knew down here. So far, but she felt reassured that, by the way things were going, she would have a new network of friends in no time.

It was 10:10 am.

She wasn't due to start her first shift until lunch time. Lilly had told her that she would cover the evening shifts for a few days, until Rachel had managed to acclimatise to her new home, and of course, the job.

So, she stretched like a cat, and languished in the warm bed while gazing at the blue sky beyond the window. She thought about her old job that she realised, she didn't miss at all.

She thought about her mother, and wondered what she'd make of her new home, in the heart of England's capital.

Probably complain about the way it's decorated.

She sighed.

It had been a long time.

She missed her parents. Maybe not on a daily basis, but at moments like these, where she was doing well for herself and wanted to share her happiness.

You should get in touch. Maybe later. Let's get settled in first.

She pushed the quilt aside, climbed out of bed and walked into the bathroom, where she brushed her teeth and mused some more about her life.

It was through the hissing of the tap and the scrubbing of the toothbrush that she heard them.

Or so she thought.

She shut off the water and listened.

Nothing... but she was sure she heard something fall, heavily, against the ceiling.

She waited and listened.

Nothing.

She was about to restart the brushing when she heard it again, something was being dropped, or more precisely from the sound of the skid, thrown to the floor in the apartment upstairs.

I thought nobody lived there.

She waited and listened a few more seconds, but there were no further sounds.

It was as if they knew she was there, as if they knew she was waiting for something else to happen... then it did, another thud.

That was not my imagination!

Without further ado, Rachel rushed back into the bedroom, pulled on clothes, grabbed one of Jason's caps and tucked her hair into it.

She checked the image in the mirror and frowned; she didn't like herself without makeup, and this morning she was looking particularly tired and washed out.

The reality was quite the opposite; Rachel didn't need to

paint her face to look pretty.

She didn't have the stereotypical angular features of a photo model, but she certainly had the clear soap and water complexion of an English rose, with brown eyes and broad facial features, that were easily softened by her shoulder length hair.

She left the apartment, made her way over to the elevator and frowned when one of the overhead lights flickered and died as she approached.

The elevator was already travelling down to the lobby, so she looked over to the opposite side where a fire door wore a plaque with the universal symbol for *Stairs*.

It was only one floor.

She took them.

Apartment 8's doorbell didn't seem to work so Rachel knocked a few times with no reply.

This frustrated her. She knew what she had heard. She did not imagine it; someone or something was in there.

It was this that led her to glance furtively around and then try the handle; the door was unlocked.

She paused to consider but had already made up her mind.

Inside, the apartment was similar to Jason's.

The front door opened to a small hallway with three doors; bedroom and bathroom, kitchen/dining room and, straight ahead, the lounge.

"Hello? Is anybody home?"

Silence.

She shivered. It was unusually cold in here. As if someone had left a window wide open.

"Hello? Anybody here?"

Nothing.

The air was still, dense and musky, as if the room could do with a good airing. This was consistent with what she had learned; nobody had lived there for a while.

Rachel knew she was trespassing. She had absolutely no business being there, but she brushed the thought aside. She was on a mission now, one sanctioned by her own sanity.

She needed to know what the noises were all about, since she was unable to reconcile these to the fact that the place was supposed to be empty.

"Hello?" She shouted, belligerently, almost annoyed that nobody was answering her.

Still nothing.

So she stepped forward. Slowly advancing into the lounge.

She was wearing training shoes, which meant that her tread was quiet, but for the wood floor that creaked nerve-jangling loud as if protesting against her intrusion.

The lounge was ablaze with daylight as there were no curtains at the picture windows, nor blinds on the balcony doors, leaving the sun to shine, intermittently, on a dazzling collection of white dust sheets that occupied the space, like sleepy ghosts.

"Is anybody home?"

No; there were no feuding neighbours, just floating dust particles.

Rachel sighed deeply as she surveyed the rest of the room, half expecting one of the dustsheets to jump out at her and yell, *"Surprise!"*

It didn't.

The room was empty but for the outlines of what Rachel could identify as a corner unit, a side unit, and a coffee table surrounded by two double sofas and an armchair.

Could she really have imagined that row yesterday, and the noises this morning? Of course not, but she reasoned that the sounds could have come from any of the apartments, not necessarily this one.

Really? Is that how you're going to sell this to yourself?

She knew that the sounds had come from the apartment directly above her.

This apartment.

Yet, she could not see any indication of that. It was clear that the place was empty and, judging from the dust, had been that way for a few weeks now.

Creak!

She spun around, just as the room was plunged into shadow, as the sun was swallowed up by a black cloud.

She swore, throwing her hand to her mouth, as if to stifle a scream, when her own reflection in a large wall mirror made her jump. It was the only thing in that room that wasn't covered.

Jesus Christ!

She laughed, nervously, but her smile disappeared when her dishevelled, washed out look gawked back at her.

Now that is scary, she thought, whilst admiring her bravery for leaving the house without a scrap of makeup. It was something she'd never done before.

Must be love, she thought with a big smile.

She moved closer to the mirror and proceeded to tuck runaway strands of hair under her cap, but froze as hot and cold shivers slithered down her back, and curled into a knot in her stomach.

There, in the mirror, she could see not just her reflection, but also that of the armchair behind her, and there, quivering under the dustsheet was the unmistakable outline of a person!

Incapacitated with fear, she could do nothing but watch whoever it was as they sat perfectly still but for the billowing of the white fabric, as they breathed in and out.

In and out.

Rachel's whole body began to tremble as the breath froze in her mouth. She willed her body to move, to run, scream but she was paralysed.

And then, slowly, and to her absolute horror, the profile shifted as the outline of a head slowly turned to look in her direction.

Creak!

"Miss!"

"Jesus Christ!" She yelled as the young security guard, the one who had reluctantly fetched her suitcases from outside, appeared in the doorway beside her.

Her heart was pickaxing its way out of her chest.

"You frightened me to death!" She said, angrily.

"What are you doing in here, Miss?" The boy asked, ignoring her tone and the terrified look on her face.

She didn't reply.

She was busy scanning the armchair. It looked perfectly innocuous with the sheet draped over it. In fact, now that she scrutinised the thing, the sun decided to make an impromptu reappearance, she couldn't even imagine how she could have mistaken that outline for anything other than what it was.

Nonetheless, she marched over to the armchair, emboldened by the presence of the security guard, and yanked the dust cover off.

"Miss!" The boy protested. "What the hell are you doin'?"

As expected, nothing but an empty leather armchair revealed itself to her.

Did I imagine that too? What about the breath? I definitely saw something breathing!

"Miss?" The young man repeated with that apathetic tone she was rapidly growing to dislike.

She was still gawking at the piece of furniture but, eventually and somewhat reluctantly, turned to face him.

"I'm sorry," she stuttered, unable to find words. She dropped the sheet back on the chair without bothering to rearrange it, "The door was open and I decided to have a look around."

"I'm gonna' have to ask you to leave," the boy said, suddenly developing a backbone.

"How come?" she asked, defiantly, still unnerved but what had just happened.

The boy, now rabbit in headlights, shrugged, "I'm just doing my job," he said.

Rachel nodded and walked over to him. Then, after glancing around the room once more, asked, "Do you know who used to live here?"

The boy gave a shrug, "Sorry, haven't worked here that long."

Rachel nodded, then left.

20 INTRUDER

When Rupert returned to the penthouse, the first thing he noticed was the stillness of the place. That and the freezing cold; it felt warmer outside.

"Ashley?"

There was no reply.

Closing the front door behind him, he called out again, "Ash?"

No answer.

He checked the dining room, the bedroom, even the bathroom, but nothing, just the dripping showerhead.

"Ashley?" He called again as he made his way back to the entrance lobby where a cold breeze rushed by him, as if seeking shelter from itself.

This time he noticed that the London bustle seemed louder here.

He moved into the lounge and noticed that the balcony door was partially open, and a gale was howling through it, bringing with it the sound of voices.

He crossed the room, slid the door open and stepped out onto the large balcony where he spotted Ashley, wrapped in a sheepskin coat, chatting to a man.

Both of them had their backs to him.

"Ash?"

Startled, the duo turned, and Rupert recognised the man as Tom from maintenance.

"Good morning, Tom," he said, quickly.

"Good Morning, Mr Harrison."

"I called you, why didn't you answer me?" Rupert asked Ashley, feeling her arms as if checking she wasn't hurt in any way.

"I'm sorry. I didn't hear you out here."

Her face looked unusually pale.

"What happened? You were on the phone one second, gone the next. I was worried."

"Yes. I'm sorry," she said, forcing a smile.

"What happened? You sounded strange on the phone."

"I know. Just silly, really. I got myself all spooked."

"Spooked?"

"I'll leave you to it," Tom said with a smile.

Ashley put her hand on Tom's arm, "Thank you so very much for coming over, Tom."

"Anything I can do to help," he said with a smile. "Mr Harrison," he nodded at Rupert, then left.

Rupert looked worriedly at Ashley. "What happened?"

"Oh," she shook her head, "nothing significant. Just got rattled."

"By what?" he asked, eagerly.

"Oh, I don't really know. I just thought somebody was in the apartment, that's all."

"What?" Rupert asked, eyes wide with concern.

"Well, at first I thought it was you. I was in the shower and I thought I heard you come home." She forced an incredulous laugh, "I even thought I smelt your aftershave and then …" she trailed off here, remembering what it felt like when the phone rang.

"What?" Rupert prompted.

"Well, I came out and then you rang me so I knew it wasn't you and…"

"…Jesus Christ! Ash, did you call the police?" He moved as if he was personally going to investigate.

"No, Rupert!" Ashley caught his arm. "Tom's already checked the place, twice, and he didn't find anything. I also called Paul at reception. He told me he hadn't sent anybody up here and, well, you know what this place is like for security. It's unlikely anyone could have snuck in without being spotted. Besides, they'd need a code."

A few seconds of silence ticked by, filled with the sound of the city.

"So, what are you saying to me?" Rupert asked.

"I don't know." Ashley shook her head. "All I know is that I thought you'd come home and you hadn't." She laughed. "I know it sounds stupid now, but it felt so real. I even heard you laugh for crying out loud! Or at least I thought I did."

Rupert smiled. "You just can't bear to be apart from me, can you?" he said, caressing her cheek.

Ashley forced a laugh. "Damn. And there's me, desperate

to be independent."

Rupert pulled her to him. "Are you sure you're okay?" he asked, seriously.

She nodded. "Yes. I'm fine. You know, I read in a magazine somewhere that autosuggestion isn't that uncommon."

"Oh yeah? What magazine was that?"

"Oh, I don't know. Some rag published by some megalomaniac who lives in a penthouse."

"Really? I like him already," he smiled, pulling out of the embrace and looking into her eyes.

"Oh, that's good because I like him too."

"Just like?"

"Yes. You see, I'm only into men who get out of bed early to buy me freshly baked pastries."

"Damn. So there's no hope for me then?"

"Afraid not."

"Oh well," he pulled away, "just have to go and eat these on my own then," he said, holding up a white paper bag.

"NO!" Ashley protested.

They laughed.

He cupped her face with his hands and looked into her eyes once more.

The meaning was silent.

She stroked his hand confirming that she was okay. "I love you," she said, and then hugged him, as if her life depended on it. As she did so, her eyes searched the shadows stalking the room inside.

21 MARTIANS

Ashley walked through the babbling buzz of the Fiction Editorial office, absentmindedly greeting members of her team as she went.

Marie was following, briefing her on the morning's events, although Ashley had barely heard a word, for her mind was elsewhere…

"…Oh and Jackie Harris has called twice for you. Would like to know if you can meet her for lunch today, she said it's important, what isn't these days? Everything is important. Finishing the painting in my spare room is also important, but do you think that makes any difference whatsoever to my son? Oh no. If I were to compare it to the modern day office equivalent, he wouldn't be email but more like a carrier pigeon. You want my advice; don't ever ask a member of your family to help you out with anything domestic, because you are ten times better off paying a stranger. At least you know he is going to get the job done on time, even if he will screw you for every penny. But at least you know you are paying for the service, and that you have some rights…" Marie broke off here as they entered Ashley's office.

She watched her boss, throw her coat onto a nearby chair, sit at her desk and switch on her computer without as much as a blink.

Thus, she continued, "And did you know that the Martians then came and beamed up my dog. Of course, they asked me to go with them, but I said hey, I've got a lazy son and a boss that takes no notice whatsoever of the things I say, why would I want to whiz around the cosmos with you lot…"

Marie stopped talking again.

Ashley looked up to see her secretary, spectacles dangling off the tip of her nose, staring down at her.

"What?" she asked.

"I may as well go home. At least I'm used to my husband ignoring me."

Ashley smiled. "I'm sorry, Marie."

"Oh don't worry, love. I'm used to it."

"No, it's not you, I promise."

TONY MARTURANO

"What then?"

"Nothing important," Ashley said, snapping out of her daze. "Did I hear you mention Jackie Harris?"

"So you weren't entirely devoid of audio intake then?" Marie shook her head. "Yes, she rang twice. She wants to know if you can meet her for lunch today, said she has something critical that she must discuss with you."

"Okay, I'll ring her."

"She said, or more appropriately, demanded that you call her on her mobile, as her home phone is out of order."

"Oh okay. I don't know..." Ashley picked up her cell phone, "if I have her number..."

"I've emailed it to you."

"Thanks, Marie."

"Glad I can be of service."

She was about to leave the room when Ashley called after her, "Be sure to let me know if they return your dog, Marie."

The woman just rolled her eyes and left the room.

Ashley opened her email and sifted through her messages until she came to the one entitled, *Grumpy Harris*."

This made her smile.

The phone was connected after two rings.

"Hello?"

"Hi Jackie, it's Ashley."

"Oh thank God. "There was relief in the woman's voice. "I've been trying to call you all morning."

"Yes, I'm sorry. I got detained."

"I need to speak with you," Jackie's voice was almost a whisper.

"Are you okay?"

"Yes. Can you meet me? Now?"

Ashley looked at her watch; it was almost noon. "Well, I just got in, Jackie and need to tie up a few things here, but I could come over..."

"...No, not here," Jackie said, decisively. "Meet me at O'Mara's."

"Okay," Ashley agreed. "Jackie, you sound very cloak-and-dagger, what's this about?"

"I'll tell you when I see you. Twelve thirty. Don't be late."

"Hang on, Jackie...."
But the line was dead.

22 BROKEN

The battle between sun and rain had been fought and lost. The weather had changed, yet again, and a dingy grey sky was now drizzling rain, as Ashley rushed across the multi-storey car park to her car.

Nearly an hour had passed since her enigmatic telephone conversation with Jackie, but she had been unable to extricate herself from the avalanche of urgent emails and phone calls. As it was, she had to push many of them back until later in the afternoon, so she could go on this spy mission to meet Jackie Harris, much to Marie's displeasure.

It was as she was negotiating her bag, umbrella and car keys that she heard Rupert's voice calling her name and it echoing around the structure.

She turned to face him, but he wasn't there; the car park was empty. Yet she had heard his voice, clear and sharp as if he'd just stepped off the elevator and had called out to her.

"Rupert?" she spoke, instinctively.

The only reply came from the hum of the traffic on the streets below and the ever familiar howling crosswind.

She hesitated for a few seconds as if expecting him to jump out from behind one of the nearby cars.

Nothing.

She turned and pressed the button on her key fob; there was a beeping sound and the vehicle's lights winked at her. She opened the back door and dumped her bag and umbrella on the passenger seat.

"*Ashley.*"

She looked up again; it was definitely Rupert's voice, albeit muffled, distant this time as if it were coming from deep inside the concrete pillars that surrounded her.

"I'm here. Rupert?"

Silence.

"Stop messing around. I'm late for a meeting," she said loudly to the open space.

The slamming of a car door made her turn to see a man and woman leave a Volvo, and chat happily with each other, as they made their way to the elevator and step inside.

She took a few steps forward and called out again, "Rupert?"

Her voice echo was the only reply.

Oh God, I'm cracking up. I must be.

She turned, climbed behind the driving wheel and pulled the car door shut, isolating herself from the sound of the city and grateful for the peace inside.

She took a few seconds to gather her thoughts. Then, she looked into the rearview mirror and gave herself a mental talking to.

Get a grip! I know. But you have to admit, it's been a pretty weird day so far.

She had to concede it had.

Then, for some peculiar reason, she felt compelled to shift her focus from her face to the rear seats of the car. You know, just to be sure they were empty.

They were.

She took a few seconds to roll her shoulders, in an effort to dispel a tension that had settled there, then clicked into her seatbelt.

Eventually, she switched the engine on, and jumped with fright as the radio bellowed a mixture of static and news at her. It bore through her fragile nervous system like an electric drill.

She hastily, and somewhat angrily, pushed it off. She hadn't been listening to the radio on her way in this morning, she was sure of that.

Or was she?

The car idled as her mind pondered.

What the hell is happening to me?

She closed her eyes and pressed fingers against her temple

in an effort to disperse a migraine that was now growing there. She pressed as deeply as she could bear it, for she had a lot to do and the last thing she needed was a bad head holding her back.

It was just as she was willing herself to calmness that the knock came; it rapped against her window and rattled around her brain causing her to leap sideways and gawk in horror.

It took a while to register the uniformed man standing outside her window.

Heart pounding, chest heaving, she eventually buzzed the window down.

"I'm terribly sorry, Miss Marshall," said the security guard. "I didn't mean to startle you. Just, you dropped this in the lift."

He handed her a key card.

"You won't be able to get out without it," he added.

She took the card from the man and said, "Thank you" with a squeak and then very quickly cleared her throat.

The guard, a fifty-year-old, overweight black man with greying hair, observed her, carefully, "Are you okay, Miss Marshall?"

"Yes, yes, I'm fine, thank you. I'm just late for an appointment, that's all," she said as calmly as she could.

The man stood back, "Okay. Well, you take care."

"Thank you, I will," she replied, shifting the car into gear.

She buzzed up the window, hesitated a few seconds then reopened it. "Sorry, could I just ask, earlier, um, did you call to me?"

The guard frowned, "I'm sorry?"

"Earlier, a few minutes ago, was it you calling my name?"

The baffled look on the man's face said it all. Ashley glanced at the clock on the dashboard; she felt foolish and was very late. "Never mind. Thank you anyway," she said, quickly.

Before long, she was exiting the car park and joining the main road, where she drove west for approximately ten minutes before reaching a retail park sandwiched between the city and the suburbs.

The retail park consisted of one department store, various

retail chains, a couple of fast food outlets and one cafe that specialised in all day breakfasts.

With real estate near the capital at a very high premium, all of the retail outlets were served but one multi-storey car park. Ashley was amazed to find a free space, and stopped short of performing a victory dance when she did.

The American diner styled eatery was on the opposite side of a very busy main road and it, like most places at lunchtime, was heaving with people on their break.

It took Ashley a while before she located Jackie. She was sitting at a small table for two, tucked away in a corner of the eatery, with a window view of the shoppers walking to and fro on the street outside.

Jackie Harris was a short woman, with a small face and long scraggly brown hair. Today, not unlike a forties spy, she was wearing sunglasses, a size too big for her face, a black overcoat, and a grey scarf over her head.

She was urgently sucking on an electronic cigarette, clearly underwhelmed by the hit it was giving her.

"Hi," Ashley said, falling into the chair opposite her. "I'm sorry I'm late, but I've had one hell of a day. Wow, are you hungry?" She asked, noticing that the table in front of them was laden with food.

"That's okay, at least you're here now," Jackie said, looking over Ashley's shoulder.

Ashley followed her gaze, "What?" she asked, suddenly feeling self-conscious.

"Nothing," Jackie said, forcing a smile. "Coffee? I ordered a pot for both of us. Black isn't it? I also ordered some scones, thought you might like some. Wasn't sure what kind to get so I just bought a couple of both types, I also bought some toasted tea cakes and some sandwiches. Again, I didn't know what you like, so I got tuna and cucumber, chicken salad, and Ploughman's but still if you don't…."

"…Jackie." Ashley interrupted.

"Yes?"

"Why am I here? What was so urgent that it couldn't wait?"

"Have some coffee and I will tell you."

As Jackie poured, Ashley noticed that her hand was

shaking.

She had met the ex-police officer several times before, but had never seen her this jittery, and it was unnerving her.

When Jackie finished pouring coffee into her cup, she spooned in a couple of sugars, regardless of the fact that Ashley enjoyed her coffee black, without, and began to stir, nervously. Then, just as Ashley was about to prompt her once more, she said, "I've finished the book."

Ashley broke into a smile, "Jackie, that's great news..."

"...But I am not going to submit it for publication."

The statement took Ashley by surprise and she was momentarily speechless. Eventually, she asked, "What do you mean?"

"Exactly what I said."

"Well, what's happened to suddenly change your mind?"

Jackie looked out of the window and her enigmatic behaviour was actually starting to irk Ashley, whose nerves were already strained.

"Jackie, I need to know why you've reached this decision, and could you please take off those glasses?"

There was a moment's hesitation, but Jackie slowly and reluctantly complied, revealing dark circles and bloodshot eyes.

She looked as she hadn't slept in days.

"My God, Jackie. Are you alright?" Ashley gasped.

"No, actually I'm not," she said in a shaky voice, as she sucked on the e-cigarette...

"Oh fuck it!" she said, plucking the device from her lips and throwing it at the table, where it bounced off the coffee cup and over to the next aisle.

The act made Ashley leap back in her chair, which pulled on her last nerve, and she was about to lose it with her lunch companion but stopped when she noticed the look in her eyes.

"I can't do this anymore, Ashley. I just can't." The woman said, fighting, back tears.

"Jackie..."

"...I think you lost this," a man in a suit said, as he placed the e-cigarette on their table. He was wearing a sour look on his face.

Ashley was torn between apologising to him or seeing to the neurotic woman in front of her, she chose the latter.

Once she was sure that the man had retaken his seat, she leaned forward, "Jackie, what happened?"

"What hasn't happened? I have been watched, followed, burgled, you name it. Ever since it was made public that I was writing this book, I haven't had a moment's peace."

"Why didn't you tell me about this before?"

"Because I thought I could cope, but last night was the last straw."

"What happened last night?"

"Somebody broke into my home, Ash. While I was asleep, in bed! Jesus Christ." She glanced at the e-cigarette but dismissed it, she wanted the real thing.

"Somebody broke into your home, who?"

Jackie cocked her head, as if Ashley had just asked the world's dumbest question.

She rephrased it, "Why would somebody break into your home?"

"Why do you think? To hack the hard drive of my computer, why else?"

"You mean they stole the manuscript?"

"Yes. Wiped the computer clean. What they don't realise is that I have a copy."

"You do? Where? On a cloud account?"

Jackie scoffed. "You think they haven't already hacked into that."

"What then?"

"I've gone off grid, as they say. And taken other precautions."

Ashley looked puzzled.

Jackie rolled her eyes. "I copied it to a pen drive. In fact, I've been working off that ever since I started writing the manuscript. There were just fragment documents on my hard disk. But you don't have to be a genius to work out that the last file I worked on was located on an external drive."

There was a pause and then Ashley asked, "So, where is it?"

"It's safe," Jackie whispered, looking around the room to make sure that nothing but the walls was listening. "I've stashed it in a secret hiding place in my bedroom. Somewhere London's finest wouldn't even have the balls to look."

"You need to go to the police."

Jackie let out an incredulous laugh. "They *are* the police, Ashley."

"There must be another, oh I don't know, branch you can talk to."

Jackie shook her head.

"...Maybe Scotland Yard or even MI5."

Jackie kept on shaking her head.

"...There must be somebody you can go to."

Jackie leaned forward, "Don't you get it? There's nobody. This is how it works, they protect their own."

"I don't believe that. It's a book, Jackie. Not national security."

"Well, you believe what you want." Jackie hissed.

Both women took the time to ponder what had just been said. Ashley wondered if any of this bore any relation to the strange things that had been happening to her. Was there really somebody in the penthouse this morning? Had someone actually been calling her name in the car park? Maybe someone was trying to scare her, make her think she was going mad.

"Now *you* seem perturbed," Jackie said, taking a despondent bite out of one of the scones.

Ashley forced a smile, "It's nothing. I'm just wondering what you're planning to do."

"I'm planning to leave the country. That's what I'm planning to do. I've already booked the ticket. I'm going to lay low for a while until this whole thing blows over."

"But what about the manuscript?" The question had come out before Ashley had a chance to think about it.

Jackie shook her head. "Is that all you're worried about?"

"No, of course it isn't. It's just that in one breath you tell me how these people have been tormenting you, making your life a misery, and in the next, you're telling me that you want to let them get away with it. I am worried, Jackie. I'm concerned to hear that the very same people we're supposed to trust to protect us are also capable of something so awful. And then, instead of remorse, have the balls to persecute you for it."

Jackie's eyes narrowed, "You don't need to lecture me," she said through gritted teeth and watery eyes, "I was there, remember?"

"Exactly. You were there. You were held down while your colleagues, members of our police force, took it in turns with you, and now you're thinking of telling them that it was okay, and that not only did they fuck you that night, but that it's okay for them to them to fuck you now too!"

Suit man looked across at them once more, but if Ashley felt his eyes on her, she ignored them.

Meanwhile, the tears had broken through, and with trembling lips, Jackie uttered, "I don't have to listen to this."

She grabbed her bag, her glasses and left the table.

Ashley could have kicked herself.

She took a few seconds to contemplate her next move. She resolved to follow the would-be author out onto the busy streets, and into the drizzle that had now metamorphosed into rain.

Jackie was hurrying along the pavement, dodging people and umbrellas as Ashley rushed after her.

"Jackie!" She called.

Nothing.

"I'm sorry, Jackie. I shouldn't have said that" Ashley gasped when she finally caught up with her.

"It's alright for you; you live in a posh penthouse with a bloody millionaire for crying out loud. The force was my life. The realisation of a dream, and it's been shattered. I have nothing left, nothing but the nightmares and the humiliation of that trial, as well as the phobia that one night I'm going to wake up to find someone standing over me. Christ, if they broke in to wipe my hard drive, they can do anything and nobody would be any the wiser. They'd be untouchable. There's no one else in a better position to fabricate or lose evidence. They could slit my throat, pass it off as suicide and nobody would give a shit," she growled through tears, "I'm not going to live like this; I can't live like this anymore. I want it over. I want them to leave me alone!"

"Running away is not going to help, Jackie. They'll be waiting for you when you come back."

"Then I won't come back!"

"And what about the others, the new recruits who come in after you? If they get away with this, they will think they can do it to anybody."

Jackie snorted and wiped the back of her hand across her eyes, "Jesus, you *really* don't get it do you? They have already got away with it. The courts set them free! Nobody is going to give a fuck whether or not I publish a book about it now."

"Well, they obviously do. Why do you think they are so hell bent on stopping you?"

This made Jackie pause for thought. Ashley hoped it would be enough to make the woman see reason, but there was a determination in her stride until Ashley caught her arm and stopped her. "Please think about this," she shouted over the din of the lunch hour traffic.

Jackie hesitated, "I have and I'm leaving today."

With that, she turned and stepped into the busy road, causing a car to swerve and yell at her with an angry blare of its horn.

Ashley hunched in terror, as she watched other cars react in the same fashion, as the crazy pedestrian slowly made her way across the busy road.

One by one, cars swerved, stopped, skidded. All to a cacophony of angry car horns that Jackie seemed oblivious to, as she slowly made her way to the other side of the road.

Then there was that Ford, the silver one, driven by the middle-aged executive who was deep in conversation with his colleague, sitting in the backseat.

They'd just had a very bad meeting with a client, and he was angrily engaging with his passenger by looking at him in the rearview mirror, rather than keeping his eyes on the road ahead.

Which meant he failed to see the crazy lady in the red coat and sunglasses cross the street, right into the path of his vehicle. It was only when his colleague, sitting in the passenger seat next to him, yelled, "Look out!" that he saw the stupid bitch.

He stomped on the brake pedal and surrendered himself to the inevitable; along with losing one of the company's most important clients, he'd be adding murderer to his C.V.

Ashley could only watch, in abject horror, as the speeding silver car proceeded on a collision with the controversial ex-police officer.

She screamed, "JACKIE!"

But her warning was too late. The silver car had already engaged its brakes, and these screeched angrily over what they were being asked to accomplish at such speed, at such a short distance.

Yet, by some miracle, just as Jackie was stepping off the road and onto the pavement, the car skidded and slowed enough to allow the driver to swerve and miss crazy lady by what must have been millimetres.

All of the occupants of the car were still screaming in stupefied high-pitched terror, even as the car came to a halt.

Meanwhile, Jackie Harris, hunched against the rain, casually made her way towards the multi-storey car park, as if nothing had happened.

Ashley was still holding her hands to her mouth in a silent scream when she felt a tap on her arm and snapped around to see Julie Emerson, Romance Editor, grinning at her. She was wearing a suede jacket and carrying a yellow umbrella.

"Hey, there you are," Julie said. "I thought it was you. Where on earth have you been all day? I've been looking for you."

She moved in closer to shelter her friend from the rain. Then, following Ashley's gaze, she asked, "Who was that?"

"That," Ashley said, not taking her eyes off Jackie until she disappeared into the building, "is Jackie Harris."

"*The* Jackie Harris, the one you've got Martin all steamed up about?"

"The very same."

"I didn't recognise her with that scarf over her head. So, has she finished the final draft?"

"I think so."

"And is it what you expected?"

"I don't know; she won't let me see it."

Julie's eyebrows lifted in an inquisitive fox kind of way.

"She doesn't want us to publish the book any more," Ashley added.

"What? But she's signed a contract."

"Somehow, Julie, I don't think she could care less about that right now."

"Oh girl, I'm so sorry. Is that why you look so tired?"

"That and a host of other things. "

"Like what?"

"Oh God, where do I start?"

"The beginning; it's normally a good place."

"I'm sorry, Julie, I can't right now. I've got so much on my plate today. What are you doing Saturday night?"

"You mean besides going out on yet another bad date?"

Ashley smiled, grateful for Julie's light humour, "Yes besides that."

"Oh, I don't know. Coming over to yours for dinner?"

They laughed.

"It's actually at Rupert's."

"Nice," Julie nodded appreciatively.

"Eight o'clock okay?"

"Sounds fine, but you have to promise to tell all."

"I promise."

What happened next was over in seconds but would haunt the two women for the rest of their lives.

The traffic moved, people walked and the rain fell, as a screeching of tyres and scraping metal pierced the air, followed by a thunderous *Whomp!*

A giant cloud of dust and mortar appeared above them as the parapet of the fifth floor of the car park exploded outward, raining blocks of concrete onto two pedestrians below; cracking the head of one woman and snapping the neck of the other.

A red SUV emerged from behind the cloud, and plunged to the road. It slammed onto the roof of a passing car then flipped forward, ejecting the driver through the windscreen and onto the wet tarmac. There, like a herd of raging animals, the oncoming traffic trampled over the body, while shunting the vehicle thirty feet down the road.

The grotesque scene unfolded to a medley of squealing brakes, screeching metal, screaming people and car horns as, one by one, cars slammed into and swerved to avoid each other.

Ashley and Julie could do nothing but watch in incredulous horror, as two more speeding cars trampled over the lifeless body in front of them. They broke bones and squished organs, before skidding or crashing to a halt.

Jackie Harris' body lay, twisted.

Her deathly, glassy gaze watched the morbid curiosity of traumatised onlookers while on the nearby tarmac, a grey scarf rolled slowly in the breeze, until it was weighted down with blood and rainwater.

23 THE LETTER

5:00 am, one week later.

William Barber walked into the Royal Mail's Cambridge sorting office and headed straight for his colleague's station and was pleased to find it empty. This meant that he wouldn't have to make small talk, nor ask for his personal mail, he could retrieve it himself.

He quickly sifted through the various items until he was left with three personal letters.

The first was a gas bill, the second, a catalogue promotion and the third... he took in a deep breath; the postmark slogan on the front read, *'Harrison - For a Good Read'*.

His heart skipped a beat. This was it; the letter he had been waiting for.

He looked around; he was standing in a corridor of yellow pigeonholes, in front of them stood grey sacks full of post, waiting to be sorted into the first mail delivery of the day.

So far, only a couple of his colleagues had arrived for their shift but it wouldn't be long before the place was teeming with postmen.

He considered taking the moment into the privacy of a toilet cubicle, but decided against it; he needed to know, now.

Don't prolong the agony, just open the thing!

Gingerly, he ripped open the envelope, pulled out the letter and studied the Harrison logo, the thick bond paper, his printed name, address and then the text:

Dear William Barber,

TALES FROM A TOMB

Thank you for giving us the opportunity to read Tales from a Tomb.

Your manuscript captured a raw and distinctive sense of horror that is quite often lacking from many of today's modern novels.

There's no doubt that you have a talent for storytelling.

However, we are driven by current market trends, budgetary constraints and of course, our own personal criteria. In order for us to accept a manuscript for publication, the editorial team has to feel very strongly about it. Unfortunately, in the case of Tales from a Tomb, we did not.

I am very sorry to have to communicate this news to you, and would like to stress that this is simply our personal opinion and that other publishing houses may feel differently.

We strongly advise that you seek the guidance of an independent editor, and perhaps a literary agent, who these days, are more than often worth their fee.

You can find a list of agents in the Writers' & Artists'

Yearbook.

Thanks again for thinking of Harrison Publishing.

Yours Sincerely,

Ashley Marshall
SENIOR FICTION EDITOR

William read the letter two more times, for he was finding it hard to digest exactly what it was saying.

Meanwhile, the early morning scram to get the first delivery sorted and prepped for delivery had started.

There were stories of the night before, laughing and somewhere, somebody was shouting at him to get a move on.

But William could not move. He had waited months for this letter and never had he allowed himself to consider the possibility that the content may treat his destiny with such harshness.

It had taken three years to complete this manuscript, another two revising it and another year sending excerpts out to every agent and publisher he could find.

All of them had rejected him. All had said that he did not fit into that year's publishing schedule, all except for Harrison Publishing.

And this is what he was finding hard to deal with.

The other publishers had just said no, they hadn't even bothered to ask for excerpts, but Harrison was different, they'd asked for more and then taken three *fucking* months to make this decision.

If no news was supposed to be good news, then what was this shit, and why had they taken so long just to reject him? It seemed that, after all this time, they had turned out to be no better than all the other heartless bastards before them. And this woman, this, this, what was her name, he looked at the letter's signature, ah yes, Ashley Marshall. She had written this letter, regurgitating the same crap he already knew off by heart. All of those empty words he had already read a hundred times before.

But she was worse.

She had twisted the knife; she had given him hope, made him believe that his dream might finally come true and then...

...He ran his hands over his balding scalp; he'd broken out in a sweat and was trembling, not from the cold but from the rage that was twisting in his gut like a coiled cobra.

Oh God. I'm trapped!

He was trapped in that shitty job and there was no way out.

He clutched his chest. It felt tight, really tight, as if someone, probably that bitch from Harrison, had placed it in a vice, and was squeezing his palpitating heart out of his throat...

...He couldn't breathe, he was choking...

...now the lights were dimming and the walls were leaning in to swallow him whole.

I'm going to die. Right here, in this place I fucking hate. In this job I despise, and it's all down to one person.

Marshall.

"Hey!"

Ashley Marshall.

"Shakespeare!"

The voice was familiar, and it cut through his thoughts like an angle grinder through sleep, first thing on a Sunday morning.

William looked up.

It was Daniel, a twenty-three-year-old lout with a shaved head. He was the ringleader of those who derived much pleasure in ridiculing his aspirations, the very same people who would whisper about him and laugh when he failed to finish his rounds on time.

Ever since he started working as a postman just over six months ago, none of them had offered so much as a word of encouragement.

They just mocked. Humiliated.

And now he was standing there, grinning that *fucking* grin the way he always did before he would say something loud enough for the others to hear, something that would elicit equally loud howls of laughter, at his expense.

Grinning, Daniel said, "Mike has called in sick so the boss

wants you to do his round for him."

If the boy was expecting a reaction, none came. The freak wouldn't even look at him; he was too busy reading the letter in his hand.

"Hello, earth to Shakespeare," Daniel sniggered.

Bloody freak is probably high on something. "Yoo hoo, lovey, did you hear what I said? I said…"

…The rest of Daniel's sentence froze in his mouth as icy, black eyes fixed on him. Such was their malevolence that the young man was reluctant to move, for fear that *the freak* might actually charge, wrestle him to the ground and pummel the life out of him.

The scene was made chilling by a blood-curdling leer he'd seen before, on Jack Nicholson in the Shining.

Eventually, Daniel found his feet, and backed away, very slowly, as the hawkish glare stayed on him, burning deep into his skull.

Finally, he found the courage to turn his back on William Barber and return to his station where, believing himself to be safe, he casually shrugged off the ice bucket of fear, that had been emptied onto his back, by playfully punching a colleague in the arm.

Then, he checked, by glancing over his shoulder, you know, just to make sure that the freak wasn't still watching him; he was.

24 DARK SKIES

The weather on Thursday was just as miserable as the day before as if to accentuate Ashley's sombre mood.

It had been a week since Jackie Harris' death, and Rupert had encouraged her to take time off, but she couldn't see the point. Jackie was dead, and moping around the apartment was not going to bring her back, nor erase the images of her last moments from her mind.

No, she needed work. She needed to stay busy, especially since the incessant police questioning did nothing to help her push the event from her mind.

As the last person who spoke to Jackie, they insisted on asking the same questions, but in different ways.

Anybody would have thought that it was she who had been driving the car.

Worse, despite all of the questions and the provisional tests performed on the vehicle, they were still unable to explain exactly what had happened. Although, they did intimate that Jackie may well have taken her own life. This was consistent with the fact that it would have taken considerable energy to smash through the parapet of the car park. This could only be achieved if Jackie had deliberated accelerated towards the wall at great speed.

Of course, investigators were quick to jump on Ashley's recounting of Jackie's assertion that she was being persecuted by the Metropolitan Police, which in turn led them to speculate that the woman's paranoia may well have pushed her to suicide.

A deduction categorically refuted by Ashley, who suggested that Jackie's death may be the result of an attack on her life by person or persons who had purportedly broken into her home, with the sole intention of stealing her manuscript.

She made no bones of sharing who exactly that might be.

And, given that it was the Metropolitan Police conducting the investigation into the author's death, it was not surprising that her comments proved to be somewhat inflammatory.

Yet, the only response she received was that the investigation was still in its early stages, was ongoing, and that Ashley should be very careful about making unfounded accusations.

"Who gives a shit," she had retorted.

Now she was gazing through the window of her office at black rain clouds promising yet more rain.

Is this weather ever going to let up?

Below, London traffic crawled forward with headlights

blazing against the darkness that was smothering the day.

"You shouldn't be here, you know," Marie said, walking into the office.

"Why not?" Ashley replied, without turning.

"Because it isn't good for you."

"What would be, sitting at home feeling sorry for myself?"

"Possibly."

Ashley turned in her chair and marvelled how, even on such miserable day, her secretary was dressed in an immaculate navy blue pinstriped jacket and skirt.

"It wasn't your fault, you know." Marie continued, dropping papers on Ashley's desk.

"Wasn't it?"

"No, it was not," she spelled out like a mother who was trying to get through to her insolent child.

"She was obviously desperate, Marie. I should have tried harder to understand what she was going through."

"I thought you did. Ashley, remember, you were her editor not her mother."

Ashley pondered on this, "Maybe you're right."

So why do I feel so bad?

"What happens to the manuscript now?"

Ashley looked up, "Marie, if I didn't know you better, I'd think that Jackie's death meant absolutely nothing to you, just as long as we can still get our hands on her manuscript."

The older lady shrugged, "Perhaps. At the end of the day, Ashley, your relationship was about business, nothing more. After all, we paid her for the manuscript. It belongs to us."

"Marie!" Ashley exclaimed, incredulously, even though she knew her secretary was right, but added, "Most of the people here didn't even want that manuscript to see the light of day. I dare say Martin is doing a jig around his office right now."

"What a hilarious thought," Marie said with a smile.

"I don't know what happens to it now. I don't even know where it is. No doubt the police will get their hands on it and…" Then it occurred to her.

If the police searched Jackie's home, which they most probably would, if they hadn't already, they would sequester the manuscript as evidence. It was what they had wanted all along, and now there was nothing to stop them from getting their hands on it.

Or was there?

25 FIRST SHIFT

The day was handing over to night when Rachel returned to the switchboard desk with a mug of coffee.

It had been a few hours since Lilly had passed responsibility for the service to her, and things had been relatively quiet but for one caller, a woman named Mrs Farmer. It was a name Rachel did not recognise and thus concluded could not have been anyone famous.

It was only now, as she sat in the operator's swivel chair, drinking from her cup, that she allowed herself to take in her new office, the place she had now dubbed *the dungeon.*

She felt isolated.

This place was in such stark contrast to the world above, where the architecture was all about light and breathtaking views.

Down here, the small sliver of a window was woefully inadequate.

Earlier in the day, she discovered that the only way to see a patch of green from the gardens was to angle her head in a specific way. Otherwise, it was just a bit of sky with a lot of concrete from neighbouring buildings.

Worse, as Lilly was showing her around the switchboard, once again, and running through all of the dos and don'ts, she'd spotted the boots and partial trouser leg of the gardener, or whoever he was, as he went about his business.

It made her feel claustrophobic.

"You'll get used to that," Lilly had said, quickly, noticing the look on her face.

But Rachel had her doubts.

Hence why now, in the absence of blinds, and as night pressed on the window, the idea of switching on the harshness of the neon light, and turning the place into a goldfish bowl, did not appeal to her. But then, nor did the thought that had suddenly popped into her head: someone watching her from the other side of the glass.

She shivered

Stop it.

It's not as if she'd forgotten her experience in the room of sleepy ghosts.

Stop it! You're going to freak yourself out!

She shook her head and shrugged her shoulders, as if to shake off all negative and creepy thoughts.

She preferred the discretion and *cosiness* of the small lamp to the harsh realism of the overhead neon light. At least this way she didn't get to see too much of the antiquities, the dust, the cobwebs and their equally creepy inhabitants.

Seriously?

This wasn't the way to start her first shift. She wouldn't last two minutes. This job was a great opportunity. It would give her independence, avoid a stressful commute to some office across the city, and no doubt might give her the opportunity spend more time with Jason since they lived in the same building.

Now, pull yourself together!

She needed to be busy.

She tapped the pencil on the notepad in front of her and willed the next call to come through, but none did.

Lilly had told her that things generally got quieter in the evenings.

So, she proceeded to untangle the headset wire while wondering if Lilly even knew what Bluetooth was.

And it was as she was fiddling with the earpiece, making sure the microphone was hanging just so over her mouth, that she caught sight of the massive carcass of the monitor that dominated the desk.

This dinosaur of the computer world must be years old. If the machine isn't working, why does she keep it on the desk?

Then again, the whole place was like that. It was as if Lilly enjoyed clinging to the memorabilia. Maybe she was. Maybe she was clinging on to how things used to be down here. Perhaps, she was hoping to wake up one day, walk in and find all of her girls busy clanking at typewriters and talking on phones.

Is this thing even plugged in?

Rachel slid the chair back and peeked under the desk, found the computer tower and switched it on; the fan was as loud as a jet engine in the still of the room.

"Shit," she whispered, looking around the room as if fearing that she would wake someone.

Seconds later, the monitor sprang to life, scrolling a list of memory checks and bios statuses.

"Okay, well that's a start."

Not surprisingly, the machine was running an ancient operating system but, to its credit, was fully booted within minutes.

Rachel found the usual desktop icons and one she didn't recognise sitting on the opposite side of the screen; Optel.

She double clicked it and the program loaded, flashing up a splash screen with a logo, and then presenting her with a login screen that requested a username, password and impatient cursor.

"Great," Rachel mumbled under her breath.

She shook her head. She had no clue.

As a guess, she typed ADMINISTRATOR as the login id and ADMIN as the password, then pressed enter, but the computer returned INVALID USERNAME OR PASSWORD.

She tried again with several other combinations, with and without passwords, upper and lowercase but nothing; the computer kept displaying the same message.

Frustrated, Rachel was about to pull the plug on the thing when a call came through, making her jump.

The light indicated Apartment 3.

"Stanton residence, good evening."

"Hi, this is Ceri Hooper from Now Magazine."

"Hello, how can I help?"

"Hi. Would it be possible to speak to Mr or Mrs Stanton?"

"I am afraid the Stanton's aren't taking any calls at the moment. Can I take a message?"

"Yes, as I said, this is Ceri from Now, Darren Stanton was expecting my call about a piece we're doing on him next month and I really need to speak with him."

"I see. Have you tried contacting his agent, as matters of this nature are typically dealt through his rep? Would you like the number?"

"Hello?"

But her reply was the dial tone and the apartment light went out.

Lilly had told her about these calls. Anyone and everyone would try all sorts of tactics to get through directly to residents by bypassing official representatives. It was their explicit job to act as gatekeepers unless explicitly told otherwise. She also went on to stress how important it was that Rachel remember this.

You're not getting through. Not on my watch, she thought with a sense of satisfaction.

As Rachel wrote the name in the call log, she found herself pondering on the name Ceri Hooper and why the name seemed oddly familiar.

Then she remembered; Ceri was the name of the girl Lilly had told her about, the one that used to work here and had gone missing.

Instinctively, she looked around herself; the room was empty, the door was closed yet, suddenly, she no longer felt alone. It was as if someone was watching her, and was it her imagination or had the shadows grown bigger?

She pushed thoughts she didn't want to entertain from her mind and turned her attention back to the monitor.

Without even thinking, she typed:

LOGIN ID: Ceri

And no password.

ACCESS DENIED, was the computer's response.

She tried again but with a variation on the spelling.

LOGIN ID: Keri

And no password.

The computer displayed: PLEASE WAIT, ACCESSING TELEPHONE MAINFRAME.

"Excellent!"

The hourglass filled and turned, filled and turned some more, but nothing happened for a minute or so until there was a beeping sound and the message:

UNABLE TO CONNECT TO TELEPHONE MAINFRAME. OK.

"Shit! No, it's not okay."

She peered under the desk, but it was way too dark.

So, she grabbed the lamp and, stirring an army of shadows, she bent onto her hands and knees, while shuddering at the thought of what might be lurking down there.

Nonetheless, resolute in her mission, she peered behind the computer tower to find tangled cables, a blanket of dust and a cobweb blowing in the breeze of the computer's fan like laundry on a washing line.

She squirmed when she wondered where the web's resident might be. Then, gingerly checked for loose cables, but finding none.

So, she got back to her feet, slapped the dust of her hands and, with a big sigh, sat back in the chair.

That's when another call came in. The light on the handwritten label said that the call was for Apartment 6.

"Mr Gallagher's residence, how may I help?"

"Hi, is Gallagher there?" It was a female voice with an American accent.

"I am sorry; Mr Gallagher isn't taking any calls right now. Can I take a message?"

"Yes, tell him that Alice Wrigley from Fox called."

"Will do, Miss Wrigley," Rachel said as she wrote on the pad. "Can I take a phone number?"

"Actually, it's *Mrs* Wrigley. He has my number. "

"Could I take your number anyway, just in case…?"

The line went dead.

"Hello? Hello?"

The apartment light went out.

"Suit yourself." She mumbled as she pulled the headset off. Maybe this job wasn't going to be as exciting as she thought.

Despondent, she turned her attention back to the computer. Its cursor was still flashing insistently, as if frustrated by the human who was incapable of using it.

Rachel grabbed the mouse and was about to shut the machine down, but stopped when, out of the corner of her eye, she noticed the telephone cable leading out of the back of the switchboard unit and onto the floor, behind the desk.

She stood up and followed it to the wall socket and that is when it occurred to her; the computer may not even be connected to a telephone line.

So she checked the back of the machine. Sure enough, it housed an empty telephone socket.

She followed the cable back up to the switchboard, where she carefully lifted the brown, antiquated contraption and turned it into the light; the telephone line was plugged into the back of it. She guessed it was this that was missing from the back of the computer, but she asked herself whether she dare risk unplugging it.

This was her first day after all.

On the other hand, how happy would Lilly be if she finally got her investment earning its money?

What if I unplug something I shouldn't? What if I can't put it back as it was? Course you can, just make a note of what you are unplugging and where.

Instinctively, she looked around the room again, and at the door.

Still closed.

Then, she unplugged the telephone wire from the back of the switchboard, and plugged it into the back of the computer.

She clicked the OK button and the login screen reappeared. She typed in KERI, with no password, and the familiar message was displayed:

PLEASE WAIT, ACCESSING TELEPHONE MAINFRAME

The egg timer restarted its acrobats.

After a few seconds, she saw a new message that read:

CONNECTION ESTABLISHED, LOADING SWITCHBOARD

"Yes!" She punched the air and then looked around, as if expecting somebody to cheer with her.

I guess college wasn't such a waste of time after all.

Within seconds, a two pane window appeared.

On the right was what looked like a blueprint for the building with a summary that read 10 floors, 21 Apartments. She assumed this included the penthouse.

Each apartment was tagged with floor and door number.

The left, smaller pane, displayed statistics, such as connection, date and time, room, operator, etcetera.

When the program had completely loaded, a prompt appeared:

TELEPHONE LOGGING IS ENABLED; PLEASE ENTER LOG NAME FOR THIS SESSION:

C:\ OPTEL\LOGS\KERI_

The cursor flashed as it waited for Rachel's input.

She hesitated a few seconds and then typed in today's date and pressed enter.

A green light appeared in the top left-hand corner of the screen and a box labelled STATUS read: WAITING CALL.

Then, an aircraft cabin-type bell sounded from the computer's speakers, startling Rachel. The status on the screen read, INCOMING CALL, and a prompt box read:

Ringing Heron Heights, Answer? YES / NO

"Oh, Shit!"

The box kept flashing and the bell kept sounding.

BONG: Ringing Heron Heights, Answer? YES / NO

But the headset was not plugged into the computer; it was still connected to the old switchboard.

She panicked and hissed repeatedly, "SHIT!"

BONG: Ringing Heron Heights, Answer? YES / NO

"SHIT!"

She scrambled behind the desk, yanked the headset out of the switchboard, snatched the lamp from the desk, fell to her knees and searched behind the computer for the jack socket. She found it and pushed the plug home.

BONG: Ringing Heron Heights, Answer? YES / NO

"YES! Damn it!"

She dragged the headset onto her head and clicked the *YES*

button.

The screen divided, information about the call was displayed on the left and an electronic notepad appeared on the right.

A discreet beep sounded in her ear; she was connected.

"Good evening, Heron Heights, sorry to keep you waiting."

"Hey, whatever happened to answering before the third ring?"

It was Jason.

"Oh god, Jason." She said breathlessly.

"What's up?"

She sighed, deeply, "Oh nothing. Just, wondering who the hell it was."

"Think it was your boss checking up on you."

"Yes, you could say…."

Rachel was unable to finish the rest of her sentence when she noticed what was on her screen.

Incredibly, another window had opened displaying fluorescent green text on a black backdrop that read:

KERI: > Good evening. Heron Heights. Sorry to keep you waiting.

HERON: > Hey whatever happened to answering before the third ring.

KERI: > O god. Jason

HERON: > Whats up.

KERI: > O nothing. Just wondering who the hell it was.

It took Rachel a few seconds to realise that it was the transcript of her telephone conversation. The window was date stamped with the time and milliseconds of the call.

"Rach?"

"I'm here." She said, gawping at the box as it transcribed her words.

"Are you okay?"

"Yeah, I'm good."

"You sure?"

"Never been better." She said as a huge grin spread across her face.

She liked this, it was cool.

It was really cool.

26 EYES

Night had enveloped the city by the time Ashley reached her destination.

She had driven east, across London, to the borough of Southwark right in the middle of rush hour. This gave her ample opportunity to consider the multiple reasons why she should make a U-turn back home.

She thought about what Rupert's reaction might be when he found out, or that of Jackie Harris' neighbours when they spotted a stranger casually walking into the dead woman's home or, if she was really lucky, that of the police who'd be keen to know why the hell the last person to speak to Jackie Harris, alive, was now snooping around her home under the cover of darkness.

All more than motivating reasons yet turning back wasn't an option, she needed to see this through.

Thus, against every shred of common sense, Ashley parked her car just down the road from St Andrew's Court and walked the rest of the way, so as to attract the least amount of attention.

Number 6, St Andrew's Court was in the middle of a clutch of older houses that were still standing in the shadow of London's newest landmark, The Shard.

Most of the nearby land had been reclaimed to build affordable flats to tackle London's ever growing housing crisis.

Ashley drew her coat around her and hunched against the bitter cold gale. It had pulled her hair and spat at her from the moment she left the warmth of the car, as if incensed by her presence here.

Hands thrust into her pockets, she gripped the concealed weapon that was the flashlight she'd retrieved from the glove compartment of her car.

Then, she crossed the court and headed for the only house that did not have its lights on and curtains drawn against the night.

All around her, windows, like giant fireflies, glowed amber in the night.

Mercifully, the surrounding streets were empty, but for a suited man who exited a red Audi. He hastily said something to the driver, and then dashed into one of the nearby flats for cover from the gathering rain.

Ashley stopped outside number 6 and casually looked around herself, trying to look as inconspicuous as she could, while making sure nobody was watching her.

She had been here just once before. It was after a lunch meeting with Jackie.

During lunch, the ex-police officer candidly stated that if Ashley wanted to read any excerpts from the manuscript, she would have to do so at her home, in front of her. She made it clear that she had no intention of letting it out of her sight, at least not before it was ready to go to print.

Ashley had obliged and remembered how, on that day, Jackie had joked that, for an ex-copper she wasn't particularly security conscious.

This was way before it was announced that she planned to expose the Metropolitan Police as institutionally corrupt.

She then proceeded to retrieve a spare key from a secret hiding place, telling Ashley to ignore everything that she was about to see.

The two black ceramic lions, mouths crafted wide in a silent roar, were still standing guard on either side of the front door.

They, Jackie explained, were an ostentatious gift from her aunt, who apparently snapped them up at a bargain sale at a local DIY store.

The sound of a car brought Ashley back to the present and she spun to catch the glowing taillights of a vehicle disappearing around the corner.

What the hell are you doing out here?

She was exposed, and she needed to get inside, fast.

She scanned the area once more; despite her paranoia, nobody seemed to care about her presence here. There were no doors opened, no curtains twitching.

I don't want to be here.

Yes, you do.

No, I don't.

Why are you here exactly? For Harrison? For Jackie? For you?

Just get on with it!

Her hands were trembling, whether this was due to the freezing rain that was now falling in sheets or the crazy act she was about to commit, Ashley did not know. However, slowly and way too surely, she willed herself to insert her hand into the mouth of one of the lions only to snatch it back, yelping and rubbing her fingers against her jeans.

Eww.

She shuddered with revulsion, shook her hand and squirmed a few times more. Whatever she had touched was cold and slimy, and could only be a slug or something equally revolting.

A snail with no shell, that's all it is.

I can't do this.

Get on with it! A woman is dead, Ash.

With that, and grimacing all the way, she forced her hand back into the lion's mouth, and this time was relieved to feel her fingers brush against a leather key fob and then the jagged edges of a key.

She walked up to the front door and, in one swift motion, unlocked it and stepped inside.

The relief was instant.

She pushed the door shut and then leant against it, as she took a few seconds to enjoy the respite from the elements. Rainwater dribbled off her hair and down her face, and her coat leaked onto the carpet.

Then she felt her nose with the back of her hand, it was numb from the cold.

The house didn't feel much better. It was unusually chilly, still and very uninviting. Everything appeared to be switched off. No hum of kitchen appliances or reassuring drone of the central heating.

Just more cold.

There was a sweet scent of artificial honeysuckle in the air; a battery operated air freshener was continuing its work somewhere, regardless of that fact that its owner was no longer alive to appreciate it.

The dim glow of streetlight filtered in through nearby windows, slowly defining silhouettes of furniture that haunted the lounge.

Directly ahead, was the couch, in front of that the TV and beyond that, an archway led to the dining room.

After pulling the curtains shut, Ashley switched on the flashlight, scaring back the shadows.

Thankfully, her orientation was aided by the memory of her recent visit.

Okay, now that you are in here. What the hell are you going to do? You don't have a clue where this thing is. The Police could have already taken it for all you know.

The beam of the torch licked across basic furniture and white walls.

Have the police actually been out here at all?

She made her way through the archway and into the small dining room. There was a little table in here with a wall unit. She opened the doors and searched inside, but found nothing but a shoebox full of cutlery and a shelf full of table linen.

Beyond the dining room was a tiny kitchen. The surfaces were clean; nothing seemed conspicuously out of place, and she doubted very much that there would be anywhere in here that Jackie would have hidden her manuscript. Besides, when she came over that day, she remembered Jackie disappearing upstairs before returning with the printed pages.

Tap! Tap! Screech!

The sound made Ashley literally jump on the spot and drop her torch, causing it to skitter then roll across the black and white tiles.

Her heart pounded and a sickly wave of hot and cold shivers skittered over her; something, outside, in the back garden, was tapping and scraping at the glass of the patio door.

Tap! Tap!

She yelped.

That's when she noticed, from bony claw shadows projected all over the walls and kitchen units, that the visitor was actually an overgrown branch. The wind was forcing the tree that towered over the house, to bend to its will.

Jesus Christ!

Ashley hastily retrieved the stricken flashlight, retraced her steps back through the lounge and then climbed the stairs but froze when one of the steps creaked particularly loudly.

There's nobody here!

Nonetheless, she listened carefully, just to make sure the whole neighbourhood hadn't heard the creak. Then, slowly and carefully resumed her journey upward, passing a water pastel painting of rivers and cornfields as well as an array of photo frames of smiling strangers.

The first room she came across was a small box bedroom which, by the presence of an ironing board and basket full of laundered clothes, doubled as an ironing room.

The second room was much bigger with a double bed, wardrobe and a desk, upon which stood a flat-screen monitor.

She noticed immediately that the curtains were open, and worried that the flashlight could be seen by the world outside. On the other hand, while the streetlight overspill was useful, it wouldn't be enough for her to conduct her search.

She'd have to risk it.

She sat down at the desk and started searching through drawers, revealing stationery items, manila folders, pens and plain paper, but nothing that resembled a manuscript or any clue as to its whereabouts.

"It's safe. I've stashed it in a secret hiding place in my bedroom. Somewhere London's finest wouldn't even have the balls to look."

She remembered Jackie's words, as she searched through diaries and various documents, in the hope of finding a clue about where the pen drive might be, but she realised she was clutching at straws.

She thought back to her meeting with Jackie and what she had said. She'd told her that they had broken into her home while she was in bed!

"Somewhere London's finest wouldn't even have the balls to look."

She allowed the torch beam to probe the shadows in the room, to violate every nook and cranny of the space that Jackie Harris once occupied, and it made her feel very sad.

This was hopeless.

Worse, a woman was dead. Another human being had met a horrific end to her life on this earth, and what was her reaction to this? To search her home, like some kind of literary scavenger; violating the dead woman's things in the hope of finding a manuscript that was, so bloody obviously, long gone!

She felt ashamed and angry at herself. Angry not only with her behaviour, but at her stupidity.

If Jackie was actually being stalked, and if somebody had the audacity to break into her home and make the woman paranoid enough to not want to copy her manuscript to her computer hard drive, then she was hardly going to leave a printed version, the pen drive, or even clues about the drive's location lying around, was she?

Shame you didn't take time out to deduce this rational conclusion before setting out for this place. You idiot!

She took a few seconds to take stock. She contemplated getting out and leaving this whole sorry story behind her. Forget the manuscript, and forget that Jackie Harris had ever gone to her with this.

But now she felt worse.

Forget Jackie Harris. Is that what she would have wanted? For you to forget her. After all of her hard work. After everything she has been through, you want to forget her?

She was so frustrated she could have screamed.

Instead, she fumbled, angrily, under the desk until she felt the front of the computer and the power button.

Instantly, the machine began to whir and booting information appeared on the computer screen.

She left her seat and went to the wardrobe. As soon as the doors were open, she flipped on the flashlight to reveal hanging garments; blouses, shirts, suits, even a police uniform.

Underneath these, was a long wooden box, it ran the length and breadth of the wardrobe.

This looks promising.

She fell to her knees, lifted the lid off the box and shone light inside, revealing shoes, trainers, boots and heels, but no manuscript.

No pen drive.

A search around and, as far as she could see, on top and behind the wardrobe, yielded the same result, as did that of the two bedside cabinets.

She returned to the computer and noticed that it was stuck the C of the DOS prompt, and the cursor was flashing, helplessly, awaiting further instructions.

She typed in DIR, but the computer returned no files or directories.

So, it was true. They really have been here, and they really have formatted the drive.

This chilled her, as the gravity of everything Jackie had said suddenly sank in. These people really would stop at nothing.

So what the hell was she doing there?

She was done.

She killed the whirring of the computer and stood up, now more than ever, eager to get out of that house and get back home.

But that's when she noticed it.

The bed.

She'd walked around it while searching the bedside cabinets but…

"Somewhere London's finest wouldn't even have the balls to look."

Jackie told her that they had broken into her home while she was in it.

Presumably, asleep, in her bed. Would they have had *the balls* to look under her bed while she was in it?

She fell to the carpet, pulled up the hanging quilt and pushed back the darkness with the flashlight to reveal the handle of a small suitcase.

Really?

She pulled it out and flipped the locks open.

The case was full of envelopes, letters, bills, insurance policies and various receipts, but no pen drive.

She rummaged through and under the paperwork, then carefully examined every inch of the case, paying particular attention to the lining, in the hope of finding some kind of hidden recess.

Nothing.

Frustrated, she slammed the case's lid shut, pushed it aside with contempt, and sulked for a few seconds.

Then, she was casting the flashlight under the bed once more.

Empty.

She swept the beam, like a searchlight, as far as the light would travel, but there was nothing else under there.

So, it was with despondence, that she kept the light trained on the space directly in front her with one hand, while sliding the case into view with the other.

She was about to push the thing back from whence it came when she noticed an irregularity in the beam; carpet fibre. Nothing too obvious, just a few strands standing conspicuously to attention right where the case once rested.

She scrambled further under the bed until her progress was impeded by the bulk of her coat. She promptly shrugged it off, and discarded it to one side, before returning to the task in hand.

It smelt dusty underneath the bed and, as she inched forward, a cloud of dust, and most likely an army of mites, she thought, drifted in front her.

She pushed any images of magnified monsters from her head, determined to stay focussed on her objective.

As her face drew closer to the strands, she could clearly see that they marked an actual tear in the carpet, maybe even a cut.

Maybe even one that had been made deliberately to house a pen drive.

She examined the slit with her fingers, and concluded that it was in fact big enough to conceal a drive, without it being obvious.

Could this be it?

She pushed her fingers further into the cavity just as the beam of her light began to fade.

"No…" She complained as if the thing could hear her.

But the traitor wasn't listening and instead it dramatically flickered a few times.

"No!" she protested again, and smacked it on the carpet, but that did little to revive the thing. If anything, the impacts finished it off since, after a few more spluttering flashes, the room was plunged into darkness, but for the jaundice light overspill from the city outside.

Ashley remained still for a few seconds, contemplating her next move. She closed her eyes, as if to transfer additional sensory powers to her fingers where, no matter how far she probed, she still felt nothing.

They've been here already. Must have....

That's when it came.

A sound so loud, a cacophony so jarring in the still of the house, that it caused Ashley's body to jolt for the second time that evening. She smacked her head against the undercarriage of the bed and winced.

The noise was coming from the stairs and sounded like smashing glass.

Jesus Christ!

Ashley extricated her body from the bed and jumped to her feet so fast, the act literally made her head spin.

She paused for a few seconds to listen. The sound had stopped.

Had somebody flipped over the wall unit downstairs?

Is it them?

Are they back?

Heart pounding and pulse racing, she reluctantly crept over to the bedroom door, that she'd had the presence of mind to push to when she entered. She had left a slit wide enough to offer a scary view of the stairs that were eerily lit in sallow yellow, thanks to a small landing window.

She neared the gap in the door as carefully and as quietly as she could, but this wasn't easy for she was breathing way too fast and way too loud for the quiet of the house.

At least it felt that way.

She slowly placed an eye to the slit in the door as a strand of her hair danced in front of her face, like a puppet on a string, as she breathed in and out.

Then, she drew in a sharp breath.

The sound she'd heard wasn't that of the wall unit being turned on its side, but that of photo frames and paintings smashing onto the stairs, and cartwheeling down to the front door.

She could just about discern shattered glass on the steps, the corner of a photo frame, and the partial dazzling smile of a photo.

Ashley stared at the damage, as her heart clawed at her chest. It wanted out, as did she from that house. Somebody was in there with her, and whoever it was, wanted to scare her by knocking down those frames.

And, it worked.

She was terrified.

Thus, hands to mouth, to stifle her hyperventilation, she took a step back from the door.

Creek!

Someone was on the stairs.

Oh God!

Fear pinpricked her skin, and her whole body began to tremble.

She knew she had to do something. She knew that if she wanted to survive, she would have to take action now, but her terror was stronger than her will to survive.

If you don't move now, Ash, you'll die here!

Hyperventilating, and shuddering, she slowly replaced her eye to the slit in the door, and instantly wished she hadn't, for there, in the gloom of the stairwell, stood the shadow of a man.

She yelped, instinctively, pushed the door shut, and turned the key.

She was under no doubt that whoever was out there was not her friend, but her enemy.

She backed away from the door and was parallel with the desk once more. The room was chillingly silent, except for the blood pumping in her ears.

She listened carefully, but the house was as still as a tomb. Even the world outside seemed to have disappeared behind a sheet of noise proof glass. What happened to the cars, the people, and the overhead planes?

Is he out there? What does he want? Maybe I imagined it. I didn't imagine it. Someone is out there. I can feel their presence! They're waiting for me!

Oh God, save me.

No sooner had she processed those thoughts; she sensed someone behind the door.

She couldn't explain how she knew, but she knew, someone was standing right outside the door and they were listening to her pounding heart, her shallow breaths.

She backed further into the room.

And then it began, at first so quiet that she thought she was imagining it. Then, her eyes, like a director's camera in one the most horrifying of movies ever, zoomed onto the key in the lock where, her now dark-accustomed eyes, could see that it was rattling!

Help me. Please. Somebody help me.

The rattling grew in strength and sound until the key fell out of the lock, and to the carpet.

Terror had swallowed Ashley's scream before it emerged from her mouth.

Who are you? Leave me alone! Leave me alone!

She looked around the room; there was nowhere else to go. She was trapped in here.

Then she spotted the rain-soaked window.

She moved over to it and looked outside; the rain was falling on a shiny wet city. She could see a car in the distance.

There was hope!

Maybe she should open the window and start screaming. One of the neighbours was bound to hear her, surely. It might even scare the intruder away, but what if it didn't? What if it made them even more determined to get in there, and do her the same unspeakable harm that they had to Jackie?

It was a subconscious thought, but the idea that Jackie had been murdered seemed most logical in that moment.

A banging on the door snapped her head around. Her whole body was shuddering in short acute spasms, her nerves were taught, and where she had been freezing just minutes before her body now burnt perspiration.

Oh, God.

Whoever was out there had started banging on the door now. Slow at first, then progressing into fast, violent, and loud impacts that threatened to knock the door from its frame.

There was no time to think; Ashley opened the window and thrust her head outside; the scent of fresh, rain-drenched air was a momentary comfort, for it symbolised freedom.

However, the sensation was temporary as she took in the roof that, from the window, sloped down towards the guttering where rainwater gurgled, noisily, down a drainpipe.

Using the bedside table as a stepladder, she stepped carefully up, out of the window and onto the slippery tiles.

Instantly, the rain began its assault as a cold wind bit into her flesh and tugged at her hair once more.

Despite this, she stepped away from the window.

She had no idea where she was going, nor did she care, as long as she was out of that room, no longer a trapped animal.

The banging seemed to have stopped, but Ashley wasn't sure if this was merely because the sound was being drowned in the din of rain on roof tiles.

She didn't care.

She just wanted away from there, now, and preferably without any broken bones.

She looked across the rooftop to the roads below and the safety that they represented. Then she looked at the lights blazing in windows all around her.

Where were all of these people? She wanted the opposite of when she had arrived there, she wanted them to stop hiding behind closed curtains and take an interest in her plight.

There's a woman on a bloody roof for God's sakes! What's wrong with you all?

She was so frustrated she wanted to scream, but something stopped her, as if doing so might compel her pursuer to *shut her up*.

Instead, she slowly inched her way forward, holding onto the arch summit that ran the length of the building, being careful not to slip.

She considered the choice: the side down towards the back garden, the tree and the slabs of the patio, or the concrete of the front door.

Which way? Back garden or front door?

Neither of the options was appealing.

In the back garden, anything could happen to her, since she would be hidden from the eyes of the main street, and the rest of the neighbours. At the front of the house, whoever had followed her up to Jackie's room, could simply stroll out of the front door, and be waiting for her as she descended.

Which brought her to her next dilemma, how exactly was she going to get down?

She could feel rain water dribbling down her belly. Her sweater was soaked through and all of her extremities were beginning to numb.

Thankfully, she'd seen the practical advantages of changing into jeans and trainers before embarking on her amateur detective adventure.

She glanced back as rain soaked hair slapped at her cheeks; nobody had followed her out of the window.

Have they gone? Maybe they thought I'd scream and attract the attention of those bastards, who are so wrapped up watching their bloody soap operas that they can't see a woman clinging for her life, on a fucking rooftop! Jesus Christ, won't somebody help me!

But Ashley had to face the fact that she was alone, and that if she did scream, her pursuer might indeed come for her.

Maybe they had already scampered off somewhere but what if they hadn't? What if they were just biding their time? Waiting for the inevitable, waiting for her to fall off the roof and to the ground, where she would without a doubt break bones; and that was if she was lucky.

Then it occurred to her; the tree in the back garden. It would be dangerous, but it was a possibility.

She glanced back at the window; still nobody following her.

They could be waiting for me, down there.

Regardless, and with soaked strands of hair dangling in front of her eyes, Ashley sat down and, much to her own astonishment, began to inch her way towards the edge of the roof.

The wind hissed at her, and the cold was starting to settle

deep into her bones, constricting her chest. But she resolved that there was no other way but forward, towards the salvation that was the branches of the tree.

She reached the edge of the roof with a sense of petrifying helplessness; if one of the tiles slipped, she would have nothing to grab, nothing to stop her fall and she would plunge down to the patio.

The branches of the tree came into view. Mercifully, because there were no leaves, she could see exactly which of the thicker branches could potentially take her weight.

She estimated that the first suitable branch was approximately six feet from her, which meant she would have to literally jump off the roof in order to reach it, as she fell.

She looked around; still nobody following her and still nobody outside, nobody walking their dog, nobody whose attention she could attract.

Just you and that tree, Ashley.

Carefully, she inched her way forward and the patio came into view.

The cold hard slabs were approximately fifteen to twenty feet below her, a vision that made her queasy.

To the left and right, she could see the light spilling from the patio doors of both next-door neighbours, and she considered screaming out to them, but even if they heard her, would they even bother coming to her aid?

She'd lost count of the articles she'd read. Surveys conducted in Harrison's own magazines outlined a frightening sign of the times that here, in the city, people would sooner turn the other way than get involved in something. The pages of newspapers were all too often awash with have-a-go heroes, losing their lives to save others.

She glanced at the gnarled branches of the tree. There was salvation in them, but Ashley knew she would have to stand up in order to get sufficient thrust to reach one that could bear her weight.

Oh my God, there is no way. Oh no, I can't! I can't! I don't have any option; I can't go back in there. I can't do that either!

"HELP!" She screamed into the night. "HELP ME!

PLEASE!"

The words just came screaming out of her mouth.

"HELP ME!" she yelled so loud that her voice choked in her throat.

Nothing.

"SOMEBODY HELP ME, PLEASE! SOMEBODY!"

Just the dinging of rain on tiles.

Tears joined the rivulets of water washing down her face. There was only one way she was going to get out of this. Only one way she was going to get down.

Ashley wept, loudly and angrily, as she very carefully began to lift herself into a crouching position.

It was a treacherous feat, but one she was managing very well until a tile slipped from beneath her.

She lost her balance and fell backward, starting off a landslide of tiles that crashed, loudly, to the patio below.

One by one, as each tile fell, it took Ashley's foothold with it, and there was absolutely nothing she could do about it.

She slid, helplessly, towards the edge, screaming as she went.

In seconds, she was sliding over the guttering.

It scraped up her right side, all the way to her arm, until she finally managed to grab a hold with her left hand until, suddenly, she was kicking the air beneath her feet, as the exertion of the acrobatics snatched the next scream from her throat.

Slowly, she managed to grab a hold with the other hand, but the strain was taking its toll on her aching arms, as she hung dizzyingly high from the hard stone of the patio.

She grunted at the pain, as the rain pummelled her face.

"Pl...please," she uttered, through the strain, "Somebody, please help me! Please!"

And that is when she heard it.

It sounded like bending metal, and it was accompanied by a popping sound.

She turned her head sideways, and her fears were confirmed; the guttering was coming away from the building, and the popping sound was that of the fixtures, wrenching free!

"Oh...no," she breathed. "No…… help me… somebody."

But the strain on her body was so great that she could just about breathe, let alone call for help.

POP!

"No!"

There was more bending and Ashley felt her body fall a few inches.

POP! POP!

A few more inches.

"Help somebody…" she groaned. But her words were whispers in the pouring rain.

POP!

She slipped further and now could see that from her far left, the guttering was hanging loose. Slowly, one by one, the fixtures were relenting and eventually when too many had been lost, she would fall.

POP!

The ground was getting closer.

She turned her head to the tree, but the branches were too far away, she would never be able to reach out to them. "Oh God… help me please... somebody help me!"

POP! POP! POP!

In quick succession, the rest of the fixtures gave way.

Ashley screamed, and kicked her legs, hopelessly, as her body plunged, in one pendulous motion, towards the patio furniture where the cold hard stone slabs, that she had been dreading, reached up and smacked her in the face.

She lay motionless as the rain bathed her. Her numb body slowly registering the pain which helped bring her back to her senses.

My legs hurt, Are they broken?

She tried to move them, it took some effort, but they moved.

Thank God.

Then, she slowly lifted her face from the pavement, and flinched, as a searing pain carved across her face, and sank into her skull.

She looked up into the rain, as blood trickled down her cheek, to see the guttering swinging in the wind.

Thankfully, it had broken her fall, by swinging her to the ground instead of dropping her.

She had made it. She hurt so badly that she wanted to cry, but she was alive.

She willed her body to stand, but couldn't.

Let me sleep. No, get home first! Get safe! No, sleep.

She strained hard to focus and eventually her vision came back, long enough for her to see something that, despite her condition, scratched fingernails down the chalkboard of her back. She was looking directly at the patio doors, into the kitchen, and what she saw froze the blood in her veins.

There, in between the blinds that adorned the patio doors, was a shadow, and it was watching her with a pair of expressionless, cold blue eyes that seemed to glow in the dark.

Such was the malevolence of the unblinking glare, that it transfixed her, as much as it suffocated the breath from her lungs.

She tried to scramble to her feet, to run, but she couldn't. A sickly merry-go-round sensation gripped her.

Within seconds, her face met the hardness of the slabs once more.

Then, a shadow drifted over her body, and the world went black.

27 TV STUDIO

Abigail Palmer tried hard not fidget as she sat in the makeup chair. The vanity lights were blinding, the air conditioning seemed to have packed up and she was finding it hard to breathe.

And she had pretty much felt that way ever since she received the call yesterday, and was asked to fill in as host on the chat show; Peter Denham and Co.

The show pulled in a seven million audience and the usual host, Peter Denham, was adored almost as much as the celebrities he interviewed.

Unfortunately, Peter was stuck in Sri Lanka. He was scheduled to return to London this morning, but his flight was grounded when the airport received a terrorist threat, which lead to the cancellation of flights in and out of the country.

Abigail Palmer, a thirty-three-year-old investigative reporter, with a few series worth of current affairs programs on her resume, was the only person they could find at such short notice. She'd also produced a few Denham specials that focused on interviewing key leaders from around the world.

The network wasn't exactly enthralled with the impromptu appointment, but she was the most *appropriate* person according to the show's executive producer. In his opinion, Abigail was a familiar face for the audience, and also had some knowledge of the format of the show. Therefore, it was a choice between putting her on, or cancelling one of their hottest bookings since Madonna.

"Five minutes!" somebody yelled.

Receiving the call yesterday had been very exciting, especially when she found out who exactly she would be interviewing; one of the most famous celebrity couples since Brad and Angelina; Darren and Leticia Aaron–Stanton.

However, as they counted down to the *On Air* sign, things were a little different; Abigail could feel butterflies in her stomach, and the need to pee was ever present.

"Abby!" a voice boomed over the intercom, "can we have you in your seat, please?"

It was the director, Harry James, a veteran of television, a no-nonsense perfectionist who, according to the makeup lady, strenuously opposed replacing his friend, Denham, even if it was only for one evening. He insisted that the producers postpone the show, but they refused on the grounds that it would be a logistical nightmare to rebook. That and the fact that they had already spent thousands of pounds on television promos. They also pointed out that, as per his contract, Harry James was obliged to direct tonight's show, whether he liked it or not.

This was according to the makeup girl, who not only cleaned and applied makeup, but laundered as much gossip as her machine gun mouth could manage.

The girl also insisted, not unlike the chauvinistic bastard in the control booth, on calling Abigail, Abby.

She almost slapped the fussing hands away, and carefully stepped her way through a minefield of cables, and a squad of technicians.

Whatever happened to health and safety, Jesus! Who gives a shit about health and safety? Okay, calm down. Just ignore what the stupid cow told you. So that arsehole up there hates your guts. What do you care? Just do the job...

"Ah at last," the voice boomed over the sound system.

Breathe.

She took a deep breath, "Where would you like me?" she asked, squinting through the set lights to the control box at the back of the studio.

"Well, in the host's chair would be a good place," was his sarcastic reply.

Abigail sat in Peter Denham's special leather chair; opposite her were two more, obviously for husband and wife. Behind her, a backdrop featured red and orange painted swirls.

A sound technician fiddled with her microphone, as the lights went on and off, in a series of checks.

"Testin', testin'," a technician's cockney voice boomed in Abigail's earpiece, making her jump.

"Sorry."

Her palms were sweating, and the adrenaline that was coursing through her body was making her tremble.

"For the love of God, sit up straight, stop slouching!"

Abigail straightened in her chair. She hated that man, and this was another reason why she had to be successful tonight.

"Two minutes!"

There was some commotion, and she turned to see the Stantons being escorted on set, as there was clapping from the studio audience.

The Stantons smiled and waved, as Abigail stood, and held out a hand to Darren Stanton, who looked as good as he did on TV. He had wavy black hair, an excellent physique, showcased by a slightly unbuttoned blue shirt, which he wore with denim jeans and suede boots.

"I'm Darren," he said with a big smile as he shook her hand.

"It's a pleasure, Darren," Abigail said with a big smile.

Next, was Mrs Stanton, the rising movie queen, rumoured to have signed up to make a Hollywood film for a cool two million pounds.

Not surprisingly, she was dressed almost identical to her husband, with shoulder length blonde hair and blue eyes.

"Hi," she said, shaking Abigail's hand.

"Hello, it's good to meet you."

They both sat in the opposite chairs, as if they'd already been briefed, and waited.

"One minute!"

Somebody thrust a list of questions in Abby's hands. She glanced at the paper, "You both know the areas we're going to cover, I take it?"

"Yes, and so do you," said Leticia, nodding at a nearby Autocue screen. "And don't you forget it," she added with a menacing smile.

I should have known that they wouldn't want me asking any questions the audience might actually want to hear. Like, tell us about how you are trying to block the release of one of your earlier films, Mrs Stanton.

Abigail knew that the questions on her sheet of paper and on the autocue would be dull and uninteresting. She also knew that she would have a hard time making them seem any different. After all, these words would have been dissected by Stanton's legal and PR team until they contained nothing remotely interesting.

But that is how things worked with celebrity interviews. Nobody was interested in the truth, just the ratings and, of course, what made the egomaniacs feel good and best pedalled their latest product.

So much for exclusive.

"HEY!" It was Harry James yelling in her ear piece, startling her for the second time that evening.

You bastard, do that one more time and I'm pulling this

fucking thing out!

"What?" she seethed.

"I need you to talk into this thing for a last minute check."

"Oh, you want me to say something? How about...."

"Thirty seconds!"

Leticia, or Mrs Stanton as she preferred to be called these days, was fussing over what was left of her husband's hair and she was starting to annoy Abigail who, if she didn't know better, would have thought the woman was parading her claim on her racing driver husband.

"Twenty seconds!"

"Try not to freeze in front of all those people, won't you, kid," came Harry's reassuring words.

Fuck you!

"Ten seconds!"

A dazzle of light flooded the set. The stage manager walked out in front of the studio audience and held up his hands; on cue, they exploded in rapturous applause.

"Five, four, three, two, one......"

"Camera one," somebody said in Abigail's ear. She turned to it and with a smile began to read the auto queue, "Good evening, ladies and gentleman, and welcome to tonight without Peter Denham, but with the co."

What?

"My name is Abigail Palmer and I will be filling in for Peter, who has been unavoidably detained somewhere with some tigers, I hear."

Smile? Are these people for real? They are actually writing in my smiles.

The audience, as if cued, laughed.

"Tonight we'll be talking to some very special guests indeed. He has been hailed as one of the best British racing car drivers since Hill, and she, as a blonde Catherine Zeta-Jones. Alone they were icons, but together they are the biggest sensation since Brad and Angelina. Ladies and gentleman, would you please welcome Darren Stanton and Leticia Aaron-Stanton!"

The floor manager appeared to be attempting flight as, behind the scenes, he waved his arms frantically up and down at the audience, who clapped and whistled in response.

A group of numbered cameras all around the trio moved in closer, one of them capturing a smiling picture of the couple and beaming it to a nearby monitor.

"Hello and welcome to the show."

"Thanks for having us," Leticia replied with a fake butter-wouldn't-melt smile.

"This is apparently the first interview you have given together since the birth of your son, Terrence, who's three years old now, is that right?"

"Three and half, yes," Leticia corrected.

"Well, it's truly a privilege to have you here with us tonight. Darren, is it true you were besieged by members of our studio audience tonight?"

He smiled, "Well, they were asking for my autograph, yeah."

"In fact, Darren, you were voted one of the sexiest racing car drivers in the world, which means literally thousands of women find you adorable. What does it feel like to be idolised by so many?"

"Well, it's great and it's really flattering, but you know, at the end of the day I just do my job. I just drive."

"What about you, Leticia? What does it feel like to have to share your husband with so many?"

Leticia shrugged, "Well, I've got to be honest with you. I'm so busy with my own career that I hardly notice it. To me, he's just Darren. My husband who, like most men, leaves the toilet seat up and underwear on the bathroom floor."

There was a cheer from some members of the audience.

Abigail looked and smiled broadly then, she turned back, "Darren, tell me about Terrence, there is no mistaking how proud you are of him. What does it feel like to be a father?"

"Yeah, it's great."

I should have added in words of more than one syllable.

"Do you think he is going to grow up to be a racer, just like you and your father before you?"

"Definitely."

"Now, Leticia, there have been these reports in the press that you refuse to leave your home without Terrence, is there any truth to that?"

"Absolutely not. You know, I'm just like most women out there. I have to earn a living. So, those that think I'm a neurotic mum who can't trust her son with anybody other than family, are just talking rubbish. In fact, Terrence is at home with his nanny right now."

The tedium of the questions, as per the script, continued for another fifteen minutes. Questions, not surprisingly, lingered on Leticia's new film in which she plays Brad Pitt's love interest. One of the reasons why the film's marketing team insisted on the comment about the couple being the new 'Brad and Angelina'.

What wasn't mentioned, is that she had a minuscule role and is killed off in the first act.

Darren's questions revolved around his career, his son, and his soon to be released line of sportswear.

All subjects that had been researched and published many times before. The whole thing was a charade. They even had her ask details about the Stanton's homes in various corners of the world. This included their residence in London where, for some obscure reason, Abigail was obliged to comment on how *normal* it was for the two to shack up in an apartment building, rather than buying their own house somewhere on the outskirts of the city.

Apparently, the reason for choosing their London pad was the convenience and security that it provided.

28 SECURITY

Back in Apartment 10, Amy, the Stanton's twenty-six-year-old nanny, sneered at the TV and then turned the volume down.

She was lying on the sofa, devouring a bar of chocolate.

Mrs Stanton had just said that she wasn't neurotic about

leaving her son, but she was. Amy had to endure no fewer than three investigations into her past, just so she could be eligible for this job. Even after that, Leticia had demanded three character and employment references, along with detailed information about any previous, current or potential boyfriends, that were strictly forbidden from going anywhere near her child at any time.

The woman was fanatical about her son and spoilt him rotten.

That said; she did pay extremely well, and the little boy was actually really cute when his mum wasn't around, and he knew who was boss.

In fact, she'd only just managed to get him to sleep for he insisted he was not tired, and did not want to go to bed. However, one fairy tale later, he'd finally succumbed.

Now, Amy was talking on her mobile phone, and explaining to her friend how tonight she had seen Darren Stanton come out of the bedroom, topless. "He is gorgeous," she said, longingly, as Darren's face appeared on the television screen, "but she's a bitch. What the hell does he see in her anyway?"

"They'll be divorced soon," her friend said, casually, on the other end of the phone, "and then she'll get all his millions."

"Oh God, I hope so," Amy said, "except for the part where she gets the millions."

"Why is it that all the best ones are either taken or out of our league?"

"Hey, speak for yourself," Amy exclaimed in mock protestation.

"Dream on, girl. You've got more chance of shagging the prime minister."

Amy pulled a face, "Eww, no thanks," she said, popping another cube of chocolate into her mouth.

"Did I tell you what happened to that queen bitch, Tracey?"

"No, what the hell is going on?"

"Well, she…"

"…No, I mean with the TV. It keeps freezing, and then clumps of people's faces keep moving. Eww, it's like painting pixels moving around a canvas."

"Are you watching Satellite TV?"

"Yes."

"That'll be it then. It always goes like that when there's bad weather."

"It's just foggy. Hardly bad weather."

"Yeah, and what's up with that. One minute, I'm freezing my tits off, thinking it's going to snow, but then we get freezing fog."

"It's global warming, innit'. Pretty soon those ice caps are gonna' melt, and we're gonna' drown in giant tsunamis."

"Great, thanks for that cheerful outlook."

"Just saying."

"Yeah, well, don't," Amy said, distractedly, as she got up from her lying position and looked around the room. She could have sworn she heard something move behind her, and she wondered if Terrence had got out of bed.

She watched as the furniture revealed itself through bursts of blue light from the TV.

The room was empty.

"I can't believe you've landed that job there. Satellite TV, all those perks and, best one of all, you get to be in the same house as that stud…"

"… and his queen bitch wife, remember," Amy added, as she rolled onto her knees and then slowly leant forward to check behind the couch.

Nothing.

"Yeah, well, I think the benefits outweigh the suffering, don't you?"

Amy didn't answer as she was still scanning the room.

"You still there?"

"Yes, I'm here," she said, resuming her prostrate position.

"What's going on with the phone?"

"What do you mean?"

"You keep cutting out, that or you sound like a Dalek. And then these bursts of static are driving me nuts. Are you not hearing that?"

"No, must be your end. You sound fine to me," Amy said, subconsciously looking at the glowing screen of her device, as if it could give her some kind of clue as to her friend's complaint.

"I can't see anything…"

The words were cut short as Amy snapped upright into sitting position as she felt someone pulling at her hair."

"What the…"

"Amy?"

Amy looked around the room.

It was empty.

"Amy?"

She reached out for a nearby lamp and felt a hand on hers. She screamed and leapt to the opposite side of the couch.

"JEEEEESUS!" She exclaimed, when she saw Terrence standing by the sofa. "Terrence! You gave me a bloody heart attack!" She snapped.

The boy just stood, watching her, with bleary eyes and dishevelled blonde hair.

"Hey, what's going on?"

Amy eventually tuned into her friend on the phone. "Nothing, he's up again. Hold on," Amy said, putting the mobile phone down and turning to the boy. "What are you doing out of bed, Terry? You gave Amy a really big fright," she said, buttoning up the jacket of his Scooby pyjamas.

"Someone keeps tapping on my window."

"It's just the wind, Terry."

"No, that man."

"What man?"

"Man outside my window."

"There's nobody outside your window, Terrence. We're way too high in the sky for anybody to be outside your window. Now, come on. We need to get you back to bed before your parents get home."

"No," the three-year-old whined. "Not tired."

"Of course you are. You were very sleepy earlier."

"No, Amy, it's cold in my room."

"Well, we'll turn up the heating, but you must get back to bed. Your mummy left strict instructions. Come on, let's go," she said, taking his hand, but the boy snatched it away and pulled one of his obstinate frowns where his nose wrinkled, his eyebrows furrowed and he stared every which way but at the person who was talking to him.

Amy grabbed her phone, "Hey."

"What's going on?"

"I'm going to have to call you back. I've got a situation here."

"What, is the hotty home?"

"Not quite."

"Okay, call me as soon as you're done."

"Will do."

Amy disconnected the call and threw her mobile device onto the sofa.

"Right, young man," she said, snapping on a lamp, and putting her hands on her hips in an obvious display of authority, "time for you to get back to bed whether you like it or not."

She scooped the protesting child into her arms, and carried him back to his bedroom, just as a close up of his smiling parents filled the television screen.

"Terry, Terrence…"Amy corrected herself.

Queen bitch actually made a point of saying that her son's name was Terrence and not Terry.

"…you gave Amy a real fright earlier. Especially when you pulled my hair, which, by the way, wasn't very nice, was it?" Amy continued as they made their way down the corridor.

"It wasn't me," the little boy, whined.

"Come on, Terrence," she said, seriously.

"It wasn't," the boy repeated, as they reached a door sporting the roaring mouth of a tyrannosaur and the words: *T-errence's Room.*

Amy felt the boy's whole body stiffen and he buried his face in her neck.

The move was palpable and it made her pause.

"Terrence? What's wrong?"

No answer.

"Terrence?"

Still no answer, just clinging.

She unravelled the little boy's grasp and looked into his big brown eyes, and felt a pang of concern; he seemed genuinely afraid.

"Oh Terrence, what's the matter? Tell Amy what's wrong."

The boy looked at his bedroom door for several seconds and then turned, leant in close to her ear and whispered, "He's...he's in there. Hiding behind the curtains."

The line chilled Amy and it took her a few seconds to compose herself.

"That's not funny, Terrence," she snapped.

Then, as if to prove a point, she pushed the door open to a dark room.

"What happened to your night light? I left it on for you."

"He switched it off."

"Terrence, I told you that isn't funny," she said, angrily. The little boy's words were really starting to creep her out.

She searched the wall for the overhead light switch, flipped it on and gasped.

All of the little boy's toys were stacked in one big pile in the centre of the room. Trains, teddy bears, Transformer figurines, Marvel figurines, skipping ropes, jigsaw puzzles, colouring books and crayons.

It was as if the boy had emptied the entire contents of his giant plastic storage boxes, and then stacked everything in one big pile, like some bizarre PG rated orgy.

"Oh my God, Terrence. What have you done?" Amy breathed. "Is this why you didn't want me to bring you back to your room?"

The boy just looked at her.

"Why would you do this?" She said, stepping closer, as if this would help her comprehend the exhibit.

She let the boy slide to the floor, but he clung on.

"No, Terrence. Amy is very cross with you right now. If your mum comes home and sees this, she's going to have a fit. I may even lose my job. Is that what you want?"

She looked at him, but the boy was too busy holding onto and burying his face in her leg.

"OK, well, it's into bed for you. I've got to clear all this up before your parents get home."

She picked him up and placed him in the bed, where the boy instantly shrank under the duvet, until just the top part of his face was showing.

Again, Amy couldn't help but notice the look in his eyes, which were now wide and full of apprehension.

She could only assume this was in response to the mess he'd made, but it nonetheless unsettled her.

She had never seen him like this before.

She brushed hair out of his face. "What's going on, Terrence, huh? What's the matter," she asked. Now wondering if perhaps the boy's behaviour was symptomatic of something else.

She'd had experience, had attended numerous courses, read and studied enough articles about childcare, to know that *acting out* was, more than often, a sign of something far more concerning.

Maybe, things weren't so fantastic in the Stanton household, and this was taking its toll on the little boy.

"Terrence?" She prompted.

But he was busy looking past her towards the picture window and the curtains.

"Seriously?"

She followed his gaze to the oversized crimson curtains, that started above the picture window and fell to the carpet.

"That does it..." Amy moved to leave the bed, but Terrence grabbed her arm.

"Don't go," the boy whined.

"It's going to be fine. I'm just going to show you that there's nobody there."

"He is.... He's....he's there....watching.... now."

She pulled away from him and stood up.

Outside, a siren wailed in the distance, as the low rumble of city life pressed against the glass, like the thick fog that had descended on the city.

Amy, was surprised to find that she was actually approaching the window with caution. She didn't even know why, since there was no way anybody could be hiding behind the curtains.

"There's nobody here," she said, quickly, turning back to the boy whose eyes could barely be seen above the covers, but were watching her, full of fear.

The overhead light flickered.

Amy looked up, pulled a face, and then turned back to the curtain.

Then, suddenly, in one big showy movement, she swiped back the fabric.

"Ta dah! See? Nobody here."

She turned back to the little boy, whose eyes drifted over to the curtain on the opposite side of the window.

Amy took her cue and walked over.

Then, she grabbed the fabric and swiped; "Ta dah! See? Nobody here either."

Whilst there, Amy felt the radiator; it was cold.

Great.

Something else to tell the Stantons. Along with the toaster that nearly caught fire, and the dead lights under the kitchen units.

It had been that way all evening, with one thing or another malfunctioning or packing up; it seemed as if the whole place were falling apart.

So much for luxury.

She turned to her charge and forced a smile, but the little boy said nothing. Instead, his eyes roved over to the walk-in wardrobe on the other side of the room.

Amy's shoulders slumped and she rolled her eyes. "Terrence, Really?"

But she knew she'd never get the boy down again, unless he was satisfied that there was no bogeyman in the closet either.

So, she picked her way around the mound of toys, marched up to the wardrobe, yanked the door open and drew in a sharp breath.

"You know, Terrence, if I could shrink myself I'd be borrowing your clothes all the time, look at this stuff", she said with mock excitement.

The closet was a fifteen-foot narrow recess, with rows of hangers on either side, full of designer shirts, jeans, suits, and trousers. Below these, were metal stands, loaded with casual and formal footwear.

She reached up and pulled on the light chord, it clicked on, hissed and died once more, plunging the cavity back into semi-darkness.

"Oh come on," Amy grumbled.

Then she turned to the little boy who was still huddled under the covers.

"There's nobody in here," She exclaimed, then added under her breath, "funny that."

There was something in here that she needed. It was on the top shelf, at the far end of the closet.

She turned to Terrence and said, in an ominous tone, "I'll be right back," although judging by the look on the boy's face, it probably wasn't the best thing to say.

She chastened herself, then walked forward, feeling her way past the humanoid silhouettes of Terrence's jackets, until she reached the other side.

There, she reached up until her fingers touched the folded blanket.

She turned to leave…

…the bedroom light flickered. She froze. Half expecting the light to die, and abandon her in the closet.

It was a prospect that she did not find appealing.

She hurried towards the light.

More flickering.

She emerged with a sigh of relief.

"Look what I found," she said with a big smile, holding up a Thomas the Tank Engine blanket.

The boy's favourite.

She actually managed to conjure a smile.

Yes!

She moved to capitalise on the moment, "So, what do you think then? Think your mum would be okay with me borrowing some of your clothes?"

The boy giggled, and she could see that his eyes had brightened.

"That's silly, Amy."

"Why is that silly?" She asked with mock seriousness, shoving the closest door shut.

"Because they're my clothes."

"So, don't you think I'd look good in your jeans? I could wear them on one leg, what do you think?" she asked, walking up to him.

The boy giggled some more. "You're silly, Amy."

"And you're just cute."

He giggled again.

"Now, do you think you can go back to sleep for Amy? Because if mummy and daddy come home, and you aren't, Amy's going to be in a lot of trouble."

The boy's face darkened.

She reacted immediately by moving over to the pile and plucking a Buzz Lightyear doll from it.

Then, she walked back to the bed, fanned the blanket out over the little boy, and sat on the bed, next to him.

"So, I need to get on, but I'm going to leave Thomas and Buzz to stand guard while I clean up this mess. Would that be okay?"

The boy nodded and clutched Buzz to him as if his life depended on it.

Amy, tucked them both in with the blanket, brushed the hair from the little boy's face as a reassuring sign of affection and said, "Sweet dreams."

Then, she stood up and turned to face the mountain of toys in the middle of the room.

She needed to get this cleared, and fast.

29 NIGHT SHIFT

A knock on the door startled Rachel, who was in the middle of reading a John Grisham novel.

"Who is it?" She called.

"It's Tom," came the muffled reply.

She smiled, and rushed over to unlock and open the door.

"Hello stranger," she said with a smile.

"Hello," came Tom's perturbed reply. "Are you worried somebody's going to break in and steal your notes or something?"

It took Rachel a second to register.

"Oh, the door. Well, the bloody thing kept opening earlier, and it was really starting to freak me out."

"Opening?" Tom asked.

"Yeah. Must be some kind of draught or something, but I had to lock it to stop it from happening."

Tom checked the latch. Tried opening and closing the door a couple of times, and it seemed to close without any problems.

He looked at her.

"I'm telling you, it kept opening earlier and was really starting to give me the creeps. Especially as the bloody thing creaks like something out of a haunted mansion. Yes, you'll have noticed that I'm not a particular fan of the night shift, and that thing isn't helping."

Tom shook his head. "I don't know what the hell's goin' on with this place. You can go weeks, maybe even months, without so much as a light bulb change, but the past week, it's like the whole building's fallin' apart."

"Anyway," Rachel said. "Shall we start again? Hello Tom, how are you?"

"I'm fine, thanks," he said with a smile.

She ushered him into the room and pushed the door shut.

"I'm not interrupting anything am I?"

"You mean apart from the jury delivering their verdict?"

"Yeah."

"No, nothing major."

"You got the computer workin' then," he said, nodding at the glowing monitor.

"Yes, made sense seeing that the thing was just sitting here. Would you like a drink? Coffee or something?"

"A coffee would be great. Thanks."

Rachel moved over to the coffee machine. "Sugar, Milk?"

"Lots of both please," he said, sitting down.

"So, how come you're all on your todd?" he asked.

"Well, Lilly and I have split up the shifts."

"No, I meant how come fella ain't with you? It being your first night, I thought he'd be here to keep you company."

"Oh, well, he had other plans. Work or something. It's actually quite good he isn't here, as he'd only get in the way, and I'm just getting used to things as it is."

She returned and placed a mug of coffee on the desk in front of her visitor, "Hope that's okay."

"Looks good," he said, glancing at it. "Cheers."

"So, this is a pleasant surprise," she said, closing her book and returning to her seat.

"Meaning, what am I doing here at this time of night and why am I not at home in front of the telly?"

"Yes that too," She smiled.

"Well, as I said, things have gone mental around here so I had some repairs to do. Light bulbs keep failing around the whole building. I'm wondering if something's up with the wiring."

Rachel put her hand up.

He looked at her and his shoulders slumped.

"You're joking?"

Rachel shook her head.

"First thing I did tonight was switch on the overhead light. I thought I could bear it in here with just the desk lamp, but I changed my mind. Anyway, it's out. Bloody thing gave me a heart attack."

"I'm sorry about that."

"It's not your fault."

"Would you believe, I'm actually out of spare bulbs, but I'll stop by tomorrow and get a new one in for you."

Rachel drank from her own cup. "So, what other strange and unusual things have been happening?"

"Well, everything and anything. Even the water system doesn't seem right. I've got showers in two of the apartments that will only run freezing cold water."

"Mine works okay."

"Count yourself lucky."

There was a pause as Tom drank from his cup.

"So, did you fix them?"

"Well, I would have," He said, scratching his head, "but I can't find anything wrong. I'm going to have to call a plumber tomorrow."

Another pause.

"Thanks for stopping by. It's really sweet of you. It's not like I don't welcome the company. Between you and me, this office gives me the creeps. For one reason or another, it's always so dark in here"

"Oh, don't worry. You'll get used to it. The other girls did."

"Ah yes, I'm glad you mentioned that."

"Right… why's that then?"

"I've been meaning to talk to you about a girl that used to work here. I was hoping you might be able to tell me a bit about her."

"Sure. If I can. Who are we talking about?"

"Um, Keri Paxton."

Tom looked at her for a long time and then drank from his cup.

Rachel noticed this. "What?"

"It's nothing."

"Oh no you don't. You know something. Spill it now," she said with mock seriousness.

Click. Creak.

They both turned in unison, as the Night & Day door suddenly sprang off the latch, and slowly creaked wide open.

They looked at it, at each other, and then promptly burst out laughing.

"See?!" Rachel said. "I told you! Now imagine sitting here, minding your own business and that happening. The first time it did it, I nearly peed myself!"

They both left their chairs on route to inspect the door, but Rachel halted when the bell on the computer demanded her attention.

BONG: Ringing Apartment 10 / Stanton Residence, Answer? YES/NO

Rachel pulled her headset on.

BONG: Ringing Apartment 10 / Stanton Residence, Answer? YES/NO

"Good evening, Stanton residence….."

There was a loud hiss, then a crackling sound as if the wires were being connected then disconnected.

"Hello? Stanton residence?" Rachel asked as she watched

Tom noisily fiddle with the door handle.

There was an ear-piercingly loud shriek of static that made Rachel cry out, and yank the headphones from her head.

"Are you okay?" Tom called from across the room.

"Ow, I think so. That was loud," she said holding her ear and cringing.

Eventually, she turned back to the screen. The call had disconnected, but what Rachel read in the transcript box made her skin crawl.

RACHEL:> Good evening Stanton residence
UNKNOWN:> f e a r m e
RACHEL:> Hello, Stanton residence
UNKNOWN:> f e a r   m e
Call ends. Save? YES/NO

30 UNSPEAKABLE

The shrill of the telephone jolted Amy awake, to a room in complete darkness.

She had fallen asleep in front of the TV, but it, along with both lamps, were now extinguished, and the room was a graveyard of silhouettes.

As the fuzziness of stasis cleared from her mind, she realised that the persistent ringing was not the house phone, but her mobile device.

She hastily hunted for it.

Eventually, it was the blue glow and a picture of her friend, with her tongue sticking out, that enabled her to home in on the device that, at the same time, was telling her that it was 22:03.

She snatched it up from the floor and answered, somewhat testily, "Hello."

"Hey, what happened to you? I thought you were going to ring me back."

"Oh yeah," she groaned, rubbing the sleep from her face. "Sorry. Terry had a bit of a moment, and I had to clear up after him."

"Is he asleep now?"

"Um, yeah."

She swung her legs down from the couch and yelped, as she stubbed her toe on something.

"Ouch! What the hell…"

"…Are you alright?"

"No! I'm not alright. I've just stubbed my toe on something, and these poxy lights have gone out again…"

She was angry; her toe really hurt, she couldn't see a thing, her friend kept asking questions and, no matter how many times she told Terry not to leave his toys lying around because his mum didn't like it, he still did it…

… *"To infinity and beyond!"*

The sound of the toy startled her.

Buzz?

Her heart skipped a beat, although she had no idea why.

"Terry?"

"Hello? What's going on?" came her friend's tinny voice.

"Terry?" Amy called out to nowhere in particular, as she scanned the shadows.

It was still fairly dark in the room, but there was enough light spilling in through the windows to see that Terrence wasn't anywhere nearby.

She flicked the lamp switch on and off a few times.

Nothing.

"Terry?"

Silence but for the tinny voice of her friend on the other end of the phone.

"Terry?"

The sudden shrill of the house's cordless phone startled her, and she reached down to the coffee-table to silence it.

"Stanton residence," she said, now completed creeped out and irritated.

Static.

"Hello?"

Screeching static!

She snatched the receiver from her ear, waiting a few seconds and then gingerly listened once more.

The static stopped, replaced by a continuous clicking sound, as if someone was messing with the cables.

Then, the line went dead.

"Hello?"

There was nobody there.

And that is when she heard it, echoing in from the hallway; somebody was at the front door, pushing and pulling at it, as if trying to wrench it open.

The sound drove a dagger of fear into Amy's heart, as a piercing scream drilled through her eardrums.

She jumped to her feet.

Then, an image slowly appeared on the TV, revealing a girl, dressed in her underwear, running down a rain drenched street while being pursued by a flying bat-like creature.

In that same moment, the two lamps sprang to life, as did the lights in the hallway, and the general hum of various household appliances.

Amy sighed with relief when she watched Leticia and her husband walk in from the hallway, babbling about a faulty card reader.

Leticia noticed the look on Amy's face and immediately asked, "What's wrong?"

"Nothing," Amy blurted.

"Then, why do you look like you've seen a ghost?"

"I haven't, it's just that…"

"…is Terrence okay?"

"He's fine. We had a moment earlier…" Amy realised she was still holding Buzz in her hand and paused.

Leticia didn't wait for her to continue. She'd already left the room.

Darren Stanton, on the other hand, looked at her and asked, "Are you okay?"

"Yes, yes, I'm okay. It's just we've had some really strange goings on tonight," Amy laughed, nervously.

"What kind of strange?"

Amy's reply was interceded by Leticia Aaron-Stanton's blood-curdling screams.

Darren raced down the hall, but froze in the doorway of his son's bedroom when he took in a scene so ghastly, so incomprehensible, that it froze the blood in his limbs, and his ability to use them.

Amy crashed into Darren's back.

Then, when she looked over his shoulder into the room beyond, she instinctively threw her hands to her mouth to suppress the scream that had already been strangled in her throat.

What Amy saw was a series of snapshots, revealed to her like the flashgun of a camera, via the flickering eerie blue hue of the nightlight.

Leticia Aaron-Stanton was emitting a wailing sound, akin to that of a wounded animal, but was actually the harrowing mourn of a grief-stricken mother.

Above her, one end of a skipping rope was wrapped around the curtain pole, the other around her son's neck while she, frantically and clumsily, attempted to take the little boy's weight in her arms.

But it was too late.

Amy's scream finally found its way out of her lips, it reverberated down the corridor until it reached her phone, and the ears of her friend.

31 RECOVERY

Rupert nearly dropped the phone when the nurse identified herself to him.

He had been trying Ashley's mobile all evening, without reply, and had actually come to dislike the sound of her voicemail greeting.

Heron Heights Security, who he'd contacted multiple times, confirmed that Ashley's key card had not been used all day.

She had not returned to the penthouse.

He'd called friends, colleagues, but all to no avail. He'd even found himself wondering if Ashley had ever mentioned a distant relative, perhaps a cousin or long-lost aunt, anybody from her past who she may have suddenly decided to visit.

No.

And this got him thinking.

Neither of them enjoyed talking about their families, and they both avoided the subject, but Ashley had hardly ever mentioned anything about any member of her family.

He contemplated calling the police, but weighed up their potential helpfulness versus his frame of mind. He wasn't in the mood to play twenty questions and deal with a couple of officers who fancied themselves as Relate counsellors.

He opted to call the city hospitals instead.

And was just about to pick up the receiver when the phone rang; it was a rather bubbly nurse from the A&E department at Guys and St Thomas' Hospital. She told him that his wife had been in an accident, and that she had been treated for a mild sprained wrist, with minor cuts and bruises. However, she was fine, and needed someone to pick her up.

The nurse had hardly finished speaking and Rupert was out the door.

The drive across London was stressful; the traffic seemed particularly bad and was made worse by failed traffic lights, road works and what seemed like an endless array of pedestrian crossings.

When Rupert finally arrived at the hospital, a whole frustrating hour had passed.

It was late, the building was relatively empty, which only emphasised the drab décor and the decadence unique to government buildings.

Rupert hated hospitals. His hatred was born from the very reason that justified their existence; curing sickness.

This is where they had brought his mother, on multiple occasions, to pump out her stomach. This was also the very place where Miriam Harrison had been snatched from the brink of death, and dragged, kicking and screaming, back into the world and to the people she had so vehemently rejected;

her only son and husband, neither of them deemed reason enough to live.

She had decided that life without her baby son, Ben, was not a life worth living.

Memories of those visits flooded into Rupert's brain, resurrected by that exclusive hospital scent that was now forcing its way into his nostrils, subconsciously urging him to want to hold his breath.

He found Ashley sitting on a plastic brown chair, with her head bowed. Opposite her, sat a man and pregnant woman, each wrapped in their own thoughts, both ignoring her presence.

Ashley also seemed a million miles away. It was only when Rupert spoke her name that she looked up, revealing a patch of gauze taped to her forehead, and a strapped wrist.

His baby was hurt.

"Oh my God, Ash," he breathed.

Their eyes locked; both of them willing to say so much yet suddenly unable to do so.

Tears immediately welled in her eyes. Her distress apparent and palpable.

She ran to him.

He folded her into his arms and allowed her to bury her head in his chest. She clung to him like a frightened child, her body a mass of shudders as she wept.

The ironic, heart-wrenching similarity of this moment was not lost on Rupert as he was immediately transported back years to the moment when a frightened thirteen-year-old boy stood in his father's embrace.

"Come on, let's get out of here," he said.

They rode home in silence, each of them lost in their own thoughts. Rupert had so many questions but knew now was not the time, maybe later when they got back to the apartment.

All that mattered right now was that she was okay.

Ashley knew that she would have to tell Rupert the truth, what she didn't know was how. How could she tell him that she had taken it upon herself to enter Jackie Harris' home, in search of a manuscript and that, whilst there, she had been pursued by someone or something?

Something?

Why that word?

Oh God.

Memories of what she had seen behind that window came back to her through the blurry headache that had dogged her ever since she had regained consciousness.

She gave mental thanks to Jackie's neighbours who, after all, had found her. If it wasn't for them, she would probably still be lying there with blood pouring from her head and that....

...She broke her thoughts; maybe she hadn't seen anything at all down there.

It all seemed so murky right now, a distant memory, distorted by the pain she was feeling, and the migraine that hurt so badly that she could see lights flashing in front of her eyes.

"...What's going on?" It was Rupert's voice interrupting her thoughts this time, as he brought the car to an abrupt halt.

Ashley sat up in her chair for she could not believe what she was seeing, nor could Rupert, in fact, for a second he thought he had taken a wrong turn, but he hadn't.

This was their street, up ahead and to their right, Heron Heights stood over the chaotic scene unfolding all around it.

BBC and SKY television trucks were parked up on the pavement on opposite sides of the road, access to which had been blocked off by several police cars. In front of them, a cordon of police tape and officers was holding back a crowd of onlookers, journalists and camera crews.

"What's going on?" Ashley asked, incredulously.

"I don't know," Rupert uttered, distractedly, thinking that none of this circus was here a couple of hours ago. He had never seen anything like it.

A short rap on his window startled them both; a police officer dressed well against the night chill shone a flashlight into the car as Rupert buzzed down his window.

"What's going on, officer?" He asked, slightly affronted by the man shining the light straight into his face.

"I'm afraid you can't get through this way, Sir," the officer said, officiously, as his breath smoked out in the bitter cold night.

"Why? What's happened?" Ashley asked, urgently.

The officer observed her and her wounds and said, slowly, "I'm afraid this road is blocked off to everyone but residents."

"We are residents," Rupert said, quickly.

"Could I see some ID, please Sir?"

"Of course," Rupert said, pulling his wallet out of his jacket and handing his driving licence over to the officer, who studied it under the beam of his torch.

"Would you like to come with me, please Sir?"

"Of course, but can you please tell us what's going on?"

"I'm afraid there's been an incident."

"What kind of incident?" Ashley asked, not believing that her amateur investigative antics could have warranted so much police and press attention.

"I'm afraid there has been a death in your building."

Ashley gasped.

"What? Who? How?" she asked, eyes wide with apprehension.

"Please follow me," is all the officer would say.

"Wait, what about the car?" Rupert asked.

"Just leave it here for now, Sir, give me the keys, we'll take care of it."

The officer led them into the throng of people, most of whom were indifferent to the newcomers, until they realised exactly who they were.

Suddenly, a microphone was shoved in front of their faces.

"… Mr Harrison, Mr Harrison, you live here, do you have any comment?"

"Mr Harrison, did you know the little boy?"

"What little boy?" Rupert found himself asking, as more officers encircled them and rushed them through the rest of the crowd.

"Miss Marshall, did you know the Stantons?"

"Mr Harrison!" "Miss Marshall!" "Any comment?" "Will you be moving out?"

Video cameras appeared out of nowhere, bright lights

dazzled them, camera flashes fired.

Eventually, they reached the entrance gate, which was guarded by more police officers. It opened, allowing them and their escort to pass through.

The walk up the path to the entrance seemed particularly long tonight. The whole building was ablaze with light and the bustle of investigating officers.

They entered the lobby to find Paul, the security guard, and his partner being interviewed at their station by two more police officers. In front of them, seated on one of the divans, was a black woman in a brown, well-worn trouser suit. She was talking to Tom, but stopped when their escort walked up to and whispered in her ear.

She looked over at Rupert and Ashley, said something to the officer, and then walked up to them.

"Mr Harrison?"

"Yes."

"I am Detective Inspector Julianne Taylor."

Rupert nodded.

"And you must be Miss Marshall," she said, weighing up Ashley's bandaged wrist, and the gauze on her forehead.

"Yes," Ashley said feeling suddenly self-conscious.

"What happened?" The D.I. asked, nodding at Ashley's forehead.

"Oh, I fell.... over," she said, quickly.

"Must have been one hell of a fall," Taylor said.

"It was."

"What's happened here, inspector?" Rupert interrupted. He hadn't even had a chance to speak to Ashley yet. He certainly didn't want the whole thing played out in front of a complete stranger.

"I'm afraid there's been an incident," Taylor said.

"We heard. But what happened? A journalist out there mentioned a young boy," Rupert said.

"Did you know the Stantons?"

"Well yes, who doesn't ...?"

Ashley gasped as realisation dawned, "Oh my God. Their little boy?"

"I am afraid so," Taylor said, gravely.

"What happened to him?" Rupert asked.

The inspector hesitated and then, nodding at a nearby divan, said, "Why don't you take a seat."

32 THE PROPOSAL

It was almost an hour later when, weary and somewhat shell-shocked, they finally found themselves riding the elevator in silence. Both, seemingly mesmerised by the perpetual change of the floor indicator, as it made its way up to the penthouse.

D.I. Taylor had asked them a battery of questions about their neighbours, building security, and even personal questions about each other, such as how long they'd been living together.

The D.I. also showed a lingering, and somewhat unnerving interest in Ashley's injuries.

However, they both did a pretty good job of steering the conversation back to the Stantons, and what they both knew about the celebrity couple, which wasn't much. They explained that they actually saw little of the Stantons and, as far as they knew, they didn't actually spend much time at Heron Heights. When they did, it was clear that they valued their privacy. They didn't speak to anybody and if they could avoid contact, they appeared to do so.

But then, most of the building's occupants were like that.

Asked about Amy, the Stanton's nanny, both denied ever meeting her.

The bell sounded and the doors slid open.

They entered the penthouse. It felt unusually cold, and oddly unwelcoming.

This didn't help Ashley's mood, for she felt lonely. It was the kind of loneliness commonly experienced by the love-stricken who are unable to eat, sleep or think about anything else other than the object of their affection.

In this case, Ashley could not settle anywhere, nor draw comfort from anything because her mind was jammed with thoughts of Jackie, the visit to her house, the events that had taken place downstairs, the manuscript, Rupert's silence so far, and the explanation he would inevitably be expecting from her.

"Ashley!"

The voice startled her. "What?" She snapped.

"Are you sure you're okay?"

"I'm all right," she said, tucking a strand of hair behind her ear.

"Only, I called you three times. You were miles away."

"I'm sorry." she said, sitting down on the sofa and pulling a white, furry throw over her.

"I've poured you a brandy," he said, handing her the glass.

"Thank you."

He checked the thermostat, which was already turned up high, then sat down opposite her, allowing that familiar silence to return once more, as he watched her sip from the glass.

Her eyes were wild, and she seemed to be looking every which way but at him.

A police siren wailed somewhere off in the distance, then, after a few more seconds of thought processing, Rupert said, "So, are you ready?"

Ashley finally gave him her eyes. They were glazy with exhaustion. "For what?" She said, although she knew full well what he meant.

"Are you going to tell me what happened to you tonight?"

Her heart skipped a beat.

For some strange reason, she was afraid. She did not know if this was due to Rupert's potential reaction, or more to do with the fact that she would have to, albeit mentally, return to that place, and she did not want to.

"Rupert, I'm exhausted and aching. I just want to have a bath. Do you mind if we do this tomorrow?"

"Of course I mind," he said, waiting patiently. And it was clear from his expression, and the anticipatory way he was leaning forward in his seat, that he wasn't going to let her go anywhere without an explanation.

Ashley set her glass down on the coffee table and looked up at him.

"I know you're going to be disappointed."

He forced a laugh. "Disappointed? I'm not your father, Ash. I just want to know what happened."

"I went over to Jackie Harris' home," she said, quickly.

Rupert frowned. "You what?" he said, incredulously, "Why?"

She shook her head slightly, and stared at the granite in the coffee table in front of her. "I don't know," she said with conviction. "I really don't know why."

"I have an idea. Could it be Harris' bloody manuscript?" He said, angrily.

Ashley flinched at his raised voice, which didn't go unnoticed.

He took a few seconds, sighed, and said, "I just don't get it. What is it with you and that woman, Ash?"

"I don't know."

"You must have some idea. You seem obsessed with her. Jesus, even after her death. Why won't you just let it rest?"

"Because I can't."

"Why can't you?"

"Because the truth needs to be told!"

Rupert stood up, "Oh for God's sakes, Ash. The truth was told in a court of law. We've been through this."

He began to pace behind the sofa.

"Only because some of them lied."

"Yep, here we go again. How do you know? Were you there?"

"I know what she told me and what I feel."

"What *you* feel? Ash, I was going out of my mind tonight, wondering where the hell you were, while you were busy breaking into some dead woman's home…"

"…I didn't break in. I had a key."

"Oh that's okay then," he said, sarcastically. "You didn't even bother calling, or even sending a text."

"I'm sorry. I didn't think I'd be that long. I left the phone in my car."

"You could have got yourself into some serious trouble tonight. Is that what you want, huh? Is it?"

"Of course not."

"Are you sure? Because from where I'm standing, it seems that you're hell bent on pissing off the police, and getting yourself killed at the same time."

He ran his hands through his hair, "I mean, Jesus Christ, Ash. I think you're at work and next thing I know, I get a call from the hospital. So, if we're talking about people's feelings, let's talk about mine. Let's talk about how bloody scared I was tonight when I thought something awful had happened, when I thought I'd lost you, or aren't my feelings important?"

Ashley was taken aback by Rupert's words and uttered, "Of course they are."

"But obviously not as important as some woman you barely knew."

"There's no comparison."

"No, she's much more important."

"Now you're being childish."

"Am I?"

"Yes, you are..."

"...And your excursion to some dead woman's house wasn't childish?"

Ashley wanted to say something, but it just so happened that she agreed with him.

I'm sorry, Rupert.

He was clearly upset. His eyes were glistening, and Ashley could not tell if they were tears or just the glaze of rage. Then, as if to hide his real feelings, he turned from her and walked over to the window, where he stared out into the night.

"I'm sorry if I worried you," she said, quietly, like a child who had just been chastised.

Rupert said nothing, and she felt his silence hurt more than any abuse he could hurl at her. She did feel thoroughly foolish for what she did, but, like most of life's greatest blunders, it seemed right at the time. And now, no matter how much they argued about it, it was too late. The damage had been done, the painkillers were wearing off, her head was pounding, her arm was aching and Rupert's heart was hurt.

I am so sorry I worried you tonight.

"Do you know what made it worse?" he asked, suddenly without turning. It was a rhetorical question and he continued, "That nurse who called me tonight, she said that they had treated *my wife.* And it struck me, anything could have happened to you. I mean, that woman could have just as well have told me that you had been killed, and I could have lost you without even having had the chance..."

His voice faltered.

Tears pricked Ashley's eyes.

He turned to her with a knot in his throat. "The thought of losing you..."

"Oh, baby." She rushed over and flung her arms around him, ignoring the shockwaves of pain the impact invoked.

"I'm sorry," She cooed. "I'm so sorry."

"I love you," he said, pulling her tightly to him. "I love you, Ashley. Please marry me."

For a perverse moment, she thought she had misheard. He, Rupert Harrison, could never have asked her to marry him. He didn't believe in all that, not after his first wife, she had jaded him, and he wasn't interested in jumping into another marriage.

He wasn't. Was he?

"Please say yes," he said as if he had heard her thoughts.

For Ashley, the room started to spin and her stomach was fluttering.

It is true; he wants me to marry him. Oh God.

Slowly, the reality of the proposition sunk in and it was quickly followed by a tidal wave of joy.

"Yes," she said breathlessly. "Of course."

He squeezed her tight and she let out a little cry of pain.

"Oh God, I'm sorry," he said, pulling away.

She laughed. "Don't worry," she said, quickly.

"I am so sorry, I didn't think. Does it hurt that bad?" he asked, anxiously, delicately feeling her arm.

"It's okay." She cupped his boyish face with one hand and shook her head, "Rupert, I'm so sorry I worried you," she said, earnestly.

"Don't apologise. You can't help being you, I suppose." He smiled, pushing her hair back from her face, exposing the patch of gauze on her forehead and placing a delicate kiss on her nose.

She closed her eyes, and gently leant her face into his hand, enjoying his touch.

"You still haven't told me what actually happened," he said softly. "How exactly did you get hurt?"

She opened her eyes as fear strummed the strings of her memory.

She remembered the eyes.

Although, after everything else that had happened tonight, they now seemed more like a distant dream, a nightmare. Had there really been someone in that house? Did she really see those eyes? It all seemed so confused, so blurred right now, and would telling Rupert all about it actually help in any way?

Probably not.

"Later." She said, kissing him full on the lips. "Right now, I just want to enjoy this moment. Remind me again, what you just said. You see, the bump on my head, I forget things really quickly."

They laughed.

Rupert considered whether or not to push Ashley on the issue. He wanted to know what happened. On the other hand, he'd just asked her to marry him and she'd said yes. Which conversation would he rather pursue right now?

"I love you," she said, interrupting his thoughts, and pretty much making the decision for him.

There would be plenty of time to talk to her tomorrow.

"You sure?" He asked.

"I'm sure. But I need a favour."

Rupert cocked his head as his wife-to-be suddenly looked serious.

"Right. What is it?"

"My head is killing me and we don't have any painkillers in the house. Well, we do, but I think I need industrial strength, if you know what I mean."

"Of course. You sure we don't..."

"I'm sure... I made a mental note to get more today then, after everything that happened..."

"No problem. I'll nip out to the 24/7 down the street and get some."

"Thank you so much," she said, kissing his hands with eager anticipation.

"Come on," he said with a wink, "let's get you undressed."

He ran the bath for her, added bath salts and an array of herbal oils, which he knew were her favourites. Then, he placed the house phone and a bottle of water by the tub, and told her to ring if she needed anything else.

Then, with the promise to bring comfort food and that he wouldn't be long, he left.

Ashley had slipped into a red silk gown, a gift from Rupert, and prepped for a bath by putting her hair up. She wished she hadn't bothered when she spotted her reflection in the half steamed up mirror.

God, I look awful.

Her eyes were puffy, her cheek grazed and purple, and her skin was slightly swollen around the gauze on her forehead.

The evening's events were starting to sink in now, but they were nothing more than hallucinations, nightmares, manufactured from the stress of the moment.

At least, that's how she preferred to remember them. However, the pain in her wrist, the throbbing in her temples and behind her eyes, reminded her that they were not, that they were real. She did go to Jackie's home, and that boy was dead.

Murdered.

She shuddered.

Don't do that. Think about Rupert's proposal. Think about being his wife!

Mrs Harrison.

She did, and it brought a big smile to her face, as she secured her hair with a bull clip and felt the bath water. It was hot, and that is just what she needed to soak her aching limbs.

She let the gown fall to the floor, and gingerly stepped in.

33 THE DARKNESS

Rupert thought he was going to get trapped in the elevator. The doors had only just closed when a power drain dipped the lights, and threatened to bring the lift to a halt. Luckily, the symptom was temporary. The hum of power returned and the elevator resumed its journey.

He made a mental note to have a chat with Tom, since this wasn't the only problem he had experienced today. Early this morning, he was taking a shower when the hot water had suddenly turned freezing cold.

The elevator stopped, the doors opened onto darkness and not the subdued lighting of the lobby. Rupert looked up; the floor indicator read *8*.

He peeked out, into the pitch black, and the proximity sensor controlled lights sprang to life.

He returned to the elevator cabin and pressed various buttons; it did not budge. Instead, he succeeded only in making the overhead light flicker and the control panel lose power and die.

He tried the intercom.

Nothing.

"Come on!" He said, frustrated.

He stepped back out into the corridor, walked over to the stairs, and flinched when he pushed on the door. The damn thing squealed like a dying pig. The sound so loud, it raked at his last nerve and echoed around the stairwell.

He swore.

Then, he began the descent with haste, his footsteps clicking loudly on the concrete steps. He was eager to get to his destination, back to the apartment, to Ashley, and bed.

He was irritated.

Talk about a bad day. Everything that could have gone wrong had gone wrong, and it all started with this morning's cold shower.

Slam!

The sound of one of the doors, several floors below, made him come to an abrupt stop.

It seemed somebody else was experiencing the same

problem with the elevator, and had joined him in the stairwell.

He looked over the railing, but couldn't see anyone. He listened, but heard nothing, just the echo of his own footsteps from moments before, ringing in his ears.

He resisted the urge to call out to whomever it was, and wondered why.

Was he scared?

A little boy was murdered tonight.

The thought pushed its way into his mind.

He swore again, and hurriedly restarted his descent for two more flights of stairs, before stopping again, to listen.

Nothing.

He was alone.

Or was he.

Rupert Harrison was unable to explain it, but while he could not hear the presence of somebody else in the stairwell, he could certainly could sense them.

Several floors below; someone was standing, perfectly still.

Someone was waiting.

He leant over the metal railing, looked and listened, carefully.

Nothing.

He squinted all the way down as far as the dingy brown light would allow, but he couldn't see anything.

Then, the lights flickered.

Oh no, not now.

On, off, on, then off, then on again.

He blinked rapidly, trying to refocus his eyes.

Did he just see something, a few floors down? Was it just a shadow, an optical artefact of the darkness? He leant further over the handrail to scrutinise the shadows.

There's someone down there.

No, there isn't. It's just your imagination!

But there was.

Down on the second floor. He could just discern the crook of an arm. Was it someone leaning on the banister? Someone in a black coat?

Pull yourself together, it's just your imagination...

The arm, or whatever it was, moved, and at that moment, a gust of freezing cold wind blew in his face, pushing his hair back and stinging his eyes.

Then, he watched in horror as, one by one, each and every light from the floors below died, plunging that level into a deathly blackness that, like a giant leviathan, rapidly ascended toward him, bringing with it the loud, nerve-jangling slam of each door.

Instinctively, he turned and raced back up the steps, away from the tsunami of darkness, as if exposure to it would drown the very life out of him.

2nd floor!
SLAM!
3rd floor!
SLAM!
Closer…4th floor!
SLAM!
Closer…5th floor!

"Nooooo!" Rupert yelled as he reached and wrenched open the door marked *Level 8,* and just as he was about to step back out into the hallway, he tripped and fell sprawling onto the carpet.

He instantly flipped over, just in time to see the door pull itself shut.

He crawled backwards, heart pounding, lungs bursting until he felt the metal cage of the lift press against his back.

He watched the dark press against the fire door glass, like a surge of crude oil.

What the fuck…?

He didn't even know what he was running from, nor did he have time to consider it, for he was distracted by a pair of raised voices.

He turned to see a slither of light peeking out from the partially open front door of Apartment 8, and while he couldn't work out exactly what was being said, it was obvious from the intonation of the voices, that the protagonists were not happy with each other.

Apartment 8 is supposed to be empty was his last thought as the shadow fell over him.

Rupert Harrison screamed.

Time evaporated as Ashley languished in the bath. The warmth of the bathwater was soothing her into a snooze.

That was until the steam shifted, and a cold draught danced across the nape of her neck.

Her eyes sprang open, she sat up and listened hard, but there was no sound, just the shifting of the steam and an unnatural quiet.

Somebody was in the other room. She couldn't hear anything, but she could sense a presence, it was as if someone was waiting outside the door.

"Rupert?" she called, suddenly wide awake.

She had been in this situation before.

She watched the door. She remained perfectly still, as if to move would be to solicit unwanted attention.

She was naked, vulnerable.

"Rupert?

No reply. Just her voice echoing around the bathroom, closely followed by her eyes, as she searched for a solution to her current predicament.

She took in the steamed up mirrors, the shower cubicle, the toilet, and the bath towel hanging nearby.

Slowly and as quietly as she could, she emerged from the sanctuary of the warm water and stood, as goose pimples instantly formed on her skin.

The room had turned as cold as a frosted winter's morning, and the lighting had dimmed, or at least it seemed that way.

The bathwater sloshed loudly as if protesting against her departure, as she reached for the towel and quickly wrapped it around her body.

Her teeth began to chatter, involuntarily.

This is all your imagination, she told herself, although she didn't believe it.

She stepped out of the bath, pulled the plug and instantly regretted the action as the water gurgled and squealed noisily, like a tortured animal, as it was sucked down into the abyss.

Eyes still on the bathroom door, Ashley inched her way across the room.

Rupert. Where are you?

A splitting sound smacked her to attention; it was cracking glass and it stung her already shredded nerves like salt on a wound.

Help me!

Her breath was now fogging in front of her. The air had turned so cold that all of the mirrors had begun to demist, slowly revealing a stranger with dripping hair, hollow, wild eyes, and a face creased into mask of abject terror.

It actually took Ashley a few seconds to realise that she was looking at her own reflection.

That's when another loud splitting sound pierced the quiet of the room. It came from beyond the door.

She began to hyperventilate.

Someone or something is in the other room!

Something? Why did you think that?

The hideous thought had pushed its way into her head, along with a snapshot of those eyes. The eyes that had watched her from beyond the glass at Jackie's home.

She jumped backward as a scream froze in her throat; the nearby full-length mirror was cracking! Then, slowly, like time-lapse footage, it frosted over.

The steam that had, just minutes before, licked then blanketed the glass surface of the mirror was being replaced by a veil of frost! It instantly turned it opaque and then white. As it did so, large cracks appeared and stretched to each extremity.

"Ashley..."

Her eyes darted to the bathroom door; somebody was calling her from the bedroom. The voice was hollow, distant; the remnants of an echo calling to her from the deep recesses of a catacomb.

"A s h l e y..." it continued, beckoning her, but now it was overhead, moving from the bedroom across the ceiling.

"Who... who is it?" she stuttered, as waves of shivers froze over her, but the only response was the sound of heavy footsteps as they fell heavily overhead.

Then, the lights flickered, beating on and off to the rhythm of her heart.

"A s h l e y..." the voice, continued, guttural and haunting.

She ran from the bathroom, clutching the towel around her, but stopped abruptly when she saw that the bedroom window no longer offered a view of the city, but that it had crystallised into a sheet of frost that glittered in the overhead lights.

She raced from the bedroom, bare feet slapping loudly on the parquet floor, as the wet footprints she left in her wake instantly froze over.

She was in the entrance lobby now, where the dome projected a view of a clear and starry sky. This was in stark contrast to everything else; glass, mirrors, picture frames, each and every item was covered in glittering frost.

And it was as Ashley turned in a 360 spin of the world around her, that she noticed it; the front door, it was wide open.

"HELP ME!" she shouted and, without thinking, sprinted for freedom, but a sudden gust of icy cold air tugged the door shut, killing the lights as it did so.

She screamed and closed her eyes, half expecting someone to rush at her, but they didn't.

The entrance lobby was tomblike still. There was no sound of curious neighbours, no footsteps from security, just the pounding of her beating heart, and the scratchy sound of her rasping breath, that continued to fog in the air in front of her.

She opened her eyes.

Slowly, they became accustomed to the dark, and the spectres of the furniture that haunted it. She was alone in the freeze of the blackness.

"ASHLEY!"

The voice was a loud whisper in her right ear. She slapped at the air in horror and leapt to her left, rubbing her ears as more tentacles of icy terror licked her skin.

"ASHLEY!"

She screamed, "No!" and leapt to her right.

"Ashley!"

"LEAVE ME ALONE!" she screamed, and retreated until

she could feel the cold wall on her back, and the frame of Miriam Harrison's painting pressing against her cheek.

"A s h l e y!"

This time the loud whisper was in front of her and when it spoke, an icy draught blew in at her face.

She shrank back, against the wall, as her shivering metamorphosed into convulsions, not just from the cold, but from fear, as she contemplated the inevitable.

"Nooo," she whimpered and squirmed, but there was nowhere else for her to go. She was literally backed up against a wall.

Then, she stared in disbelief, as slowly and hideously, one of the shadows began to stretch and expand, like a giant ink stain. It ebbed, flowed and swelled until it smothered the starry dome view of the sky and replaced it with the thick inky blackness of eternal sleep, from which, Ashley knew, there would be no awaking.

Then, out of the dark, they slowly began to form, like the negative of a photograph, eyes, narrow and full of malice.

They glowered in the dark while drifting closer.

"NOOOOOO!"

Closer.

"A s h l e y..."

She slapped, maniacally, at the air in front of her.

"NO!"

"Ashley!"

"Let go of me!"

"ASH!"

She felt strong arms shaking her eyes open to dazzling spotlights.

Then, she was back in the bath.

Rupert was standing over her, his face full of worry.

"Oh Jesus, Ash, are you alright?"

She could say nothing; she just lay, shivering in the freezing cold bath water.

Rupert didn't hesitate.

He snatched the towel from its hook, wrapped it around her, lifted her into his arms, and carried her dripping naked body through to the bedroom, but not before she managed to catch sight of the mirror; the cracks were like giant tentacles, stretching from the centre outwards.

34 THE MORNING AFTER

What was left of the night had been restless.

Ashley, despite her apparent exhaustion, had tossed and turned.

Rupert was awoken twice by her screams. Both times, she had been clawing at the air above the bed. Both times, he took her in his arms, and held her to his chest where, eventually, she would return to a fitful slumber.

It was, for this reason that morning came too soon for the company director who had a day full of meetings.

He had planned on getting to the office early, but refused to leave Ashley alone or let her out of the security of the apartment.

Something terrible had happened to his fiancé yesterday. The result was giving her nightmares, and he was anxious. He resolved that if Ashley wouldn't share with him, then he would push to have her speak to his doctor, perhaps even his therapist. He'd already contacted them both, as a precaution.

He stopped short of telling her to take the day off. He knew that wouldn't go down well, but insisted that she have a lie in, and when Ashley mumbled that she needed to go back to her flat, to collect post and other items. He insisted that she let him go instead.

"Stay home. Rest," he told her. "I'll take care of everything else."

And he was very glad he did. There was no doubt in his mind that Ashley was in no fit state to deal with what he found there.

In fact, what he discovered scared him to the point where he actually considered hiring a personal security detail, since there was no longer any doubt that he, and the woman he loved, were being targeted, for whatever reason, by someone.

He immediately placed two calls.

One to the police, and the other home, where he spoke to Maria, the Italian maid, who confirmed that Ashley was yet to emerge from the bedroom.

He renewed his instructions that she was to rest, undisturbed, until he returned home, and had managed to speak to her.

When he eventually made it to the office, his mind was on everything but the day ahead, no matter how much his assistant tried to prep him for it.

Simply too much had happened in one day, and he needed some time to rationalise it all. To understand.

What had happened to Ashley that was so traumatic that it was causing her nightmares? And what had happened at her flat? Did she know about it, and kept it from him?

Was she attacked and feels like she can't tell me?

This latest thought had dogged him most of the morning, and it made him worry. He wasn't sure how he'd feel if he learned that Ashley couldn't trust him with something like that.

He reached into the inside pocket of his jacket, pulled out a wad of paper, unfolded it, and placed it on the desk in front of him.

Then, he took a few seconds to consider his actions, and what exactly these entailed.

Too late now, he thought.

The so-called damage had already been done.

Worse, now that he had seen them, he couldn't get the content out of his head, along with the myriad of other chaotic thoughts that had taken residence there.

He comforted himself with the fact that the paper that was in front of him was not a direct result of his snooping, but a ghastly by-product of the actions of some unidentified scum bag, who had taken it upon him, or herself, to break into Ashley's home.

The first to greet him was a mound of post, flyers and newspapers.

The second, was a scene of complete devastation.

The lounge had been turned upside-down.

Drawers had been pulled from cupboards, and contents emptied. Furniture had been turned over, pictures had been pulled off walls, and curtains ripped from windows. Even the cushions had been dragged from the sofa, ripped apart and their stuffing scattered, dusting the place in synthetic yellow snow.

It was a similar situation in the bedroom, where clothes had been pulled from hangers and dumped, in a heap, in the middle of the room.

It was amongst this mess, peeking out from under a pair of jeans, that Rupert noticed the crumpled shoebox. It had been tipped upside down. Underneath it, he found letters, documents, and a wad of bank statements.

His first instinct was to reconstruct the box and refill it, but it was as he began to do so, that something from one of the bank statements caught his eye. So, he paused to examine it.

It did not cross his mind for one second that he was prying, for the impact of what he had just discovered was far greater.

The bottom line of Ashley's bank statement was overdrawn by four thousand three hundred and thirty pounds. Hooked by this discovery, he proceeded to examine the other documents.

These were letters from Ashley's bank, demanding that she bring her account back inline, and threatening to freeze future withdrawals until she did so.

He checked the dates, some were a few months old, others were recent, and one of them was dated last week.

Am I so unapproachable? Couldn't you have spoken to me about this?

And now, as he sat at his desk and studied another bank statement, his heart sank.

He'd failed Ashley.

Yes, she valued her independence, but this. She knew he had the money, but she didn't feel that she could approach him. What did this say about him? What did it say about their relationship?

Everything and nothing.

Her not coming to you about this means nothing. If anything, it's consistent with the type of person she is.

Where is all the money going anyway?

He studied the paper in his hand. Living in London was notoriously expensive, but Ashley didn't exactly lead an extravagant lifestyle.

It was as he churned through these thoughts that he noticed it; the thirty-first of the month, a significant withdrawal, a direct debit, paid to the Whitehouse Group.

He picked up another statement, it was a few months old; same date, same company, same direct debit, same amount.

The 'Whitehouse Group'.

Who were these people, and why was Ashley paying them so much money every month? He needed to know. He might even be able to help.

He booted up his computer, opened the web browser, typed *'The Whitehouse'* into the search engine, and waited.

His assistant deposited a mug of steaming coffee on his desk and reminded him, for the second time, he was running late.

Most of the links related to The Whitehouse in Washington DC.

Really? The Whitehouse, Washington? Surely not.

He tried his search again, only this time he typed *'Whitehouse Group'*.

The results were an advertising agency, a Wikipedia page for a band, a firm of accountants, a care home, a car parts company, a medical practice, and various other pieces of information that made no sense to him whatsoever.

He scrolled down and tried the next page.

"Well, nice to see you actually made it into the office."

The voice made Rupert jump, and he looked up to see James standing in the doorway.

"Blimey, I haven't caught you surfing those porn sites again, have I?" James asked, walking up to Rupert's desk.

"Foiled again," Rupert said, forcing a smile.

James looked at him curiously and then said, "Rough night, huh? I heard about that little boy on the news. I couldn't believe it. Are you okay? I tried to call you and Ash, left several messages for both of you, but no answer. I was worried."

"You did? I didn't receive any messages from you."

"Yes, left messages for you both to check in, make sure you were okay and let me know if you needed anything."

"Well, Thanks. I'm sorry, I didn't get the messages and I don't even know where Ashley's mobile is…"

"Forget her mobile. Where the hell is she? Her guys told me that she wasn't going to be in today."

"No, no, she's not feeling well," Rupert said, suddenly feeling extremely self-conscious, as he realised that the bank statements were sitting on his desk.

"Really? What's up with her?"

"Long story."

"Well, I'm all ears. I had to cancel the breakfast meeting because you weren't here."

"Yeah, I know, sorry."

"What's up?"

"Anything and everything."

"Such as?"

Rupert's assistant appeared at the door. "Mr Harrison, they're still waiting for you."

"We'd better go."

"Hang on a minute, you still haven't told me about what's going on."

"I'll tell you later," Rupert said, standing up. He grabbed the statements, stuffed them into his pocket and switched off his computer monitor.

"I may be dead later," James complained.

Rupert walked his friend to the door.

"No, that's not dark at all, James. Although, I suppose at your age, one has to consider such things," Rupert said, putting his arm around his friend. "Either way, you'll have to put that on hold, because I have a lot to tell you, and that's much more important."

TONY MARTURANO

35 FRIDAY

Friday morning seemed dazzlingly bright, yet the muted
television, standing on a cabinet at the foot of the bed, was
beaming a map of the UK, smothered with black clouds.

Rachel rolled over in bed, reached out to Jason's side, and
was surprised to actually feel his chest beneath her fingers.

She opened her eyes to see him smiling down at her.

He was propped up against a pillow with the TV remote
control in his hand.

"Good morning, sleepy head," he said with a smile, "or
should I be saying, good afternoon?"

"Hey," Rachel smiled. It was good to see his face.

"Sleep well? You've been spark out since you got in."

"What time is it?"

"Just coming up to lunchtime."

"Shit, really?"

She groaned, pulled herself up into a sitting position, and
ran both hands through her hair, blinking in an effort to wake
from her sleepy stupor.

"Rough night?" Jason asked, brightly.

"Oh, you could say that," she said with a big sigh, as
memories of the evening came flooding back to her.

"Yeah, I heard about what happened. It's intense. Kettle's
just boiled. I'll get you some coffee, and you can tell me all
about it," he said brightly, getting up from the bed and
leaving the room.

Rachel vacantly watched the news anchor on the TV. She
still couldn't get her head around the fact that the man was
talking about something that had actually taken place there,
in her apartment building.

It was this contemplation that slowly brought the events of
last night, back into focus.

To say that it had been a strange shift was an
understatement. It had been downright weird.

And it all started when her detective work revealed clues
into the past of the stranger that was her former colleague.

Which reminded her; Tom didn't look particularly thrilled
when she'd asked about Keri.

What does he know? Do they have a past?

She realised now, that the subject had got buried, as soon as all hell broke loose.

The most frustrating thing was that, from her dungeon, she had no clue of what was actually happening. She could only hear the wailing of sirens and see flashing blue lights.

Things got particularly creepy, in a War of The Worlds kind of way, when the beam of a flashlight shone through the window, and proceeded to scan them and the rest of the room.

It was promptly followed by a visit from two young cops, and an interrogation about what they both may or may not have seen or heard.

Of course, their frustrated reply had been *nothing!*

In exchange, the policemen had been tight-lipped. They refused to share anything about the events of the world above, other than the fact that a crime was being investigated.

Lilly made an appearance shortly after, and brought with her the devastating news about the little boy.

News that chilled Rachel, as she recalled the transcribed words on her computer screen.

A close up of a small boy in his father's arms appeared next to the news anchor who, grim-faced, mouthed something, before the picture cut to wobbly images of a couple, dressed in black, with matching shades, jostling their way through a crowd, before boarding a car, and driving off at great speed.

Rachel hunted for the remote, but the picture had already changed to a series of adverts. She gawped at them as her mind wandered back to last night, and that phone call.

She wondered about the Stanton's nanny; did she really do this? And if so, why? How could anybody do something like that to an innocent child? She could only imagine what the Stantons must be going through right now.

And what about the other residents? Were they, like her, in shock right now? Would more of them move out?

Then, her thoughts turned to Ashley, and she wondered what her only friend down here thought of all of this.

Rachel's eyes widened, *Dinner tomorrow!*

She'd actually forgotten about it. What the hell was she going to wear?

It might be cancelled.

Jason, dressed in jeans and a white shirt, walked into the room and handed Rachel a mug of coffee. She sat up straight before taking the mug from him.

"So, how come you're here today?" She asked, after taking a sip.

He smiled. "I live here, remember?"

"You know what I mean. You're normally at work."

He frowned, "Is that your way of telling me I'm never here for you?"

"No, of course not, but if the cap fits," she said, teasingly.

"Yeah. Thanks very much. So now I'm being penalised for wanting the best for us."

Us. I like the way you say that.

"Of course not. I'd just like to see more of you."

"Well, that is why I decided to stay home today. Thought we could go shopping together."

"Shopping?" Rachel's face lit up.

"Yes, for tomorrow. The dinner party."

"Oh wow, you didn't forget."

"Of course I didn't forget."

She grinned, and kissed him on the cheek, while he glanced at the TV, "Bloody hell, not this again."

Rachel followed his gaze, and saw pictures of Darren, and his wife with their son, dressed in a miniature version of his father's racing uniform. A caption in the right-hand corner of the screen, read, *Library Pictures.*

"Turn it up! Turn it up!" she said quickly.

"Why bother, I can already recite, verbatim, what they have been saying. They've been showing this segment all bloody day."

"Jay!"

"Alright," he said, begrudgingly, picking the remote up from the floor and pointing it at the TV.

".... Honoured in the sixties for outstanding contribution to the sport. It wasn't long before his teenage son, Darren, seen here Go Karting, followed his father's footsteps, and began to carve his own niche in the racing world by winning several professional Karting championships.

However, tragedy struck in the late eighties, Terrence Stanton was killed in a racing accident. Darren took the death of his father very badly, which led him to shun the media spotlight. It was only a few years later, that Darren Stanton raced back onto our screens by winning Silverstone.

Five years ago, he was voted Britain's sexiest male. That's when he met the actress Leticia Aaron, seen here at the premiere of her latest film, Desperate Motive. They were married within a year. Two years later, Leticia Aaron-Stanton gave birth to a baby boy. He was named after his famous grandfather, Terrence.

The scene on the TV then changed to a black anchorman addressing a TV screen. It showed an image of a reporter, standing outside the gates of Heron Heights.

"Wow, can you believe this?" Rachel breathed.

"...And we can now join Abigail Palmer live from the Stanton's residence in London. Abigail, this is shocking to say the least, and something that has a personal element for you. Right?"

"Well, yes Peter, it does, in that I was interviewing the Stantons only last night. Darren Stanton, in particular, spoke about his relationship with, and affection for, his son. We can only imagine how the family must be feeling right now."

"Quite right. Abigail, are the police any closer to ascertaining exactly what happened, and indeed, who might be responsible?"

"Well Peter, as you can imagine, the police are not prepared to disclose any information at this time. What we do know is that the Stantons left our studio at approximately 10:00 PM yesterday, and went straight home, where the discovery was made. The Stanton's nanny, Amy Cumberland, is currently being questioned by police."

"Do we have any idea why the police are questioning her?"

"Well, Peter, what we have are unconfirmed reports that Amy Cumberland was the last person to see Terrence Stanton alive, since she was on duty last night. So, some pretty tough questions will need to be asked before any more can be established."

"Abigail Palmer, thank you very much. And now for the

rest of the headlines. The prime minister is facing yet…"

Jason muted the TV once again.

"She said the same thing this morning." He commented.

"I just can't believe it. This is awful, and it happened here, in this building!"

"I know. The police have already been on the phone. They want us to give a statement. I wasn't even here."

"I know. We were questioned at length last night," Rachel said, flatly, still unable to pull her eyes off the television's muted screen.

"We?"

"Yes, Tom and I."

It took Rachel a few seconds before she tuned into Jason's glare.

"He was down fixing the boiler or something. I tell you, for a luxury building, this place is actually falling apart."

"I'm more interested in what the fuck that guy was doing hanging out with you down there last night."

Jason's tone was flat and annoyed. The change in his tone was sudden and it took her by surprise.

"I told you. He was down there fixing stuff."

"What stuff?"

"Are you serious? A little boy is dead, and the only thing you're talking about is why Tom was down in the basement doing his job?"

"No, the only thing I can talk about is why he was down in the basement with you."

"I told you. He was fixing the door. The place is falling apart."

"What's wrong with your door?"

She looked into his brown eyes to make sure he wasn't just teasing her.

He wasn't.

He was angry.

"I'm not having this conversation with you," she said, eventually. He was annoying her and she wasn't in the mood. She turned her attention back to the silent images on the television screen.

"I take it you've handed in your notice," he said, getting off the bed.

Rachel laughed. "No, of course I haven't."

"Why not?"

"Well," she stumbled to find the words. "I need the money for a start."

"You don't need the money, I earn enough for us both. Just call and tell them you won't be going back."

Rachel was about to respond, but instead she thought about it. The place was creepy, and she didn't particularly enjoy the night shift.

On the other hand, she'd only just started the job, and she needed to give it a chance. At least, until she found something else. And, most importantly, she wasn't going to be told what to do.

"No."

"What do you mean, no?" Jason asked, incredulously.

"I mean, I can't just hand in my notice, Jay."

"So, my opinion doesn't mean anything to you, is that it?"

"No, that isn't it, but I've only just started there, I should at least give the place a chance and, despite what you just said, I need my own money. My own independence. You know how I feel about that."

"Fine," he threw back, petulantly.

"Oh come on, please don't be like that. I'm pretty freaked out about all of this as it is. I don't want us to fall out."

He walked up to the bed, looked down at her with cold eyes and said as dramatically as possible, "What if it wasn't her? What if there's some kind of psychopath running around out there?"

It took Rachel a few moments to recover from Jason's icy stare, after which she said, "Yeah, thanks for that. I feel much better now."

"Well, you need to understand the seriousness of this."

"You're joking, right? I was here, remember? I think I appreciate the seriousness, perfectly."

"Then, quit."

"And do what?"

"I have contacts. I'll have you lined up for a job in no time."

Rachel thought about this.

And Jason thought he'd actually managed to convince her.

"No. As I said, for all of its weirdness, I like this job. And I like Lilly."

"Fine… just remember that you came down here to be with me, and I am not sure I like the idea of you working nights and sleeping during the day. I never get to see you."

"Well, what's the difference? I never get to see you anyway. You're out most nights, as it is."

Jason nodded. "Right, so that's what this is all about is it."

"No, I…"

"…You've taken on this job just to prove a point."

"…of course not…"

"…So, now you want me to give up my work."

"No, Jay I didn't say that," Rachel protested.

"What are you saying then, Rach?"

"I'm just saying that if you're out, then there's no point me being here, on my own."

"Jesus Christ, you haven't even been here a week, and you're already asking me to give up my job."

"No, that's what you're asking me to do."

He looked at her, as if he was about to say something, but instead, he waved his hand at her and mumbled, "Whatever, just do as you fucking well please."

With that, he left the room.

"Jay!"

She called after him, but he didn't reply.

Moments later, she heard the door slam.

Once again, she was alone.

36 THE INVESTIGATION

Ashley awoke to the rumble of an aeroplane as it flew overhead and to a relatively bright day. It seemed the sun was actually shining, albeit with lacklustre enthusiasm.

The bedside clock surprised her; it was well after lunchtime. She'd drifted in and out of consciousness so many times, yet still felt somewhat groggy.

She glanced over at Rupert's side of the bed; it was empty. This made her sad.

She sighed, as memories of last night cranked into action, drifting in front of her consciousness, like the white fluffy clouds she was watching in the autumnal blue sky, outside.

Daylight was as comforting as the homely smell of baking that drifted down the corridor to her.

She slipped out of the bed and padded over to the wardrobe where she was reminded, once again, that she still hadn't retrieved all of her clothes from her flat. She hoped Rupert would manage to swing by there today, as promised.

In the meantime, she had an excuse to wear another of Rupert's shirts.

She made her way up the short hall, to the dining room, where all the surfaces had been polished and now gleamed, as if excited by the sunshine's return.

Everything seemed in order until a loud clanging sound caught her attention; it was coming from the kitchen.

She approached the restaurant-style doors just as they flew open. She screamed, which in turned startled the maid, who promptly dropped the vase she was carrying; it smashed onto the parquet flooring, sending shards skittering to the far extremities of the room.

"Oh Maria," Ashley gasped, holding her hand to her heart.

"Oh Jesu mio, Signora, you give me art' attack."

"Oh I'm sorry," Ashley laughed, nervously, "I'm so sorry, Maria, I thought you were..." she left the words unspoken and then, realising, she asked, "Where's Rupert?"

"He gone to work, Signora. He ask that you call in the office as soon as you awake, and told me to take good care of you. I make lunch as soon as I clean this," she said, holding her hands out, as if she were about to cast a spell on the broken pieces. "Oh Dio, I hope not expensive." The woman said, "I go fetch a brush."

"Oh Maria, I'm so sorry," Ashley repeated, feeling guilty. "I'll help," she added, and began to hunt down the fugitive shards.

It was after Maria had disappeared back into the kitchen that the doorbell rang.

Ashley looked at what she was wearing, and then at the kitchen doors, that were still swinging after Maria, and decided she would answer the front door.

It took her a few seconds to recognise the woman.

She was accompanied by a young man, in his early thirties, dressed in a blue suit, and sporting a military-style crew cut.

His hazel eyes took in her legs and her chest, where the top button of the shirt had been unintentionally left undone.

"Good morning, Miss Marshall," it was Detective Inspector Taylor. "This is Detective Sergeant Warner," she said, discreetly glaring at the man; she had noticed his roaming eyes. "May we come in?"

Ashley hesitated, whilst subconsciously clasping the shirt collars together. She wasn't dressed to receive visitors yet, reluctantly, stood aside.

"Please, take a seat," she said, gesturing to the lounge, "I'll be right with you."

With that, she hurried back down the hall where Maria was re-emerging from the kitchen, dustpan and brush in hand. "Who is it? I hear the doorbell."

"Yes Maria, I just need to get some clothes on. There are people in the lounge; could you offer them a drink for me, please?"

"Of course," Maria complied, putting down her tools and rubbing her hands on her apron.

The detective and her companion declined Maria's offer, causing the Italian woman to shrug her shoulders and return to her duties, mumbling something in her mother tongue.

Minutes later, dressed in cut down jeans and one of Rupert's cream sweaters, Ashley returned.

"Sorry about that," she said.

Mark smiled at Ashley in such a way that made the Detective Inspector want to roll her eyes.

"What can I do for you?" Ashley asked, gesturing at the sofas, and taking a seat opposite her guests.

"Well, we were hoping to ask you some questions about

what happened yesterday," Taylor said.

"I'm sorry, Detective. I've already told you everything I know."

Taylor consulted her notes. "No, not really. We have a statement from Mr Harrison but not from you."

Ashley frowned. "But we talked last night. Rupert and I, we saw you as soon as we came home."

Taylor smiled. "Oh I'm sorry, Miss Marshall, there's obviously a misunderstanding. We're here to see you about the break-in at your home, not what happened here."

"I'm sorry. What?" Ashley's eyes widened, "Somebody broke into my flat?"

She pushed the hair off her face, as a headache, and a throbbing in her arm, suddenly began their assault.

"Well, not exactly…" The Detective Sergeant interjected.

"May I ask what happened?" Taylor spoke, as she eyed the plaster on Ashley's forehead.

Ashley's heart leapt. "We've had this discussion, Detective. I… I fell down."

"Nasty fall," Warner commented.

"Yes, yes it was, but you were telling me about my flat," she said quickly in an effort to change the subject.

"I'm afraid so. Mr Harrison has already made a statement…"

"…Wait… Rupert knows about this?"

"Well yes, he reported it."

"When?"

"This morning."

"And he didn't tell me?"

Taylor fell silent. She exchanged glances with Warner. It was clear, from the expression on Ashley's face, that she genuinely did not know anything about what had happened at her flat.

Ashley stood up. "I want to see."

"Miss Marshall, perhaps now isn't the best time."

"Why not?" Ashley snapped.

"Well, you seem upset…" Warner started.

"Upset! Of course I'm bloody upset, somebody broke into my flat, and nobody bothered to tell me." She took in a sharp breath. "Do you think there might be some link with what happened to that little boy? Is that why you're here?" She looked down at the detectives.

"I doubt it very much," Taylor said, calmly.

"Then why are you here? Do you normally investigate burglaries?"

"No…"

"…Then why are you here?"

"It's just a courtesy, Miss Marshall. I'd already spoken to you last night, we were already here, and it made sense for us to come and talk to you about this. It really isn't anything more than that," Taylor said, as soothingly as she could. Then, gesturing to the sofa, "Please."

Ashley took her cue and sat back down.

"So, do you have any leads?"

"Not yet. Hence why we're here. We're hoping you could answer some questions. Perhaps shed some light."

"What kind of questions?"

"There are a few irregularities that we need to resolve," Warner said, way too eagerly for both women, who looked at him.

"What kind of irregularities?" Ashley asked.

"Well, there doesn't appear to be any sign of forced entry, which would lead us to believe that whoever trashed your flat had a key," it was Warner again.

Ashley suddenly felt cold.

"Somebody trashed my flat? What exactly did they do?"

"Well," Warner began, finally finding sympathetic mode, "they've turned over furniture, emptied drawers and vandalised a few things."

Ashley gasped, incredulously, "Why?"

"That is what we are trying to find out," Taylor said.

"Can you think of anybody who might have a grudge, an old boyfriend or something?" Warner asked.

Ashley took a few seconds and then shook her head, "No, I can't think of anybody."

"Nobody you gave a key to or had access to yours?"

"No, nobody, except for Rupert."

"Mr Harrison?"

"Yes. And that was only today. He offered to go over there and collect a few things for me."

"And he's told you nothing about what he saw there?"

"No. Why?"

"Any idea why Mr Harrison withheld this information from you?"

Ashley shook her head. "No."

"You work as an editor, don't you, for your boyfriend's company?"

"Yes, I do."

"And what is it you do exactly?"

"Well, I read manuscripts."

"For publication?"

"Of course," Ashley said, irritably.

Why is she asking such stupid questions?

"You must get through quite a few of those."

"Yes."

"Most are probably a load of dross."

"Some, yes."

"Do you reject a lot of them?"

"Yes, yes, Detective, what's your point?" Ashley asked.

"Well, I'm just wondering about the possibility of the visitor being a writer. Writer spurned, and all that," Warner added with a smile.

Ashley considered this. "But, I've never met any of them. None of them know where I live."

"Sadly, Miss Marshall, these days, it wouldn't be that hard to find out," Taylor said, delicately.

Ashley's headache worsened.

"Now, Miss Marshall…"

"Please call me Ashley," she said, quickly. The formality was actually starting to grate.

"M…Ashley, can you think of anybody that you may have had a run in with, lately?"

Ashley laughed. "Jesus, am I to include drivers? Because if so, there's half a dozen of those. Let me think, there was a taxi driver yesterday, a bus driver the day before and let's not forget that woman on her bicycle. Oh, yes, the porter I didn't tip, the waitress who was shit and…" Ashley paused and ran her hands through her hair.

Both detectives noticed that the woman was trembling.

There was a long pause, then, "I'm sorry, Detective; I didn't mean to be flippant. It's just, well it's frightening to think that some sick bastard has been out there all this time scaring the shit out of me."

The words slipped out of her mouth before she had a chance to reel them back in. She looked up; her guests were watching her, with interest.

"Is there something you would like to tell us, Ashley?" Taylor asked.

Ashley sighed.

How could she even begin to tell this woman about the events of the past few days? The visit to Jackie's house, her weird dream and all the other happenings? After all, she was one of them; Julianne Taylor and her sidekick were both police. For all she knew, all this could be their doing. They might be trying to scare her. She had said some damaging things about them. She had denounced them publicly, accused them of committing an unspeakable crime against one of their own, and vowed to publish a book about it.

"Ashley?" Julianne prompted.

"I'm sorry. It's just. Well, I have a terrible headache, and I am finding it hard to think right now. Is there any chance we can finish this conversation later?"

"Well, I think we should stay with this. After all, we still don't actually have a full statement…"

"Please… I just need to have a lie-down."

Taylor exchanged looks with Warner who said, in his most sensitive tone yet, "How about I come back later this evening?"

"That'll be fine," Ashley said, forcing a smile.

Just get out!

Reluctantly, Taylor stood up.

Mark followed suit.

Ashley escorted them to the door.

Just before they left, Warner turned to Ashley and handed her one of his business cards. "Ashley, I know it all may seem a bit overwhelming right now, but we're here to help. If you remember or need to talk about anything, I can be reached at this number, any time."

He smiled at her.

"Thank you," she said, returning the smile, before promptly closing the door.

The detectives walked to the lift in silence, pausing momentarily to let a young lad in a security uniform pass them.

"Seriously?" Taylor asked, as they made their way to the elevator.

"What?" Was Warner's response.

Taylor rolled her eyes, "I can be reached on this number, anytime." Taylor mocked.

Warner smiled. "I was just being supportive. The woman's obviously rattled."

"Yes, she is. The question is, by what."

The elevator's doors slid shut, and it began its descent just as the penthouse doorbell rang once more.

Ashley hadn't even left the entrance lobby, her head was pounding and she'd had enough.

She snatched the door open, "Detectives, I've already told you that…" she stopped mid-sentence, when she realised it was Paul's security sidekick.

The young man took in her bare legs then cleared his throat and said, "This just arrived for you, Miss Marshall. Special delivery. I tried to buzz you, but I don't think your phone is working properly, so I thought I'd bring it up here, personally."

"Thank you," Ashley said, taking the packet from the young man, "That's kind."

"My pleasure," the boy said, snatching another glimpse of her legs.

Then, he turned and left.

Ashley smiled and closed the door behind him.

She studied the packet; it was a small, yellow Jiffy bag. Other than the typed address on the front, it bore no details of the sender, nor was it big enough to accommodate a manuscript, yet it was heavy.

She carefully pried open the flap, which was folded over

and stapled down, as she walked over to the window. It took a while, but eventually she managed to create an opening wide enough to push her hand inside.

However, when her fingers touched something cold and squishy, she snatched them out and instinctively threw the bag to the floor.

That is when she smelt it, burning her nostrils, like a noxious chemical; the putrid stench of rotten flesh.

She backed away, still watching the bag in horror, when she felt something tickling her fingers; wriggling maggots.

They were on her hands and now crawling over the carpet.

Ashley's scream was so loud, it pierced the penthouse door and echoed down the lift shaft.

37 SCHEDULES

Over three hours had passed before Rupert emerged from a meeting with senior managers from Harrison's Finance and Legal departments.

During the meeting, they discussed many matters relating to the Harrison Group's daily operations. However, also on the agenda was the fact that an unknown Swiss company had shown a sudden and 'peculiar' interest in Harrison stock.

While James played down his concerns, he told meeting delegates that, as a precaution, he had set up a small task force to investigate.

He went on to report that preliminary investigations, through conventional channels, had revealed that the stock was being purchased via a very well-known group of stockbrokers who were buying on behalf of a 5-year-old 'Shelf Company'.

A company that had been incorporated many years before, but had not reported any finance transactions, until now.

James added that the investigation was ongoing, that he had

also enlisted the help of some key contacts, and that he expected more information soon, when he'd be sure to keep those present updated.

Asked whether the board should be informed, Rupert categorically refused, saying that at this stage, there was nothing to tell. He did confirm that it would be added to the agenda of the next board meeting.

Presently, Rupert was at his desk, scanning through his email messages. There were thirty one new messages, of which ten were marked urgent.

One of them was from Ashley, asking him to ring her as soon as possible.

The house phone was answered by Maria, who explained that Ashley had showered, dressed and left the house not so long ago.

"Why the hell did you let her out of the house?" Rupert yelled.

At least he did in his mind since it was clear to him that while he could charge the housekeeper with taking care of Ashley, he couldn't expect her to restrain the woman.

More's the pity.

He tried Ashley's mobile phone, but that kept going to voicemail.

It was all he could do not to throw the thing against the wall.

At that moment, his assistant brought him a most welcome cup of coffee and commented on how tired he looked. Then, somewhat callously, went on to tell him that his next meeting, with the Managing Director of a rival publishing house, would be in ten minutes.

Noticing his blank expression, the woman pressed that this was the third attempt at a meeting between the two companies, and that it was regarding the title alliance they'd discussed late last year.

With that, she left.

Rupert stared after her.

Ashley had gone out again. Where had she gone this time? *And since when have you been checking up on her? You'll be hiring a private investigator next!*

He turned back to his messages.

That's when he noticed that the internet browser on his machine was still open, but minimised at the foot of the screen.

He clicked on it and the results of his search engine query appeared.

Of course, he had been searching for information on the Whitehouse Group when he had been interrupted by James.

He read the results again, in no particular order, *advertising company, Wikipedia page, firm of accountants, care home.*

The Whitehouse; Residential Care Home.

He clicked the link and an image appeared. It was a basic website, constructed in pastel colours. The picture was of a Georgian style house, with a black roof and gleaming white walls. The header read:

'THE WHITEHOUSE – Care is our distinction.'

He read some of the guff on the ABOUT US page which went on to tell him that the company was professional and that the nurses were all registered carers. They worked hard to ensure that, when the time came, you were in the best hands in a spectacularly beautiful setting.

The contact details were at the foot of the screen.

Could this be The Whitehouse he was looking for? Judging by the appearance of the place, and the amount of money debited from Ashley bank account, it was a distinct possibility.

What the heck, without even thinking, he dialled the number.

"Whitehouse Group, good afternoon."

"Yes, hello, I was wondering… I'm enquiring about one of your residents."

"Name please."

Shit! Name? "Umm, Marshall."

"Marshall, just a moment..."

Pan-pipe music blared out of the receiver as Rupert asked himself what the hell he was doing. Not so long ago, he had been angry with Ashley for conducting her amateur investigation and now he was doing the exact same thing.

He pushed the thought from his mind, explaining it away

with the fact that he had a good reason.

And she didn't?

"I'm sorry. We don't have anybody here by that name."

"Oh, ok, well thank you anyway." Rupert was about to hang up but then added, "Who could I speak to about monthly fees."

"Monthly fees?"

"Yes, your fees."

"One moment…"

There was silence and then ringing on the line as he was transferred, but the ringing continued for nearly a minute and there was no answer.

"Mr Harrison?" Rupert was startled by his ninja assistant who suddenly appeared in the doorway. And he, for some obscure reason, like an employee who had just been caught using the phone without permission, hung up.

"Yes?" he said, as casually as he could.

"Your appointment is here. I've put him in the meeting room."

"Thank you. I'll be right there."

The woman nodded and, after glancing at him curiously, left the room.

Rupert closed down the browser then stood up, but not before sending details to his mobile device.

38 EMAIL

It was afternoon when James returned to his office.

He checked his emails. There weren't many. This was a refreshing change for the corporate lawyer, whose daily workload sometimes equalled the weekly average of other men of his profession.

Like many workaholics, James didn't have much of a social life; not that this mattered to him since, despite all its pressures, he loved his job. Indeed, he had fallen madly in love with it, around about the time he had fallen madly out of love with his ex.

Theirs had been a particularly acrimonious break up that started with the lament of abandonment, and ended with a baby fathered by someone else. This was particularly painful for a man who adored children, and had always dreamt of having a couple of his own.

Although his wife had supplicated him to forgive her and consider raising the child together, his heart had been broken, the damage irreparable.

In the end, his marriage was terminated with a few strokes of a pen.

Since then, James refused to give his heart to anyone or anything else but the corporation that he reportedly treated as his own. He had fought, bought, settled and devoured any company or individual that threatened it.

James Howard had grown from a corner shop lawyer to one of the most influential men in his industry, and by surrounding himself with some of the best brains available, he gained a reputation revered by many, and feared by all. This obsession elicited numerous rumours that James harboured unnatural interests towards the ownership of Harrison Publishing. It was even alleged that he one day planned to take control of the company.

Rumours dismissed by Rupert, since he could not imagine anything of the sort, from the man that had been nothing but the paragon of loyalty, both to him and his father before him.

Now, as James vacantly scrolled through his messages, his mind returned to the meeting he had with Rupert earlier in the day, and the casual way in which his friend had dismissed him.

The two had often disagreed, but today, for some strange reason, James had taken particular exception to Rupert's attitude. Whether this was due to the fact that the man was distracted by something else, James did not know. What he did know, was that he was troubled by the casual way in which Rupert kept playing down his concerns about a potential hostile takeover of the company.

He sighed, and wondered if it was he who was being hypersensitive as he clicked on an email from Jerry Blenheim.

Jerry was a fifty-five-year-old retired stockbroker, who had made his millions working the markets, and now toured the world giving classes on killer tactics.

The American had met James at a corporate Christmas party, and the two found that they had a lot in common.

The email was in response to a message from James, in which he asked Jerry to keep his eyes open and ears to the ground regarding Harrison stock.

This was his reply:

Hi James,
I spoke to a friend of mine today about what you
mentioned in your previous email.
You need to call me... NOW!

Now, was over three hours ago. James dialled the number, but it was answered by the philanthropist's voicemail. Apparently, he had gone stock car racing, but would be sure to get back to him as soon as possible.

James left a message, slammed the phone down and swore.

39 THE WHITEHOUSE

The sun was playing peekaboo behind the clouds on its way towards the horizon, when Rupert found himself sitting at his desk once more.

It had been a long day so far. He was tired and there was still a lot more on his schedule. He asked himself if he could actually face another two to three hours of tedious meetings, when all he really wanted to do was go home to Ashley, to bed.

He was contemplating this as he looked out of his window, and watched London's industry cogs turn in the late afternoon.

"Mr Harrison?" It was his assistant.

He suppressed a sigh and turned in his chair. "Yes."

"You are…"

"…Running late for my next meeting, I know."

"And I've…"

"…emailed my messages, yes, thank you."

The woman pulled a face, and was about to leave when he turned and said, "I'm sorry. I didn't mean to be rude."

The secretary sighed.

Rupert, with his usual talent, had managed to disarm her.

"It's fine. I understand. You've had a lot on your plate in the past few days. If you don't mind me saying so, I'm surprised you came in at all."

"Yes, well, things still have to be done. Otherwise, I would have you to contend with," he said, mustering up his most cheeky grin.

The secretary smiled. "True," she replied, "but even I could let you off occasionally. Would you like me to clear the rest of your schedule?"

Rupert was surprised. "Sorry?"

"You look tired, Mr Harrison."

"Thanks."

"Don't mention it."

He considered her suggestion. "No, I think I should see the day through."

The woman shrugged and left the room.

Rupert checked his phone for messages from Ashley. There were none, although there was an email message from himself to himself.

He opened it.

Of course, The Whitehouse residential home. He contemplated the idea for a few seconds and then glanced at his watch. It would take a couple of hours to get east of the city, to Canvey Island, but that's exactly where he was heading.

Mercifully, traffic was good, and it wasn't long before the concrete rises of London boroughs gave way to the green county of Essex.

Even the prematurely setting sun put in the occasional appearance, which in turn lifted Rupert's spirits and made him glad to be out of the office.

He was free, or at least that is how he felt until he rounded yet another bend. The grey flatness of the Thames estuary came into view, and he was reminded of the true purpose of his escapade.

As daylight faded, the car's satnav instructed him to drive by several clumps of houses, a golf course, a national park, and then turn left.

He drove down a narrow, windy road that opened up to green fields, and a washed-out view of the Thames River.

The road continued downhill, towards a white building perched on a cliff top.

As he neared the square forecourt, he passed a faded signpost that read, *The Whitehouse.*

He pulled into a parking space, switched off the engine and then sat, motionless, as he gathered his thoughts.

He had absolutely no idea what, if anything, he was going to find here, and he realised that it was this unknown that actually scared him.

Whatever it was, Ashley had felt compelled to hide it from him.

Which reminded him.

He spoke to the car, and asked it to dial Ashley's mobile phone for the third time since starting his journey.

Her voicemail.

He swore; a mixture of anger and apprehension. Why wasn't she answering her phone? Was she okay? Maria told him that she'd left the house, but she didn't say where she was going.

He called the Penthouse.

No reply.

He checked the time; early evening. Maria will have gone home.

Well, you're here now.

He stepped out of the car and into a cold breeze that brought with it the scent of the sea. He pulled the sheepskin jacket, a gift from Ashley, from the passenger seat and put it on. As he did so, he couldn't help but wonder if he had, in some indirect way, contributed to her financial crisis.

The house was smothered in withered, naked vines. Their dried wrinkled clothes were lying in clumps on the ground, with a few items blowing lazily around the forecourt, which was empty but for a few small cars and a battered Land Rover.

The house was still handsome, but looked weather battered, and much more tired than it did in the pictures on its website.

Rupert walked up to the large front door, and was about to ring the bell but decided against it. Instead, he turned the handle; it was unlocked. He walked in, as if he owned the place, and was instantly met by a gust of warm, musky air. As if nobody had bothered to open a window in weeks.

He was in the lobby; to his left, stairs led up to the first floor, to his right was the battered dark wood of the front desk and directly ahead, the corridor led to a brighter room, presumably the conservatory.

The front desk was unmanned.

Rupert was about to step forward but froze, when a loud groaning sound rushed down the stairs at him. It seemed one of the residents was kicking up a fuss about something, since his petulant whine was followed by the measured, patronising tone of what could only be one of the carers.

"Can I help you?" a voice said, startling him to the point where he physically jumped.

He suppressed a swear word.

"Oh hello," he said, as calmly as he could.

Suddenly, his jacket felt very heavy.

He was looking at a short, dumpy woman in a nurse's uniform, who wore her black hair slicked back in an old matron kind of way, which aged her beyond what could only have been her late twenties.

She was observing him as one would a trapped animal.

"Yes, I was wondering if you could help, please." He

flashed one of his best charismatic smiles, which the grey-eyed gaze of the woman appeared to deflect.

"I've come to see one of your residents."

"Last visits are at four o' clock."

Rupert looked at his watch; it had just gone that, "Really?"

"Yes."

"Oh, I'm sorry, I didn't know. See, I've just driven from the city and was wondering if there was any chance…"

"…Last visits are at four," the woman repeated, firmly.

"Yes, you said, but I was just wondering if there was any chance I could just pay a quick visit…"

"…the residents are having their dinner right now."

"What if I promise not to be long?"

"What if I told you that you should have checked visiting hours before driving down here," she said with a wolverine smile.

"Then, I would be very sad, as I had been looking forward to this visit for weeks, and it's so hard to get the time off." Rupert followed up the comment with his best puppy-eyed look.

The woman observed him for a few seconds and then, with a big sigh, and without looking at him, but at the computer behind the front desk, said, "Who've you come to see? If they're not eating, you can have a few minutes."

Rupert beamed, gratefully. "Thanks very much, that's very kind."

The woman simply stood, expectantly, as Rupert kept on grinning.

A few seconds went by until she cocked her head, "The name?"

"Oh I'm sorry," he forced a foolish laugh.

Shit, what name.

"Um, yes…"

Mr? Mrs?

"…Um, Marshall," he finally said, leaning casually on the front desk.

The woman tapped on the computer keyboard, waited a few seconds until there was a beep, and then looked up. "What was that name again?"

"M… Marshall," He repeated, as the walls started to cave in.

The woman tapped on the keyboard once more, but the computer beeped. "Sorry; no one here by that name."

"Are you sure?"

The woman looked at him as if he had just insulted her.

"What I mean is; could there be a mistake?"

"No mistake. What's the first name?"

Oh shit!

"You mean you don't know?"

Eh?

The words just came out of his mouth. The woman gave him a look.

"That's just perfect, after all the money I pay you people…"

"Well, if you gave me the person's first name…"

"I shouldn't have to," Rupert said with mock distress.

"Look, if you want to…"

"…Too right I want to make a complaint."

The woman just gaped at him.

"If it's such a big problem for you to let me visit after travelling this far."

"I didn't say it was a problem."

"Do you own this place?"

"No, I don't."

"Okay, so maybe I should talk with the manager, I'm sure he'll be much more helpful."

What the hell are you talking about?

"I already told you, we could try to make an exception but for that I'm going to need a name," the woman repeated.

"I told you, it's Marshall."

"And I told you that nothing's coming up under that name. Maybe you've mistaken us for somewhere else."

"There's no mistaking the direct debit you're taking every month from my bank account."

"Okay, so why don't we try that?" The woman asked with another of her impatient sighs. "Maybe we'll have better luck with that. Why don't you give me *your* full name," she looked at him, expectantly, once more.

"Mine?"

"Yes, yours."

Panicked, Rupert said, "Marshall."

"Yes, I know that. What's ya' first name?"

It wasn't lost on Rupert that the more impatient she was becoming, the more her Estuary English accent was shining through.

"Ashley," Rupert said tentatively, half expecting the woman to burst out laughing, but she didn't. And, after tapping more keys, said, "Right. Here you are."

Rupert nodded.

"Well, no wonder we couldn't find him."

Him? Father? Uncle? Brother?

"…it says here, his name is Burton, Andrew Burton."

Burton?

The woman looked up at Rupert, who could feel his face flushing as he searched desperately for something to say. Eventually, he said, "Of course he's registered under another name. That was the whole point of him coming out here in the middle of nowhere. He wanted the anonymity."

There is no way she is going to swallow that. Oh, what the heck, nothing to lose now. "That's why I didn't want to give you his first name. I was just making sure that nobody could just walk in here, and find out about him. And could I just say that I was very impressed with the way you dealt with me."

Rupert beamed a smile and leant closer to the woman who, despite her icy demeanour, could not help but notice those lovely brown eyes.

Her lips creased slightly, as if forced with a pair of pliers, and she asked, "Why wouldn't he want anybody to know his real name?"

"What?"

"Why doesn't he go by his real name?"

Rupert had to think fast, he shook his head in mock disapproval, as he thought of what to say next, "What is the point? If you don't know then what's the point," he said, shrugging his shoulders, and shaking his head in mock exasperation.

The woman leant forward. "I'm sorry, I haven't been here that long," she offered, now curious about the enigmatic patient's résumé.

Excellent!

"Well," Rupert began, looking around the room as another holler drifted its way to him from the second floor. "He was dubbed as one of the greatest literary geniuses of our time."

"He was a writer?"

"IS a writer."

"And was that before or after the accident?"

"Accident?"

Rupert looked up at her as the wailing from upstairs continued.

Five minutes later, the carer, whose name tag introduced her as Alison, was walking Rupert into the bright room.

Turns out it wasn't a conservatory, but a large lounge with picture windows, overlooking a green hill that sloped down to the grey, still river.

The sun lounge, as Alison called it, was carpeted in faded brown that looked as if it had been laid in the seventies. It clashed with the flowered wallpaper seemingly from the same era. The furniture was dark, and it too had seen better days.

The room was empty.

"As I told you, all the other residents are eating their dinner. He doesn't like to eat with them and, no matter how freezing it may be, he prefers to sit outside most of the time. You're his first visitor since I started working here, over three months ago."

It could have been his imagination, but it seemed as if she was trying to make a point with the way she delivered the last part of that sentence.

"Yes, I try to visit more often, but you know what it's like with work and everything," Rupert said, following her out into the cold.

They walked down a footpath, through a rose garden, passed a pond and then a hedge. Behind it, a man in a wheelchair sat with his back to them.

"Andrew," the carer called and then, as if she had suddenly had a personality transplant, beamed a happy smile, as one would to amuse an infant, "You have a visitor."

The man did not turn, and Rupert noticed that Alison had to stand in front of him, in order to get his attention. Therefore, he followed.

Andrew Burton was a thin man in his late sixties. He was wrapped in a thick black overcoat, complete with woolly hat and large dark sunglasses. A blanket was draped over his legs, on top of that rested long bony hands.

Although, what drew Rupert's attention, was the welted scar that slashed from left to right, down the man's face. It began in his eyebrow, travelled down his cheek and across his mouth, where it curled his lip into a snarl.

He appeared to be staring out to sea.

"Andrew?" Alison prompted, crouching down to the wheelchair. "You have a visitor; your son is here to see you."

It took a few seconds, but this comment appeared to conjure some kind of a reaction. The man's gaze seemed to shift to the woman in front of him, and then up to the man standing nearby, prompting Rupert's heart to skip a beat.

I'm screwed!

Burton shifted his hand, and Rupert noticed that it was curled up in a claw-like fashion, as if he had been the victim of a stroke.

The claw slowly shifted up the man's body until Alison intervened.

"No, Andrew, you know the sun irritates your eyes when you take off your glasses."

But Burton wasn't listening and, slowly, he pulled off the shades to reveal large ocular cavities. The iris, in his healthy right eye, was a cloudy grey, whilst the other was albino white, as if the eyeball had rotated to the back of his head.

Rupert tried hard not to flinch, as the good eyeball observed him with suspicion, making him think that, despite the cold, he had broken out in a sweat.

What the hell am I doing here anyway? What am I expecting to learn from this man? What happened to him?

Rupert forced a smile, "Hello. How are you feeling?" he asked, kneeling down next to the wheelchair. But the man did not respond.

"He doesn't say much our Andrew," Alison chimed in and then, with a big smile for the old man's sake, added, "except for when he's hungry that is."

So, is this Ashley's father?

He didn't know. And that was exactly it. Now that he had snooped through Ashley's things and driven out here on a knee-jerk reaction, was he any the wiser? Of course he wasn't. He couldn't exactly rush back and talk to her about it. She wouldn't exactly be thrilled to learn that he had launched his own amateur investigation into her life.

He felt guilty.

So Ashley had some secrets, many people did. Not everyone was prepared to bare all in a relationship. If anything, it was a reflection on him. If Ashley felt compelled to keep all this a secret, then he hadn't done a very good job of earning her trust.

Alison's voice broke through Rupert's thoughts, and he noticed that she had been joined by a bright young girl in a blue smock.

"I'm sorry, Andrew, but you should come inside now. It's getting chilly out here and you haven't had anything to eat today."

The man's impassive face seemed to somehow darken as the girl took her place behind the wheelchair, removed the brake and carefully manoeuvred it away.

It was as she was doing this that Rupert's blood froze, for as the chair turned, so did the old man's eyeball, it watched him with an expressionless gaze, but one that unsettled him nonetheless.

Rupert and Alison slowly followed the chair from a distance, as if they were following cortege.

"He seemed very pleased to see you," she said, suddenly.

"Yes, he did. I was happy to see him too."

"Not happy enough to give him a hug, though," she added quickly.

They both stopped walking and she turned to look into his

eyes.

"I was told that Andrew hasn't received visitors since he arrived here, years ago. Who are you?"

Rupert considered the question, and was about to continue with his charade, but decided against it. The truth was just too obvious.

He shrugged and squinted at her in what was left of the setting sun. "My name's Rupert Harrison. I guess you could say I'm an acquaintance."

"*The* Rupert Harrison. As in Harrison publishing?"

Rupert nodded, coyly, as if used to his celebrity preceding him.

"I thought you looked familiar. I read an article about you in one of the Sunday supplements. I've also read a lot of your books. I'm reading one now."

Rupert smiled. Not sure what to say. If the woman was star struck, she was doing a good job of hiding it.

"So, Mr Harrison. How well exactly do you know Andrew?"

Rupert shrugged. "To be honest, I don't know him at all. That's why I'm here. I was hoping to learn more about him."

"Why would you want to do that?"

"My fiancé is the one paying for his care and I'm trying to find out why she is doing that."

"Why don't you ask her?" the carer asked, flatly.

Rupert smiled. That was a good point. "I don't know why. It wasn't exactly something we discussed, I sort of found out by accident."

Alison nodded.

"Look, I know you probably can't tell me, but I would really appreciate any information you may have."

She hesitated. "I told you, he hasn't had any visitors except you. At least not since I've been here."

"Do you know where he came from? Where he lived before?"

"No idea."

"What exactly is wrong with him?"

She paused and Rupert continued, "Please."

"I could get the sack."

"I appreciate that," Rupert said and then added with a sigh, "I'm not interested in getting you into trouble, but you are the only person who can help me."

The hesitation continued as the carer sized him up, as if considering that he was, after all, some kind of celebrity. That, and the fact that his deep brown eyes appeared to be glistening with sadness, or was that shame?

"I can only tell you what I've heard."

Rupert nodded.

"Most of it is hearsay anyway. You could pick it up from anyone here," The carer added, as if justifying what she was about to share. She leaned in closer, "There's a seal on Andrew Burton's identity."

"A seal?"

"Yes."

"What does that mean exactly?"

"It means that somebody somewhere has asked that his real identity be concealed."

"You mean a relative?"

"No, I mean a court."

Rupert frowned. "You mean he's under some kind of witness protection program?"

Alison shrugged, "I don't know if it's anything as dramatic as that. All I know is that normally we would have access to all of his medical history, but in his case we're only aware of the essentials."

"Which are?"

"That he was the victim of some kind of vicious knife attack. He was stabbed multiple times."

Rupert's eyes widened.

"Who…"

"As I say, we don't know. What we do know is that one of the puncture wounds crippled him."

"Jesus," Rupert whispered. "And you don't know anything at all about his family?"

"No, as I said, the file's sealed; we don't have access to that kind of stuff."

"You don't even know where he came from before this?"

The carer shook her head.

"What about time? How long's he been here?"

Alison considered the question, and then said, gravely, "A long time. A very long time."

40 NOWHERE

By the time Rupert left The Whitehouse, darkness had smothered the land, bringing with it a thick blanket of fog.

For some reason, when he used voice command to call Ashley, it didn't respond.

So he checked his mobile phone, and was surprised to find that there was no signal, yet he distinctly remembered using it on the way down.

He flung the thing onto the passenger seat.

It was getting late and there's no doubt that Ashley would be wondering where he was and, like him, had probably left a collection of messages on his voicemail.

He couldn't help but smile at the irony; only yesterday he was angry at her for disappearing on him yet today, he had done exactly that. What was worse, is that he could not even tell her where he had been, or could he?

He considered this as he turned up the heating.

What exactly did he know? What exactly had he discovered?

Not much really.

He had discovered a man in a nursing home who may, or may not, be her father. If he was her father then why did she hardly mention him, and why had she told him that he had died?

Who exactly was Andrew Burton? How exactly did he get those terrible injuries? And why had the man's file been sealed by a court?

Once again, so many questions, to which only one person knew the answers.

Should I just talk to her? Just come clean, tell her about my trip down here, about what I found in her apartment. After all, I wasn't snooping. Or was I?

His confusion was as chaotic as his guilt was heavy.

With everything that has happened in the past few days. What do I do? I take off from work and embark on my own amateur investigation into the woman I love and want to marry. What a fucking hypocrite! I'm so sorry, Ash.

The fog hung in blankets in front of the headlights, making the road ahead as clear as the conundrum in his brain.

The drive home felt miserable, in stark contrast to the drive out of the city, and he suddenly missed Ashley. He wanted to speak to her, tell her everything, and explain that the only thing he was interested in was her welfare.

He dialled the heating higher, as the chill from outside seemed to have taken up residence in the car.

He checked his mobile again.

No signal.

Bloody thing! Out of a so-called ninety eight percent coverage, I would have to drive through the 2 percent!

It was when he returned his eyes to the road that the shadow appeared, out of the mist, causing him to stamp on the breaks, and swerve to avoid it.

Tyres screeched, he yelled, and the car fishtailed a few times before it came to an abrupt halt, with its nose dangerously close to a ditch.

"JESUS CHRIST!" was all he could say when the ordeal was over.

He sat there, nerves taught, heart pounding, and breathing so heavily, he was on the verge of hyperventilation.

Seconds drifted by, as the engine idled and hot air hissed loudly out of vents.

Through the windscreen, the headlights illuminated part of a ditch and a field, before the view disappeared into fog.

He looked around the car; more fog.

He checked the rearview mirror and froze, when he saw that the shadow was actually a person.

He could see the outline of an individual, standing about ten feet back, at the edge of the road.

He or she stood, unmoving, as if watching him.

He glanced at his phone; no signal.

So, he took a few seconds to consider what to do next.

Eventually, he pulled the door handle and pushed the door open.

The sound of the engine rushed in, along with a crisp fresh scent of...

..Frost?

He instantly recognised the scent, as it always brought back memories of his childhood.

Reluctantly, he left the car and looked down the road.

That shadow had not moved.

"Hello?" he called, and waited for an answer.

Walk over there or just drive off?

Drive off!

It was obvious that, whoever was standing opposite him, was, for some obscure reason, determined to spook him, and it was working.

He glanced at the open car door and then back at the shadow, and nearly screamed; the shadow had moved, closer, much closer.

No more than five feet away.

Now, he could see that the shadow was actually a man. He was wearing a long back coat, with a hood pulled up, overhanging his forehead and concealing his eyes.

Rupert's heart pounded in his chest.

He just wanted to get into the car and drive off at great speed, but common decency prevailed. He had, after all, nearly run this person down.

Yes, he could be a freak. and his behaviour was certainly substantiating this thought, but what if he wasn't. What if he was just an innocent farmer whose tractor, or whatever, had broken down, and he was just trying to get home, out of the freezing cold...

..."I frightened you."

The stranger's voice, deep with no inflection, no discernible accent, was like an alarm bell in the still of the night, and it jolted Rupert's tongue to life.

"Yes, you did." he said, then added, "...just, with the fog...

you appeared out of nowhere."

The need to make eye contact was instinctive in the businessman, and his inability to do so made his skin crawl.

It was all he could do not to cock his head, and peer under the man's hood.

"Can," he croaked, quickly clearing his throat, "Can I give you a lift somewhere?"

But the stranger said nothing, and Rupert could only watch, aghast, as the man walked over to the back seat of the Lexus, pulled the door open and climbed inside.

Rupert hesitated for a few seconds, as he considered what to do, but he had no choice.

Reluctantly, he slid behind the driving wheel and then, with a curse about ever leaving the sanctuary of the vehicle, he reversed and straightened the car.

The stranger was just too bloody weird, and now he was sitting in the backseat, smelling of musty old clothes.

What have I done?

Rupert fixed the rear mirror so that he could see his passenger and smiled, almost embarrassed, when, for the first time, their eyes met.

The stranger had intense blue eyes that appeared to shimmer in the dim light of the dashboard. Now, they were watching, observing him, locking him in some kind of stare off, until Rupert tore his eyes away.

Now, thoroughly unnerved, he threw the car into gear and resumed the journey.

They drove in silence as Rupert focused on the road ahead. The fog was getting worse, and he was finding it hard to see more than five feet in front of the bonnet.

He flipped on the fog lamps, tinging the world with an eerie yellow hue.

The atmosphere in the car was almost as dense as the mist outside.

Although Rupert wasn't looking directly at the stranger, he could feel those eyes, like giant cockroaches, crawling all over him; in his hair, on his skin.

At one point he had to suppress a scream, for he could have sworn he felt cold fingernails tracing the nape of his neck, molesting the hairs that were already bristling there.

It's all in your mind.

But was it?

Rupert, an expert in the art of dealing with awkward clients and fabricating small talk, was unable to find words on this occasion, no matter how hard he racked his brains.

Then, finally, he heard himself stutter, "So, so, where are you going? Where can I drop you?"

There was a nail-bitingly long pause and then the stranger said, in the same monotonous drone, "Ware."

Rupert smiled, nervously, "Ware. I don't think I've ever heard of it," he said, with a nod of the head. "You'll have to give me directions."

"Soon."

"Okay," Rupert said brightly, trying very hard to suppress a note of hysteria. "Are we close?"

"We're already there."

"Really?" Rupert asked, peering into the windscreen. "I can't see anything."

There was another dramatic pause before he heard the stranger say something.

"I'm sorry, what was that?" Rupert asked, glancing up at the rear view mirror, and instantly performing a double-take.

But the reflection was not lying to him. What he saw made his eyes water, his stomach turn over, and sent shivers scraping down his spine.

For the second time that evening, Rupert Harrison stomped on the car brakes. The action thrust him forward, into the restraint of his seatbelt, then violently back into his seat, as the car came to a screeching halt in the middle of the road once more.

He clicked himself free, yanked the door handle and fell out, onto the cold tarmac. He spun around, while simultaneously crawling backward, away from the car.

Then, he scrambling to his feet and gawked at the back passenger seat, now perfectly illuminated by the vanity light; it was empty.

The stranger had vanished.

"What the…." He breathed, incredulously.

His mind reeled, his heart throbbed and the small hairs on his body prickled as he tried to comprehend what he was, or more precisely, what he was no longer seeing.

The open door alarm chimed loudly in the still of the night, as he slowly and carefully approached the vehicle, and yanked the door open.

He saw what the courtesy light had already shown him; the back seat was empty.

"Oh God, help me," he muttered. "Oh God."

His legs buckled.

He doubled over, and put his hands on his knees, in an attempt to calm his breathing, for he was starting to feel light-headed, and his chest tightened.

"This isn't possible... this isn't possible," he chanted over and over again as he stared at the empty passenger seat.

That's when an icy cold breeze ruffled his hair, and he noticed, the fog had lifted.

The road and the surrounding fields gleamed, as if washed clean, beneath a clear moonlit sky in which stars winked like white diamonds.

And it wasn't long before Rupert Harrison realised exactly where he was; in the middle of *no-Ware*.

41 INVESTIGATION CONTINUES

Ashley wished she never decided to visit her apartment. What she saw there filled her with total and utter horror. It wasn't just the devastation, but the thought that someone, unknown to her, had entered her home and been through her things, and then wreaked such devastation with such malice.

Who could possibly feel that way about her?

The police concluded, that while burglary would have been obvious motivation for the attack, it was an unlikely one, given the senseless vandalism.

The typical modus operandi for a burglar was to take as much as possible with the highest value and get out. Not hang around to cause mayhem. This was substantiated by the fact that Ashley couldn't see anything obvious missing. The television, DVD player and other such items were still there. In fact, everything of high value was still in situ, albeit defaced or broken.

There was no doubt; somebody was harbouring a grudge against Ashley.

Which then brought them back to the latest event; someone had sent the editor a putrefying heart. Initial inspection suggested that it was actually an animal's heart, most likely that of a pig. It had been allowed to begin decomposition, before it was carefully sealed in a Jiffy bag and mailed to her.

Whoever it was, they were sending Ashley a clear message; they felt wronged and they wanted her to know about it.

The most frustrating part of the whole sorry affair, was that regardless of the UK's CCTV obsession, none of the cameras in nearby streets actually recorded anything. Nobody loitering in the area, no one entering or leaving the flat. At least, nobody who couldn't be accounted for, although the investigation was ongoing.

So how the hell did they get in?

"Miss Marshall?"

"I don't know what could have motivated it, Detective. I've already told you that today," Ashley said, making no effort to mask the irritation in her voice.

They were sitting in exactly the same place they had been earlier in the day, only now it was dark outside, and Mark, the Detective Sergeant, was on his own.

He looked quite handsome with his dishevelled hair, stubbly strong jaw and a now rumpled navy blue suit.

"And you don't feel different even after visiting your flat? Nothing has jogged your memory or anything?"

"No, nothing. I just know that whoever it was needs hanging. I mean, Jesus Christ they even crapped all over my bed!"

"You saw that?"

"No Detective, I smelt it. In fact, the whole apartment reeks of it. Do you mean to tell me that none of your men noticed it?"

"No, not that anybody reported. This only substantiates the theory that it's got to be somebody with a grudge, an ex, maybe even someone you may be…"

…Ashley cut the man's sentence short with a glare and then stood up.

She was agitated now, and Mark could see this.

"What is it with you people? Something's unexplainable and you instantly assume I'm fucking someone, is that it?"

Mark was taken aback. For as much as Ashley looked feisty, it was only tonight that he noticed that she wasn't afraid to speak her thoughts.

He liked that.

"I'm sorry. I wasn't implying anything, Miss Marshall. I'm just investigating all possible angles."

"I told you, there isn't anybody, nobody obvious anyway. For all I know, it could be one of you lot."

Mark cocked his head, not comprehending, "One of us?"

"Yes," Ashley said.

She was pacing now.

"It's not like you lot didn't make it clear you'd do anything to stop Harrison publishing this book."

Ashley challenged him with a smug smile, which was returned by the young man who said, "Well, there you go, there's a suspect after all. You just said you couldn't think of any."

She threw him a look.

"Why do you think somebody from the Met would risk breaking into your home…"

"I thought you said they didn't break in."

"They didn't."

"So why are you now saying that they did?"

Mark was about to come back with another remark, but he stopped himself and, after taking a deep breath, said, "Miss Marshall…"

"Jesus, could you sound any more condescending? Just call me Ashley."

"Ashley, I'm not sure exactly what your experience has

been with my colleagues, but I can assure you, I'm here for one reason, and one reason alone, to find the truth."

"Oh good, because I was starting to wonder," she said flippantly, and then stopped.

Why the hell was she being so mean to this man anyway? He was only doing his job.

But he's one of them! One of who?

And he's annoying!

She ran her hand through her hair, rolled her aching shoulders, as if switching into a different gear and said, "I'm so sorry, Detective. I don't even know why I'm taking it out on you. It's just, well, it's terrifying. Just the thought that there's someone out there who hates me enough, to go to the length of trashing my flat, and breaking in here, just to scare the shit out of me, well it's..."

Ashley trailed off here, realising what she had just said.

"Here?" Mark asked.

Their eyes met.

There was a pause. "Ashley, is there something you're not telling me?"

"I've already told you all I know."

"Are you sure about that?" He asked, seriously.

They looked at each other for the longest time, during which, Ashley noticed his eyes.

He had very kind eyes.

"It's nothing," she finally said.

She couldn't see any point in discussing the fact that she thought someone had broken into the penthouse.

It was nigh on impossible for anybody to get into the building, without being noticed by security, and even if they did manage to get through, they'd have to have known the code to the penthouse, and their movements would have been recorded on CCTV.

"Really." She reaffirmed. "I just thought someone had broken into the apartment but, well, you've seen what security's like here."

Mark observed her and then, eventually, he asked, "What about Jackie Harris?"

Ashley looked surprised, "What about her?"

"Why did you visit her home?"

"What?"

"We learned from neighbours that a woman, fitting your description, was found outside her home and taken to hospital with a head wound."

Mark nodded at her wound.

"And pain in her arm."

He looked at her arm, where she was subconsciously rubbing a dull ache.

Ashley snatched her hand away, but it was too late. She may as well come clean. "I was looking for the manuscript."

"What manuscript?"

"The one you lot are trying to get blocked."

"And did you find it?"

"No, you got there before I did and formatted the hard drive."

Mark appeared impervious to the jibes to the point that Ashley suddenly felt childish.

"So, how did you get those?" he asked, referring to her wounds once more.

"Somebody was in Jackie's house with me."

"Who?"

Ashley allowed her shoulders to slump and eyed him as if he were the most naïve of men. "I don't know."

"So, you were attacked?"

"No, not exactly."

"Not exactly? Either you were or you weren't. How did you get those injuries?"

"I fell."

"Must have been a pretty bad fall."

"It was."

Mark paused for a few seconds and then, in his most professional tone said, "breaking and entering is a serious offence, Miss Marshall."

Ashley tried hard not to scoff at his tone and retorted, "I didn't break and enter."

"How did you get in then?"

"I had a key."

"Did Jackie Harris give it to you?"

"No."

"Then how did you get hold of it."

She hesitated. "I knew where she hid it."

"And took it upon yourself to go in?"

She was feeling suitably chastised. To her surprise, the detective was actually starting to make her feel bad about what she had done. As if she had betrayed him, personally.

"What do you know about the Stantons?"

Ashley paused, surprised by the sudden change in his line of questioning. "What most of the nation knows, he's a racing driver and she's an actress."

"You never met them?"

"Only a few times, in the lobby, they seemed friendly. Or at least, he did. She was always a bit of a cold fish."

"And you never had any other dealings with them, other than meeting them in the lobby?"

Ashley screwed up her nose, "Detective, I've already had this conversation with you and your boss."

"It isn't such an unusual question; considering you live in the same building."

"We share a building and that's about it. People here like their privacy."

Ashley closed her eyes and breathed deeply.

"I can't even begin to imagine what they must be going through right now. So, while we're on it, how about you stop interrogating me, and I ask you a question. Are you any closer to finding out what happened?"

"It's an ongoing investigation."

"Now, where have I heard that before?"

Ashley allowed herself to look into his eyes once more.

Mark continued, calmly, "It's still early days. Hence why I'm here."

"Oh, and there's me thinking you were here because you were worried about me..." there was a pause and Ashley quickly added, "and what happened in my flat."

What's wrong with me?

If Mark read into the comment, he didn't show it. Instead he asked, earnestly, "Do you really think that the Met has something against you?"

Ashley pretended to think about this, and then said, "Um, yes. The Met are worried about this book by Jackie Harris, and have sought to silence anyone who is instrumental in publishing it."

"You know, Ashley, you should really watch what you say. Those kind of comments could get you into a whole world of trouble."

"Is that a threat?"

Mark smiled. "It's a warning, Ashley. Some of those MET lads are fanatical."

"Fanatical enough to trash my home?"

It was another throwaway remark, but this time Mark noticed that it was accompanied by a faint smile.

He watched her for a while. Her long auburn hair, that looked much darker in the lamplight, her long legs and those fiery eyes. As obnoxious as this woman was, he could see why Rupert Harrison had fallen for her.

There was a silence until she noticed the way he was looking at her.

"Are we done, Detective?"

"Do you have an appointment?"

"You could say that. My fiancé has not returned my calls and is late home; I'm worried."

It was the first sign of vulnerability that Mark had seen since he'd arrived.

"Almost. Just a few more questions. You started to tell me about how you believed somebody was in Jackie Harris' house with you. Tell me…"

…they were interrupted by the sound of the front door slamming shut.

Ashley froze, like a rabbit in the headlights, while Mark jumped to his feet. Then Ashley's eyes lit up when Rupert walked into the room.

"Oh my God, where have you been?" she asked, flinging her arms around him.

She hugged him tight, but emerged when she felt that he wasn't reciprocating.

She studied his face. He looked pale, haunted.

"Rupert," she said worriedly, feeling his arms and his face,

"What's wrong? What happened?"

He shook his head. "It's just freezing outside."

"Are you sure? You look pale." She felt his forehead like a worried mother. "Do you feel okay?"

"Yes, I'm fine, really," he said, forcing a smile.

"Where have you been? I've been trying to get a hold of you all day."

"Me too. I've left messages with Maria because you weren't here."

"I had to go to the flat. I wanted to see for myself."

It took Rupert a few moments to realise. "You know?"

"Yes. Why didn't you tell me?"

"I tried. But I didn't get a chance."

Ashley hugged him. "Oh God, I've missed you. I was worried. Everything's turned so ugly."

Rupert was about to respond when he noticed Mark standing by the sofa.

Ashley spoke, "Oh, this is Detective…"

"Warner," Mark said.

They walked over to him.

"It's the Detective and his colleague that came to see me earlier today. They told me about the apartment."

"I see. Any ideas?"

"As you can expect, we're looking into it. One of the reasons I'm here."

"One of the reasons?" Rupert asked. His head was fuzzy. He still hadn't recovered from his encounter on the road, and he really wanted to talk to Ashley, but now this guy was here.

"How well do you know the Stantons?"

"We've already had this conversation, Detective," Rupert said, dismissively. "I've told you, they're a private couple, kept themselves to themselves."

"Yes, ironic really," Mark said.

"What is?"

"Well, that you should share the same apartment building, and that your company has published books about them, yet you've never actually met them."

Rupert didn't really know what to make of Mark's comments but said, "My company publishes many books about many people, Detective. I don't make a point of meeting all of them."

"Not even if you live in the same building?"

Rupert looked at him. He wasn't in the mood, but he measured his words. "I *do* know them, but, as I've already told you, it's just in passing."

"Did you ever meet their nanny?"

"No, why would I?"

"Not even in passing?"

"No not even in passing. As I said…"

"…You didn't have much to do with them, yeah, I remember." Mark thought about this, and then looked at Ashley, but the question was to Rupert, "What about Miss Marshall? Any idea who may have wanted to turn over her flat?"

Rupert thought about the question and then shook his head. "Isn't that your job?" He asked.

Mark ignored the question and offered one of his own, "You can't think of anyone who may bear a grudge?"

Ashley spoke up, "Detective? We've been through this…"

"…Dislike her enough to send rotting meat in the post."

"What?" Rupert asked, incredulously.

"Maybe an ex-wife, perhaps?"

Ashley glared at Mark and then took in a deep breath; this was the last thing Rupert needed to hear right now, and she could have slapped Mark for mentioning it. It seemed he was going out of his way to piss him off. That or prove some kind of a point.

"You didn't know?" Mark asked.

"Know what?" Rupert said, anxiously, looking at each of them for a response.

"This morning…"

"…This morning," Ashley jumped in, irritated by Mark's bullish attitude. "I received a packet in the post, it wasn't anything really, just someone playing a prank…"

"…Somebody thought they would send your fiancé a Jiffy bag full of a decomposing heart."

Rupert's eyes widened.

Ashley was furious.

"Why didn't you tell me about this, Ash?"

"I tried to get hold of you, Rupert, just like you did me, remember? It's nothing, really. The Detective suggested it might be disgruntled author, and I'm inclined to agree."

"Ash, you've been doing this job for years, nobody's sent you packets in the post before!" Rupert said.

"Which brings me back to my original question, Mr Harrison, any idea who this person might be?"

"We seem to be going round in circles... I can't think of anyone..."

Mark smiled. "Not even someone from the Metropolitan Police?"

The remark was obviously a dig at Ashley, but before she could respond, he followed it up with. "Well, I think that's everything for now. I should get going. Give you two a chance to finally catch up. I hope you won't mind me stopping by again."

Ashley bit her lip, when she really wanted to hurl abuse at the arrogant pig. Instead, she smiled, "I'll see you out, Detective."

She couldn't open the door fast enough. Mark stepped out and then turned to her. "I've annoyed you, haven't I?"

"What on earth makes you think that, Detective?" Ashley said, sarcastically, as she stood back with one hand on the door.

"I'm just doing my job."

"Does that include being a dick?" She clipped.

For the second time, her words surprised him, and then, almost as if she'd read his mind, she added, "You think just because we live up here, we feel entitled. That we're unaffected. Home trashed, we'll just redecorate. Psychos send you stuff in the post, just hire more security."

"I didn't say that..."

"...You didn't need to. It's written all over your face."

"It's part of the process. I need to establish if..."

"..You have no idea what we've been through, yet you come in here, lording your badge over us like we're the villains and not the victims..."

"...Hey, you two aren't even talking to each other. In my

profession, when we see that kind of stuff, we're trained to ask why."

She glared at him.

Seconds drifted by, and the tension between them was palpable.

Mark began, "Look, Ashley…I'm sorry if…"

"…Save it." She interrupted. "Have a good evening, Detective."

With that, she pushed the door shut, took a few seconds to recompose herself, and returned to the lounge.

"That man's an arrogant pig."

Rupert walked over to the bar and fixed himself a brandy,

"I suppose he's just doing his job. He's investigating a murder. I guess he can't exactly go around treating everyone with kid gloves."

"Yeah, well, there are ways of doing your job," Ashley said, walking up to him. "Where were you tonight? I was worried."

He took a swig from his glass, and let the alcohol burn its way to his stomach before replying, but surprised himself when he spoke the words, "I had a late meeting."

"With who?"

He forced a laugh. "Are you checking up on me now?" He said, avoiding eye contact with her, and heading over to the couch."

"No, of course not. It's a reasonable question, though. I called the office and your secretary said you'd left early. You never leave early, unless it's with me. If you do, you normally stay in contact."

"I tell you what, rather than worrying where I was, let's talk about you."

Ashley followed him over to the opposite sofa.

Their eyes met.

"What about me?"

Rupert realised what he had just said, and wondered if now was a good time to go into this, and decided against it. He was tired, angry, and confused.

Much had happened in such a short space of time, and he was still spinning from it all. He needed to work it through in his mind first, before he actually verbalised it to anyone, especially her.

Instead, he said, "You still haven't told me what happened at Jackie's."

Ashley looked at the coffee table in front of her, as if mesmerised by the glittering of the crystal. "Oh God, don't you start as well. I have just got through that dissection with him."

"Yes, well, I think if anyone deserves to know, it's me."

"Somebody was at Jackie's house with me." The words just fell out of her mouth.

Rupert frowned. "What do you mean? Someone went to the house with you?

"No, someone chased me out of the house. It's how I fell and hurt myself."

"Who?"

"I don't know."

"The Met?"

"I don't know."

"Why didn't you tell me this before?"

"I'm telling you now."

"Somebody tried to hurt you," he said in amazement, "and you're just telling me now?"

"Rupert, come on. We haven't exactly had ample opportunity to talk."

"What else?"

She looked at him, puzzled, "What do you mean, what else?"

"What else haven't you been telling me?"

"Nothing else," Ashley said decisively.

Liar!

"Did you tell the police about what happened to you there?"

"Kind of…"

"…But you couldn't tell me?"

"Hang on. You're making it sound like I didn't want to tell you."

"Maybe because that's how it feels."

"Don't be ridiculous. It isn't like that."

"Then why didn't you tell me?"

"I've already answered that. What's the matter with you?"

"What's the matter with me is that my fiancé, whilst playing amateur detective, was chased and attacked by person unknown, and she didn't see fit to tell me about it."

"I wasn't attacked…"

"Then how did you get hurt?"

"I told you. I fell."

"Where?"

"What do you mean where?" Ashley asked. She was feeling persecuted.

"Where did you fall?"

"I told you."

"Tell me again…"

"No."

"Tell me!"

"No!"

Rupert stood up and propelled his glass at the opposite wall, smashing the crystal into hundreds of pieces.

Ashley instinctively ducked, and put her hands to her ears, as if protecting them from the shower of glass.

She stayed that way for a few seconds as the very air around them crackled with tension.

It was an awkward moment, one where she would not have hesitated to retreat to her flat, but now she couldn't, she couldn't go anywhere, she was trapped here.

Eventually, she looked up at him, dumbfounded.

He was watching her, but not with anger, nor frustration, but something else.

Pain?

She could see it in his eyes, as if he was wrestling with some hideous inner turmoil.

He was clenching his fists.

Rupert Harrison thought he knew all he needed to know about this beautiful woman he loved, but today he'd learned that he did not. That she had in fact been keeping secrets from him. Secrets about her past, about her finances, and he had been totally oblivious to all of it.

But not anymore.

He loved her too much.

Now he knew exactly what he needed to do, and it would start tomorrow, without delay.

42 COLD EMBRACE

Ashley went to bed shortly after Rupert's glass smashing episode leaving him thoroughly appalled by his own behaviour.

Yes, he was frustrated and yes he was still reeling from the incident in his car, but did this justify his outburst?

The answer was no.

After all, he didn't exactly rush home and share everything that had happened to him.

And he asked himself why.

Easy. Because he was afraid.

Whether this was fear of the event itself, or Ashley's most likely reaction to his snooping into her past, or both, he did not know. But then, what kind of reaction could he expect since he was still struggling to process the details.

Did I fall asleep at the wheel?

It wasn't possible.

But then, picking up a complete stranger that literally *vanished* from the backseat of his car wasn't possible either, yet it happened.

Or at least it seemed that way.

He still couldn't believe it.

So, how could she?

Even now, in the safety of his home, he was still trying to rationalise, to understand it.

Could he have had some kind of psychosis brought on by fatigue? Because there was no doubt that he felt exhausted, both physically and mentally. He so desperately wanted to accept this as an explanation.

But this theory didn't seem to go far enough to explain why

the man's features appeared so distinctive, so real, nor did it seem to explain his inimitable odour.

But then, isn't that the whole point of a delusion?

Once again, his mind was a quagmire of questions without answers and he was drowning.

The worst thing was that he had attacked the woman he loved, for the very same thing he was guilty of. This made him feel rotten inside.

His self-loathing was compounded by the fact that things were already strained between them. He couldn't explain it, but things hadn't felt right ever since they returned from that weekend at Kenning Hall.

Maybe that was what they needed. Some time away. Just the two of them. Time to recharge their batteries and get away from everything and everyone.

He liked that idea.

But not now. Right now, he just needed to sleep.

He wearily shuffled down the hall, unbuttoning his shirt and unbuckling his belt as he went.

He slid between the sheets and instantly felt better.

The cotton felt gloriously soft, smelt deliciously fresh, and the downy pillow under his cheek was fluffily fabulous.

Through his droopy eyelids, he could see the glow of the bathroom light. This would normally be an irritation, but tonight, such was his exhaustion, that he simply did not care.

What he did care about was that Ashley had made sure she was furthest away from him in the king sized bed. Even in semi-consciousness, he felt this; the gaping metaphorical distance between them.

He had hurt her. He deserved this right now, but vowed to make it better in the morning.

He rolled over, giving her his back.

Slowly, his brain began to switch off, like lights in a warehouse, but still the questions continued like demanding children. Not even now, in the twilight of sleep, would they let him rest.

It was only when he felt Ashley move, and her arm around him, that he finally began to relax.

Oh, Ashley.

It was her white flag.

Everything was going to be okay.

She had forgiven him, and tomorrow, when he could open his eyes again, he would make it better. He would make everything so much better, but for now, he just needed to sleep, and he did.

But, it was only for a few seconds.

Only until the sound drifted to him from across the room, from inside the bathroom; it was the hissing sound of a snake.

He waited for Ashley to react to the noise, but she didn't stir.

Now, his once heavy eyelids sprang open, and he looked directly across the room; the bathroom door was wide open and light flooded out of it.

A shiver scampered down his back as he watched the door's threshold.

Wide awake now, his brain processed the situation; there was an intruder in his home, his fiancé was lying unaware of this, behind him.

What was he to do?

By the time he'd woken her and explained what was happening, the intruder would be upon them.

Oh God.

His heart had also roused from its slumber, and was back at work; pumping adrenaline around his body.

The hissing, which his conscious brain was now able to process as the sound of a running tap, was suddenly silenced.

Then, to his horror, a shadow fell across the doorway. It was the outline of a woman.

It was Ashley!

A current of shivers electrocuted his body.

Then, he heard it, behind him, heavy breathing, deep and guttural, with a spittle rattle akin to that of a reptile. And, he could feel it; cold, fetid breath, blowing slow and strong on the nape of his neck, prickling the roots of his scalp and freezing the blood in his veins.

He swallowed hard with a parched throat, petrified to move for fear of what action this may invoke.

But Ashley had switched off the bathroom light, plunging

the room into darkness, but for the murky overspill from the city outside.

He thought about her climbing into bed with this *thing* behind him.

Beads of cold sweat formed on his brow as he contemplated his next move…

…She was pulling back the covers.

His protective instinct overrode his terror.

In one swift action, he spun around, while simultaneously propelling himself out from under the covers, off the bed and to the floor.

"ASHLEY! RUUUUUUUUNNNNN!" He yelled, just before slamming his head against the bedside cabinet with a loud smack.

He landed on the carpet with a heavy thud, and snapped his head back up just in time to see two disembodied malevolent blue eyes, watching him from under the covers.

Then the overhead light came on; the bed was empty!

Ashley rushed over and fell to her knees beside him.

"Rupert! What's wrong? Rupert!"

There was panic in her voice, as she felt her man's face; it was barely recognisable.

His eyes were bulging. His skin was ashen, drained of blood. Gone was his handsome boyish looks, replaced by a white mask of abject fear.

He looked so unwell, Ashley thought he was having some kind of seizure.

She contemplated ringing for an ambulance.

"Rupert!" she screamed as he stared passed her, at the empty bed.

She grabbed both his arms and shook him in an attempt to make him refocus, then cupped his face once more.

"RUPERT!"

Slowly, he turned to her, eyes wide with terror.

He was freezing to the touch, his whole body a mass of shudders.

"Rupert? Rupert, talk to me. What's wrong? Rupert!"

He was staring through her now.

"Tell me, baby, what's the matter?" She cried, anxiously.

"Tell me, what's wrong?"

But Rupert Harrison was unable to speak. Such was the awfulness of the moment, he had lost all ability to articulate.

43 SHOPPING DELIGHT

It was hot, beautiful and just what he needed to wash away sleep, and the lingering memory of his hideous nightmare.

That was until he opened his eyes and instinctively jolted backward; through the cubicle glass, he could see a distorted shadow.

It stood, motionless. It was watching him.

Oh God, no.

Last night wasn't a terrifying dream after all.

And now, he was naked, vulnerable. He was at the mercy of whoever or whatever was standing out there, biding its time, waiting to strike, while he was locked inside the glass cage that was now shrinking in on him, smaller and smaller...

"...Rupert, are you planning on staying in that shower all day?"

The cubicle door opened and Ashley appeared, dressed in jeans and blue knitted sweater. She was holding a mug of tea.

"Your tea's getting cold," she said, with a smile.

He let out the breath that he was unconsciously holding.

"Everything okay?" She asked with a frown.

"Yeah, yes," he smiled. "Just made me jump, that's all."

"Oh, I'm sorry. But are you going to be much longer?"

"No, I'm done."

She handed him a towel as he shut off the water. "Ok. Hurry please," she turned to leave.

"Hey, where's the fire?" He asked, as he left the cubicle and began to dry himself.

"We're going out."

"Out? Out where?"

"Shopping," she said, gleefully, as she watched him dry his midriff and resisting the urge to put her hands on him.

They were already running late and there was no time for that.

She sat down on the lid of the toilet seat, as he moved to the basin and began brushing his teeth.

"So, what's brought this on?" he asked.

"Oh, I just think you and I both need it. Oh, I've called the caterers to confirm and they'll be here around three-thirty this afternoon. Everything's set for tonight."

"Tonight?"

She pulled a quizzical face, "Dinner, Rupert!"

"Oh God, I'm sorry, Ash. I forgot all about it."

"Ha, well it's a good job I haven't. Don't worry about it. It's all in hand. Hence why we need to hurry because I want to be here when they arrive." She paused for thought and then added, "Although, I have been wondering, do you think this is still a good idea?"

Rupert looked at her with a mouth full of toothpaste and garbled, "Why wouldn't it be? As you say, we both need some cheering up, right? It's been a bloody intense week."

"Yeah, well, cheering up and your cousin," she shook her head, "not necessarily synonymous."

Rupert rolled his eyes and proceeded to brush his teeth.

"OK, happy hosts it is." Then, she had another thought, "Hey, it occurred to me. This is going to be the first dinner party we host here, together," she said with a big smile.

"You're right," he said, spitting out toothpaste. "I like the idea even more now."

He winked at her.

She looked at him with deep affection and touched his bare arm "Are you okay, baby?"

"Never been better," he said, forcing a smile, and giving her another of his trademark winks that he knew she loved.

She stood up, hugged him from behind and kissed his shoulders.

The squeeze carried a lot of words and he smiled at her in the mirror.

There was so much they needed to talk about, but neither

wanted to contemplate that right now. They both just wanted, needed to be who they usually were.

"I love you," she said.

"You sure?"

"I'm....Ew, you're all wet!" She squealed, pulling away, abruptly. "Hurry up!" she added, tapping his backside and smiling mischievously before leaving the room.

His reflection returned her smile, but it disappeared the moment she was no longer in sight.

Half an hour later, they were both riding a cab to London's shopping mecca, Oxford Street, which was already packed with Saturday, and early Christmas, bargain hunters.

London's Oxford Street shopping is a wonderful experience, but early Christmas shopping is a whole different thing.

Granted, there are hordes of people, and yes there's way too much jostling, waiting, and queueing, but the atmosphere is unique. The sights, sounds, and the exhilaration of Christmas shopping in the city is unparalleled, and an event anticipated and enjoyed by thousands each and every year.

They stepped out of the cab, into a crisp morning, and a breeze that brought with it the fresh scent of cinnamon.

Above them, hanging across the streets, were giant white spheres, and the skeletons of stars and umbrellas patiently awaiting the official switch on, that would eventually dazzle late night shoppers in a seasonally magical technicolor.

Presently, the sun was performing that task, shining brightly in a clear autumnal sky, and it worked wonders to lift Rupert's and Ashley's spirits.

They held hands as they made their way through the throng. It felt surprisingly good to be around other people, as they both felt as if they'd been confined to some kind of three-dimensional nightmare over the last week. They'd moved from building to building, peculiarity after peculiarity and, unlike them, had communicated through a collection of terse conversations.

They had both secretly decided to put the events of the past week behind them, to enjoy the day and consign whatever spectres haunting their thoughts to one side as they enjoyed the simple act of being together.

And enjoy they did.

They shopped, snapped selfies, sang with street performers, and, much to Ashley's surprise and utter delight, detoured to Tiffany & Co. on Old Bond Street, where they selected his and hers engagement rings.

Needless to say, that the usually tough auburn-haired beauty became as gooey as she was excited, as emotional as she was in love.

When they left Tiffany's, before she'd even had a chance to speak to Rupert about what had just happened, he spontaneously pulled her to him and kissed her, passionately.

The kiss was long, lingering and deep, as if these were their very final moments together. Both, were completely oblivious to the world around them, and the fact that they happened to be standing in the middle of the street and had brought both cars and people to a standstill. Some cheered, some clapped while others looked for movie cameras, wondering if the couple were actors shooting a scene.

The moment was memorable as it was magical, and stayed with them, as they now sat sharing an iced bun and sipping hot chocolate, in a department store café.

Of course, there were moments where their thoughts strayed to the events of the past week, but both refused to entertain these right now.

Soon maybe, but not now.

So, the conversation changed to the evening's dinner party and what they'd both be wearing.

Outside, an armada of black rain clouds moved into position and prepared for the assault.

Meanwhile, three stories below, in Menswear, Rachel and Jason were discussing that very same thing.

They had already stopped by Womenswear, and had spent much longer than Jason would have liked choosing Rachel's dress for the evening. It was an expensive gift from him.

Now, it was his turn to try on a suit, leaving Rachel with her thoughts.

After yesterday's argument, she'd actually wondered what would become of them, since things didn't appear to be turning out as she had expected. They certainly hadn't lived up to her romanticised view of what life would be like, living in London.

Rachel appreciated that it would take some time for them both to find their role in the city, and their place in each other's lives.

But so far, they hadn't really seen much of each other and when they did, they argued.

She knew noone. All she had was that creepy job in the basement which, on the surface, seemed like Lifestyle of the Rich and Famous but was more like...

...She shivered at the thought of what had taken place in their building just a few days ago.

Do you even want to live here anymore? Where would you go? And what about your boyfriend?

Exactly.

But then, he hadn't turned out to be the knight in shining armour she believed him to be or, more precisely, that he had shown himself to be.

Ever since she had arrived in the city, Jason seemed different. Yes, he was the same person, and all of the things she loved about him were still there, but now there seemed to be something else. He was often distracted, as if he was with her, but his thoughts were elsewhere.

And this left her feeling alone.

That was until about an hour after Jason had stormed out. She was mindlessly watched a black and white movie, when she heard the front door slam. But she didn't move from her position on the bed, not even when she heard him calling to her.

In fact, it was only when Jason walked into the room, and she could gauge the humble tone in his voice, that she shifted her focus and spontaneously giggled; Jason was hiding his face behind one of the biggest bouquets of flowers she had ever seen. In front of them, a label read, *SORRY.*

In his other hand, he held a big box of chocolates, and it was only after he was inspired by her giggles, that he peeked out from behind the foliage, and batted supplicating eyelashes for forgiveness.

He followed that up by saying he was an idiot (or in his words, a dick) and that he was really sorry, and added that if she agreed to go shopping with him, he would buy her any outfit she fancied.

They hugged, and nearly an hour later, they were here.

"...Rach?"

It was Jason calling to her from the changing room hallway. He was wearing a pair of black trousers underneath a denim shirt. The appearance was somewhat odd, but failed in no way to diminish his good looks.

"What do you think?"

He twirled for her.

She admired the way the trousers hugged his backside and then said, thoughtfully, "They look good, but the others may be less tight around your thighs."

"Okay," he said with a smile. Then, he jerked his head. "Come down here. That way it'll be easier for me to show you, rather than having to walk out each time."

She looked around. There were shoppers nearby, but none paying attention to them. "Um, not sure I'm allowed in the men's dressing room," she said, quietly.

"Don't worry," he winked. "I won't tell anyone."

With a giggle, she followed him down the hall and leant on the wall opposite the changing cubicle as Jason, all but his feet, disappeared behind a blue curtain.

She kept a lookout for staff members and or other customers, but there were none.

As she was distracted doing that, a hand shot out from the cubicle and tugged her inside.

Jason, pulled the curtain shut behind them.

"Shhh," he said, putting his finger over her mouth. He was naked but for a pair of tight white briefs that betrayed his arousal.

Partially because he wanted to, but also because it was somewhat cramped inside the cubicle, he pressed up against

her.

"We are going to get into serious trouble," she whispered with a giggle.

"Only if you aren't quiet," he said with sparklingly mischievous eyes.

"Oh yeah?"

"Yeah," he said, pulling at her jeans.

She giggled. "Jay!"

"Shhh," he put a finger to her mouth, and then traced it down her body and in between her legs, making her draw a sharp breath.

She giggled some more. "Your hands are cold!"

"They won't be soon," he whispered as his finger probed deeper, causing her to close her eyes and gasp.

"Hmm, that's it," he said, "Just checking we're both on the same wavelength."

He fumbled with her tight jeans until he eventually yanked them down, aggressively.

"Careful!" she complained.

"Shhh," was his only response.

He had that look in his eyes, the same one he had the day she arrived.

On the other hand, she hadn't really looked him in the eyes during their lovemaking. Most of their encounters were either in the dark, or early in the morning when she wasn't facing him.

Just as well, because there was something about that look, that lustful glazed stare that unnerved her, as if he only had one thing on his mind.

Something that had to be satisfied. Something that she could not deny him. She was, after all, his woman and he had needs, as did she, although she did wish he would take things a bit slower.

He would, she told herself, in time. Just be patient.

Something stung between her legs, and it yanked her back to the present; Jason hadn't removed her panties, but was merely pulling the crotch to one side, causing the lining to bite into her flesh.

"Wait!"

But he'd already pushed his way deep inside causing her to yelp.

He grunted in her ear as the warm satisfaction of the act spread up through his loins.

He pulled out, teased her with his tip and then thrust deep once more.

He was hurting.

Not only was her flesh being chaffed, but her panties were restricting her movement which in turn kept her thighs together, tightening and thus amplifying his pleasure, but pinching her skin.

"Ja...aa.....so...n ... .s to p...." she mumbled, as he moved inside her, urgently, desperately.

He was like a wild animal, panting against her face. He kissed and licked it, while his muscular forearms pulled at her underwear; the strain tighter and tighter, the cut in her skin, deeper and deeper. The thrill of doing her there, in the cubicle, in that public place where anyone, at any moment could pull back the curtain and see them, accentuated his excitement.

He was breathing heavily, working much faster now and, suddenly, she was aroused; the pain, his passion, his breathing was turning her on, engorging her with desire, flooding her with love.

Her mouth fell open, and she began to moan in between short, shallow breaths, that were silenced by the clamp of his hand over her lips.

She urged him to continue, as they both grappled for the best position with the minimum amount of noise. She licked his hand, desperate for his mouth on hers, she wanted to cry out, beg him not to stop, tell him never to stop, and she was there, almost there, and then...

...There was one sudden thrust, a groan, a shudder, and then nothing.

He remained that way, panting and swallowing for a few seconds, then, he kissed her on the cheek, released her thigh and withdrew back into his briefs.

He smiled his sleepy, sexy smile that for her, at that moment, was empty; full of promise and no substance.

Then, as soon as she recomposed herself, pulled her jeans back up, he kissed her on the mouth.

"That was fucking awesome!" he whispered, excitedly, with a big grin.

She said nothing.

"I love you," he said, pecking her on the cheek once more.

Then, he peeked out of the cubicle to find two lads grinning at him. He exchanged a knowing look, gave them a wink and then called back, "All clear."

He took Rachel's hand, "Now, let's go get my suit."

44 THE DINNER

Saturday night was bitterly cold, but the rain that seemed incessant of late had gone, leaving a glistening and relatively quiet street, but for the sound of water rushing to nearby drains.

The black Jaguar stopped outside of the Heron Heights gates, and idled, as its passengers alighted.

Elisabeth Harrison; nails painted red, carefully stepped out of the car in an effort to avoid splashing dirty rainwater over her white pantsuit ensemble.

"Fucking weather...." She mumbled wrapping herself in a black cashmere pashmina as Adam, dressed in a black suit, joined her.

"Are you sure you're okay?" He asked.

"I already told you. I'm fine," she retorted.

Adam's concern had stemmed from the fact that earlier, as they were dressing for dinner, Elisabeth had complained about being nauseous, and had even come close to retching.

Elisabeth had been feeling like this for over a week now, and the symptoms seemed to be getting progressively worse. Not that she shared that information with Adam. She told him that her state was a reaction to knowing she was going to be spending yet another evening with Ashley and, as if to make matters worse, two of her newfound friends.

Why did that woman have to hang around her cousin anyway? And why was he too blind to see her for what she really was; a gold digging slut.

These thoughts, and others, had continued to churn through her mind, even while she prayed to the porcelain god in the bathroom.

She knew she couldn't be pregnant. She had lost that ability with the miscarriage many years before. Not that anybody knew; the love that had left her heart as baron as her womb was her secret pain to bear.

Craig was a barman at one of London's most exclusive clubs. One that, back then, was frequented by pop stars, actors, politicians and Elisabeth Harrison.

He was nearly twenty years her junior and towered over six feet, with scraggly blonde hair, a crooked nose that had been broken sometime during his teens, and grey eyes.

He hailed from the Northwest of England. His ambition was to become a stunt double, which saw him gym train daily.

In fact, it was his drive to hit the big time that compelled him to emigrate south, to work. Eventually, he landed a job in a place where he hoped a chance encounter would change his fortunes forever.

Yet Craig's best asset wasn't his ambition, nor his fit body, but his cheeky charm. He was a confident northern lad, who wasn't afraid to speak to, or flirt with, anyone when he was behind the bar. In fact, someone once told him that he had enough charisma to charm candy from a pouting child.

He liked that.

That person was Elisabeth.

She was smitten the moment he flashed his trademark grin at her. She'd never met anyone like him. Nobody who met her sarcasm with his own, who could breathe fire on fire.

And *she* liked that.

She had to have him.

That's why she returned to the club night after night, week after week, until he finally led her out to the backstreet alleyway, and serviced her against a damp, moss-riddled wall.

Now that was passion.

She was tired of dating the stuffy Giles, and the repressed Piers of the world, she wanted, she needed, hungered for a *bit of rough,* and, most importantly, a man who wasn't intimidated by her. Someone who was, or at least believed himself to be, her equal.

And the fact that the cocky bastard had the audacity to lead her, Elisabeth Harrison, outside and do that to her that night told her everything she needed to know.

They spent the next few months enjoying each other. They jetted away for lusty weekends, and for shopping in some of the most expensive boutiques on earth. She loved being with him, he made her laugh, as well as marvel at his ability to engage with, and amuse, complete strangers.

He was everything she'd ever wanted. Maybe not as cultured as her ideal husband, but what he lacked in social graces, he more than made up for everywhere else.

One time, they had been driving through Devon, in the brand new BMW she had bought him. Craig stopped at a small fishing village he used to visit as a child.

There, he had parked in a space overlooking the harbour, and bought them fish and chips.

They ate as the sun set and the trawlers drifted in.

The town had been full of tourists, but that hadn't stopped him claiming her as his desert.

The farmhand's son, had no qualms about pulling the millionairess into a sitting position on top of him and, despite her initial embarrassed protestations, making her climax in full view of the passing public, many of whom didn't even notice the rocking car, or the moans coming from therein.

It was this simplicity, this spontaneity that Elisabeth loved and wanted forever.

"Aye, you enjoy slumming it with me, don't you princess?" he had asked her that day.

Her response was to kiss him passionately, *"I do. I love you."*

However, things began to change.

More specifically, they changed the moment Elisabeth asked *told* Craig to give up his bar job.

To her, it was the natural next step, but to him, it meant giving up a way of life and a job that he had come to love.

It complimented everything about his personality. He loved meeting new people, he adored rubbing shoulders with the celebs, and he had no intention of packing it in.

Thus, the personality that began as an endearing accolade, quickly became a major irritation. It was inconceivable to Elisabeth, that Craig should want to continue working in the meat market that was the club. After all, they were happy together, weren't they?

And so, the accusations of infidelity and ingratitude began. These brought on late nights from Craig, who stayed out purposefully to avoid further confrontations, and, although he was bedding down at his friend's house, his absence fed Elisabeth's suspicions.

She became obsessive, ringing him all the time and checking for background noise to establish where he might be.

In two months, she had thrown him out more times than there were weeks, only to beg him to return.

Elisabeth wrongly believed, that Craig belonged to her, as much as she wanted to belong to him. But the truth was, Craig was still very young, and he didn't believe he belonged to anyone, but himself.

Eventually, after she had choked to death whatever feelings he had for her, she kicked him out and told him never to return.

He didn't.

A few days later, during which Elisabeth had kept herself busy with professional engagements, she, and her companion, alcohol, had her convinced; kicking Craig to the curb was the best thing she had ever done. However, it was on the third night, when her dinner engagement was cancelled and she found herself alone in the apartment that the reality of the situation hit home.

She hated drinking alone.

It was only after she had demolished nearly a bottle of

vodka that she decided to go to the club where, with titillated anticipation, she had pushed her way to the bar only to see, with bitter disappointed, that Craig was not there.

Eventually, she managed to get the attention of his colleague who, over the din of the music, gestured at the fire doors at the back of the building.

Elisabeth pushed her way through the crowd, and eventually reached the door. It was with trepidation, that she pushed on the bar handle and swung it open.

Night's cold, damp air smacked her in the face. The wet brick walls swayed and blended with the blue of a nearby skip. It reached out to her with its big yawning mouth, but she pulled back just in time to tune into the echo of nearby sounds.

She strained to focus, but she didn't need to, she knew who it was. She recognised his grunts of pleasure, but did not recognise the squealing that accompanied them.

Oh, God. No.

The wall across the alley reached in once more, the music throbbed inside her skull, and the nearby moaning pierced her ears and her brain like an ice pick.

"NO," was all she could moan, as the gaping mouth of the skip reached up and swallowed her, whole.

A cleaner found Elisabeth the next day. The first blurry image that came into focus was the hairy mole on the woman's chin as she gaped down at her.

Slowly, as bright daylight registered and the overhung cogs of her brain began to grind, the memories of the night before began to dribble into her mind; a bitter cocktail of dread, sadness, anger and embarrassment.

Elisabeth had to muster every bit of strength, and what remained of her dignity, to crawl out of that skip and on with her life.

A few days later, she began to bleed...

..." Elisabeth!" Adam was calling to her.

She looked at him.

"Are you sure you're okay?"

"Yes, I'm fine. Stop fussing."

"It's just you spaced out. I was calling and you'd

disappeared somewhere."

Elisabeth rolled her eyes. "What does that tell you?"

Adam pressed the intercom button.

Seconds later, they had identified themselves, and were walking through the garden, towards the entrance, as the moon emerged from behind the veil of a rain cloud, and creepily silhouetted the towers, high above them.

They had traveled in the lift for a while before Adam spoke, "So, are you planning on making an effort tonight, or should we expect more of the same?"

Elisabeth let out a short cackle as she admired herself in the full-length mirror. "Are *you* giving *me* a pep talk?"

"Yes I am, Elisabeth. It isn't fair to our hosts."

She turned on him and said through gritted teeth, "This is my cousin we are talking about. I grew up with him. I love him. I shall be how I please, and you shall stop talking down to me as if I were a child. When I want your opinion, Adam, I shall give it to you," she said, with flashing eyes and waited for a reaction, but none came.

She sighed and turned back to admiring her slender body in the mirror.

That's the problem with you, beautifully built with so much promise, but then you leave me wanting. Like a pre-packed chocolate cake; delicious, mouth-watering, but you taste like cardboard.

There was no doubt in her mind; she had settled for Adam. But then, although she'd never admit it, he was the only other man she actually cared about beyond her cousin and, of course, the man who would have been her husband.

She honestly believed that if Adam was just a tad wilder, feistier, more passionate, he actually had the potential to become the future Mr Harrison.

And the fact that she'd even allowed herself to contemplate such a thought was a significant milestone considering that she had sworn off men a long time ago.

This, coupled with the fact that he put up with her whims, didn't make any demands, listened patiently to the pains of her past, and indulged her in almost everything, actually made her pause for thought. There weren't many gorgeous men like him that would put up with that kind of shit.

Behind all the bravado, Elisabeth knew this. That's why each and every time she told him to get out, a part of her, rooted for him to pass the test, to stay and not give up on her.

And so far, unlike Craig, he had not.

The bell sounded and the doors slid open.

Adam rang the penthouse's doorbell.

Seconds later, a fresh looking girl in a black and white uniform, opened the door and smiled at them.

"Good evening," she said.

"Hello," Adam replied.

Elisabeth just pushed passed her.

Behind them, the elevator responded to the press of the call button; it was Jason and Rachel.

He was immaculately dressed in a new black suit whilst she was wearing a cross-back dress to match.

The dress was clingy, and hung temptingly close to her every curve. Her hair was tied loosely into a bun, from which carefully planned strands had escaped, and draped themselves across her eyes and down to her luscious red-coloured lips.

"You look stunning," Jason said, admiring her. It was the second time he had said that tonight.

"Thank you, kind sir." she beamed, "you look pretty handsome yourself."

And he did in his suit, gelled hair and eyes that sparkled in the overhead light.

The disappointment from the event that had taken place inside the department store, earlier in the day, was still with Rachel, but she pushed it to the back of her mind. She rationalised that it may have been difficult for him to consider both their needs in such a confined space, although she did plan to address this at the right time, but this wasn't it.

Therefore, she reached over, kissed him on the mouth and then dabbed his lips with her finger, ensuring they were lipstick free.

The elevator arrived, the bell sounded and the door swished open.

They stepped inside, and Rachel derived much pleasure in pressing the button marked, *Penthouse,* followed by the special pin number Ashley had sent her.

She smiled broadly as the lift began its ascent.

"So, how many other toffee-noses do you think are going to be there tonight?"

"Toffee-nose? They aren't like that."

Jason shook his head. "Remind me why we're going again."

"Because it's going to be fun, besides, I've never been in a penthouse before."

"It's just another apartment. Only bigger," Jason said, subconsciously checking his looks in the mirrors.

Then, he shifted his weight, admiring one side of his suit and then the other, as Rachel brushed lint from his shoulders.

"Relax," she said, sensing that he was working himself up. "They are our friends; you aren't going for a job interview."

Jason blew air from his mouth as Rachel wondered why he was so nervous.

She hadn't seen him like this, but then they'd never been to a millionaire's penthouse before either. It was then that she caught his bug, and the butterflies began fluttering in her stomach.

They are just ordinary people. Ashley isn't like that anyway, and nor is he for that matter.

Suddenly, the whirring stopped, the lift shuddered and the lights dipped.

"Fuck! What the hell was that?" Jason exclaimed.

"It's alright, it always does this," Rachel said brightly.

"What?"

"Don't worry; it will start again in a sec…"

And sure enough, the whirring recommenced and the light returned.

"See?"

"I've never noticed that before."

"Oh yeah, it's been doing it ever since I got here."

"Yeah, well it shouldn't and they need to fix it," Jason grumbled, shrugging inside his suit as if his manliness had just been tested.

The bell sounded and the elevator doors opened. In unison, they both took a deep breath and stepped out.

When one of the hired help opened the front door, Rachel's mouth dropped open.

"Amazing," she uttered, as they stepped into the entrance lobby, where all of the paintings shone under their respective lights. Above them, the moon beamed through the dome, like a giant searchlight.

They heard talking and laughing as they were led into the lounge, where Rachel suppressed a gasp; the entire opposite wall, a construction of black steel and glass, offered an unprecedented view of the city.

Rachel was awestruck when she walked into Jason's apartment, but this was something else. Oatmeal rugs, leather sofas, and a granite coffee table that sparkled under the light from the glass chandelier, that hung from a ceiling, that sprouted into two towers, like horns!

To the left of the room, was a small bar, decked out in mahogany, complete with optics. Most of the guests had congregated here, each holding a drink, as the strings of Vaughan Williams filled in any silences.

The Harrison penthouse was an exquisite blend of gothic meets twenty-first century décor.

And it was awesome!

Neither Rachel nor Jason had ever been in anything like it, that wasn't a public building.

"Hi, so glad you could come," Ashley said, moving over to the new arrivals, and kissing them on both cheeks.

"Good to see you again," Rupert said, shaking Jason's hand and kissing Rachel's cheeks.

"I, I'm lost for words," Rachel stuttered, still gawping at the splendour around her.

"It's alright. Bit ostentatious, if you ask me," Ashley said. "Come with me, I'll introduce you to the others, and give you the grand tour, if you like."

Ashley led Rachel away.

"Wow," Jason said.

Rupert smiled. "You wouldn't mind taking your shoes off for me, would you?"

Jason looked surprised but started to comply, "Oh, of course…" he replied, about to reach for his shoes.

Rupert laughed. "I'm only kidding, Jason." He put his arm around the lad's shoulder, "Come on, let's get you a drink. I get the feeling it'll help."

Rupert led Jason over to the bar where a barman served him, at his request, a beer.

To relax his guest, Rupert joined him.

Meanwhile, after giving her a brief tour, collecting an orange juice on the way, Ashley introduced Rachel to Julie Emerson who was enjoying the view of the city. Then, she excused herself explaining that she needed to check on the caterers and dinner.

"It's beautiful, isn't it?" Julie said, gazing out of the glass.

"Absolutely stunning; the view from our apartment is spectacular, but nowhere near as good as this," Rachel said, peering down at the city.

"You live here?" Julie asked.

"Yes, a few floors down."

"Wow, you lucky thing. Am I the only person who can't afford a place like this?"

Rachel smiled, "Well, it's my boyfriend's place, really."

"Oh," Julie said, knowingly, glancing across the room, "you mean that hunk over there with Rupert?"

Rachel nodded.

"Oh, he's gorgeous. It's just my luck isn't it, three dreamy men in this room and each of them taken. The only available guy is the bartender and," she leant in closer and whispered, "Between you, me and this column, I think he's gay."

Rachel laughed.

"So, what exactly does your Jason do besides looking lovely in that suit?"

"He's a software developer. He's just started up his own business."

"Really? What kind of programs does he write?"

Rachel thought about this and it occurred to her; she had no idea. She said, with a laugh of embarrassment, "I don't actually know. Finance, I think. "

"Oh, I like that. As long as he brings in the dough, you don't particularly care what he does. Girl after my own heart."

Rachel sipped from her glass and then asked, "How long have you known Rupert and Ashley?"

"Oh, ages now. Since I joined Harrison, and that was many years ago, more than I'd care to remember. They are so good together," she added, as they watched Ashley slide her arm around Rupert's shoulder, and say something amusing to Jason.

"Yes, they are," Rachel agreed. "And he is so down to earth."

"Oh, he's wonderful. He's just the same at the office. You wouldn't have thought he owned the place. If anything, Ashley seems to be more at the forefront of things. I can't believe she's finally decided to move in here."

"Really? She's only just moved in?"

"Yes, she's always had a thing about keeping her own independence but, luckily, it looks like she's caved."

"Right," was all Rachel could say; the similarity between Ashley and her own outlook on independence was not lost on her. Although, unlike Ashley, she had surrendered everything and moved many miles to be with the man she loved.

It was the right decision.

"How about you? How long have you and Jason been together?"

Rachel didn't get a chance to reply and was grateful, for she suddenly felt uncomfortable verbalising that she'd given up everything to be here.

Ashley asked, "What's going on over here then?"

"I was just asking Rachel if there's any chance of sharing her gorgeous boyfriend," Julie said.

Ashley laughed, "Julie, you are bad."

"Hey, it's alright for you. You're not sexually frustrated."

"And nor are you. You're just sex mad. Now come on, Elisabeth has already dropped hints that dinner is running late."

"Ash, remember, whatever you do tonight, please don't sit me next to her," Julie said in an urgent, hushed tone.

"What's it worth?" Ashley teased, leading them away from

the window.

"Anything, oh please, Ash, I have enough of her at work."

Rachel smiled, "Why, what's wrong with her?"

The other two women exchanged glances.

"You'll find out soon enough," Ashley said, taking her arm.

The guests filed into the dining room, where a banquet-style table had been downsized, and covered with a pristine snow-white tablecloth. It was adorned by china crockery and silverware.

Overhead, modern tubular lamps hung low, casting pools of light that made the whole table gleam in a haze of brightness.

The seating arrangements had been determined according to custom: boy-girl, boy-girl.

Rupert, at the head of the table, then Ashley, Adam and Elisabeth on one side, with Rachel, Jason, and then Julie on the other.

There was one empty place setting for James.

Rupert explained that Isabella wasn't in the country, and then joked that she had probably been scared back to Poland after her weekend with them. He then added that James, his lawyer and chum, was hoping to attend, but was running late, would be over as soon as possible, but that they should start without him.

On cue, a duo of waitresses served the entrée: Poppy seed-crusted seared tuna, with ponzu dipping sauce.

The dinner had begun.

45 DISCOVERY

In the Harrison Publishing building, James was dictating the last paragraph of a letter, when the phone rang.

His desk clock told him that he was running late. No doubt, this was Rupert calling to find out where the hell he was, so he picked up the receiver, "Yes, I know, I'm on my way…"

But the call wasn't from Rupert. It was a long distance call from the United States where, on the East Coast, it was still the middle of the afternoon.

Jerry Blenheim had just got back from a long lunch with some of his buddies. The American asked James if he was sitting down, and proceeded to lay out news that made the lawyer's stomach turn over.

James asked Jerry to repeat the information a couple of times, to ensure that he hadn't misunderstood, since he was struggling to accept what he was hearing.

He questioned the American about his sources and if they were trustworthy. Jerry explained that he had obtained the same information from two independent sources, both of which, he trusted implicitly.

Both sources stated that, in their opinion, the organisation that was acquiring large chunks of Harrison stock, had dusted off the shelf company specifically for this purpose. There was no doubt that the entity was being used as a device for a possible hostile takeover of Harrison Publishing.

Jerry asked James if he knew whether or not either of the two major shareholders was considering selling their controlling shares. James replied that, as far as he knew, neither was planning on doing so, although what he had just heard, may well suggest otherwise.

Jerry sighed, stating that it didn't make sense.

But to James it did. To him, it all made perfect sense.

He thanked his friend, told him he owed him one and hung up.

Then, he took a few minutes to consider his next move.

He had been right. His concerns well founded.

He grabbed his coat. He'd have plenty of time to think about things on his way over there.

"…Of course we're going to talk about it, Elisabeth, it's big news," Rupert said, as he poured wine into Adam's glass.

"It all feels rather macabre to me, considering it only happened yesterday," Elisabeth replied.

"Nonsense, Elisabeth. I think it's all rather exciting," Julie said, excitedly.

"Julie", Ashley complained. "My thoughts are with those poor parents."

"Are the police any closer to finding out what happened?" Rachel asked.

"Well, according to what I heard, it is an open and shut case," Julie said. "The nanny was the only person in that apartment. Assuming it wasn't a ghost of course."

"Oh, don't say that," Rachel said, quickly.

"How are you settling in, Rachel?" Ashley jumped in, eager to change the subject.

Rachel forced a smile, "Oh yes, good, thank you."

"You don't sound too sure," Rupert said.

"Oh well, you know, what happened with that little boy and all the other weird stuff with neighbours…"

Jason groaned inwardly.

"Other weird stuff. What other weird stuff? Tell us about it," Julie said, eagerly.

Rachel looked at Jason as if seeking his approval.

He had already heard her stories today, while they were out shopping, and sought to play down her speculation that something sinister might be afoot in the building. So, he gave her a faint smile as if to say, *it's your credibility.*

"Well, you know I told you I'd heard those voices coming from the apartment above us?"

Ashley nodded.

"No, I don't know this, tell all." Julie leaned forward.

Ashley rolled her eyes, playfully, "Rachel said, she heard voices coming from the apartment above her."

"So?" Julie shrugged.

"The apartment's been empty for months now."

"No!" Julie said, excitedly, taking a sip of wine. "You heard voices?"

"Yes, well, things got really creepy the other day when I heard footsteps on the ceiling too. It sounded like two people running after each other. So I decided to go and investigate."

She paused here as she remembered what she saw, or what she believed she had seen, and now she was wondering whether or not sharing this with a group of strangers was a good idea.

"Well?" Julie asked, taking another sip of her wine.

"Well, I don't know. The apartment's definitely empty. Dust sheets everywhere."

"Wait a minute? You went in there, how did you get in?" Ashley asked.

"The door was open."

"Really? And...?"

Rachel allowed the room to fall silent. Even the hired help had stopped what they were doing.

"Well, I don't know if it was my imagination, which, of course, it most likely was," Rachel forced a laugh, "But I think I saw something or someone."

"Like what? You mean, like a ghost?" It was Julie talking again.

"I don't know. I just think I saw one of the sheets move."

"As in, flap in a breeze or move across the room, move?"

"Well, neither really. It more like a feeling, like someone was in the room with me. Then my imagination took over."

"Oh God, you've just given me goose pimples!" Julie said.

"Yeah, Rach. You're freaking everybody out," Jason said.

Ashley forced a nervous laugh, as memories of her ordeal at Jackie's house were instantly resurrected, and it unsettled her.

"Which apartment's this, again?" Rupert asked as he allowed one of the servers to refill his glass.

"The apartment above us. Eight, I think."

Rupert looked up as he remembered his encounter in the stairwell. He'd seen a light in apartment eight, moments before he was found cowering, on the floor, by security.

"So, what's the deal with apartment eight?" Julie asked.

"It's been empty for some time," Rupert explained, absentmindedly. "Some girl used to live there."

"Wait, it isn't that girl that went missing, is it?" Julie asked, once again, excited.

Rachel looked up. "What girl?"

"Didn't Jason tell you?" Julie asked, looking at him.

Jason held up his hands in a surrendering gesture, "I didn't want to spook her," he said, masking his irritation.

But Julie wasn't deterred. She was having fun, and bursting to impart gossip, "The girl who used to live there, what was her name" She looked around the table, but nobody could help, "… Paxton. Keri Paxton… she disappeared…it was all over the news. One night she just upped sticks and left never to be seen again. There were all kinds of speculation. There's even a rumour that she was murdered by one of her punters."

"Julie!" Ashley complained again. "You seem to know more than me and you don't even live here."

"Yes, more's the pity. Although with all of these goings on, I'm not sure I'd want to now," she said, taking another drink from her glass.

"You are bad, Julie. You're probably scaring poor Rachel half to death," Ashley said. "Take no notice of her. You can tell she works in fiction and enjoys her wine," she added, making eyes at her friend.

Julie stuck her tongue out. "I just say it as I know it. Besides, why else would the girl just up and leave?"

"Holiday perhaps?"

"Perhaps. Only one problem. She left all of her clothes behind. And she didn't tell anyone. Not her family, not one of her friends."

Rachel looked at Jason, "Why didn't you tell me about this?"

"Because it didn't seem that important. I was hardly going to say welcome and, by the way, did you know some girl's gone missing. It's London, people go missing all the time."

"Jason's right. She's probably run off with one of her clients," Rupert said.

"Clients?" Rachel echoed. "Why do you keep saying clients?"

Ashley glared at Rupert, playfully.

"Uh-oh, now you've done it," Julie said, ominously. "But now that you mention it… apparently, the naughty little thing ran a business from her pad, if you know what I mean," Julie added, winking at Rachel.

"An escort service?"

"Something like that, yes." Rupert replied.

"Allegedly," Ashley interjected.

"High class, of course," Julie said with a scoff. "I think she'd even given her business a name. Now, what was that?" Julie mused.

"Is Elisabeth alright?" Ashley asked Adam, in an effort to change the subject. She had noticed that her number one nemesis still hadn't joined them at the table, after detouring to the bathroom.

"I think so. She hasn't been feeling too well, lately," Adam explained.

"I thought she seemed off," Ashley said.

"Should we check on her?" Rupert asked.

"No," Adam said, "best to leave her. You know how she gets when anyone fusses around her."

"Has she seen a doctor?"

"Well, I've suggested it to her a few times, but you know Elisabeth, she'll do what she wants to…"

"…Night and Day!" Julie exclaimed. "That's what the business was called. Police found her card there."

Rachel said nothing. Instead, she drank from her glass; suddenly, her mouth had gone dry.

46 THE ANNOUNCEMENT

Adam smiled warmly as Elisabeth retook her seat next to him.

"Are you ok?" he asked, looking at her bloodshot eyes that betrayed the fresh coat of makeup on her face.

"Yes, I told you, I'm fine."

"Elisabeth?" Rupert asked with concern.

"I'm okay, honestly." She said, smiling at him, and then gingerly picking up some food with her fork and popping it in her mouth.

But Elisabeth was far from fine.

The overwhelming feeling of nausea had rapidly deteriorated the moment she set foot in Heron Heights. She had barely made it to the penthouse before rushing to the bathroom, where she dropped to the floor and embraced the cold ceramic of the toilet vase, as if it were a long lost love.

Her body told her she needed to vomit, so she would heave, her stomach would spasm, her throat would thicken, her eyes would bulge and water, but nothing.

And it was an awful sensation.

Disgustingly familiar as it was painful, not physically, but mentally, as it regurgitated memories and vulnerabilities, she spent the majority of her waking time suppressing.

Memories of the man she had loved, the chosen one, her would-be husband, the father of her child.

And this is how the cycle went; what she had, how she lost it, the pain numbing binge drinking, and the aftermath. What she had, how she lost it, the pain numbing binge drinking, the aftermath, and the guilt, so much guilt.

It smothered the will to live out of her, like a pillow on her face.

I drove him away. I killed my baby.

Baron. Bereft.

She had nothing left now but her cousin. The only other man she had ever loved.

The forbidden.

And Adam.

Yet despite the two years they'd been together, she was still struggling to come to terms with the idea of becoming his bride.

Struggling with the idea, but getting used to it. As one does an odious family member, or the person that you're supposed to love?

She was tired. So tired. Sometimes, she just wanted somebody to take care of her. Someone to tell her that everything was going to be okay.

"I'll always be here for you, Elisabeth. If and when you decide to see it. Love Adam x."

The words on Adam's card.

"Elisabeth?"

Adam was calling to her again.

"What's going on? You keep disappearing."

She put a hand on his arm.

"I'm fine, she said," and smiled. Then calmly dabbed the beads of perspiration from her forehead with her napkin.

Adam cocked his head, unsure how to react to that spontaneous act of affection. He watched, as she finished mopping her brow, and then proceeded to play with her food.

She was interrupted by the sound of a fork chinking on a wine glass.

It was Rupert, and he was now standing at the head of the table.

"Ladies and gentlemen. I have a very special announcement to make."

Elisabeth slapped away the waitress who was fussing around her, and looked up.

"I was hoping that James would be here, because I know he'd want to hear this." Rupert looked at his watch. "Sadly, it looks like the old workaholic isn't going to make it. So…"

He took Ashley's hand and looked down the table.

"The past few days, well week, hasn't been the easiest for us. There's been a whole raft of things that, quite frankly, I don't even want to think about right now. Yet, these very things have made me realise something important."

He looked at Ashley, and then back at the table.

"Life really is too short. There's no way of knowing what tomorrow has in store. I was reminded of this the other day, and that's why I asked Ashley Marshall to marry me, and her answer was…" he broke off deliberately here and looked at Ashley, expectantly.

Ashley, choked with emotion, took several dramatic seconds to articulate, and when she did, it came out as a croak.

"Y-es."

The others laughed.

She cleared her throat, and stood up.

"Sorry about that," she said with a big smile. "I nearly

choked on my food!" She turned to Rupert, "Yes, I would love to marry you."

The would-be groom grinned, reached into his pocket and pulled out Ashley's ring. It winked under the overhead lights as he removed it from its box and placed it on his fiancé's finger.

Then, he held up Ashley's hand so they could all see the ring, and then, they kissed, as the table exploded into rapturous applause.

All with the exception of Elisabeth, of course. Her mind was clouding over as incredulous rage boiled, like a witch's cauldron, deep in the pit of her stomach.

How could you, Rupert? How could you of all people do this to me?

Her vision blurred as the applauding diners slipped in and out of focus and that familiar knot formed in her throat. She was going to vomit. Here and now. There was no time to get to the bathroom.

No time.

She closed her eyes as her face drained of the little colour she had regained since her last attack. She felt very ill, as if she was going to die right there, at that every moment. Not that anybody would notice. Nobody was interested in her, they were all too interested in hearing Rupert's words, the same words that were now echoing in her head, hollow, distant, unspeakable words.

No! Rupert! Rupert, wait!

But he wasn't, he was too busy telling everybody about his plans, about his engagement to her.

HER!

The guests rose from their seats to hug, kiss and congratulate the happy duo, while Elisabeth sat, blankly staring ahead.

Finally, as the others retook their seats and chatted excitedly, Rupert's gaze fell on his cousin. She had not said a word, nor reacted in any way. He also noticed that her normally immaculately made up face looked gaunt and sallow.

"Elisabeth?"

No answer.

"Elisabeth?"

Almost in slow motion, she looked up, revealing dark circles around bulging, bloodshot eyes.

He knew she would be disappointed, but he had so desperately hoped that once he had made the announcement, and she had seen how happy he was, that she might have a change of heart.

But that clearly wasn't the case, and he could slowly feel his excitement ebb.

"Are you alright?" He asked.

"Is this what you brought me here for?" she uttered in a rasping voice.

"Elisabeth…"

"…You brought me here to humiliate me, is that it?"

The table went quiet.

"We could have been happy together, Rupert," she whined, "What's wrong with you?" She added, incredulously.

Rupert frowned. "I love Ashley, Elisabeth."

"What about me? What about us?"

"Nothing will ever change that," he said, quickly. "We'll always be close."

"This will. This changes everything! Can't you see? This will change us all," her voice was loud.

"Only for the better."

"Says who? You? This is an abomination. This is a slur on the Harrison name!"

Elisabeth's voice was shrill, as if she were giving an enraptured sermon.

"That's enough!" Rupert said, severely. "Look, you're clearly feeling unwell. Let's get you home, we can discuss this when you're feeling better."

Elisabeth bowed her head, which could have been construed as her retreat, but instead was a direct response to the throbbing in her temples. A migraine had gripped her skull, and was crushing it.

Her heart was pounding, her veins were throbbing, and the merry-go-round of the room would not stop, no matter how much she put her head down.

Meanwhile, the table remained silent; Ashley wanted to go over and slap the bitch, Jason felt awkward, Rachel felt sorry for Ashley, Julie was appalled and Adam embarrassed.

"Well, at least we now know to send out one less invitation," Ashley said, in an effort to diffuse the atmosphere that was as thick as gelatine.

But that was precisely the wrong thing to say.

Elisabeth slowly raised her head and fixed Ashley with a glare so full of menace, it stung. "Rot in hell," Elisabeth seethed…

There was an audible gasp.

… "Rot in hell, you whore!"

"Right, that's it, Elisabeth. You've had your say," it was Adam talking and he touched her arm, "time to get you home..."

"…Get your filthy hands off me!" she screeched, swinging a back-handed slap at his face with such force, it sent him toppling backwards in his chair.

There were more gasps from the others as Elisabeth jumped to her feet, "Don't touch me, you disgust me!" She shrilled down at him, and then turned on the others, some of which had moved to help the stricken man, but were stopped in their tracks by her icy glare.

"Each and every one of you, you all disgust me!" she said with a hiss as she swayed on her feet.

Rupert was about to say something, but stopped, when he noticed her face crease into a whole new expression. It wasn't rage, nor menace…it was fear.

"Elisabeth?"

But she couldn't respond. Instead, her eyes rolled back in their sockets, until only the whites could be seen.

Then, she began to heave.

The deep muscular spasms travelled, like shockwaves, up from her diaphragm to her throat, as incredulous beseeching terror returned to her veiny eyes.

The retching continued, growing in intensity, as a lump, the size of a golf ball, appeared in her throat, and gradually squeezed its way up her oesophagus.

It filled her mouth with bile, built the pressure in her head, and distended her eyeballs.

Then, she began to whine like a disgruntled cat. Low at first then slowly getting louder until the sound was replaced by the squishing of cartilage as she began to choke.

Rupert finally found his feet, as did Adam. They moved to assist, but they were both too late. They could only watch, in stupefied horror, as the gagging metamorphosed into a loud wheeze.

What happened next was so shocking it seemed to unfold in slow motion, yet was over in seconds.

Gagging and choking, Elisabeth Harrison doubled over in one final, painful spasm, before lifting her head and vomiting over the brilliantly white table.

The black, sticky fluid spattered the centrepiece of flowers, and sprayed Julie and Rachel's faces, freezing both of them in shock.

The second expulsion of thick black liquid was accompanied by large clots of coagulated blood that squelched as they hit the table in front of her.

The third joined it, creating what looked like a crude-oil slick that oozed over the table and dripped to the floor.

Then, Elisabeth's eyes rolled white once more, and she collapsed to the floor.

Adam and Rupert fell by her side.

Ashley rushed for the phone, while all Rachel, Julie and Jason could do was stare in disbelief.

The plates of food, the crystal wine glasses, and the once luminously white table cloth were now coated in putrid, sticky blackness.

47 DISEASE

They had been at the hospital for nearly two hours, and were yet to receive any news from doctors, who had rushed Elisabeth through to the Intensive Care Unit.

Adam had spent most of the time sitting in the metal chair in the corridor, with his face in his hands.

Rupert had alternated between sitting, pacing and drinking machine-bought coffee.

Ashley did her best to tend to both men, and provide as much support as she could, but she felt inadequate.

She was probably with the only two men in the world who loved Elisabeth. She was under no illusion that there was no amount of comforting hugs, words of encouragement or coffee fetching that could possibly make either of them feel better.

For Rupert, it wasn't just about his cousin, it was also about being back in the very place that reduced him to a young man once more.

The smells, the waiting, the anticipation, the dread, and the fear of what the world might be, without someone who meant everything.

Miriam Harrison had been admitted to this very hospital on three separate occasions after attempting to take her own life.

The first two times, doctors had pumped her stomach, given her a talking to, recommended another therapist and sent her on her merry way.

The third time, things started out pretty much in the same vein, with young Rupert oblivious to the damaging effects of excessive medication on the human body. He had no reason to believe that things would work out differently this time.

That was until a solemn-faced doctor came out to speak with his father. He told him, somewhat casually, that, given his wife's history of abuse, her liver was failing, and that she would need a transplant to make it through the night.

But the waiting list was long.

All they could do was pray for somebody else's disaster to become their miracle.

It didn't.

Presently, exhausted from all the pacing, Rupert sat down, and, like a frightened little boy, rang his hands together.

Ashley stroked his hair and rubbed his back with affection. He looked pale, haunted with grief, and she so desperately wished there was something she could do to take his away his pain.

But there was nothing.

It was another half hour before the doctor, a balding, gangly man with spectacles walked up to them.

"Mr Harrison?"

Rupert, like a soldier who had been caught sleeping on duty, jumped to his feet.

"Yes, that's me."

Adam and Ashley stood close to him.

"How is she?" Rupert asked.

The doctor, whose face was alarmingly grim, thrust his hands into his pockets and said, "I am very sorry, but Miss Harrison has suffered severe organ failure."

Rupert's stared.

"What, what," he stammered, "What does that mean, doctor, what happened? Specifically, I mean."

"Well, specifically, Miss Harrison's primary organs have been eroded so severely, that they can no longer function without the aid of life support."

Rupert cocked his head as if the doctor were speaking another language and uttered, "Eroded, how, by what? You mean cancer or something, what do you mean?"

"I am very sorry, at this time, Mr Harrison, we don't know. We're still running tests. My diagnosis, and it's really just a guess at this stage, is that we're dealing with some kind of voracious organism that has been feeding off her. Has Miss Harrison travelled abroad recently, say during the past six months?"

Rupert shook his head. "No, not that I know of…"

He looked at Adam, who also shook his head, but said nothing as if he had lost the power of speech. He simply stared at the doctor with wild eyes.

Ashley was worried about him and wondered if he should be left alone tonight.

"Anywhere she may have gone without you knowing?"

"I doubt it," Rupert said, "we work together; I normally know everything about her travel. Adam's her boyfriend, he'd know if there was anything else."

Adam merely shook his head again.

The doctor nodded.

"Why? What are you thinking; she may have picked up some kind of illness, a bug of some sort?"

"It really is too early to say. I have asked a specialist to come down and see her. I am hoping he will be able to tell us more."

There was quiet but for the paging of a Dr Ferguson who was being asked to report to reception, and the giggling of a couple of nurses, as they walked by.

"Look, we've stabilised her for now. There really isn't much else you can do for her tonight. Go home. We'll contact you as soon as the specialist has seen her and we know more."

Rupert shook his head. He wasn't going to leave.

"There really isn't much more we can do right now but wait…"

"…For her to die?" Rupert snapped.

The doctor weighed his answer carefully. "Until some of the tests come back and my colleague has examined her."

"But you don't think she's going to make it, though, I mean primary organ failure, doesn't bode well, does it?" Rupert said, caustically, anxiety thick in his voice.

The doctor did not respond. He left Rupert to draw his own conclusions.

That's when that familiar sense of dread began to suffocate him, just as it had all of those years before. It made him weak at the knees and want to collapse to the floor and weep.

"I'll be in touch," the doctor said, turned and walked away, leaving Rupert standing in the middle of the corridor, no longer a powerful businessman, but a frightened teenager once more.

48 LTN NEWS

It was past ten in the evening and freezing rain was spitting against the window.

Abigail Palmer was sitting at her computer in the deserted offices of London Television Network.

Saturday night, and like many weekends before, Abigail was working. Her latest story was the Stantons and the tragic death of their son.

The best thing was that, through an unprecedented stroke of luck, she happened to have interviewed them the actual night their son died. Therefore, she was already coming at the story from a different angle; star denies being overprotective on show while son is murdered.

Of course, her editor thought the headline was '*Over sensational*'.

His comment didn't surprise Abigail, since it was coming from the man who also resisted her pitch for a one hour special on the grounds of good taste, which was a joke coming from him. That guy would strip his mother and put her onscreen if he thought it'd improve ratings.

She argued that a special about the celebrity couple and what had happened to their son, was a must, because if they didn't do it, one of the other broadcasters would.

It was only towards the end of the ridiculous conversation, when the fifty-something started grinning like a freakish Cheshire Cat that she realised; it wasn't that Miles Toomey disliked the idea of the special, he just didn't want *her* to produce it.

And it wasn't the first time that her blonde hair, big blue eyes and pendulous breasts had had an impact on her career.

It always went one of two ways; they either fast-tracked her to her ultimate goal or they got in the way of it. The latter normally happened when she refused to sleep with men in power. Men who wanted to have it both ways; keep their marriages as well as a bit on the side,

This time, while her sexuality had a bearing on the situation, it wasn't for the usual reasons.

Miles, an 'out and proud' homosexual, was in no way

TONY MARTURANO

interested in her curves, other than how they attracted men for him to ogle.

He didn't want Abigail to produce the segment because there were a couple of other producers with penises that he would much rather give the job to, despite the fact that she was clearly the best choice. Everybody knew it. Hell, he even knew it, and it had absolutely nothing to do with her physical appearance, and everything to do with her impeccable journalistic record.

"People see enough depressing crap in their dreary everyday lives, they don't want to watch more of it when they turn on the TV," he had said after viewing a six-month-in-the-making documentary about homeless people.

When Abigail asked him why he hadn't mentioned anything before, the man turned to her with that smile and those thin lips and said, *"I needed a basic tutorial on how documentaries should not be made and I thank you for creating such a masterpiece."*

After that, the whole room went quiet.

That's right, Miles didn't mock her work in the privacy of his office, that wasn't his style. He told her during the morning briefing.

And for a seasoned reporter such as her, it was more than a humiliating experience. It was one that actually made her want to burst into tears and run screaming from the room, but only after she'd kicked the wanker's teeth in.

Sadly, he was the new Editor-in-Chief, and she couldn't afford that luxury, not if she wanted to keep her job.

Now, nearly a year and several award-winning documentaries later, Abigail was back. She had landed an exclusive with the Stanton interview. Admittedly, she had only got the job because nobody else was available at such short notice. Yet, she had pulled it off, despite the crap she had to endure from the director, who just happened to be from Miles' neck of the woods.

It had taken a lot of courage for her to walk into Miles' office today and pitch the idea of a feature, and she was ready for the knockback.

"Come on, Miles. Let's not piss about. You know I'm the

right person for the job. Don't let your penis come between us."

"Don't you worry, there's no chance of that happening, love," he clipped.

"I know, because you'll probably be too busy showing it to Matt Warren."

His eyes lit up.

"That's right. My chum from school. The one you've had a crush on for the best part of two years..."

"...I've had no such thing..."

"...Seriously, Miles?"

She looked at him, expectantly.

He shrugged, irked by the fact that she'd come to know him so damn well, and that she no longer feared him, yet he'd actually come to respect that.

"What do you want?" He said, impatiently.

"You know what I want," she said with a grin.

"Done. But do we even know if Matt's..."

"...Hey, I'll just bring the horse to water, and all that. The rest is up to you."

"Fine," he agreed, like a petulant child.

She sat on his desk and spent the next ten minutes reeling off all the reasons why this special would work, and why Heron Heights was the perfect backdrop to it all. There were so many angles. She would pack it with detail, research and would have an outline with him in a few days.

"You have until Monday."

"That's what I said."

She winked.

"Get out, you annoying little girl," he said, feigning interest in his laptop.

Abigail moved to leave the room, but stopped at the door and turned, "Oh and Miles, you and I both know that this whole Matt thing is just a sweetener. You were going to give me this job anyway."

"If you say so."

And that's how she now found herself scouring the web and the archives, for as much detail as she could find about the Stantons, the Harrison dynasty, and Jackie Harris. She was going to need to dig up every shred of original detail to impress Miles.

She drank from her cup and flinched, her coffee had turned cold, and it was with a heavy heart that she walked over to the coffee machine for a refill.

The challenge ahead was daunting. She was going to need to outline interviews, places, collate evidence and script it all into a 1-hour show. There was no way she could get it all done by Monday, but then maybe that's why Miles had agreed to give it to her.

He enjoyed nothing more than to hand her a bomb, and see if she was smart enough to diffuse it before the thing exploded in her face.

Bitten off more than you can chew?

Hell no!

She sat back at her computer; she had already collated as much as she could on the Stantons; his driving and her acting career.

Thankfully, she had already conducted some research for the interview that was never used. Now, she needed to take a look at Heron Heights, its history, owners and security. Then, she would move on to the tenants.

She made notes on a pad:

Jackie Harris' death; How did she die? Was it suicide or was she killed? Conspiracy angle; The Met tried to ban the book, what's in it? Where's the manuscript now? Damaging manuscript mysteriously disappears; that will go down well with Miles. Look into that.

Rupert Harrison; millionaire publisher, twin brother died in freak accident. Mother died of an overdose. A lot here. Concentrate on this bloke!

Ashley Marshall, editor at Harrison Publishing and also Harrison's girlfriend. Controversial already, for wanting to publish a book about the Met rape case. Otherwise, don't know much about her?? Find out more. Need more background.

Other tenants at Heron Heights. Know nothing about them. Find out more, visit the place.

Abigail looked at her notes and smiled; there was so much

here, if she did her work properly, she would have Miles by the balls.

She shuddered at the literal thought of that and went back to work.

49 SUNDAY

Sunday morning reflected Rachel's mood; grey with freezing drizzle.

She didn't want to get out of bed. In fact, when the alarm went off, she just rolled over, and actually contemplated never returning to the dungeon. Especially since she could hear Jason's deep breathing beside her.

She just wanted to snuggle up to him.

Instead, she reluctantly extricated herself from under the covers and sleepwalked to the shower, where all of her memories began to parade themselves in front of her like a grotesque fashion show.

First, not surprisingly, was the dinner.

She still had the vivid memory of the warm stickiness of Elisabeth's vomit, as it slapped her face, as well as the pungent odour that had rapidly filled the room and her nostrils.

She shuddered then scrubbed a little harder.

Then, she felt guilty, as if her reaction was some kind of disrespect to the woman who had obviously suffered, and, of course, her hosts.

She wondered how everybody was doing today and made a mental note to ring Ashley.

Then, she promptly pushed that particular set of thoughts from her mind, because she was already feeling rough; the vision of Elisabeth, no matter how guilty she felt, was making her feel physically ill.

Her thoughts then turned to the argument she'd had with

Jason about Night & Day. It was obvious that he didn't want her to work there, and that he did have the money to support them both. On the other hand, she didn't like being told what to do, but was she cutting her proverbial nose off to spite her face?

Maybe she should have a conversation with Lilly today, be honest, and explain how unsettling recent events had been, and how her boyfriend was worried about her…

…Come on Rachel, this is all a cop out and you know it!

And she was right.

She told herself to shut up and put up, or get out. She'd been there but days, and hadn't even given the place a chance. But then, she hadn't really had the opportunity. It was as if the whole world had gone to crap the moment she arrived here.

Ultimately, she decided she'd take a look at some job sites at the end of her shift. Hell, if things were quiet, she might even take a look while she was there.

And so, thirty minutes later, after running the gauntlet of the creepy hallway that she absolutely hated, she arrived at the office to find the door unlocked.

She pushed on it, and it swung open with that hateful, loud creak.

"Good morning, Lilly?" She said, cheerily.

Silence.

"Lilly?" She called again as she entered the office, but it was empty.

As always, it was dark in there but for that strip of grey sky through the window.

She flicked on the wall light, but it spat at her and died. She tried the same with the overhead light, but it, true to its usual self, did the same.

"What a surprise."

She stepped back out and peered down the gloomy corridor. "Lilly?"

Empty.

It was way too early on a Sunday morning for anybody to be down here.

So, she stepped back into the office and closed the door

behind her.

"Lilly?" She called again. This time loud with mock exasperation, since she wasn't expecting a response. ·

She was frustrated.

Freaked out about last night, unnerved by the perpetual gloom, and irked that Lilly had left her post and gone home, without waiting for her.

The day she arrived, Lilly lectured her about never leaving the desk unmanned, yet...

Are you looking for a reason to quit?

She sighed. It was that obvious even to herself.

She switched on the computer, turned on the only desk lamp that ever seemed to work down here, and rubbed her arms.

Rachel had become accustomed to the cold in the dungeon, and often dressed to compensate, but today seemed much colder than usual.

She walked over to the radiator and touched it, it was hot.

So why's it so bloody cold?

She made hot chocolate, while her mind drifted back to everything that had happened since she'd arrived; Jason, the dungeon, Lilly, and last night's freak show.

It was particularly quiet this morning.

Creepier.

As if the whole of London was sleeping in. The traffic had stopped rolling, people had stopped talking, and the planes had stopped flying.

Or at least it feels that way.

She zipped up her fleece, sat down at the desk, and hugged the hot mug of chocolate for a few seconds, before taking a sip from it.

She signed into the switchboard and checked the daily log which was empty, as she expected.

Because it didn't matter if she'd gone to the trouble of reconnecting, and reprogramming the switchboard, Lilly refused to use it, stating she much preferred, and was used to, using a pen and notepad.

But then, there were no notes from the night before either. No messages to pass on.

Nothing.

She sighed as her attention was drawn to the flashing cursor that, like an anxious puppy, wanted her to play with it.

She looked at it and then the button above that read, *View Logs*.

Of course.

Maybe she could find out more information about the mysterious phone call she'd received on Friday night.

She explored Optel's directory for the log folder then clicked on it. Several files, each ending with the extension of .log presented themselves.

She checked the dates. All the files were recent, from when she'd reconnected the computer to the switchboard.

She spent the next fifteen minutes checking each and every log but found nothing of interest. None of them were for the night in question, certainly not around the time when Tom was with her.

Tom. Yes, what happened to you, and what was with that look on your face when I asked about Keri? You know something about her, don't you?

She made a mental note to seek him out when her shift was over.

She slowly slouched back in her chair, only to lunge forward once more!

She turned and looked behind her.

"Lilly?"

The room was empty, but Rachel definitely sensed a presence in the room. It was as if somebody had walked up to and was standing behind her.

She searched the room with her eyes: the drinks table, the toilet door, the filing cabinets, empty desks, the coat stand, the closed door, more desks, the patch of grey sky, the radiator, and her station.

The room was empty.

Yet she could have sworn that somebody had moved, displacing the air behind her.

She shivered.

After several seconds, she returned to the computer screen, then quickly glanced behind her, and then back at the computer once more.

On the monitor, she studied the files for a few seconds longer, as if expecting to see something she had missed, but she knew she hadn't overlooked anything. There weren't that many files.

You checked every single one, there's nothing here. There's no record of that call.

But then she had another thought. What if the file had been saved somewhere else?

She clicked the search button and typed in *.log - she knew that the computer would have to return everything on its hard drive that ended in that extension - and pressed return.

As she waited, she took a sip from her cup, flinched and spat the contents back out; the chocolate was stone cold, as if it had been sitting there all night.

She dumped the mug on the table; it was so cold in here even hot drinks turned cold in minutes.

The computer began to render its results, and Rachel held her breath as the list of files appeared, like a train station board, on the screen.

It had found all the files she had already examined, the ones contained inside the LOGS directory, but it was still searching. That was a good sign. Although, it was slowly reaching the end of the alphabet.

Rachel was about to close down the window when, suddenly, a batch of files appeared, all starting with the prefix of X and all stored within a folder on the root of the C: Drive, called *Untitled.*

She clicked it open and was elated to find almost 100 files with varying creation dates. Some as recent as a few months back, others from over a year ago.

These must be Keri's files.

Rachel clicked open the first one:

KERI:> Night and day

0207 373822:> hi keri its laura

KERI:> oh hi. whats up

0207 373822:> I was just calling to check if everything is still okay for tomorrow

KERI:> Yeah thats fine am I still bringing my own stuff

0207 373822:> yeah if you could
KERI:> kay will do see you then bye
0207 373822:> bye
Rachel closed that transcript and clicked on the next.
KERI:> Night and day
UNKNOWN NUMBER:> hello sexy
KERI:> hmm you've come back
UNKNOWN NUMBER:>how are you?
KERI:> Im good a bit lonely
UNKNOWN NUMBER:> me too
KERI:> fancy some company
UNKNOWN NUMBER:> hmm yeah what are you wearing
KERI:> oh the usual when I am at home panties bra
UNKNOWN NUMBER:>hmm where are you
KERI> Im lying on the sofa with my legs over the arm rest its really hot
UNKNOWN NUMBER:>what else
KERI> well i just couldn't wait any longer for your call I started without you I hope you don't mind
UNKNOWN NUMBER:>hmmm no I don't mind tell me what you did
KERI:> well at first cos i was so hot i got some ice from the fridge and I played with it
UNKNOWN NUMBER:> where where
KERI:> my neck. my skin my breasts and my nipples
UNKNOWN NUMBER:> how did it feel?
KERI:> it felt sooo good but not as good as your tongue i love the thought of your tongue
UNKNOWN NUMBER:> tell me
KERI:> well...

The rest of the transcript carried on in the same vein, eventually leading to full blown telephone sex.

Rachel couldn't believe what she was reading. Not that she was a prude, far from it, but she could not believe Keri was taking this kind of call from her boyfriend while at the office. And, most surprisingly, actually enabling and storing the transcripts.

It was only when Rachel clicked on the second, the third and the fourth log file that she realised that the calls were not from Keri's boyfriend, but from different phone numbers and different men. All with different aliases. There was no doubt that they were calling her with one obvious intention.

The length of the telephone calls varied, from ten minutes to an hour, some with identifiable phone numbers, and others which were *"number withheld"*.

Who are these sad people?

The next thought that popped into Rachel's head was dismissed before it could settle there, because that was one treacherous road she did not want to venture down.

But the thought returned moments later as she stared at the onscreen transcript. Keri was running some kind of sex line, and had managed to amass quite a client list, but who exactly were these people?

There was one obvious way of finding out. That would entail ringing each and every log with an actual phone number and seeing who answered, but that would mean disclosing her own number and identity.

Not if you withhold it like they did.

It was true.

She questioned her motive. What good would it do to know who these people were anyway?

Keri disappeared without a trace.

The thought presented itself.

There may well be information inside the logs that would assist the police in finding out exactly what had happened to her.

Now that was a scary thought. The idea of being on the other end of a phone, to a potential homicidal maniac, made her heart skip a beat.

She rejected the idea of ringing anyone, and opted instead to call Jason and tell him all about her discovery. But when she tried, her call went to voicemail. He was probably still asleep.

She glanced at the rest of the files on the screen.

Why not?

She opened more transcripts, and they read like something straight out of a sex film. Nothing was spared, no words left unused, to describe the ecstasy Keri was allegedly experiencing, while talking to the stranger at the other end of the line.

And, whilst erotic, the transcripts did absolutely nothing for Rachel, who could only imagine seedy men in their underpants doing things to themselves.

She clicked on the next file, and was about to open it when she felt fingers trace the nape of her neck!

She jumped out of her seat, and turned to look behind her, but there was nobody there.

The room was empty.

But she did feel them; cold fingers, or, more specifically, what felt like the jagged edge of fingernails, scraping across her skin, raking the small hairs that resided there. The same hairs that were bristling right now.

There's nobody here, Rach, it's just your imagination!

She subconsciously rubbed the back of her neck to dissolve the sensation that was still lingering there, like a phantom limb.

She was breathing heavily, and her heart was thumping so fast, she put her hand on her chest to calm it, and that's when she noticed.

Like fog in the headlamps of a car, her breath, in the dim light of the desk lamp, was billowing out in clouds.

The room had turned ice cold.

She zipped the fleece as high as it would go.

She looked at the door, then at her desk, and then back at the door again.

Reluctantly, she walked away from the brightest part of the room, and tested the handle to make sure the door was still locked.

It was.

This made her feel slightly better.

She turned and looked back into the room.

It's empty.

Then why did it feel like somebody was watching her?

Nobody's here.

But she didn't believe it.

She stood, back against the door, and watched the empty room, as if expecting someone or something to jump out at

her.

Nothing. Just the whirring of the computer.

Eventually, she willed herself to return to the desk, and sat down, while still surveying the room with her eyes.

Okay, I'm done. If Lilly can abandon her post then so can I.

She grabbed the mouse to shut the computer down but something caught her eye. It sent a hot and cold shiver over her skin.

She stared at the screen, incredulously, wondering if her brain was misreading the transcript in front of her, but it wasn't.

Without thinking, Rachel picked up her mobile phone and opened the address book.

The two matched.

Her stomach turned over.

She read the text:

KERI:> night and day
07700 374872:> hi its me
KERI:> hello you
07700 374872:> what time will you be back
KERI:> i don't know why
07700 374872:> just wondering
KERI:> oh you missing me?
07700 374872:> what do you think?
KERI:> Ill see you soon big boy
07700 374872:> cant wait
KERI:> kay bye

Rachel gawked at the screen, and then read the transcript again, and again, and one more time.

Each time, it hit her with the same force; Jason, her boyfriend, had called here to speak with Keri. He knew her and, by the sounds of it, he knew her quite well.

It took a while for it to sink in and, as it did so, she was suddenly presented with one hideous reality. No matter how much she believed she knew about her boyfriend, she really knew nothing.

He had known Keri and he didn't tell her about it. Why? What did he have to hide?

Is he involved in her disappearance?

The thought came to her out of nowhere and it made her feel sick.

There could be a perfectly rational explanation for this. Which is?

Regardless of anything else, he lied to you. Did he lie, though? I can't remember if I asked him about Keri. Well, he certainly didn't volunteer the information.

There was only one way to find out the truth.

So, with her heart in her throat, Rachel proceeded to open the rest of the messages.

She found more graphic phone calls between Keri and her so-called clients, and a couple more between her and Jason.

Interestingly, while suggestive, the phone calls between Jason and Keri were nothing like the others, which would imply that the two were either seeing each other, or working together.

Some also mentioned Laura a few times.

Rachel remembered reading that name before. In fact, she'd seen a transcript in which Laura calls to ask Keri if she was '*on for tomorrow*'.

Rachel clicked back to the original log and wrote down the phone number. Then, she traced back through some of the other logs and, where available, wrote down some of these numbers too.

First, she dialled Laura's number and was both relieved and terrified. She was connected to a female voicemail that told her that nobody was available to take her call, to leave a message and someone would call her back.

Rachel disconnected and waited a few seconds.

She was shaking now, not just from the cold, but from the adrenaline that was surging through her veins.

Worse, she was feeling paranoid. What if she had incorrectly withheld her own caller ID? Laura, whoever she was, might be able to trace her.

She waited a few minutes.

No return call.

She paused for thought and then dialled another number, but got the voicemail of Michael Peters.

A quick search on Wikipedia told her that Michael Peters was a prominent right-wing politician. He was well known for his views on protecting the traditional institution of marriage from the perceived threat of same-sex unions. And, despite being totally turned off by politics, Rachel actually recognised the bushy white hair and teeth-filled grin.

She couldn't help but smile.

Hypocrite. Bet you thought phone sex was much safer than trawling the streets for a hooker. But you had no idea that Keri was recording your telephone conversations.

There was no doubt in Rachel's mind that the audio recordings of each call was being stored, in the same way the transcripts were, but for what purpose?

Blackmail?

She dialled other numbers, and was surprised to find herself connected to a whole group of public, and not so public, figures: judges, bankers, businessmen.

The list was long.

So that is what you were, Keri? Some kind of classy phone sex prostitute, slash blackmailer. What the hell is your connection to my boyfriend?

Rachel knew there was only one way to find out. She was going to have to confront him, but her thoughts were interrupted by a sound across the room.

She looked up and watched, in stupefied wonder, as the once locked door clicked, and slowly creaked wide open.

50 ALIVE

The patter of soft shoes, the scuffing sound of a wheeling trolley, and the faint smell of cooked breakfast wafted in from the corridor. It signalled the start of a new day at the hospital where, during the night, Elisabeth Harrison had been moved to a side room.

To those close to her, the move felt like a positive sign when, in reality, it was simply the hospital's way of freeing up vital space in Intensive Care.

Elisabeth was still tethered to an array of machines that the doctor, somewhat pragmatically, explained were the only things keeping her alive.

He had returned during the night, and had ordered regular visits by nurses, as well as hourly updates on the patient's condition.

Adam had taken the opportunity to ask the doctor if there was any more he could share about his girlfriend's condition. The doctor shook his head, and repeated that they would not know anything else until later in the morning, when the specialist had examined Elisabeth, and they had managed to discuss test results.

That was nearly five hours ago.

Now, from his position on the armchair, with his jacket over him as a makeshift blanket, Adam's eyes fluttered open, and joy spread through him like rapid pain relief.

Elisabeth was looking at him.

He sprang to his feet, and was at her bedside in one movement.

"Elisabeth, oh my God, Elisabeth," was all he could say, as he bent down to caress her matted hair.

Adam masked the fact that she was almost unrecognisable. The face that refused to be seen make-up free was now scrubbed clean, leaving behind jaundiced skin and yellow eyes. There were various lines and tubes leading in and out of her body, and an oxygen mask, affixed to her face, hissed loudly like a reptilian sentinel.

She tried to speak.

"No, no, no…don't try to speak, Elisabeth, just rest. Everything's going to be okay. You're going to be okay." He was beaming, as he caressed her hair and wiped a runaway tear off her cheek.

He was so glad to see her conscious, he could have hugged her, but he was afraid of causing pain, so instead he held her hand as his eyes began to well, "Thank God. Thank God you're still alive," he muttered.

51 HISTORY

Abbey yawned as she poured more coffee. It felt as if she had been awake for hours.

It was Sunday morning; she had been up at five and in the office by six.

She was sitting at her computer and was logged into the central archives database.

First up, would be Heron Heights. It seemed to her that the one thing that everybody had in common, was that building. Given its history with celebrities, she knew it would make an excellent backdrop to her story.

She would start with the place, and how it became so attractive to the rich and famous, then move on to introduce the tenants. It could work a bit like a soap opera; the building and the characters that existed within it.

Good.

She typed Heron Heights into the search box, and anxiously tapped her pencil as she waited for the results.

I'm never going to make the deadline. No matter how much I fool myself, I'm never going to be able to collate enough research and write the thing up before tomorrow morning, there's no…

The results were returned, and what immediately struck Abigail was how many there were.

She was hoping for some plans of the place, maybe a few articles, but instead what she received was over thirty pages filed by category; planning, building, newspaper articles.

She clicked on the articles; a series of headlines filled the page. A caption at the top of the screen informed her that the links were sorted by date:

1. LOCAL ARCHITECT WINS CONTRACT FOR TOWER BUILDING. (1936)

2. SPIRITUALIST REFUSES TO GIVE UP HOME FOR TOWER BUILDING PROJECT DESPITE RECORD PAY-OUT OFFER. (1937)

3. SPIRITUALIST DIES CLEARING THE WAY FOR TOWER BUILDING PROJECT. (1937)

4. BUILDING SITE OF TOWER BUILDING MARRED BY FATAL ACCIDENTS. (1940)

5. TOWER BUILDING TO BE EXCLUSIVE HOTEL. (1942)

6. TOWER BUILDING "AN ABOMINATION" SAYS LOCAL CLERGY. (1943)

7. TOWER BUILDING ATTRACTS RECORD MEDIA INTEREST. (1943)

8. PRE-BOOKINGS AT FAMOUS TOWER BUILDING PUTS OCCUPANCY. AT 80%. (1943)

9. RICH AND FAMOUS TURN OUT FOR OPENING OF TOWER HOTEL. (1946)

10. MOVIE STAR DIES IN MYSTERIOUS FALL. (1947)

The headlines went on and Abigail could hardly believe her eyes for each and every one of them was sensational.

She read and took notes.

The spiritualist, an eighty-six year old woman, dubbed a witch, refused to give up her home to the tower project. She was rumoured to have put a hex on all those who dared to desecrate it, and any of the land it stood on.

Stories about strange fires breaking out all over the building site went unchecked, until two men lost their lives. Fears that an arsonist may have set his or her sights on the infamous building prompted security fears; a firm was hired.

But one night, these men reported seeing 'strange blue lights'. They appeared and disappeared all over the building. They also heard the sound of a *'phantom hammerer'*, who would vanish as soon as anybody approached to investigate. Some of the men also claimed to have seen some of the building's famous gargoyles come to life.

By day, workers reported the spontaneous disappearance and reappearance of tools, from one side of the building site to another. As well as nails and other objects mysteriously falling from ceilings.

Abby laughed out loud. She could not believe what she was reading, for the content seemed much more suited to a supernatural novel than the feature pages of a major tabloid. Nonetheless, she read on.

A local clergyman had branded the gothic design of Heron Heights, *"An abomination - the foetus of a devil worshipper. Satan has built his palace on earth."*

Yet, despite all of the negative publicity, it seemed that The Obelisk, as it was then called, went from strength to strength. It attracted a lot of publicity because of its unusual and rather ostentatious design, as well as the amount of money that was spent building and fitting it with the most opulent décor.

It became the talk of the city. The place to stay for anybody who was anybody.

But disaster struck, seven years ago, when a mysterious fire started in one of the apartments. Four people died in the blaze, and the water devastation inflicted, in the effort to bring the blaze under control, caused millions of pounds worth of damage.

However, the real controversy came when it emerged that The Obelisk's owners had falsified certain documents, invalidating their insurance. The scam was all over the papers, and soon after, the consortium that owned the building went into receivership, throwing the building's future into uncertainty. That was until a buyer stepped in: Harrison Enterprises; a division of the Harrison Publishing group.

Abigail nearly choked on her coffee. She couldn't have dreamed up such a brilliant twist.

He owns the place.

She read on; five years ago, they shut the building down and launched a major rebuild and refurbishment program. The hotel rooms were merged and converted into spacious, luxurious apartments with all of today's modern conveniences, and a few special touches. State of the art technology was installed, not only to secure the building, but to monitor everything from lighting to climate control. Everything that could be done was done to dispel the building's bad reputation, and to inspire confidence in future tenants.

Two years later, The Obelisk was re-launched as Heron Heights, named after what should have been a series of stone bird sculptures, built into the summit of the building. However, a commissioning error at the time led to the delivery of a collection of grotesque gargoyles that, after much litigation, were eventually installed in their stead, thus contributing to the building's gothic design and demonic repute.

Heron Height's marketing literature described it as a modern apartment building in the heart of London, boasting all of the mod cons, whilst retaining the original charm that had, over the years, made the building the go-to destination for dignitaries and celebrities from around the world.

The rebrand worked.

Before long, the apartment building had achieved ninety percent occupancy, despite overinflated rental fees.

Thus, indirectly, Heron Heights had, once again, established its presence in magazines around the world since everybody who had lived in it, loved it, and everybody who hadn't, wanted to.

And, as if that wasn't enough, there was still a regular stream of articles to keep the building well and truly in the media spotlight.

Such as, the recent mysterious disappearance of Keri Paxton, and now, the death of the Stanton's boy.

Abigail was grinning from ear to ear.

This was all so bloody incredible! There was enough drama in the building alone to make her story work and the best was yet to come; Rupert Harrison, the multi-millionaire, who lost his brother in a tragic accident and his mother to suicide, owned the building. He had met this unknown, Ashley Marshall, who was making a name by publishing highly controversial books; from adulterous politicians to

Metropolitan Police scandals.

But what else do we know about her?

Nothing, until now.

This is brilliant! The script is literally writing itself!

Abigail started tapping away at her keyboard. Her treatment included everything about the building, the mysterious happenings, the construction tragedies, the Harrison tragedies, and even the gargoyle blunder.

When she had done that, she refuelled on coffee and went back to the archive.

There wasn't much about Ashley Marshall. Nothing that she hadn't already picked up from the papers regarding the Jackie Harris book, which wasn't much.

Then again, there was the disappearance of Jackie Harris' manuscript. Now that was another story, she would link the two but she needed more background on Marshall first.

She went back to work.

52 COMPANY

Ashley had mooched around the apartment on her own for most of the afternoon, after dropping Rupert off at the hospital.

He knew he wouldn't be able to see Elisabeth the whole time, but just being at the hospital and being there to support Adam made him feel better.

Ashley knew there was no chance of her getting in to see Elisabeth and every chance of Elisabeth not wanting to see her. So, she decided to spend the rest of the day back at the penthouse, supervising the army of professional cleaners drafted in to return the dining room to its former glory.

She had barely closed the door on the workers when she received the phone call from Rupert. He was in very high spirits and it was infectious; he'd, relatively speaking -

through rudimentary sign language - managed to communicate with Elisabeth.

Ashley's heart soared. To hear him so happy after what had happened was just wonderful.

He told her that he would get a cab home, but she refused, saying she could do with the fresh air and would be right over to pick him up.

That was over half an hour ago.

Now, as twilight descended to collect another day, and after multiple laps around the multi-storey to find a free parking space, she finally found one and killed the engine.

She picked up her phone to text her location to Rupert and smiled at the thought of him. While keen to give him his space at a time like this, she also felt an overwhelming compulsion to be near him, and she'd missed him.

His text reply came back immediately, stating he was already walking towards her.

She returned her phone to her handbag and, whilst there, rummaged inside for lipstick.

Then, she unfolded the sun visor, slid open the mirror and drew in a sharp breath, when she saw the reflection of a pair of blue eyes glaring at her from the backseat!

Ashley screamed, wrenched the door handle, and almost fell out of the car, just as a young couple were walking by.

They momentarily paused their chatter to give her an odd look.

She was about to call to them, but when she glanced back at her car, door still ajar, key-alarm ringing and courtesy lights shining brightly, she saw that the backseat was empty.

She ran trembling fingers through her hair as she inspected the space around her.

There was nobody there, but the couple who were just getting into a small vehicle three cars down.

On the street below, teenagers in baggy clothing laughed at something amusing, as the streetlights clicked on; darkness was nigh.

She turned back to the innocent-looking empty car, as a cold wind blew up out of nowhere.

"Ash?"

The voice shot through her, and she whirled around to see Rupert with a big smile that instantly faded the moment he saw her expression.

"Oh, I'm sorry," he said, walking up to her, "I didn't mean to make you jump."

She threw her arms around him, without responding.

"Hey, now that's a welcome. It's good to see you too," he said, squeezing her tightly. "Thanks for coming to get me."

Ashley said nothing. She just held him.

Sensing the lingering embrace, Rupert said, "It's okay. She's going to be okay."

Eventually, she emerged from the embrace and he searched her face.

"Are you alright?"

Ashley glanced at the car door, and then back at him. He seemed so happy, did she really want to ruin that right now?

"I'm fine," she said, tucking her hair behind her ears. "I'm all right. Just pleased things are looking better. How is she?"

"Well, she isn't out of the woods yet, but at least she's conscious and communicating."

"Are the doctors any the wiser?"

He shook his head, gravely. "Not really, but they're still looking, and she's stable for now so, in the absence of anything else, I'm happy to take that. Adam's still with her."

"He looked grief stricken yesterday."

"He was. Is. That guy hasn't left her side."

Ashley was going to retort that she didn't deserve him, but instead she just nodded, "He loves her."

"As much as you love me?" He asked.

"I don't think that's possible," she said, touching his cheek, tenderly.

He nuzzled against her hand. Then, studied her in the fading light; there was definitely something there. In her eyes. "Are you sure you're okay?" He asked, angling himself so he could see better.

She thought about it. She wanted to tell him, and she would, but there was a time and a place, this simply wasn't the time. "Yes, I'm fine, honestly."

"Good."

He walked over to the passenger side of the car, opened the door and was about to climb in when he noticed that she wasn't following him. Instead, she was standing, staring at the driver's door.

"Ash?"

She looked up.

"Sorry," she said, "just daydreaming," yet she still wasn't moving.

Rupert cocked his head and smiled, "Okay, so are you going to get in or did you want to stay here?"

Reluctantly, she climbed in, glancing, as casually as she could at the empty backseat.

"I'm so hungry; I really fancy a steak right now." He stated, rubbing his cold hands together. "Are you hungry? Shall we get something to eat on the way home? Better still, let's stop off somewhere," he said, excitedly.

"Okay," she said, pulling then clicking in her seatbelt and starting the engine.

She reversed the car, giving the backseat a thorough look as she did so, and then drove off, out of the car park and away from there.

53 THE END

"Doctor says I shouldn't stay too long," Adam said with a smile, as he stroked Elisabeth's forehead.

Elisabeth's response was to close her eyes and turn her face away from him for, even in the dim light of the small room, she felt ugly and strange.

Everything around her seemed blurry, like a dream; the bedside table, the flowers that Rupert had bought her, the lamp, the phone, the swing doors, and the sofa. Everything was there, tangible yet dreamlike, as if she wasn't really lying in bed but was standing outside, looking through a dirty window.

Somewhere in the distance, she could hear the hollow beep of the heart monitor, and the demonic slow downed voice of a doctor being paged, and what sounded like Adam rambling on about getting her on her feet again soon.

The sounds continued to slur and jumble, but Elisabeth wasn't listening, her gaze had fallen on the fire glass portal in the door, and what she saw beyond it; a pair of steely blue eyes.

The same eyes she had seen in the club that night, the same ones that belonged to the man that had violated her. The one that had planted something inside her, something so malignant, it fed off her very being.

Her eyes widened with terror, tears leaked down her face, and a shrill alarm from one of the machines pierced the air.

Adam stopped his mumbling and was calling her name, but he noticed that she wasn't listening; she was too busy staring at the double doors, as if she could see someone beyond them, something behind the glass.

"Elisabeth?" He called, but she was not responding. "Elisabeth? Elisabeth?"

He would have shaken her, but he was afraid of hurting her. Instead, he moved into her line of vision, with his back to the door.

But her staring continued, to the point where she angled her head so that her wild eyes could look around him.

More alarms filled the air as the beeping of her heart monitor increased in speed, anxiously demanding attention.

Adam ran to the door, pushed it open and looked up and down the corridor.

The lights had been dimmed. It was deserted, as if everybody had abandoned them.

"HELP!" He yelled. "NURSE! SOMEONE! I NEED SOME HELP HERE!"

He stepped back into the room.

Elisabeth was still staring through him with glassy eyes full of fear. Eyes that saw someone standing directly behind him.

Her gaze was so convincing, he actually turned to check, but he could see no one.

But there was someone or something. It stood in the shadows, wearing a long black coat, and it was grinning.

Like the grim reaper, it was waiting to possess, to claim its latest soul, and the anticipation of this filled it exquisite anticipation.

Adam rushed back to the bed and spoke desperately, "Elisabeth? Elisabeth, darling, what's wrong? What's wrong?"

But his only reply was the cacophony of alarm bells and buzzers that resonated loudly around the room and his brain.

He slammed his hand against the red alarm button on the wall, as the pupils of Elisabeth's eyes rolled back into her skull.

"NOOO! No, Elisabeth, don't you do this to me! Don't you do this! Come back!" he yelled, gripping her arms, and almost pulling her up from the bed.

But she was unresponsive.

"Elisabeth! Elisabeth! Don't you do this to me! Don't you fucking do this to me!" he hissed. His voice no longer fearful, but full of rage. "Get back here right now, you selfish bitch! I didn't spend the last two years putting up with your shit for nothing! NO! You can't leave. I won't let you! I won't let you!"

He was shaking her now. Her lifeless body moving, like a rag doll, in his grip.

Suddenly, he felt hands on him, pulling him backwards; a night porter strained to tear him away as two nurses and a doctor rushed around the bed and desperately tried to revive their patient.

Adam was still yelling obscenities as the porter dragged him, literally kicking and screaming, out of the room and down the corridor, where they planned to administer a sedative to the man, they believed, was so traumatised by the loss of his girlfriend, he was having a psychotic break.

Little did they know that Adam's violent reaction was not to the passing of his lover, but to the fact that his plan, several years in the making, had – to the sound of a flatlining heart monitor - come to an abrupt end.

54 BAD THINGS

When Rupert and Ashley entered the lobby, they saw a woman sitting on the leather divan, with her head bowed in her hands.

Ashley recognised her immediately and went over.

"Isabella?"

The woman looked up with a mixture of relief and concern on her face.

"Oh thank God, you are here." Her Polish accent was thick in her desperation.

"What's wrong?" Ashley asked, sitting next to her whilst Rupert was called away by one of the security men.

"I have been so worried, Ashley. I don't know where else to go. I tried to call you, but you weren't home, and I have tried his office but no answer."

Ashley took the woman's hands and notice that she was trembling. "Now, Isabella, calm down, and tell me what happened."

"It's James. I haven't heard from him since yesterday, and he was supposed to pick me up from the airport this morning, but he no show. I know he come to see you for dinner yesterday, but when he didn't call or answer his phone…"

She trailed off here as tears filled her eyes.

Ashley looked across at Rupert, who was standing by the security desk, using the phone. "When did you last hear from him?" she asked.

"Last night. He called me from the office and told me that he was coming over to see you."

"No," Ashley bit her lip. "We didn't see him last night. He was supposed to come over, but he didn't show and then…"

Ashley didn't finish here sentence. She didn't really know how to explain what happened, and how they'd all completely forgotten about James, as a result.

"…I keep calling you, him and no answer…" Isabella was continuing. "I even went round his home and there's no sign of his car. I'm worried, Ashley. I see bad things."

"What?"

Isabella looked into Ashley's eyes and froze. "My Got."

"What?" Ashley asked, alarmed.

"You too."

"Me too what?"

"Bad things."

She didn't know what to say, but Isabella's words were making her feel very anxious.

"Isabella, I don't know…"

Ashley broke off here when she noticed Rupert walking back to them. His face, stoical, ashen.

She jumped up from her seat. "What's wrong?"

He looked at her with vacant eyes, and said, "Elisabeth is dead."

Ashley gasped, and Isabella began to cry.

55 THE CONFESSION

"I told you, Jay, I don't want to go," Rachel said, dumping the dishes into the sink and squirting them with detergent.

It was Monday evening. They had just finished eating dinner.

Rachel had had over a day to consider how, exactly, she was going to confront her boyfriend about his relationship with Keri, the same Keri who had mysteriously vanished.

And it was precisely that last bit that she struggled with. Each and every time she thought about the two of them, she couldn't help but wonder if her boyfriend had had anything do with her disappearance. But then she'd go on to question why she'd even had the thought in the first place. Was her subconscious trying to tell her something or had she merely watched way too many thrillers?

Either way, the last thing she fancied doing right now was going to another one of those parties, and sucking up to Jason's so-called business colleagues.

At least not until they had this out.

She scrubbed the dishes.

"Why not?"

"I told you, I just don't feel like it."

"Why not?"

"Because those places make me feel uncomfortable, Jay. Last time I walked in on two women doing lines in the bloody toilets!"

"That's not everyone, Rach," Jason said as casually as he could, thrusting his hands into his pockets.

She looked at him, incredulously. "It was two more than I expected."

Jason reeled in his irritation, "So what? If they do drugs, it's their business, not ours."

"Well, it becomes our business, Jay, when we start to socialise with them."

"It didn't bother you the last two times we've been there."

She threw him an indignant look, "Well it bothers me now. And I didn't say anything because you told me those people were your investors. Why else do you think I put up with the slimy bastards feeling me up? I wanted to make a good impression for you."

"Yes, exactly," Jason leant over the sink, trying to distract her attention from the washing up to look at him. "And you did so well, babe. They were really impressed with you. Think about what this could do for my career. A bit of harmless flirtation isn't going to hurt anybody, is it?"

She stopped what she was doing. "Do you know what astounds me, Jay?"

He shrugged.

"How normal this all seems to you. Let them touch your butt, let them paw you, soon you'll be asking me to give out blowjobs!"

Jason said nothing.

Rachel looked up at him, and a thought crossed her mind. A terrible thought, one she wanted to dismiss as quickly as it had appeared, but she couldn't. She could not dismiss it, for there was something in Jason's expression that made her think she wasn't that far from the truth.

She shook her head. "You're fucking unbelievable," she

seethed, then snapped back to her dishwashing.

Jason just stared at her. "What the hell is wrong with you?"

No reply. Just scrubbing.

"Rach? What's the problem?"

"You're the fucking problem!" She yelled, finally giving him her eyes.

She was angry. He could see it now, and this wasn't just about the party. This was about something else.

He watched her scrub and rescrub the same pan.

"Rach, if you don't…"

"…did you have something to do with Keri Paxton's disappearance?" She blurted.

"What?"

"You heard me, Jay. Did you have something to do with Keri Paxton's disappearance, yes or no? It's a simple question."

"Is that what this is about? Some bird we don't even know."

"You know her," Rachel threw at him. "You seemed to know her really well, despite the fact that you've been acting like you didn't."

"Rach, I don't know what you think you know but…"

"…I don't think I know, Jay. I know it. I have the transcripts and recordings of your conversations with her."

He straightened. "What?"

"That's right. She kept a record of all of her conversations with all of her men, including you."

Jason's face had suddenly lost its colour.

Rachel nodded, "Thought so."

"It's not what you think," he said, quickly.

"Then why don't you tell me, Jay, because right now, right now I could quite easily report you to the police."

He looked at her, aghast, "And tell them what? That I happened to know some girl who decided to up and leave without telling anyone."

"I think we both know that you knew her better than most."

"So what, you think I killed her, is that it?"

"Did you?"

She met his gaze.

"Jesus," he whispered. He looked hurt. "You really think

that little of me, Rach? I thought you loved me."

She felt the look on his face dilute her resolve, but she resisted it. "Why didn't you tell me you knew her?"

He swallowed. "What the fuck did you expect me to say, Rach? Oh hello, thanks for giving up everything you know to come down here and be with me, oh and by the way, you know that bird that's gone missing? Well, I happened to bang her a couple of times? Come on, Rach, I was scared. You'd just got here and you were so excited. Then all the weird shit started to happen..."

"...You could have said something..."

"...What? Why? What possible reason could I have to tell you about that?"

"How about because I asked?"

"You didn't ask, Rach. Not directly. You just kept talking about her."

"Now you're just splitting hairs," she turned back to the dishes.

"I'm not. Think about it, babe. It just isn't relevant to us. It was in the past. You're my future, Rachel, can't you see that?"

She looked at him. His eyes were welling up, and she wanted to fling her arms around him, but not so fast. She was still processing all of this.

He was right, though, wasn't he? There was nothing in the transcripts to suggest that Keri was anything more than some girl he used to see. And, his not telling her may well seem like he had something to hide but, seriously, could this man, the one she knew she wanted to marry, really be involved in the girl's disappearance?

She said nothing.

Instead, she proceeded to scrub the obstinate encrustation from the pan.

"Rach?"

He could tell that her stance had changed, because the tension in her shoulders had disappeared now.

He watched as the vigorous scrubbing shook her body, causing the runaway strands of hair from her ponytail to wiggle in front of her face, and her backside to move so enticingly, he wanted to unzip and push up behind her. But he knew now wasn't the time, she wouldn't be receptive and, besides, he had a job to do.

He sighed heavily, leaned up against the sink, folded his arms and then spoke, "I didn't want to tell you this, Rach. But given the amount of hurt I've already caused you, I think it's time I told you everything."

He waited for her to stop and turn to him. She didn't, but he knew she was listening. "Things aren't going as well as I've made out."

Now she stopped and looked up.

He forced a laugh. "In fact, things are pretty shitty, actually."

"What do you mean?" she asked, warily.

Yes!

"Well, I didn't want to say anything because I didn't want you to be disappointed. I wanted you to be proud of me."

"Jay, what are you talking about?" She said, sternly. Then, noticing her tone, she added, "You know I'm proud of you."

"I know, but you probably won't feel the same, once I tell you the truth about the kind of fuck up I am." He shook his head away from her, "I thought I could pull off this deal but I, well, I overstretched, financially. And now the bank doesn't want to know me anymore," he said, sadly.

Rachel heard pain in his voice and it tugged at her love for him.

"Oh Jay," she wiped her hands on her shorts. Then, she turned his head to face her, and wanted to crumble when she saw the tears in his eyes. His lovely, brown eyes that were now brimming with sadness. A little boy that had lost the one thing he treasured most.

"Oh baby." She touched his arms and then caressed his face.

Go for the kill!

"I'm sorry, Rach. I'm sorry I'm such a disappointment to you."

"Stop saying that. You aren't a disappointment to me. I love you."

"I just wanted to give you more. I wanted to give you the

life that you deserve. Show you how much you mean to me, and I fucked it up."

He screwed his face in anger.

"Oh, you dope. You think I fell in love with you for what you could give me? It's not that, Jay. It's you. You know me, I'm a survivor. Working is all I know. I didn't want to be a kept woman anyway."

He nodded while allowing a few tears to escape. Then, a great idea popped into his head.

He swallowed hard, "Just, you seemed really into that Harrison bloke and his missus and I just wanted to…"

"Shhh," she hushed him by placing a finger on his mouth, and smiled with deep affection. "You think I want you to be like Rupert?"

He nodded, for he was unable to speak, such were the emotions he seemed to be wrestling with.

Gotcha!

"You couldn't be wronger. Of course I admire Rupert, he's a good man and he's achieved a lot. But that's only admiration. But you, I love you, Jay. I gave up my life to be with you. And, as much as I love this stuff, it's nowhere near as important to me as you are, but you need to be honest with me, Jay. We need to be in this together."

He pulled her to him. "I am sorry, Rach. I'm so sorry if I've been a bastard recently. Just with all this going on and not being able to tell you, it's been killing me."

She kissed his ear and his cheek. "Good, then let that be a lesson to you. I love you. You should know that you can tell me anything, *anything.*" She reiterated. "Just like now, I want you to tell me everything about the business, so we can decide on the next step, *together.*"

Jason smiled a sly smile that changed instantly, to a mixture of sadness and hope, as soon as he broke the embrace, and their eyes met.

And so they sat on the sofa and talked.

Rachel listened patiently as Jason weaved his story about how much his product had suffered, and how difficult it was to get people to invest in his computer programs.

He went on to explain how, these days, it wasn't just about

the product's capabilities, but it was also about the brand. He told her how he had neglected the importance of this at his peril, and how he was now suffering for it.

The only way to truly get on in his business was to woo the real titans of the industry, and have them recommend him to their peers. But to do that, he needed money and the right connections.

After a lot of hard work, he'd managed to forge the right contacts, and had even convinced some of them to invest. In fact, it was their money that paid for the apartment at Heron Heights, and financed work on his computer program, but he couldn't afford to sit back, he had to keep networking with these people, and make his presence felt to other potential investors and buyers.

So what was involved?

Nothing much.

Just keep attending these functions, small talk the fat cats, charm them and, yes if necessary, even flirt a little. Anything to get them to write the cheques.

This event, the one he had asked her to go to, would be major. Anybody who was anybody would be there, and he'd managed to get an invite.

All Rachel had to do was, be her usual charming self, and if the crusty old men took a fancy to her, so what? It's not as if they could have her. But a bit of charm, and yes, flirting may well seduce the cash that he so desperately needed out of them.

"You mean, like a prostitute?" She asked, bluntly.

He stared at her.

This was going to be harder than he thought.

56 THE CROWS

Elisabeth's funeral took place a week after her death.

Her body was laid to rest on the family's estate, next to her parents' graves.

Adam insisted that the funeral happen as soon as possible, since Elisabeth would not have wanted to have been kept waiting even in death. Similarly, he campaigned to have the will read, without delay, as the whole thing was distressing enough without having to unnecessarily draw it out longer than need be.

Rupert agreed.

Thus, on a blustery cold Sunday morning, the small cortège slowly snaked its way to a copse at the top of a hill that overlooked the estate. There, among gnarled and naked trees, that had long been stripped of their summer beauty, a grave had been neatly carved out of the earth.

The parish pastor spoke kind words about a strong woman, beloved cousin and friend, who would be dearly missed. All to the cawing soundtrack of a murder of crows that, like the ravens at the Tower of London, had lived among these trees for generations.

These professional mourners added a unique sombreness to the occasion that had, very few of those gathered, in floods of tears.

Rupert, dressed in a black suit, stood at the edge of his cousin's grave, and wept openly for the woman who had become a sister and surrogate mother to him.

Elisabeth Harrison may have been the queen bitch to many, but she was the queen of hearts to him.

Rupert was most likely one of the very few who truly understood that her worse fault was that she cared too deeply. She gave her heart completely and her love unreservedly. Ironically, it was these very things that, over the years, would prove to be her weakness, and the source of much emotional pain that, in turn, made her the caustic person that everybody knew.

The gale that was blowing around the mourners, pulling at hats and tugging at clothes, snatched the rose from Rupert's hand and tossed it onto the coffin as Ashley slid a comforting arm around the man who was, once again, being subjected to the anguish of loss.

Opposite them, also dressed in a tight-fitting black suit, with pale white fists, an expressionless and composed demeanour, Adam stood against the blustery onslaught that had now released a shower of sleet. He was visibly trembling from the cold, but he felt nothing for his mind was elsewhere, crawling over various thoughts like fingers on a glass casket, behind which, lay the documents to his salvation.

The only question was, how soon could he get at them?

At three o' clock that same afternoon, the few people mentioned in Elisabeth's will, congregated in the library, where Rupert had spent most of his time, when visiting his uncle as a child.

As per Elisabeth's last wishes, just two chairs had been set out in front of her father's desk. Her lawyer, a tall man with a mop of salt and pepper hair, sat where her father once sat and, without any further ado, read the contents of the will.

Ashley, who had specifically been asked not to attend the reading, sat outside amongst the artefacts that had shaped Elisabeth's life; family portraits, antique furnishings, and everything else that symbolised power and wealth.

It hadn't been ten minutes since Ashley had watched Rupert and Adam disappear behind a thick wooden door, when an ear-piercing shrill smashed through it and reverberated around the building.

It was Adam, and he was racked with grief.

The same grief that Ashley later learned was not a derivative of the death of his girlfriend, but the cold fact that, although recently modified, Elisabeth Harrison's will left him absolutely nothing.

She had even been specific enough to say that, although his obliging behaviour may have suggested the contrary, it was her belief that Adam had been with her just for her money. It was for this reason that, should he outlive her, she wanted him thrown out like the trash that he was, penniless.

As for the rest of her estate: two million was to go to her favourite charity, Alcoholics Anonymous, and the rest was to go to the one person who meant everything in the world to her, Rupert.

Rupert went on to explain that the will was relatively new, and it was believed that Elisabeth wrote it the day after a booze binge that had poisoned her blood, and nearly killed her.

Apparently, it was that near death experience that prompted her to summon her lawyer, and have him witness her scribble her final wishes.

Ashley couldn't help but wonder, had the will been updated more recently, if Elisabeth would have been spiteful enough to exclude Rupert for wanting to marry her. He dismissed the idea, stating that Elisabeth may not have liked Ashley, but it was only because she felt protective of him, and that she would never have been so vindictive.

Ashley nodded, thoughtfully, as they drove home towards London.

57 THE CURTAIN CALL

The bistro was situated on one of the many quiet back streets of London's West End.

Frequented mostly by theatregoers, *'The Curtain Call'* was a tidy little place bustling with activity, the aroma of coffee and fresh baked cookies.

It was lunchtime and the place was packed with people.

Rupert had to push his way through the throng to get to the annex at the back where his contact agreed to meet him. The idea was that there would be so many people in the eatery, nobody would notice them tucked away in a small cubicle.

When Rupert arrived, his contact, a short man in his late forties with cropped black hair and a pair of spectacles, was drinking tea and munching his way through a bacon sandwich.

When he saw Rupert, he smiled, wiped his hands on a paper napkin, and quickly swallowed his food to speak. "Good to see you again, Mr Harrison," he mumbled, still chewing and shaking Rupert's hand.

"Hello," Rupert said, squeezing into the seat opposite.

"Sorry to drag you out here, but when you specified absolute discretion, I figured this might be a good place to meet."

Rupert didn't particularly agree, but he said nothing. After all, this man was supposed to be the professional.

"I love this place," he said, taking another bite from his sandwich and then garbling, "Excellent bacon rolls, and the chocolate chip muffins, hmm," he closed his beady green eyes in ecstasy, "absolutely pukka."

He gestured to a plate of them on the table.

Rupert declined with a smile. He felt uncomfortable sitting opposite that man. He didn't like the situation, it felt wrong.

He felt that he was being deceitful, but what other choice did he have? He needed to know the truth, and he had made a pact with himself to do whatever he could to find out, including hiring a private investigator.

But that was two weeks ago, before everything else, before he buried his cousin. In fact, he'd actually forgotten about the man until he left several voicemail messages on his phone. He told him that he had the information he requested, and that he would find it very interesting.

So Rupert told himself that he wasn't spying on Ashley, but just wanted to ensure that his fiancé was alright. Of course, he could have just asked her but, like most affairs of the heart, that would have been too easy, and probably wouldn't have revealed the whole truth.

And he needed to know everything because he loved her. He wanted to move on with their life together, and he couldn't do that if he was constantly wondering about secrets. That's why he wanted this man to dispense with the small talk and just get down to business.

"What do you have for me?"

The man laughed. "I see, just want to get down to business. That's fine, I'm like that too. I like to just cut to the chase, none of that small talk crap. I just thought that if we had a cup of tea, you know, maybe some of these lovely muffins, you would be able to relax…"

The man stopped in mid-sentence when he noticed the look on Rupert's face. He reached down, into a rucksack, and pulled out an orange A4 envelope.

"Of course, you only asked for the generic service so I have only compiled the basics. But, if you wanted to upgrade to the premium service, I would be more than happy to…"

"…What did you find out?" Rupert asked, as quietly as was possible, considering the din in the room.

The man pulled out a piece of paper, and handed it across to Rupert, who studied it with deep interest as his companion narrated.

"It seems that Ashley Marshall was a bit of a rebel as a kid. She was born into a relatively wealthy family, her father owned a construction company; she's had a fairly privileged upbringing."

"Owned?"

"Yeah, he died a few years back. I think I included it in there, construction accident. Built the business from scratch, turned over a couple of million in the first year, and it took off from there. Had a bit of a reputation for being a control freak, though, you know the kind that likes to keep his hands dirty. He often helped on construction. Only, one day, a crucial safety check was missed, and Robert Marshall died, along with two other men, when the scaffolding collapsed."

My God, Ashley.

"Apparently, the girl was kind of brainy, what you would call a 'straight A' student. She was studying law at Kings when the accident happened. She was your typical daddy's girl, never got over losing im'. The two of them were close. After the funeral, she refused to go back to college, opted instead to travel the world with some of her inheritance. Seems she didn't get on with her mum; hasn't seen her since she left home."

The man took another bite from his sandwich and washed it down with tea.

Rupert's mind reeled as he attempted to process everything

he was hearing.

"What about a picture?" he asked.

The man smiled. "Sorry, you asked for the generic package. And that is just text. If you wanted…"

Rupert waved the man quiet.

It wasn't that he begrudged spending the money. Rupert wanted the generics because he somehow thought that by not asking this man to dig up every personal aspect of her life, he would somehow feel less of a shit.

It hadn't worked.

But he needed to know. After all, this was one of the reasons why his first marriage had failed.

His ex, along with being a gold digger, failed to tell Rupert that she was madly in love, and that it wasn't with him, but a slimy club owner, who cared for her less than he did the scantily-dressed girls he employed.

"Have you been there?" Rupert asked.

The investigator stopped his chewing and looked up. "Been where?"

"To her house."

The investigator paused. "Well yeah, it's standard practice when investigating…"

"I want the address."

"What?"

"I want the family's address."

The investigator shook his head. "Oh no, mate, I don't think you should…"

"…Why not?"

"Well, for a start, her mum still lives there, and you know, in cases like these, you have to be discreet. You can't just drop by for tea and biscuits. Especially if you don't want your lady to know that you know. No, not a good idea, not a good idea at all."

Rupert thought about this and then said, "You know, I often think that some of my best decisions have stemmed from bad ideas, but I still hired you, didn't I?"

Rupert leaned forward and repeated very slowly, "I want that address."

58 ASHLEY MARSHALL

Half an hour later, Rupert was steering the Lexus out of London and onto the M2, southeast towards Canterbury.

He drove fast under a thick cotton wool sky of grey clouds, that some forecasters believed would bring early snow.

The drive took longer than the satnav had originally predicted, with traffic and road works.

He'd been on the road for nearly two hours before he turned off the motorway, and onto a narrow winding B-road that snaked through woods and grassy hills. It delivered him somewhere in the Kent Downs, before the chequered flag on his car's digital map told him that he was finally nearing his destination.

He drove through an archway of spindly trees where branches, like long bony fingers, reached down and almost touched the car.

To his left, a deep glassy river raced him, to his right, yet another copse of trees.

After rounding another bend, he turned right and drove down a steep road, into a valley, parallel with the river.

A sign welcomed him to *'Acorn Falls.'*

He drove through an avenue of manicured lawns leading to an array of large stone houses, set back amidst the cover of old oak trees.

There was no doubt that Acorn Falls was exclusive to those with a healthy bank account.

It became apparent to Rupert why Ashley never appeared remotely interested in his wealth. It was so obviously something that she had grown up with and had most probably tried to escape, as rebel children often do, for most of her life.

He turned at the post office corner, passed a field called Acorn Green and then turned left into Erdington Road, where he stopped the car outside number one.

It was a large stone building that resembled more a plantation mansion than a typically British house.

He emerged from the car to the roar of rushing water. It seemed that the river had followed him here. He looked over to see it cascading over a mini waterfall that sent a cloud of mist fizzing into the air.

He looked around, the place was surrounded by trees, each standing tall and regal, like centurions on patrol.

He imagined what it might be like here in the summer, when the sun shone in a blue sky and warmed the colours of this Constable painting of a place. The place where Ashley had grown up.

Suddenly, he felt sad.

Why Ashley? Why didn't you want me to see this place with you? Why didn't you want to tell me about your parents?

He looked up to the double front doors of the house. He did not doubt that the answer would be found behind them.

He walked up the few stone steps and rang the doorbell.

Within seconds, he could hear footsteps and then the door opened, revealing a tall woman in her late sixties.

She was elegantly dressed in grey trousers, white blouse and red cardigan, with shoulder length silver-white hair that hung neatly over a slim face housing lucid grey eyes. A bead of pearls hung around her delicate long neck, complimenting an identical set of earrings.

Ashley's mother?

"Can I help you?" the woman asked in a cultured husky voice.

"Mrs Marshall?"

"Yes," the woman replied, curiously.

Rupert froze.

Of all the thoughts that had coursed through his mind on the way down here, he had not considered this moment, the moment where he would come face-to-face with Ashley's mother.

What should he do? Introduce himself as her fiancé?

And give her a heart attack? No!

"My name is Rupert Harrison," he blurted out, as if the name would mean something to this woman, who stood, patiently waiting for him to speak. "I'm here about your daughter."

There was a flicker of interest behind the woman's eyes.

"My daughter?"

"Yes, Ashley, Ashley Marshall."

"What about her?" the woman asked without emotion.

Rupert looked around them and then back at the woman. "May I come inside?"

Mrs Marshall looked Rupert up and down, as if she could discern his intentions by checking him over. And he did look respectable enough, in his blue corduroys and cashmere pullover. Moreover, there was something vaguely familiar about this man, although Mrs Marshall couldn't quite put her finger on it.

"What did you say your name was?" she asked.

"Rupert Harrison."

"Rupert Harrison as in Harrison Publishing?" she asked dubiously.

Rupert smiled and nodded.

"Why, of course," she said, in amazement, "I saw you on TV the other day. Do come in," she added, stepping aside.

The house could have been straight out of a luscious movie set; grey flagstone flooring, a sweeping mahogany staircase, with magnolia painted walls, and canvasses depicting life across the centuries.

Rupert took everything in for this was Ashley's childhood home and this elegant woman, who was leading him through the hall, was her mother.

The lounge was spacious, and tastefully decorated in creams and reds, with a gigantic window seat that offered a view over the river.

"You have a very beautiful home, Mrs Marshall," Rupert said, appreciatively.

"Thank you. How very nice of you to say. May I offer you a beverage of some kind? Some tea perhaps?"

"That would be nice, thank you," Rupert said, admiring the view from the window, all the time imagining Ashley here as a little girl.

"I'll be right back. In the meantime, please make yourself comfortable," the woman said, and left the room.

Rupert pulled himself away from the window and looked around. He wasn't surprised to see a gleaming, black Steinway piano to one side of the room. On top of it, were silver photo frames depicting smiling people in various casual and formal poses. Many of them were of a heavy set man with grey hair, dressed in a tuxedo. Rupert had to look twice, because in one of them it looked like he was shaking the hand of a well-known politician, and he was.

In other pictures, the man, who presumably was Mr Marshall, was posing with a woman Rupert recognised as his elegant hostess, only a few years younger. There were also some older looking pictures, tinged in sepia. One of them, in particular, caught his eye. It was the only one of its kind and it had captured a happy family beach scene; a fit young man with black hair was holding a little girl in his arms. They were laughing and looking towards the camera, as was a familiar looking blonde. Both were tickling the little girl who was doubled over in fits of laughter, but whose eyes just happened to be looking past the camera's lens. It was a charming family portrait, and it tugged at Rupert's heart.

Ashley.

He took the frame in his hands and smiled; the little girl couldn't have been much older than ten with pigtails. Given the tone of the image, he couldn't tell the pigmentation of the eyes or the hair.

This picture was taken a long time ago, fifteen, twenty years or more. The hair could be different now.

"Margate," the woman said, as she deposited a silver tray on the coffee table.

Rupert turned around still clutching the picture.

"You know, people always turn their noses up at Margate, but I'm quite fond of the place, it reminds me of very happy times."

Rupert smiled. "Yes, you all do look very happy in this picture."

"We were," Mrs Marshall fondly agreed.

"Is this your husband?"

"Robert, yes. Such a wonderful man too, beautiful and very kind," she said fondly. "Please, come and sit down."

Rupert carefully replaced the picture and complied.

He sat in an armchair opposite Mrs Marshall, and with his back to the window, so that what little daylight that was left shone off the woman's hair, and sparkled in her grey misty eyes.

Mrs Marshall was an attractive woman, but far from the blonde beauty Rupert had just been admiring in the photograph.

"Sugar?" she asked as she poured the tea.

"No, thank you, just white."

There was silence, but for the humming of the river and the chinking of china, as Mrs Marshall prepared the beverage.

"So, what's on your mind, Mr Harrison?" she asked, handing Rupert his tea.

Rupert smiled at the woman's directness and couldn't help but think of Ashley, "Well, I'm not quite sure how to put this."

Mrs Marshall smiled encouragingly. "Anyway you like."

"Well, Ashley and I, um, wow, I feel like a teenager. We've been seeing each other for some time now."

"You have?" Mrs Marshall asked with a raising of a thin eyebrow.

Rupert smiled, almost with embarrassment. "Yes. Just she's never mentioned you and I was wondering…"

"…How you managed to convert her?"

"I'm sorry?"

Mrs Marshall forced a laugh. "I think there's been some confusion here, Mr Harrison."

"Please, call me Rupert. What makes you say that?"

"Well, you seem to believe that your girlfriend is my daughter, but that cannot be."

"Why not?"

"Why, my daughter is a lesbian, Mr Harrison, has been since she was a teenager. And she isn't even in the country right now. She's travelling around Australia with her partner, I think. I've lost track."

Rupert could feel his excitement ebb.

He was so keen on coming out here to find out more about Ashley, that he hadn't even stopped to consider if the information he had been given could be trusted.

He felt foolish.

Mrs Marshall continued, "If you don't mind me saying so, you look as stunned as I did the day she told me. I dare say the circumstances didn't make it any easier. It was the day after her father's funeral. I suppose she didn't think I was already hurting enough, she decided to throw that bit of news at me too.

You see, things have always been a bit strained between us. She had always been a bit of a daddy's girl and, of course, when he died, well, it was just me. She left as soon as she was able to cash her inheritance. Took off to travel around the world and I haven't heard from her since. Oh, except for the odd postcard, of course, just to let me know how much she is enjoying life away from me."

Rupert was ready for the floor to open up and swallow him. How could he have been so stupid? How could he have trusted that waster so implicitly, and barged into this woman's home, her life?

"I'm sorry, Mr Harrison. I must confess, as soon as you told me about Ashley, I realised the mistake, but I was just too curious. You see, nothing much exciting happens around here, apart from Bridge and the odd charity appearance. So, of course, when a handsome celebrity such as you arrives on my doorstep, telling me you wanted to talk about Ashley. Well, I couldn't resist. Please forgive me," she said.

Rupert smiled politely. He felt hurt, angry. "No, it's okay. It's my fault, really, for not checking the facts before rushing over here."

Mrs Marshall smiled like a proud mother. "If it's any consolation, I'm sure I would have been delighted to learn that that beautiful woman I saw you with was my girl, and you her fiancé."

Rupert smiled warmly. "Thank you." He sighed. "Well, I guess I have already wasted enough of your time. I'd better be on my way."

"Oh no, please, won't you stay and finish your tea?"

Rupert considered this and smiled, "Well, I wouldn't want to intrude."

"It would be my pleasure," Mrs Marshall smiled.

"Of course."

They drank their tea in silence and then the idea popped into Rupert's head, he dismissed it but it returned.

Before he knew it, he was speaking, "Mrs Marshall, would it be possible to see a recent picture of your daughter?"

She shrugged, "Well, I suppose so. Although I don't have any very recent pictures, just a few she sent a couple of years back."

"That would be fine," Rupert said.

He was finding it difficult to accept that this had all been some cruel coincidence.

Then he heard Mrs Marshall ask, "Would you like to see her room?" When she noticed the surprise on his face, she added with a smile, "They always say that in the movies, don't they?"

Rupert smiled, "Sure."

When Mrs Marshall turned on the light, it illuminated a spacious room with maroon coloured walls adorned with posters of book covers.

The bed wore a black quilt with gold pentagram style symbols all over it. A heap of teddy bears sat on the floor nearby, and shelves loaded with paperback books ran the length of one wall.

"She liked to read, especially after her father's death," Mrs Marshall offered.

Rupert smiled. "May I?" he asked, gesturing into the room. "Of course."

Rupert walked over to the bookshelf to find an array of supernatural and horror novels. He recognised most of the authors; they were published by Harrison.

He looked up.

The woman smiled, warmly, "One of the reasons why your name meant something to me."

He walked passed an arched window that ensured that this Ashley awoke every morning to a majestic view of the river.

"When's the last time you saw your daughter, Mrs Marshall?"

She pondered the question. "I wouldn't know exactly, but it has been quite a few years now."

"You must miss her."

"I do. We may have rarely seen eye to eye, but she's still my daughter." She nodded at a heavy looking dresser, "The pictures are over there," she said, as if she were afraid to approach them.

Rupert walked over to the dresser where everything seemed in place, as if the girl still lived here; hairbrush, perfume, makeup, all stood eagerly awaiting their use. Beside them was a selection of photo frames of all shapes and sizes.

Mrs Marshall joined Rupert and picked up a heart-shaped silver frame. In it, a young lady, with spiky blonde hair and a nose stud, pulled a fake smile for the camera; this was Ashley Marshall. She was stocky, wore cargo pants and a white T-shirt.

Rupert looked up; Mrs Marshall forced the smile of a mother who wasn't exactly proud of, but grateful for, the daughter she did have.

He almost apologised to her, but didn't know why. Maybe it was the way she had spoken to him downstairs, maybe it was the way she wished that his Ashley, the woman he loved, was her daughter.

It felt as if Mrs Marshall had had nothing but hurt from this stranger whose picture he was holding.

He replaced it amongst the other photo frames and picked up another; a little girl in a lilac dress, playing somewhere outside by the trees.

"Ten years old." Mrs Marshall offered. "She was an angel then."

Some of the other pictures were taken a few years later. A class photo, one of Ashley riding a bike with her father in the background, another of her staring at the camera with a sulky look on her face, and one with her arm around another girl.

"She looks very happy," Rupert said.

"She was," Mrs Marshall replied, thoughtfully, "until she lost her father, then everything changed."

"I'm sorry."

"You don't have to be sorry," she said with a motherly smile, "From what I hear, you have had your own share of unhappiness."

They shared an empathetic look, then Rupert sighed and said, "I'd better get going."

"Of course. I'll see you out."

They walked down the stairs in silence until they reached the front door. Mrs Marshall opened it and a bitter cold wind licked at them both.

"They've forecast snow," she said, looking out into the early stages of night.

"That would explain the cold," Rupert said and then added, gratefully, "Thank you for seeing me today."

She smiled her motherly smile, "Thank you for coming over, it was a true pleasure to meet you. I'm only sorry you didn't find what you were looking for.

"Me too," Rupert said. "Please take care of yourself."

"You too."

Mrs Marshall watched Rupert climb behind the wheel of his car and pull the door shut.

He took a few moments to gather his thoughts. What exactly had just happened here? What had happened was that the investigator he had hired had failed him, and made Rupert look like a complete fool!

He felt angry, very angry because he had been instrumental in resurrecting painful memories for a complete stranger. In fact, now that he sat in the freezing cold of his car, the reality of what he had just done sunk in. What the hell had possessed him to walk into that woman's house, march into that little girl's room and then start looking through her things...

...That is when it occurred to him; the pictures.

He leapt out of the car and back up the steps where the door had been closed once more. He rapped on it urgently until Mrs Marshall reappeared.

Rupert gave her no time to think, he said, "The pictures!"

"I'm sorry?"

"The pictures, Mrs Marshall, may I see them again?"

"Why, of course," she said utterly bemused. She stood aside, and Rupert darted up the stairs and into Ashley's bedroom. He rushed over to the dresser, picked up the photo of Ashley and her friend and studied it; it was a faded colour picture, taken many years before judging by the clothes the two girls were wearing. Both must have been in their early teens, and were leaning on each other as they smiled at the camera.

Rupert studied the faces; Ashley with the straggly blonde hair and her friend, the one with the unforgettable pixie nose and dark hair. The picture was taken from a distance and was blurry, making it difficult to make out eye colour, but that face looked too familiar to him.

Mrs Marshall appeared in the doorway. Rupert turned to her and asked, without taking his eyes off the photo, "Where is she now?"

"I told you, somewhere in Australia."

Rupert shook his head. "No, not Ashley, her." He pointed at the other girl, "Ashley's friend."

Mrs Marshall frowned and took the photo from him, "I don't know."

"Do you remember her name?" He asked.

"Well, of course, I remember her name; it's Tracey, Tracey Skelton. She was Ashley's best friend. They were inseparable as children. They even used to read to each other."

"Harrison books?" Rupert asked.

Mrs Marshall frowned again, "I suppose so, yes."

"Tracey," Rupert whispered, running his finger down the image of the girl.

"What is this all about?"

"What else can you tell me about this girl?"

"What else do you want to know?"

"Where does she live?"

"Mr Harrison…"

"…Please," Rupert supplicated, "it's very important."

She observed him, carefully. "Well, she used to live on a farm just outside of Fordwich until the incident."

Rupert looked up. "What incident?"

Mrs Marshall was about to speak but caught herself. "I'm sorry, it was such a long time ago, I really can't recall."

"Please," he urged.

She thought about this and he saw a struggle behind her eyes, he could tell that the woman knew something, but couldn't decide whether or not to tell him about it.

Eventually, she said with deep sadness, "All I can tell you is that when they took that little girl away, it broke Ashley's heart."

"What happened, Mrs Marshall? What happened to Tracey?" Rupert prompted.

The woman hesitated as tears brimmed in her eyes, then, suddenly, she shook her head decisively. "No, I'm sorry; I really can't tell you any more."

"Mrs Marshall…"

"…No, I can't," she said firmly.

Rupert was about to press the issue, but his experience as a negotiator told him that this meeting was over. He handed the photo back to her and smiled.

"Thank you anyway. You've been a great help."

She nodded, stoically.

At the front door, they were greeted by snowflakes dancing in the porch light against a backdrop of darkness.

"Thank you for everything, Mrs Marshall," Rupert said, warmly.

"I'm sorry I couldn't help you anymore," she offered.

Rupert smiled and left.

As he pulled the car door open, she called to him, "Mr Harrison?"

He turned around and looked up to see her standing on the doorstep as a gale tugged at her silky silver hair. "Say hello to Tracey, won't you, please."

Rupert smiled and got into his car once more.

He picked up his mobile phone and dialled Open Eyes Investigations Ltd.

A woman answered, and told him that Graham wouldn't be in until later in the evening. Rupert asked her to take a message, told her he had an urgent job, and that he needed Graham to investigate. He said, he wanted the same again, only this time the name was Skelton, Tracey Skelton, of Fordwich.

He was about to hang up, but then added, "Oh, and please tell him that this time, I'd like the premium service."

He disconnected the call, started the car and drove off, into the falling snow.

59 FOXBERRY HALL

The drive to Foxberry Hall was long.

To Rachel, it felt as if they had been driving for hours. They were heading southwest of London, as the snow fell, heavily, in front of the car's headlights.

"How much further is it?" she asked.

"Any second now," Jason said, intently studying the road.

"I don't fancy the idea of getting snowed in here. It's falling really heavily," Rachel said, peering through the windscreen.

"Don't worry. There's plenty of space if we need to stay over."

"Stay over…"

"…Here it is," he interrupted, steering the BMW left, off the main road and onto a private drive, where it stopped in front of two large iron gates.

The golden words, *'Foxberry Hall'*, glinted in the headlights. Above them, a close circuit camera whirred as it turned to focus on them.

Jason buzzed down his window and held up an identity card. Instantly, there was a click and the gates hummed open.

"Ooh, very swish," Rachel marvelled as Jason piloted the car through the gates.

They rode up the ghostly drive of snow covered trees, until they reached a large forecourt that resembled an outdoor showroom of luxury automobiles.

Jason parked the BMW next to a Jaguar and killed the engine.

"Here we are," he said with a smile.

Rachel looked out of the window and grinned. "I thought you said you weren't into this snobby lifestyle."

"I'm not," Jason said with a wink, "it's just business."

"Yeah, yeah," Rachel teased, as she stepped out of the warm car and into a cold breeze that snatched her breath, and made snowflakes dart here and there, like a panicked shoal of fish.

She pulled a shawl around her and was grateful that she had opted to wear a long dress. It was made of velour, crimson in colour. It accentuated every curve of her body, but provided limited protection against the elements.

"Oooh, it's cold," she shivered.

Jason put his arm around her and, together, they crunched through snow covered gravel towards the front door.

It was too dark to make out much of the building, but Rachel felt a sense of its enormity from the pair of giant concrete pillars that led to a spacious balcony, and a symmetrical row of large square windows. They ran the length of the building and disappeared into darkness.

Rachel hesitated at the front door.

Jason looked at her, "What's wrong?"

"Nothing," she said, forcing a smile.

He took her chin in his hand and looked at her inquisitively, letting her know that he knew something was on her mind.

She hesitated a few more seconds and then spoke, "It's nothing, really. I just, well I just want this night to be a success for you. I don't want to let you down."

Jason chuckled and then said, affectionately, "I don't think you could let me down even if you tried, Rach." He kissed her on the mouth as snowflakes settled in their hair.

She smiled at him and took a deep breath, indicating she was ready for the night ahead.

Jason pulled on the bell rope and, moments later, the door opened, wafting a medley of classical music and the scent of perfume their way.

They entered and the door was shut and locked behind them.

60 THE CALL

Ashley gazed out of the window and watched how London had slowed to a crawl, as it negotiated the foreign substance that had blanketed the city in cotton wool whiteness.

She looked at the clock, it was getting late. She hadn't

heard from Rupert since the afternoon, and she wondered if he was one of the many trying to make his way home.

She dialled his mobile phone but, yet again, was immediately diverted to voicemail after just a couple of rings.

This time she began to leave a message, explaining that she hadn't heard anything since her last message, and was starting to worry, and to please call as soon as…

…the doorbell interrupted her.

"….let me know you're okay," she said quickly. Then disconnected and hurried to the door.

She felt inexplicably nervous. It couldn't be Rupert because he would have a key, which meant it must be somebody else known to her, for security to let them up without announcing them first.

She looked through the spy hole, smiled and then pulled the door open; it was Adam.

He looked unkempt as if he hadn't groomed in days.

"Adam," was all Ashley could say with surprise.

"I'm sorry to barge in on you like this…"

"…Oh no, don't be silly. You're not barging in at all. Please," she stood aside, "come in. It's good to see you."

Ashley hadn't seen Adam since Elisabeth's funeral. He'd requested a leave of absence from her, but hadn't returned any of her calls since. She was pleased to see that, albeit a bit worse for wear, he was okay.

He slipped his hands into the pockets of his jeans and surveyed the apartment, as if seeing it for the first time.

"How are you holding up?" she asked, affectionately.

He turned to her and shrugged, "Oh, you know."

Ashley felt for him. She couldn't even begin to imagine how he must be feeling right now.

She spontaneously hugged him, tightly.

The embrace lasted a while and when it broke, he smiled at her and said, "Thanks, I needed that."

She returned the smile, "Anytime. Please."

She ushered him through to the lounge. "Can I get you something to drink? I've already got a pot of coffee on the go, or would you like something else?"

Adam nodded, "No, coffee is good, thanks."

"I'll be right back," she said, and disappeared into to the kitchen, leaving him alone with his thoughts, one of which turned his stomach.

The dinner scene, here in this very penthouse. The images returned in shocking vivid detail, replaying like a stuttering projector image on the whiteboard of his mind.

And it hurt, sweet God it hurt.

All his dreams, all his hopes, destroyed. He blinked back tears and begged the visions for some respite, but they were unrelenting like a swarm of enraged bees, they returned to sting again and again.

"Adam?"

He refocused; Ashley was standing in front of him with a mug of steaming coffee in her hand. "Are you alright?" She asked.

He forced a smile, nodded and sat on the sofa.

Ashley sat opposite.

There was an awkward silence as cars honked loudly somewhere on the streets below.

Mercifully, Adam spoke, "Is Rupert still at the office?"

Ashley frowned, "I don't really know. I can't seem to get hold of him," she said.

"Is he out of town?"

"I'm not sure. He isn't answering his mobile. I've no idea where he is. And with this snow, I have to admit, I'm starting to get a bit worried."

"I'm sure he's just been caught up in traffic somewhere. It was hell trying to get over here. You know what the Brits are like, a bit of white stuff and they fall to pieces. He's probably stuck in a jam somewhere."

"I suppose so. It was coming down quite fast earlier," she said, looking out of the window.

"Typical, isn't it? We never get weather like this at Christmas."

"No, we don't," Ashley smiled.

"Bizarre really when you think about it."

"That we don't get snow?"

"No, that Elisabeth will never see another Christmas."

Ashley surprised by Adam's candour. She studied his face;

she had known this man for over a year, but she hardly recognised him now with those sunken eyes and that troubled expression. She felt sorry for him, yet she didn't know what else to do or say right now. Adam was going through something that only he could deal with. All she could do, as his friend, was be there for him.

"I am so very sorry, Adam," she said, earnestly.

"Thanks. But it wasn't exactly your fault. It's just another one of those tragic facts of life. You devote yourself to someone, think nothing can separate you, nothing can tear you apart, yet life... well... it has other plans. It doesn't matter how much you plan or prepare, something or someone can easily come along at the last minute and turn the whole thing to shit."

Ashley wasn't sure she understood exactly what Adam was saying.

"For example," he continued then paused, as if to add drama to the moment, "What would you do? If something precious was taken away from you? What would you do to get it back?"

He looked at her, expectantly. Ashley blurted out, "I don't think there's anything I wouldn't do."

"Exactly," Adam said, holding her gaze for a few seconds and then taking a sip from his cup.

He pulled a face.

"What's wrong?"

"Oh no, don't worry."

"What is it?" She asked.

"Well, just the coffee." he smiled with embarrassment, "Over the past few days I've developed a taste for sugar and, well..."

"Oh, of course, sorry, just I thought you always took it black without," she said, standing up.

"If you just tell me where it is, I'll get it."

"No, don't be silly," she said and hurried towards the kitchen.

She was just about to leave the room when the house phone rang, and she turned instantly to see Adam snatch the cordless phone from the coffee table.

She watched on, anxiously.

"Hello? Oh, hi…. Yes, Ashley's been worried, where are you?"

Pause.

"Oh, I see… I thought it would be something like that. Of course, no problem, hold tight, we'll be right there. Okay… bye."

He hung up.

By this time, Ashley had walked up to him.

"Was that Rupert? Is he alright? Is he okay?"

"Don't worry, he's okay. Told me to let you know that he had to go out of town on business, but that he's having trouble. Apparently, the AA have been inundated with calls and can't get anyone out to him for some time. He wants to know if we can swing by and rescue him.

"I'll just get my coat," Ashley said.

"Okay," Adam smiled as she hurried out of the room.

61 THE NEWS

The snow was falling fast and the radio had reported that somewhere, a few miles up ahead, a road accident between two cars and a truck was causing major delays.

This explained the snake of glowing red tail lights that Rupert could see far into the distance. It was clear to him that the traffic wouldn't start moving again any time soon.

To his right, he noticed a slip road leading up a hill to a service station. So, with a bit of careful manoeuvring, he managed to squeeze the Lexus through the gap between a car and a transit van.

At the petrol station, he refuelled, bought coffee, and a sandwich. Then, he hurried back to the car where, from his elevated viewpoint, he was now able to see that traffic was at a standstill, for approximately five miles, and ended with several flashing blue lights.

He kept the engine running to stay warm and distractedly mulled over the day's events.

How exactly could he drive back to London and confront Ashley with all of this? He had no idea, but what he did know is that it had to be done. In his opinion, they'd both spent weeks dodging emotional projectiles, and were no better for it. In fact, it was this very thing that had led him here in the first place.

If he had been any other man, he would have confronted Ashley with the Burton discovery right from the start, but he didn't. He had been so wrapped up with everything else that was happening, that now the world as he knew it was disintegrating around him.

His thoughts touched on Elisabeth and the reality that she was gone forever, and that hurt. It hurt to think that he would never see her again.

He put down his half eaten sandwich. He'd suddenly lost his appetite, and the head that had started as an ache felt like it was going to turn into a migraine.

He squeezed his eyes shut as thoughts fluttered in his mind like butterflies in a jar.

He wondered about Ashley, Elisabeth, James, work, the accident in the apartment, the traffic jam, the pictures he had seen of Ashley as a child, Elisabeth, the traffic jam, James, the pictures of Ashley, the pictures of Ashley, and, once again, the pictures of Ashley.

He snapped his eyes open to a snow-covered windscreen and reached over for his mobile device. That's when he noticed that it had been switched off since his visit with Mrs Marshall.

He turned it on and when the network logo finally appeared, a beeping sound alerted him to five messages. He checked the numbers; three of them were from Ashley, one from the office and another from an old school friend.

He pressed connect and called Ashley's mobile, but it rang out until it was diverted to voicemail. He rang home until the answering machine picked up.

"Ashley? Are you there? It's me, pick up the phone."

But after waiting a few seconds of nothing, he left a message, telling her he was ok, about the traffic jam, and that he would get home as soon as possible. He also added that he loved her and that they needed to talk. The machine beeped an acknowledgement and then flashed the red *message* diode at the empty penthouse.

Then he opened his phone's browser. The odds weren't good, but there was a chance that if there had been an accident in a small village, it would have been reported, and or posted somewhere.

Luckily, the reception on the main highway was good and, before long, eight results were returned.

He tapped each one, in turn, and found that the majority of them related to an author and a university professor, with respective links to their websites and social media pages.

Three other links were from a national newspaper archive that Rupert had never heard of.

He tapped the first article.

It was from the Canterbury Times. It talked about a man and his girlfriend, who had become victims of a frenzied knife attack while in bed with each other.

The female victim, who suffered minor injuries, was a local resident, Sally Matthews.

The male victim was one Andy Skelton, he suffered severe lacerations to the face, and two stab wounds in the back, one of which had paralysed him.

The second article was from another newspaper, and it expanded on the Skelton story.

It talked about Andy Skelton's history, and how his wife had abandoned him and their eight-year-old daughter many years before. It was believed that Mrs Skelton left the family home because of her husband's gambling and alcohol abuse.

Skelton didn't start dating again until a few years later, just weeks before the knife attack.

The paper then went on to describe the assailant, based on the description provided by Skelton's daughter, Tracey Skelton.

Rupert noticed that the third and final article had been posted several years later. It rehashed the details of the attack at the Skelton farm, but then went on to tell a new story, one that made his blood run cold.

62 OPULENCE

Foxberry Hall was resplendent with 18th Century décor. It featured high ceilings, gem encrusted candelabras, ornate borders, and glimmering marble floors.

To Rachel, it was so exquisite it seemed unreal.

She looked at Jason, who smiled knowingly as if he had anticipated her reaction. Then, he linked her arm and led her into a spacious ballroom with an equally refined décor.

The room was full of people, Rachel estimated approximately thirty, all dressed in elegant evening wear, and all chatting animatedly in various groups.

"This is awesome," she breathed.

Unlike previous dinner parties, she didn't feel intimidated by her surroundings, nor the pressure to perform. Here, she felt like she belonged, and it was exhilarating.

There was a good chance that each and every one these people had the power to change Jason's, their, life forever.

And Rachel was determined.

It was her mission to ingratiate and charm the funding that they desperately needed, and she was going to succeed.

Right after some Dutch courage.

She grabbed two flutes of champagne from a passing waiter as they crossed the floor.

"You okay?" Jason asked through a gritted smile.

"I'm good, just petrified," she replied in the same tone.

"You'll be okay after a few more glasses of this," he said. "Come on, I'll introduce you to a few people."

He slipped his arm proudly around her and they mingled.

63 UNEXPECTED

They had been travelling southwest for nearly an hour and the snow was still falling, albeit not as hard.

"What was he doing all the way out here anyway?" Ashley asked, suddenly.

"He didn't say," Adam replied glumly, eyes intent on the road.

Ashley looked across at him, but his eyes did not betray anything as he peered through the windscreen.

She hoped he was okay. Right up until they left London, he wouldn't stop talking, as if he was nervous about making the journey in this weather. And now, now that they were in the middle of nowhere and she was growing nervous, he had fallen silent.

"I hate that Rupert's out here alone. Where did he say he was exactly? I noticed you didn't put anything in the satnav. Do you know where we're going?"

"He didn't say, exactly" was Adam's reply, eyes still fixed on the road.

Ashley forced a laugh. "What do you mean he didn't say?" Adam didn't reply.

"If he didn't say, how do you know where we're going?"

"He said it was somewhere along this road."

"Somewhere?" She questioned peering out of the glass. "He could be anywhere," she said, irritably.

Adam turned to her as if to say something and Ashley caught a look in his eyes, one she couldn't quite decipher. It did little to ease her edginess.

"Adam...?" she began but the words were stifled when he stamped on the brakes, causing the car to swerve and fishtail a couple of times, before skidding to a sudden halt. The motion threw her forward, against the restraint of her seatbelt, and then back again.

He turned to her and waited for her to recover.

Ashley, still reeling from the moment, garbled, "What happened? What's wrong?"

"We're here." Adam said, calmly.

"Here? Where?" she asked, rubbing the misty glass on her

side of the vehicle and peering out of it. "I can't see anything."

She turned to him, about to speak, but instead saw the blurry white of his fist power towards her face.

The impact smacked her in the nose with such force that it slammed the back of her head against the glass of the passenger window, and turned her world black.

64 THE ROOM

When Rachel first saw Daniel Bayliss, she did not recognise him. The forty year old politician, with sleeked red hair and sparkly blue eyes, looked nothing like the man on TV; this man looked much more handsome, as did Alan Chapman, MP. Then there was Gemma McCarthy, TV presenter, and Janet Roark, a senior executive for British Petroleum.

It was exactly as Jason had told her; everybody who was anybody was here tonight, and Rachel was awestruck. She was rubbing shoulders with some of the world's most powerful and influential people, and, although she didn't voice it, she couldn't help but wonder how on earth Jason had managed to get them a pass to such a gathering.

And things got even better when she was introduced to Robert Hicks, the famous veteran broadcaster, and they chatted about his show.

He was actually one of the few good memories Rachel had of her childhood. Her mother was a very big fan and she'd often come home to the smell of baking and the sound of Hicks' radio show.

Robert then moved onto his favourite subject; himself, and stories of his rise to fame, which Rachel found absolutely fascinating.

If only her mother could see her now.

Rachel had become so involved in Hicks' stories that she didn't even notice that Jason had left her side. He was across the room now. She looked up to see him deep in conversation with a particularly tall man, with bushy black hair, thick eye brows and deep, recessed panda eyes.

He reminded her of Lurch from The Addams Family.

The man did not smile once throughout his conversation with Jason, and then, suddenly, they both looked her way, she instinctively waved, but neither acknowledged her.

She wanted to go over and find out what they were talking about, but Robert's droning drew her back to him. She didn't want to appear rude so she smiled sweetly and nodded, as if she'd been engrossed the whole time.

Half an hour later, Rachel was growing restless.

Hicks was still talking about himself, and she could only handle so many glasses of champagne before she started to lose the plot.

So, with a very courteous apology and a big smile, she excused herself, explaining that she needed the girl's room.

She scanned faces as she made for the door, but could not see Jason, nor Lurch.

Finally, she emerged into the hallway and breathed a sigh of relief. Pleased to have put some distance between her, and the egomaniac she'd spent the last thirty minutes of her life with.

She looked around; the hallway was empty and she wondered where the hell Jason could have got to.

She was starting to get anxious.

He'd just disappeared on her without so much as a word, despite the fact that he had promised never to leave her side. In fact, this was an express condition of her agreeing to accompany him there, yet, here she was, alone.

She considered what to do next. One thing was for sure, she wasn't going back into the ballroom, at least not on her own.

She looked up the stairs; maybe she did need the ladies' room after all.

She clutched onto the banister and nearly missed her first step.

Her effort to drown out Hicks had turned into a light head. She promised herself no more drink for a while. Then, slowly and gingerly made her way up the stairs.

On the landing, she admired a few paintings of unsmiling portraits with judgmental eyes. She gave them one of her overused fake smiles.

Then, just as she was about to move on, she heard something. It seemed to be coming from a room, a few doors down, what appeared to be, an infinite corridor.

She couldn't identify what it was, but it sounded like a person. Someone unwell.

Instinctively, she moved closer to the door and paused to listen. Although the sound was akin to someone in pain, she was old and wise enough to know that it could well be something else. Which meant that, despite her tipsiness, she wasn't going to burst in there and make a complete fool of herself.

Instead, she furtively glanced around, to make sure nobody was watching, and then she put her eye to the two inch gap in the door, and her mouth dropped open.

The lighting in the room was subdued, but she could clearly see a video camera mounted on a tripod.

Beyond that, a skinny female in her twenties, with long blonde hair and a blindfold over her eyes, lay spread eagled across the bed, bound by leather straps.

Her partner, a middle aged man with a large gut spilling over tight briefs, was doing something between her legs. Rachel couldn't quite see what exactly because he had his back to her but whatever it was, it was making him grunt and chuckle satisfactorily. The girl, on the other hand, mouth wide open, was moaning loudly as if she were about to give birth.

Rachel's eyes widened and she pushed her face closer to the gap to get a better look.

What the hell are you doing to her? Is she enjoying it?

Rachel could not tell.

Then, he stood up, causing his fat belly to wobble while his hands caught the light and glistened.

Rachel's hand shot to her mouth to suppress a scream. She

could now see that both the man's hands and the girl's thighs were covered in what looked like blood!

"Can I help you, madam?"

The voice startled Rachel, she turned too quickly, lost her balance and fell to the floor as Lurch, all seven feet of him, towered over her.

65 UNTHINKABLE

Ashley's eyes were still closed when she felt the tingling in her fingers. It slowly metamorphosed into a stinging pain on her lip, and then a numbness throughout the extremities of her shivering body.

Her head hurt, she couldn't move her arms and wherever she was lying, it was freezing cold, damp and smelt of earth and pine.

Somewhere in the distance, she could hear someone talking, a man maybe, on his own, talking on the phone.

She very slowly managed to peel her eyes open, but squeezed them shut again when she was dazzled by a powerful shard of light above her.

Where am I?

She tried to lift her pounding head, but it was too heavy and she was forced to lie back again. She waited a few seconds, willed the energy back into her limbs, and opened her eyes once more to see the blurry beam of light shining across the sky above her.

A flashlight? Where am I?

The talking stopped and the glare of light eased on her eyelids as it was picked up and moved.

She opened her eyes fully now to see the gigantic silhouette of a man towering over her as a handful of dirt fell onto her face, causing her to flinch and spit.

"Ah, brilliant you're awake," said a cheery tone.

"Adam?" she croaked with a dry mouth.

"That's me."

"What, where am I?" she asked, feeling a trickle of energy and apprehension as memories slowly began to return, incredulous memories in which Adam had looked at her with icy cold eyes and then…. And then he had struck her!

Oh God.

Slowly, her surroundings came into focus: she could see a star glittered sky, snow covered tree branches, and walls made of hardened soil, with a cross patch of twigs and hibernating larvae.

The air was snow fresh, laced with the heavy scent of freshly dug earth!

Towering above her, was the gigantic silhouette of a man.

She was fully alert now, as adrenaline began to rush around her body.

She was afraid, very afraid.

Her body had been squeezed into a hole, approximately six feet long, three wide, and four deep.

"Oh God, no," she murmured, weakly.

"This is just perfect," Adam said, gleefully. "For a moment there, I thought I was going to have to go through this part without audience participation."

Ashley couldn't see his face, since the flashlight was in his hand, and either dazzling her or shining on the ground next to him, but, from the intonation of his voice, he was probably grinning.

"What are you doing, Adam?" she asked, incredulously as she tried to move, but couldn't.

Not only was her body heavy and her limbs weak, but her legs and hands were bound together with Gaffer tape.

"You remember William Barber, don't you, Ash?"

"Who… who?" she stuttered.

"You know, the postman guy, the one who sent us that manuscript, the Tales from a Tomb bloke."

"What…what about him?" she shivered.

"Remember what he did to his mother?"

A lightning bolt of terror shot through her, as a dust cloud of snow spontaneously fell on her like frozen tears.

"Adam …"

"…You see, that is exactly it, Ash. That is exactly what was missing from Barber's manuscript. There was not enough description, like for example right now, your eyes are bulging wide with tears of terror, because you know what's coming next. You know that any second now, I am going to cover this hole up with wooden planks, seal it shut with a mound of soil, and then, if we're lucky, it might even snow to top that."

"No," Ashley whined, in disbelief, as her eyes welled with tears. "Please, Adam, Please don't do this..."

"That's exactly it! Terror. In that scene, Barber failed to capture the terror that his mum felt when he put her in her grave. Of course, she was already dead at the time. Or was she? I don't remember, do you?"

Freezing crystals of tears formed around Ashley's eyes.

"That's brilliant, Ash!" Adam exclaimed, excitedly, "Tears of terror! On the other hand, please don't cry. I may just start feeling sorry for you, and I don't want that. I don't want to feel sorry for you, I just want terror. You know, the kind that makes me feel better, makes me feel in control for a change. Because you know something, I am sick of not being in control. I spent all this time with that bitch, trying to get some control, and what does she do at the last minute? She fucking goes and carks on me, which would have been fine, I suppose, if only the greedy bitch had seen it somewhere in that miserable black heart of hers to leave me something. You know, I wasn't asking for much, maybe a million or two, I mean, come on, Ash, what harm could that have done, huh? A few million quid to her would have meant nothing, especially as I did everything for the miserable bitch..!"

He hissed the last words through gritted teeth, as the memory of her perceived betrayal enraged him.

"…But no, that would have been too good, too decent of her. So instead, what does she do? She decides to give the whole fucking lot to your boyfriend!"

His incredulous laughter echoed around the surrounding forest, scaring some night creature to flight in a flutter of wings.

For a second, Ashley thought somebody had joined them

until she realised that it was Adam's manic cackle; the unmistakable cackle of a mad man.

"Can you see the irony in that, Ash? As if the man doesn't have enough money as it is! Did she really think he needed several more million? Well, they do say that money goes to money. It's the same old story. The rich just keep on getting richer and the poor; well they just keep on dreaming of becoming rich, but not me, not anymore. I've found a way to make my money and that way is lying in this hole beneath me right now."

Ashley's teeth were chattering, her whole body was shaking and she wanted to cry, but couldn't, such was the coldness and the shock.

What she did try to say came out as a stutter and Adam laughed.

"Please……Ple.. ple…"

"Don't worry, Ash. As long as lover boy pays up, you're going to be just fine. Providing they get to you before the frostbite, of course."

Adam paused, and looked at his watch. "Oh well, it's time. I best get going if I am going to get out of sunny England tonight."

"No... no... Adam, wait."

"Don't worry; you'll be fairly cosy in here. Until your air runs out and your limbs freeze over. In the meantime, just to prove I'm not a complete shit, I've brought this for you"

He dropped a thin car blanket on top of her legs and midriff. "Snuggle up, you're going to be here a while."

"Nooooo!" Ashley shrieked as the sobs finally emerged.

"Shhh…. You'll wake up the animals," he said, leaning over the mound of dirt and dazzling her with torchlight as he picked up a plank of wood.

"No…no… please, Adam… please…" she begged.

"Stop begging, Ashley, it's pathetic. Besides, I told you, as long as lover boy follows his instructions on time, you're going to be fine."

"Noooooo!" Ashley screamed as she saw the wooden plank float over her. "Heeelp! Somebody heeelp me! Please! Help!

Adam paused, "Come on, Ashley, stop being silly. Don't

waste what little energy you have left, you're going to need it if you want to survive."

"Ple.. please, Don't do this to me. Please, Adam…Don't."

"It's nothing personal, Ash, nothing personal."

"NOOO!" HELP ME!" She screamed with all her energy, as another plank of wood floated into place, "SOMEBODY PLEASE HELP ME!"

"It's no use, nobody's going to hear you, Ash. Nobody has any idea you're even out here, and, in the infamous words of Annie Wilkes, you better pray nothing happens to me, because if it does… Is that how it went? I can't remember…"

Another plank was pushed into place, leaving just a slither of a starlit sky.

"Now, how the hell did it go? Do you remember?" Adam asked, picking up the last plank, "Oh yeah, I've got it, I've got it; you better pray nothing happens to me because if I die, you die."

With that, he pushed the last plank into place and Ashley's world turned black once more.

She tried to move, she tried to sit up but to no avail. Her bound hands and legs were making it impossible to move as she lay on her back, all but wedged into her shallow grave.

"Nooooo!" She screamed, huskily, through frozen vocal chords as the hopelessness of her plight became clear to her.

"NOOO!"

But nobody was listening.

The world above was silent, but for the distant thud of earth as it fell in clumps onto the planks. Some, sifted through the gaps and fell onto her face, as if her last rites were being read.

The thuds continued, shovel after shovel, until the planks were firmly secured in place turning her screams into nothing but murmurs to the rest of the world.

Ashley Marshall was entombed.

Adam grunted satisfactorily when the work was done. Then, he zipped his coat up against the freezing still of the night and whistled as he made his way back up the path, from the lake to the mansion.

66 RANSOM

The snow had stopped falling and the skies had cleared, leaving the sub-zero temperatures to ice over the already treacherous roads.

When Rupert received the call on his mobile, he nearly crashed into the car in front of him; Adam, his dead cousin's boyfriend, was telling him that unless he transferred two million pounds into an offshore bank account, details of which would be text messaged to him, he would never see Ashley alive again.

Of course, Rupert's initial reaction was to think that Adam was playing a practical joke. It was only after considering the man's voice that he fully understood what was being demanded of him.

The cars behind the Lexus honked as he absorbed the instructions in stunned silence.

"You have roughly an hour, maybe two before your beloved either freezes or suffocates to death. Now, you can use that time playing heroics, Rupert, trying to get the police and all their bureaucracy involved, or you can just pay the money and get her back. It's not like you can't afford it. The choice is yours."

"Adam, I don't understand....Why?"

"All you need to know is, if you don't get that money organised soon, Ashley will die, and it will be because you didn't think she was worth it."

Rupert flared, "Adam, I just don't understand…"

"…You're wasting time. Right now, she's probably passed out from the shock. Eventually, she will come round to realise the predicament she's in, and I guarantee you, if the cold doesn't claim her then a heart attack will."

"Please Adam, I will give you whatever you want, just don't hurt her."

"Then do as I said, and everything will be fine. As soon as I'm safe, I'll let you know where she is."

"How do I know I can trust you?"

"You don't. But all you have to do is transfer the cash, and pray nothing happens to me, because if I so much as get a whiff of the police anywhere near me, I swear, she's dead, and it'll be on you. I have nothing left to lose while you, on the other hand, stand to lose the only thing you have left. Can you live with that? Can you lose another person so close? Can you live with both hers and your brother's death on your conscience?"

"You fuck..!"

"…Your time starts now."

"Adam…? Adam?" Rupert yelled into his mobile but the line went dead.

Meanwhile, the honking continued while he gripped the steering wheel in an effort to stave off the rage and fear that had enveloped him.

It was all so surreal. This couldn't be happening to him, but it was.

67 VANISHED

Lurch fixed Rachel with a stare as he reached out to the bedroom door and pulled it shut.

Rachel crawled backwards before blurting out, "I was looking for my boyfriend, Jason Tyler. You were talking to him earlier."

She managed to scramble to her feet.

"I believe he's downstairs," Lurch said in a slow, unaffected tone.

"I couldn't find him down there," Rachel said, dusting her clothes self-consciously.

"Rachel?"

She turned around, Jason was walking up to her, and she rushed over and threw her arms around him.

"Where did you go?" she asked, quickly.

"I went to the toilet, why?"

Rachel looked behind her; Lurch was still standing there.

She grabbed Jason's hand and led him past the giant, and back down the stairs.

"You won't believe what I've just seen," she said under her breath, glancing back to make sure they weren't being followed.

"What?"

"Oh God, Jay, you won't believe it."

"What?"

"I just saw something happening in one of the bedrooms."

"Something? Like what?"

"I don't know. Some bloke was doing something to some girl."

Jason stopped and turned to look at her.

"Don't stop!" she whispered loudly, pulling him after her.

"Rachel, what are you talking about?"

"I saw something in one of the upstairs bedrooms. Some bloke was doing something to some girl."

"Yeah, you said. But doing what exactly?"

"I don't know. Just, his hands were covered in blood!"

"What?"

Jason stopped again.

She pulled his hand, "We need to go home."

"Rachel…"

"Now, Jay, we need to go home now!"

"Don't be stupid," Jason said, as they reached the foot of the stairs. "I can't go home now, you know I can't."

"Please Jay; I don't want to be here anymore. I saw something up there."

"What? You mean like two people going at it?"

"No, no, it was more than that. He was doing something to her, she was bleeding."

Jason smiled at a couple that walked by and then looked at her and added, seriously, "Look Rach, I don't know what you think you saw up there, but babe, I can't go home, not yet. You know how important these people are to me."

"Of course I do, but…." She stopped in midsentence as Lurch appeared on the stairs, and began to descend towards them. "Oh My God, he's coming."

Jason looked up and smiled. "You mean, Jerry?" he asked

her.

He then moved to greet the man.

"No!" Rachel hissed, but it was too late.

"Is everything okay, Sir?" Lurch asked.

"Yes, everything's cool. Just my girlfriend thinks she saw something in one of the upstairs bedrooms."

Rachel closed her eyes as her cheeks burned.

Lurch asked, "What exactly did you see?"

Rachel shot evil eyes at Jason, swallowed and said, "I saw a man up there doing something to a girl."

"Doing something?" Lurch repeated as his bushy eyebrows lifted, inquisitively. "What exactly was he doing to her?"

"I don't know. He was just, well, there was blood all over his hands."

"Really?" Lurch asked, unperturbed.

"Yes." Rachel said, petulantly. She really hated Jason right now. "You saw them anyway."

"I did?"

"Yes, you closed the door."

Lurch smiled. "Yes, I did. I'm sorry, but it isn't appropriate for guests to wander around the bedrooms. Especially as it's very easy to get lost in this house," he said, looking at her. "However, back to the girl, the man and the blood. We must go investigate at once," he said, climbing the stairs.

Jason followed up a few steps and then stopped and turned to her. "Are you coming?" He asked with an outstretched hand.

Rachel hesitated, but followed.

When they reached the landing, the door to the bedroom was already open and Lurch inside.

Rachel gasped; the room was empty, all the lights were on, and the bed looked like it hadn't been disturbed in days.

"No," she said, shaking her head. "There is no way."

She walked into the room and up to the bed and felt it; it was cold. "I saw them, they were both on this bed, and she was strapped down.

"Strapped down?" Lurch echoed.

Jason smiled, embarrassed. "Steady on, babe."

"I am telling you, Jay. They were on this bed. He must have

moved them," she said, looking at Lurch with accusatory eyes.

Jason bowed his head as if he had just seen his favourite car smashed to pieces. He grabbed Rachel's hand, smiled at Lurch and led her out into the corridor.

"Jesus Christ, Rach." he said in an angry hushed tone. "What the hell are you trying to do? That man is our host for Christ sake!"

"I don't care who he is, Jay. I know what I saw."

"So do I. Too many glasses of champagne and no bloody food. I also know that if you carry on like this, you may as well piss all over any chance of us getting any funding. Is that what you want?"

Rachel hesitated, avoiding his gaze for a few seconds and then she looked at him, sheepishly, "Of course not. But I know what I saw in there."

"Fine. If you really think it's going to make a difference, we can press that point on our host."

She hesitated. She had had a few and she was feeling light-headed, but could she really have imagined what she saw?

"Is everything alright?" Lurch asked, joining them out in the corridor.

Jason said nothing but looked at her, pointedly.

Rachel hesitated an agonisingly long time before finally saying, "I'm sorry. I don't know what I saw." She forced a smile. "I think the champagne truly got the best of me."

Lurch smiled. "Not to worry, my dear." He glanced at Jason. "Now," he added with a sigh and holding out his arm, "would you do me the honour of accompanying me downstairs where, I promise you, the real fun awaits us." Lurch's lips curved into a rare smile as he waited.

Reluctantly, Rachel took his arm and they descended the stairs back to the party, back to the fun.

68 ESCAPE

Adam was parked at a service station approximately three miles southwest of London Heathrow Airport.

It had been just over an hour since he had placed the call to Rupert's mobile and it was with a great deal of trepidation that he tapped the icon on his mobile phone. He entered his credentials and waited for his bank to log him in.

Seconds ticked by until a summary of his accounts and their respective balances appeared on the screen, and a smile spread across his face.

It took him a few more seconds to truly register what it meant but, ultimately, it was true; Rupert had complied and transferred the money as instructed.

"YES!" He yelled, punching the roof the car. "I'M FUCKING RICH!"

Okay, maybe not as rich as I would have been had we taken over the bastard's company, but this will do nicely. Fuck you, Elisabeth Bitch!

He held up his middle finger at the empty passenger seat.

Adam was overwhelmed with excitement. His pulse was racing, his heart thumping.

All he needed to do now was drive the short distance to the airport, dump his car, and get on the plane out of the country.

And, he concluded, given that Rupert had transferred the money so quickly, it was highly unlikely that he planned to call the police. After all, it's not as if he'd miss the money.

This meant that he should be able to get on the plane without any problems.

He looked at the clock on the dashboard.

His flight closed in two hours.

It had been over an hour since he had left Ashley. With a bit of luck she was still okay, but if she wasn't, he didn't give a shit. He had got what he wanted.

He started the car.

The traffic report, he had made a point of listening to, had forecast hazardous road conditions, and the last thing he wanted was to get stuck in a jam.

69 THE TRUTH

D.S. Mark Warner shared a couch with a uniformed officer who took notes as they talked.

Rupert was already regretting the call, as it seemed that the police were way too busy interrogating him, rather than getting out there to search for his fiancé.

But he was desperate with nowhere to turn. He had transferred the money, but hadn't heard anything from Adam.

"So, when did you transfer the money?" Warner asked.

"About fifteen minutes ago."

"To the offshore account…?"

"Yes, I've already told you and given you that information, Detective. And, as I've already told you, I am not worried about the money, I just want my fiancé back. Jesus!" Rupert sat forward on the sofa and ran his hands through his hair.

"I can understand what you…."

Rupert held up a hand to silence Mark. "You don't know what I'm going through right now so just, please, just don't patronise me okay. I would rather you spend your time finding her, than dispensing textbook sympathy."

"Well, we've alerted all our patrols, it's only a matter of time before we pick him up," Warner said, calmly.

"But that's exactly it. We don't have time! He said she had an hour, maybe two, before she froze or ran out of fucking air!"

"Is that exactly what he said?"

"Yes! I think so."

"Think Mr Harrison, it's very important, were those his exact words?"

"Yes they were. I think! Fuck!" Rupert jumped to his feet. "Jesus Christ I can't remember! I was in shock at the time; I couldn't believe the little shit was serious, or that he was capable of something like this!"

He paced by the window, absentmindedly, gazing out onto London. He thought about all of the people out there, who were going about their lives oblivious to his plight.

Mark nodded at the officer, who then proceeded to pull his

mobile phone out of his pocket and walk to the corner of the room to make a call.

"Mr Harrison, what do you know about this man?"

Rupert thought about the question. "I've already told you... he'd been seeing my cousin for over a year."

"What did you know about him before this time?"

Rupert thought some more, "Well, not much, I suppose. James, my lawyer, he..." Rupert faltered, "...he told me..."

I can't deal with this. Not again, I can't! Oh God, Ashley. Ashley, please be alright.

"Mr Harrison," Warner continued.

"What?" Rupert snapped.

"This Adam character is a convicted felon; he's got a very long record with us. He's been charged in the past with extortion, coercion, fraud, to name just a few." Warner paused here and then added, "We're talking big time fraud, Mr Harrison. This man's a professional, and his speciality is relieving rich woman *and men* of their money."

"Jesus Christ.," Rupert said under his breath. He then went over to the bar and poured himself a drink.

Warner hesitated, reluctant to continue, for he could see that Rupert was having a hard time dealing with the situation and was wary of pushing the man over the edge.

He proceeded, carefully, "You see, we've been looking into this man's past and, well, quite frankly, his associates aren't the most savoury of characters either. As I said, these aren't have-a-go villains, they are specialists. We believe that he was dating your cousin for one reason..."

"...Really?" Rupert asked sarcastically; it was obvious now that Adam had been dating Elisabeth for her money.

"...To get at you," Mark finished.

Rupert looked up. "What?"

"To give you an idea of how meticulous and patient these people are, this guy, and his associates, formed a company many years ago with the sole purpose of taking over yours."

Rupert walked over to Warner. He was squeezing the tumbler so tight, he thought the glass was going to implode in his hand.

He shook his head, "That's impossible. They could never

take over my company, Elisabeth and I are, were, are, oh for fuck's sake, were major shareholders."

Warner said nothing.

"Oh my God, that was why he was with her," Rupert laughed, "did he really think he could get my own cousin to betray me?" He took a sip of the brandy and laughed some more, but he noticed that Warner was not laughing with him. "What?"

"I don't think that was his intention," the detective said, gravely.

"What do you mean?"

"We think that Adam Lewis' intention was to marry your cousin and, therefore, become her husband."

"And?" Rupert asked although he already knew the answer.

"And, if something terrible happened to her, Lewis would have inherited her stake in your company, add to that the stocks owned by this other company…"

"…and he would have become a major shareholder," Rupert uttered.

"Afraid so."

"My God."

"What's more is, we think that your lawyer found out about this."

Mark pulled a piece of paper out of his pocket.

"This is an email that was found on his computer, after his disappearance."

Rupert took the piece of paper and read it. "Why wasn't I told about this before?"

"We wanted to check its validity," Mark said, casually.

Rupert's eyes flashed with anger, "I had a right to know about this before!" he yelled, and was about to continue his tirade when the officer walked over to Mark and whispered in his ear.

"What is it?" Rupert asked, anxiously.

Mark looked up and replied, "They've spotted Lewis' car."

70 DEPARTURE

Adam broke out in a sweat as he joined the motorway. He was so close to his ultimate goal that he could already taste the cocktails and feel the sun on his skin.

He could also feel the pressure to the point where it was making his head throb, but he had a word with himself. This wasn't his first time and it probably wouldn't be his last. He'd been in worse situations, with even worse odds before, and had always emerged triumphant.

He just needed to take a breath, stay focused, and before he knew it, he'd be on a flight out of this freezing cold and on to a tropical beach.

Rupert was a smart man. He knew that involving the police would jeopardise his chances of seeing Ashley alive again. He wouldn't take that risk. Two million pounds was nothing to him.

He wouldn't be so stupid, would he?

The traffic was crawling agonisingly slow and Adam watched as a queue of aeroplanes climbed, lights flashing, into a moonlit night.

He swore.

It was this freak weather that was causing all the havoc. First it dumps snow, and then it decides to freeze the bloody thing over. This meant that most of the roads were untreated, which, in turn, was causing a numerous vehicle collisions.

He'd already witnessed two prangs which meant the police were out in force, and each and every time he saw a flashing blue light his heart somersaulted.

He talked to himself again.

The only reason there's so much police presence is because of the accidents. It has absolutely nothing to do with you.

Then, he heard the yelp of a siren behind him, and it was all he could do not to swerve and crash into the centre barrier.

He looked up in the rearview mirror to see blue lights and headlights blink.

The police car was almost on his bumper.

He was in what would normally be classed as the fast lane, but the traffic was bumper-to-bumper. There was no escape.

He was sandwiched in.

So, he indicated and slowly tucked himself behind another car, a Mini, in the hope that he might be able to use the layby to make an escape.

More siren yelping and lights flashing.

"FUCK!"

Slowly, like a shark in the water, the patrol car drew up alongside him. The driver scrutinized his face for a few seconds, but then, as soon as the cars in front parted, it sped off, lights flashing, siren wailing once more.

Adam exhaled and wiped his forehead with the back of his sleeve.

Calm down, you're getting hysterical.

Has he told them?

Of course, he hasn't. If he had, they would have pulled you over.

Relax.

He looked in the rearview mirror and swore again; there was yet another patrol vehicle, just two cars behind only this one didn't seem to be in any particular hurry.

They aren't following you. But what if they are? If they are, they will never see her again.

He kept his speed even and his heading level for a couple of minutes, as he followed the column of traffic. He was temporarily lulled by the crunching and slushing sound of melted snow under his tyres, but actually yelped when a machine gun *rat tat tat tat* strafed the metal of his door.

He turned to see that a gritting truck was overtaking him, whilst hastily spraying its cargo of crushed rock and salt. It sped by with flashing yellow lights, that intermittently freeze- framed the anxiety on his face.

It was all he could do not to ram the asshole. His nerves were already stretched beyond what he knew he could handle.

Then, the traffic slowed once more, which prompted him to slap his steering wheel in anger, as it was slowly revealed that this was due to the fact that the drivers ahead of him were distracted by a stricken lorry, in the opposite lane. It appeared to have slid, crashed and twisted into the central reservation.

Fuck this!

He mopped his brow with the back of his hand; it was getting so bloody hot in the car, despite the fact that the gauge was telling him that it was minus 2°C outside.

He turned on the radio, but all they could talk about was the sudden '*cold snap*' that had paralysed Britain. The radio show host then went on to tell people not to travel unless absolutely necessary.

Adam looked in the rear view mirror. The cop car was still there.

He angrily shut the radio off. The babbling was making it hard for him to concentrate.

It was taking way too long to get to the airport. He felt like overtaking all of the cars in front by using the hard shoulder, but that would undoubtedly attract unnecessary attention.

So, instead, he stuffed a piece of chewing gum in his mouth, buzzed down the window and gulped in the fresh air which made him think of Ashley.

The fluorescent digits of the dashboard clock told him that she must be running out of time and air by now. If he didn't get to the airport soon, he wouldn't be able to call and let Rupert know where she was, she would die and he would have killed her.

He considered this, but only for a few seconds before he pushed it to the back of his mind.

Just one of those things. She's just the means to an end. Don't start feeling guilty about her. I don't feel guilty at all.

Mercifully, the traffic picked up speed once more, and he passed a road sign that told him to turn off now for London *Heathrow, Terminal 5*.

He smiled, indicated and steered off the motorway and onto Airport Way.

He could almost hear the P.A. system, the hustle and bustle of travellers, the clicking sound of luggage wheels, and the animated discussions of fellow passengers, as they made their way to their departure gate.

I'm rich! And soon I'll be rich and free!

The thought made him feel warm inside.

That was until he looked up and noticed, after his eyes

became accustomed to the glare of the headlights, that the same police patrol car that was following him on the motorway was still tailing him now.

Coincidence?

Unlikely.

He accelerated and overtook the car in front of him and then looked in the side mirror; the police car was keeping its distance, but it was still there.

Calm down, you're imagining things.

He had to know for sure, he had to satisfy himself.

He took the next exit, steering the car off Airport Road and onto a minor road that ran parallel with one of the airport parking lots.

The road here hadn't been cleared of snow, nor had it been treated.

You're fine, you've got a four by four, and this is what it's for.

The cars in the lot winked and glistened enticingly in the overhead lights. The only problem was; he was travelling in the wrong direction.

He glanced in his review mirror and smiled; the patrol car had disappeared. It had apparently pulled off onto some other road.

He sighed with relief and then sped up once more, following the road for a couple of miles until he reached a slip road that would take him up, onto the main road and back on course to his original destination.

However, once he'd made it up the icy incline, he discovered that traffic was much heavier and moving much faster than he had anticipated.

Obviously, this main artery had been gritted sooner and much more effectively.

He set the handbrake and waited patiently for an opportunity to join the busy stream.

A glance at the clock told him he was running out of time; the flight would close soon. He needed to ditch the SUV and check in.

He looked left and finally spotted a large gap, between a bus and a vehicle transporter.

He pushed the vehicle into gear, gunned the engine and waited for the bus to pass, but just as it was about to do so, just as he was preparing to pull out behind it, he spotted them; about two cars back.

It was another patrol car! The officer in the passenger seat, face glowing red from the tail lights of the car in front, was looking directly at him and talking on the radio.

Fuck!

They were tailing him after all.

Instinctively, he pushed on the accelerator, the Range Rover lurched forward, but then lost traction and began to spin on the frozen terrain, launching a cloud of mist and ice into the air.

The move was enough to scare the bus driver into swerving to avoid a collision, but he overcompensated on the black ice and crashed into the central reservation.

"SHIT!"

Adam shifted gears and stomped on the accelerator, the SUV heaved forward, in a growl of tyres, just as the deep guttural blast of an angry claxon demanded his attention.

He looked left, just in time to see two large rectangular headlamps speeding towards him.

"NOOO!" he breathed as the vehicle carrier slid inexorably towards him.

The impact was as violent as it was deafening. The monolith slammed into the side of the Range Rover, flipping it over and then rolling it, like a football, twenty metres down the road. Then, it clipped its mangled undercarriage and steamrollered over it, before groaning like a prehistoric creature and collapsing onto its side, spilling its car cargo like ball bearings.

The officers in the patrol car could only watch in horror as, one by one, more cars slammed into what was left of the Range Rover, until it was no longer identifiable among the wreckage.

The passenger seat officer picked up the radio and requested immediate assistance, although, judging by the mangled mess of the Range Rover, he doubted much could be done for its driver.

71 CLAUSTROPHOBIA

Ashley had gained and lost consciousness countless times.

Mercifully, each awakening had not been long enough for her to absorb the reality of where she was, but this time it was different. This time she was compos mentis enough to fully appreciate the horror of her predicament, and she cried for help, but choked on the air that was beginning to taste bitter.

Her extremities were frozen numb and she had lost sensation in her arms. The rest of her body felt okay, inside the coat she was wearing, the very same coat that was bulking her up and wedging her inside her tomb. This made it nigh on impossible for her to move without the aid of the hands that were bound in front of her.

The darkness was palpable as was the claustrophobia and the thought of dying alone, buried alive in a makeshift tomb without any hope of anybody ever finding her, without ever seeing Rupert again, his smile, his laugh...

"NOOOOO!" She screamed and choked again.

She rocked her body and attempted to sit up, but she simply couldn't, especially now, since her energy was freezing over just like the world above.

She wept once more.

"Help me!" She sobbed, "SOMEBODY, PLEASE HELP ME!", but the only reply was her own voice, ringing in her ears as she listened carefully for a possible answer.

And then she felt movement.

At first she thought she imagined it but then, suddenly, it moved again, scuttling across her hair in the darkness and then down her forehead.

She opened her mouth to scream, but the beetle fell through her lips! She gagged with revulsion, which caused her to involuntarily bite down, bursting the insect, and spilling its innards into her mouth.

She spat, choked, coughed and screamed in abject terror, until her energy reserves dwindled, and she lost consciousness once more.

72 THE NIGHTMARE

Rachel tried to forget what she had seen in the bedroom, and some food and a few glasses of champagne later, she had succeeded.

It was Jason's idea that she should drink some more, as she seemed tense and it was important that she loosen up. So, she accepted each glass as it was brought to her.

He was right. It did help; most of the dull people were turning into colourful characters, and those people she would have normally avoided were suddenly becoming more agreeable, and their double entendres less repulsive.

This included comments made by Trevor Branson, a lawyer from a top London firm.

He was a forty-year-old man in decent shape with a tendency to laugh at his own jokes. He had joined Rachel and Jason as they stood at the bar.

But, once again, before she knew what was happening, she found herself abandoned, talking to the man, while Jay chatted up some woman, old enough to be his mother, on the other side of the room.

Still, Rachel didn't mind. She had come to learn that there was no harm in flirting.

Besides, Trevor knew she was with Jason, and that meant that even if she did play him at his own game of sexual innuendo, there could never be any risk of him jumping her.

That's why when Trevor suggested they move to a quiet anteroom, she accepted, although she did take more booze with her, just in case she needed him to become more interesting.

He closed the door behind them, sat on a leather couch and patted the seat beside him. Rachel, head still buzzing from the champagne, nearly fell on top of him.

"Hmmm, steady," he said with a laugh, running his hands over her rear, and manoeuvring her into the seat next to him.

"Oops, sorry, it's this champagne. I think it's a bit rich for me," she giggled, "Rich? You get that?"

"Hmm, I like your laugh," Trevor said with a big smile as he ogled Rachel's cleavage. "So, this is your first time here."

It was more of a statement than a question.

"Yes, it is."

"Have you enjoyed yourself so far?"

Rachel hiccupped, "Oh yeah, so far, despite the fact that my boyfriend keeps disappearing."

"He does?"

"Yes," Rachel said, petulantly.

"Oh well, never mind," Trevor said with a smile and patting her leg. "We'll just have to amuse ourselves without him."

This, of course, in Rachel's inebriated state was highly amusing and she erupted into fits of laughter. As she did so, her breasts wobbled inside the fabric of her dress and Trevor enjoyed this, he enjoyed this very much.

He did like her laugh, he especially liked it when she leant back into the sofa, propping both her hands for support on the headrest. It was as if she were ready, almost as if she were inviting him to crawl on top of her, but he didn't, not just yet, he wanted to savour the moment first. He planned to deny himself, because that made the rest much more exciting.

Instead, he settled for feeling her knee. Then, graduated to her leg and then, the inside of her thighs.

"Where have you been all this time my delicious Rachel?"

"Working."

"Working?"

"Yes, you know, switchboard, and before that it was accounts and before that computer science. I know what you are going to say, it's not necessarily an attractive subject for a girl, but I liked it, and it opens doors to lots of opportunities."

"Fascinating," Trevor agreed, totally uninterested, as his hand tickled up the inside of Rachel's thigh. "So you like the anatomy of computers then. Fixing them and all that. And how do you feel about me fixing you?" he said with lusty eyes.

Rachel giggled, "Fix me? I'm unfixable, mate," she stated, sitting forward, but fell back again when Trevor pressed a hand on her chest.

"Hey!" she protested with a laugh and pushed up once more.

"Oh no, I prefer you much more when you lean back," he

said, placing a hand on her tummy.

"I don't like leaning back," Rachel said, "Makes me feel woozy."

"That's okay," Trevor whispered, licking his lips and tasting her curvy breasts with his eyes, "Woozy is nice."

"Not this kind of woozy, I feel like I'm going to puke!"

She tried to sit up again, but Trevor's powerful hand stopped her once more.

"Hey, stop that," she protested.

"No, I'm ready," he stated. "I'm ready for it, now," he said, grabbing her hand in his.

Rachel laughed, "Ready for what?"

"To have you," he replied with another lick of his thin lips that, even in her stupor, made Rachel recoil.

She forced a laugh, "Uh, I don't think so," she said, pushing his hand off.

She moved to stand up, but a sharp tug on the hem of her dress brought her back down again, right into the lawyer's lap, where Rachel could feel his hardness through her dress.

"Eww, let go of me!" she protested, but Trevor had other plans and, with hands on her thighs, manhandled her rear to rub him, while simultaneously pushing his face into her breasts.

He moaned appreciatively as he did so.

"Get off me!"

"Oh yes, yes," he cheered, "I like it feisty!"

"Get your fucking hands off me!" she screamed, tugging at his hair forcing him loosen his grip; she fell to the floor with a thump.

"You bitch, that hurt! You're going to pay for that," he said, still inebriated with lust, as if it were all part of the game.

Rachel scrambled to her feet and moved to leave the room, but before she could get to the door, strong hands grabbed her hair and yanked her back, making her cry out in pain.

"Hmm that's it, I like to hear you scream," he said and propelled her, face first, back onto the sofa. Then, before Rachel could collect herself, he was on her back, like a randy dog, rubbing himself up against her, sucking the air in over his teeth and snorting like a pig.

"Get off me! Get off!" She protested now as vehemently as her head pounded.

"Yes, that's it, fight me bitch, fight me," he said, slapping her backside and then pulling up her dress to expose part of her legs. "Oh yes, me likey, yes," he appreciated as he held one hand on the back of her neck, to keep her doubled over, and ran the other over her rear.

He licked his lips, "Hmm, fresh meat," he moaned as he slid his hand under her dress and fingered her panties.

Meanwhile, face down in one of the cushions, Rachel squirmed to get free. She was screaming, but her voice was muffled as her mouth was grotesquely pressed into the cushion's fluffy cover.

"Geeett ooooff me! Get off!"

But Trevor was having none of it. Instead, he released her temporarily, long enough to pull himself out of his trousers, but it was long enough for her to lift herself up.

However, before she could turn around, he was mounting her again like a repulsive, slobbering animal.

He rubbed against her now bare flesh, and kept telling her how he was going to give it to her and how she was going to love it.

He yanked at her dress, ripped part of it and then at her panties, expecting them to tear also, but they didn't. Instead they cut into Rachel's thigh, making her scream.

"GET THE FUCK OFF ME!"

"Yes, fight me, my beauty, fight me," he chanted, as he attempted to barge his way between her legs. That's when Rachel put all the strength she could muster into elbowing him in the chest.

He made a choking sound and slowly slithered off, eventually falling back onto the sofa.

Rachel, now panting from the exertion, wrenched herself up into a standing position and then turned to see the lawyer, slumped on the couch. He was clutching his chest with both hands, while his pink erection poked grotesquely up from his zipper.

The sight of it sickened and enraged her, and she swiftly brought her shoe up between his legs, smashing into his hanging testicles.

He cried out, but there was no sound, as the sickening sensation, that gripped the pit of his stomach, sucked the air from his lungs.

Rachel ran to the door, yanked it open and froze, as her brain struggled to translate the spectacle before her.

The lights had been dimmed, dipping the hallway in an eerie, jaundice yellow.

At the foot of the stairs, a couple chatted casually. Nearby, on a chaise longue, a man was lying back, with his arms tucked under his head while a gaunt, anaemic looking woman, in her sixties, hitched up her baggy navy dress, and straddled him. She then proceeded to flick her thighs, as if she were having a seizure.

Rachel found her feet, and ran forward, towards the ballroom.

The chatting couple paused temporarily to look at her, as if she'd been caught running in the school corridor.

The overhead lights had been switched off. The only illumination was thrown by candelabras, strategically positioned around the room.

Rachel's mouth dropped open when she spotted, tangled in the velvet curtains across the room, a young man in his twenties with a woman, many years his senior.

He had one of her legs flung over his arm, as he pounded her against the backdrop of fabric, making it shake with every thrust. He was loud in his pleasure while she, thin lips pursed and eyes shut, grinned maniacally.

On a rug near them, a black woman's head bobbed between the legs of an old man, whose face was contorted in spasms of pleasure, while his shiny wet tongue slithered over chapped lips.

Rachel blinked, convinced that this was all some hideous nightmare. Any second now, the horror was going to dissolve and she was going to wake up in bed to a sun-drenched bedroom.

But it wasn't.

Minutes before, these people were dolled up, like some of the finest people of high society and now, now, they were half naked and copulating freely, like members of some kind of sex sect.

Sect?

Oh God.

This is where he had brought her, and these were the favours he wanted, and this was how much he loved her.

An angry wail brought her crashing back to the present. She turned to see her drinking companion stumble, hands between his legs, towards her, his face creased into a mask of rage.

She didn't know what to do, where to go from here. Should she find Jason? Should she just run? Where to? She was in the middle of nowhere and she didn't have the keys to the car.

She had no choice but to find Jason.

Where is he? With whom?

With a mixture of trepidation and rage, she raced up the stairs, as angry shouts were thrown after her.

"Jason!"

She ran down the corridor, opening doors as she went.

The first room was empty. The second revealed a semi naked woman. She was wearing rubber boots and gloves while a man, Rachel recognised as one of the politicians she had met earlier, lay sprawled on the bed pleasuring himself as he ogled her.

Both of them looked up as the intruder stormed into the room.

Rachel gaped but said nothing, she just turned on her heels and fled.

"Jason!" She shouted again, as she entered another room with subdued lighting, blacked out windows, and chains hanging from the ceiling.

Inside, a middle-aged, wafer thin man stood in his white underpants, with his hands chained up in a crucified pose, while a woman, in a leather outfit, shrieked obscenities at him. Both looked up when the door burst open and Rachel appeared on the threshold.

"JASON!" she screamed through horrified tears. "JASON!"

Another room; a man was crawling around in a giant nappy whilst an overweight woman, bulging out of a black nightdress fed him with a bottle.

They glared at her.

"JASON!"

Another door; middle-aged woman lay on her back as a young girl, two times her junior, in nothing but stiletto heels, crawled over her on all fours.

"JASON!"

Rachel was sobbing now. It was the house of horrors. Her boyfriend was nowhere in sight. She was alone.

Terrified.

That was until she barged into the next room, and instantly threw her hand to her mouth, not to stifle a scream but to stop the bile from spewing out of her mouth.

Jason was so busy, he didn't even notice his girlfriend enter the room.

He was on the bed, naked, along with a scrawny old woman and a thin young blonde.

Rachel could only watch as Jason's, her boyfriend's bare backside moved up and down, as he worked between the old lady's legs.

She quivered with disgust as she watched the young girl lick her lips and run her hands all over her boyfriend, all over the man she had planned to marry, whose children she had planned to bear.

Rachel could no longer keep the contents of her stomach, and promptly vomited onto the carpet.

She remained doubled over for a while until she spotted it. Across the room, opposite the bed, a tripod-mounted video camera was recording everything in sickening detail.

The old woman's bony fingers were entangled in Jason's hair, and pushing his face towards the camera lens, as she ordered him to push deeper, faster.

Suddenly, the girl stopped caressing the copulating duo and looked up. Almost telepathically, Jason stopped what he was doing and turned around.

Rachel drew in a sharp breath, as if *she* had just been caught spying on them.

TONY MARTURANO

Their eyes met and the true weight of what was happening hit home.

She ran from the room and back down the corridor. She wanted out of that place. She wanted out of there, now.

"Rachel!" Jason called, but she had gone.

The woman pulled him back into her, but he refused. Then, much to her discontent, he withdrew.

He slid into his clothes, and was about to race out of the room, when Lurch and a couple of the others appeared on the threshold.

He skidded to a halt, then looked up, sheepishly, into Lurch's solemn face.

Behind him, Trevor was ranting about how the girl had denied him, how he had been exposed by an *outsider*, and how the whole group was going to be outed.

Lurch silenced him with a wave of his hand.

"I... I'm sorry." Jason said while, behind him, his sex partner hissed angrily.

"You brought a reject into our midst, Jason," Lurch said.

"I, I didn't know."

"You know the rules," someone piped up from the corridor.

"You have exposed us all!" Someone else shouted.

"I can fix it, really I can," Jason said in a panic.

"Just like you fixed the other one?" Lurch asked, calmly.

"She was different," Jason said.

"Different how?"

"She must be silenced!" Someone shouted.

"Silenced like the other one," someone else agreed.

"She will expose us all!" someone else whined.

Jason shrank back as Lurch loomed closer, "Fix her like you did the other, or we'll fix you," he growled.

Jason, who was shaking now, nodded, scuttled out of the room and down the corridor, leaving the rest of the congregation to converge and chat, animatedly.

Rachel found the group of people at the foot of the stairs intimidating. They reminded her of a coven of witches. Especially the way in which they chattered to each other until they saw her, then the buzz ended and they settled for staring, instead. Burning holes in her body with accusatory eyes.

She hesitated, as she wiped tears from her face. Her mind was still swimming with alcohol, although recent events had gone some way to sobering her.

The reality of her predicament was as palpable as the atmosphere, as she slowly made her way down the stairs, closer to the sea of glowering faces.

I hate you too!

She thought.

She resented being here, hated what she had seen, and despised these creatures, for taking from her the only thing she had ever wanted.

She swallowed hard.

She felt cheap, betrayed and enraged, and if any of these freaks tried so much as to lift a finger to her, she would rip their fucking heads off!

It was with that thought that she descended the rest of the stairs and, much to her astonishment, the sea of bodies parted and allowed her to pass.

She hurried to the front door and, without looking back, yanked it open.

She stood there for a few moments, sucking in the freezing cold freshness of the outside world that suddenly made her feel so giddy, she had to lean onto the doorframe for support.

But there was no time to rest; voices were gathering behind her. One, in particular, was calling out her name; she recognised it, but didn't care, she was done, and launched herself into the freezing cold night.

She grabbed handfuls of snow off cars, chewed, then spat it out, and repeated the process two or three times before actually swallowing some.

The air was still, and a supernatural moon shone brightly like a giant spotlight in a star-filled sky, glittering the winter wonderland around her.

She felt cold and the material of her dress was little defence against the chill, but such was the amount of adrenaline pumping through her body that the effect was diluted.

Suddenly, she heard footsteps crunching the snow behind her and so, without even looking back, she increased her speed, even though she had absolutely no idea where she was going. She figured, that as long as it was far away from here, she didn't care.

"Rachel!"

She ignored him.

"Rachel, wait!"

"Get away from me, Jason!" She warned.

"Wait!"

"Fuck you!"

Jason had to jog to catch up with her and when he did, she was half way down the drive where frosted trees appeared to lean in, as if to listen to what was about to be said.

Jason grabbed her arm and spun her around to face him. "Where the hell are you going?" he asked as his breath fogged out into the night. He was wearing his jacket and carrying her shawl.

"As far away as I can get from you and the rest of those freaks!"

She snatched the shawl off him; she was mad, but not stupid. It was freezing out there.

"Rachel…" he put his hand on her arm, but she pushed it off. "Come on, Rach…"

"Come on? What do you mean, come on?"

"I mean come back to the house, let's talk about this."

"Oh My God, Jason. Do you really think we actually have anything left to talk about?"

"I love you, Rachel. What you saw back there doesn't mean I love you any less."

Rachel snorted, and her face creased into an incredulous glare, she wanted to say something, but was so enraged by his comment that she couldn't find the words. Instead, she turned and started walking again.

"Rachel…" Jason called as he caught her arm.

"I told you to stop fucking touching me!" she yelled at him as her voice boomed into the night.

"Rach, this isn't funny anymore."

She looked at him, baffled by his statement.

"Everybody does it, Rach," he stated calmly. "One way or another. You just don't see it."

"I can't believe I'm hearing this. Everyone may do it,

Jason, but normally it's with someone they care about or even fancy. You can't tell me that you fancied that old hag back there. Oh God!" she put her hand to her mouth, as she felt sick again.

"No, I don't fancy her, but that's the whole point. That's the whole point of this place; you are allowed to indulge your fantasy and nobody asks questions, and in return…"

"…And yours was to shag that bitch? Jesus Christ!"

"Of course it wasn't. But I was doing my part, making my contribution to the group. By helping each other this way, we get other rewards."

"Oh, so what you mean is if you whore yourself out to those deviants, they do you favours in return, is that it?" Rachel's voice was calm and understanding.

"Yes, sort of," Jason agreed.

"Oh, oh well, now that you've explained it. I feel much better, thanks," she said sarcastically with a big smile that rapidly changed into a sneer and she spat, "You make me sick!"

With that, she turned and started walking again.

"Where are you going?" Jason shouted after her. "We're in the middle of nowhere. You can't walk back to the city?"

"Watch me."

"There's nobody else out here, Rachel. You'll freeze to death."

"That's just a risk I am going to have to take."

"Rach, stop being so fucking stupid!" Jason yelled, his anger boiling over.

She wasn't stopping and this was annoying him. It was bad enough that the bitch had embarrassed him in front of the others, now she was making him stand out there in the freezing fucking cold.

He ran after her, grabbed her arm forcefully and spun her to face him yet again.

Rachel cried out, "You're hurting me!"

"Good," Jason said, eyes narrowing, angrily. "Do you have any idea how much trouble you've fucking caused me?"

"No," she said through a grimace of pain, "I don't, and I don't give a shit either!"

"Well you better, you selfish bitch!" He held both of her arms, leant into her face menacingly and said through gritted teeth, "Do you have any idea who you're dealing with here? They're society's richest and most powerful. Do you really think they want the rest of the world to know what goes on in there?"

"Like I said before," Rachel's grimace increased as she tried to pull away, "You're mistaking me for someone who gives a shit!"

And that is when it came, hitting the side of her cold numbed face like a meteor. The slap was so hard, it knocked her sideways, into the snow.

White light flashed in front of her eyes as blood oozed from a cut on her lip and dripped to the ground, dying the snow black in the moonlight.

She lay, unmoving, as a freezing wetness seeped through her dress and kissed the skin of her trembling body.

Jason's shadow fell over her as he stepped forward. "Get up." He ordered, but Rachel didn't move. "I said get up!" he yelled, his voice laden with rage.

Slowly, Rachel turned her face and looked up into his silhouette.

"Now get back in there," he ordered, and then added, incredulously, "Fuck! What is it with you stupid bitches? You just aren't able to appreciate a good thing when you see it. It was the same with that other stupid cow. To make things worse, she gets herself knocked up," he said with disgust. "And just like you, she wanted more. She actually wanted the guy to give up his family and career for her. Can you believe it?"

Rachel held the shawl to her mouth.

"What? Well, you wanted to know about her, didn't you? Fuck! And she was a whore, Rach, a top class whore, but she was too greedy and had a big mouth. And that's what happens when you cross these people, Rachel, you disappear, never to be seen again. Now, if you don't want the same thing to happen to you, I suggest you get your fucking arse back in there right now and that you play good." Jason's voice was low and menacing.

Rachel, lip quivering, said something that, in her stupor, came out as a mumble.

"What was that?" Jason asked, leaning forward.

"I said, FUCK YOU!"

With that, he reached down and grabbed her by the hair, "You bet you will… And anyone else I tell you to," He said as he yanked her up, making her cry out in pain. "Get used to it, there's plenty more where that came from," he murmured as he led her forward by the hair.

However, Rachel had decided that she wasn't going to go back to that place, at least not alive. With that she turned her face to Jason's hand, and gave every scrap of strength into the bite she sank into his skin.

The clamp of her teeth was so deep, she thought she had reached the bone.

He shrieked and instantly released his grip, attempted to shake away the pain, and then proceeded to inspect the damage.

Rachel did not hesitate to take advantage of the moment, and as he stood, gawking at his hand, she swung a right uppercut into his nose.

The shock and force of the blow propelled him backwards, into a snow covered bush.

Rachel did not hang around to inspect her deed. Instead, she clutched the shawl to her and ran for, what she believed, was her life, into the woods and the unknown.

But she hadn't got far when Jason's enraged rant reached her.

He was screamed many things, but the two words that chilled her more than the very air around her were, "…..kill you!"

73 TALES FROM A TOMB

When news of Adam's death arrived at the Harrison Penthouse, Rupert's legs buckled beneath him and he had to be escorted to the sofa.

He'd sealed Ashley's fate the moment he transferred the money. His actions, albeit indirectly, may well have contributed to the death of the woman he loved.

Warner did his best to reassure him. He told Rupert that he had all the police officers that he could spare, following up on any and all possible leads in the effort to find Ashley, but this was little comfort, for he knew that the police had no leads.

But that is when he noticed one of the officers walk up to Mark Warner, and whisper something in his ear. The news made the Detective Sergeant shake his head.

Rupert sprung to his feet, "If you lot have something to say, why don't you just say it?" he said, angrily.

"Mr Harrison…"

"…forget the Harrison shit; just tell me what the hell is going on!"

"Okay, I will, just calm down…"

"…Don't tell me to calm down, my fiancé's out there," Rupert said through gritted teeth. "Jesus Christ," he wrestled with tears, "my fiancé is out there somewhere and we have no idea where she might be."

Mark sighed. "I'm sorry, Mr Harrison…"

"…Rupert, my name is Rupert and my fiancé's name is Ashley."

Mark nodded, "Rupert. I ordered a trace on Adam Lewis' mobile phone. There's a slim chance that we may be able to triangulate where he was when he made that call to you."

"Really?" Rupert's face brightened.

But Warner was quick to stress caution. "Please, it's just a possibility. Unlike what you may have heard or seen in movies, the technology isn't that accurate."

Rupert looked perplexed.

"You see, when you make a call from your mobile phone, the tower it's directed to is dependent on multiple factors and software algorithms."

"But there must be a chance, I've heard of people being convicted on that kind of data."

"Yes, they have, often wrongly. For example, if I were to pick up my phone right now and make a call, it wouldn't necessarily be routed through the nearest mast, since how my request is handled is subject to the load on that particular mast in that particular moment. If the load is high, there's a distinct possibility that the call may be routed through another tower, miles away."

Rupert's shoulders slumped once more.

"I'm sorry," Warner said. "I just don't want you to get your hopes up too high."

"Some hope is better than none, Mark. So please, from now on, no more Mr Harrison and no more whispering, just tell it to me exactly how it is," Rupert said, wearily.

Mark smiled and nodded.

There was silence for a few seconds before Mark spoke again. "Mr....Rupert, there's something else."

Rupert looked up.

"It's about the package Ashley received here."

"You think it was Adam?"

"No, we know it was somebody else."

"Who?"

"Have you ever heard of a man called William Barber?"

Rupert thought for a few seconds and then shook his head.

"Well, during our investigation into the incident at Ashley's flat, and the package she was sent, we routinely looked into some of the authors that she had turned down recently. William Barber happened to be one of them. In his home, we found newspaper clippings about the book Ashley wants to publish about The Met, among other things. We also found your address scribbled on a notepad, along with a copy of the actual manuscript Ashley turned down. Do you have any idea what Barber's manuscript was about?"

Rupert shook his head. "I told you, I've never heard of him."

"It was about a man that lives with his mother, but one day flips out and buries her alive in the back garden. Adam Lewis was on your fiancé's team, the team who turned down this man's manuscript, he will have undoubtedly read it."

Rupert breathed in, "Oh God."

Mark continued, "There's more." Mark paused, then, "We found William Barber dead tonight; he was hanging from the banister of the home he shared with his mother. There was no sign of her so, on a hunch, we checked the back garden, and, well, let's just say that his book wasn't fiction. It was a true story," Mark said, gravely. "We also have reason to believe that it was he who sent the package to Ashley."

"So, do you think he was also responsible for what happened at her flat too?"

"There's no evidence to suggest that."

"Who was it then? Adam?"

Mark paused. "Well, at the moment, we don't know."

74 THE BEACON

Rachel had lost track of time.

It felt as if she had been wandering through the woods for over an hour when, in reality, it had not been more than fifteen minutes.

She had run, stumbled and walked through the woods aided only by the light of the full moon.

She was tired, her head thumped and despite the fact that her body was burning from the exertion, the rest of her extremities were numbed by the sub-zero temperatures.

She stopped by a fallen tree as her rasping breath rang loudly in the still of the night.

A bird screeched from somewhere in the shadows, making her jump. She looked around and began to appreciate the hopelessness of her predicament; she was in the middle of nowhere, cold, unwell, and without a clue.

A snapping sound snatched her from her thoughts. She turned quickly in its direction, and panic gripped her. He was here, he was close and he was going to kill her.

Oh God, the same way he killed Keri. And nobody will ever know. Nobody even knows I'm out here!

Another snap and then a fluttering sound in the shadows.

She began to breathe fast and heavy, and she could swear she heard the sound of her beating heart echoing around her.

She listened hard, her eyes darting all over the place, as she half expected Jason to pounce at her from behind a tree, donning that same maniacal glare, but nothing happened.

That didn't stop her breaking into yet another run.

The forest seemed endless, albeit mercifully sparse, yet populated by the giant spectres of naked trees with long creature-like talons that occasionally seemed to reach down and pull at her hair and her shawl.

She stopped, momentarily, and snatched the garment from the clutches of a branch, but when she turned, it took its revenge by tripping her up with one of its roots. She fell, once more, into the snow.

It was as she was lying there that she broke into a sob.

She remained that way as a few minutes melted by. The awfulness of all that had happened to her in the past hour, in the past weeks, finally taking its toll.

You're gonna' die out here.

No, I'm not.

And it was as she was wearily pulling herself to her feet that she saw it; a light, shining through the trees like a beacon.

She made her way towards it, like a moth to a flame. Slowly, the amber glow took its place inside the silhouette of a building; hope in the winter wilderness.

Like a warm shower, relief washed over her as she emerged from the forest into a small meadow. Directly ahead, a light shone brightly from one of the mansion's upstairs windows.

She raced across the blanket of snow, around the building and up to the front door.

She hammered on it just as a shadow emerged from the woods behind her.

"Hello! Hello!"

But there was no answer.

She stepped back from the steps and looked up and around the building; all of the windows were in black.

All lights extinguished.

"NO!"

She retraced her steps to the side of the house.

Nothing.

No lights. No beacon.

This isn't happening!

She ran up to the front door once more.

"PLEASE! HELLO! PLEASE! OPEN UP! I NEED HELP!"

Nothing.

So she grasped the door handle in frustration and felt part relief, part apprehension when it clicked open.

"Hello!" she called as she pushed the door open with a loud creak.

"Is anybody here? Hello?"

Just silence.

In the gloom of what appeared to be a large entrance hall, she could just about make out a table and two armchairs. Next to them, the outline of a staircase disappeared up to the next floor.

The air was musty with a strong scent of lavender.

She walked in and scanned the shadows for the outline of a phone.

She could hardly see, so she searched for a light switch. Found it, flipped it on and off a few times but nothing happened.

"Hello? Please! Somebody!" she called desperately into the darkness. She was suddenly overwhelmed by a strong sense of foreboding that the house may be uninhabited, with no phone, and nobody to help.

But she refused to believe this. She'd seen the upstairs light.

She crossed to the foot of the stairs, and nearly squealed with excitement, when she spotted a small table under the staircase, and a phone!

She rushed over to it, snatched the receiver from its cradle and cried with relief when she heard a dial tone, but with it came the sound of muffled footsteps in the snow outside.

"No," she breathed.

Oh God. He followed my footprints here!

She looked around in the gloom trying to decide what to do next, where to hide.

The footsteps were getting louder, closer; he was just

outside the door.

The staircase; without hesitation, she rushed to it and climbed the stairs, as quickly and as quietly, as she could, just as the doorframe filled with the scary shadow of a man.

From her position on the landing, Rachel watched as the figure remained unmoving as if sniffing the air for her.

She struggled to stifle her breathing as she waited for its next move.

For a fleeting second, she even considered giving herself up, trying to reason with him. He was her boyfriend after all. He was the man who was supposed to love her. The one for whom she had given up everything.

But he was also a desperate man, someone who would stop at nothing to protect a secret that could send him to prison and ruin the lives of those he consorted with.

He wouldn't hesitate to hurt you. You found that out tonight. He killed Keri!

She touched her thick lip in the darkness as if to remind herself. The welt was a stark reminder that her boyfriend was not the man she believed him to be.

This is why Keri took out insurance against them. This is why she recorded all of her telephone conversations.

Rachel drew in a sharp breath, as the shadow moved from the door. For one horrifying moment, she thought it was going to climb the stairs.

Mercifully, it didn't. Instead, the footsteps clicked into one of the downstairs rooms.

She looked around; the stairs, the balcony directly in front of her and the long, dark corridor to her right at the end of which she could see a slither of a moonbeam, like gold at the end of a rainbow.

She knew she would have to move from her position, it would only be a matter of time before he came up to search for her.

Slowly and quietly, she moved away from the banister and crept down to the end of the corridor, and looked out of the window. The moon glistened on a snow covered world, but offered no way out of there.

She heard a creak and spun around.

He's coming up the stairs!

She quickly and as quietly as possible, opened the first door she could find and darted inside.

Like the rest of the house, the room was stalked by shadows; she could just about make out a bed and some furniture.

She pushed the door to, careful not to click it shut, and then listened carefully, but it was difficult with her rasping breaths and the pounding of the blood in her ears.

She willed herself to calm down.

Then she heard it, that eerie creaking sound, one of a person creeping quietly down the corridor, someone searching for her, someone who could not and would not stop until she was found.

She looked around the room and spotted a door, presumably a closet or bathroom. It would be foolish to corner herself that way, but she had no choice.

She hurried over to it, pulled the door open and felt ahead of herself; wire hangers jangled loudly.

Flinching at the sound, she stepped inside.

She closed her eyes and listened carefully, but she was still breathing too loudly. Even the swallowing sound she made, to moisten her dry mouth, seemed deafeningly loud in the still of the stale closet.

She tried to stifle her breathing, by putting her hand over her mouth, yet the more she suppressed the urge to gulp in the dank air, the louder the sound seemed to get.

Then, suddenly, she felt a freezing cold draught blow on her right ear, followed by a short, sharp whisper, "R a c h e l!"

Somebody was in the wardrobe with her!

She screamed, and literally fell out of the door, crashing to the floor, where she scrambled backwards until her back was pressed up against a bedside cabinet.

Eyes wide with terror, she turned to look at the swinging wardrobe door.

How did he get in there? Oh, God save me! Save me!

Rachel was so intent in detecting movement from the closet, that she didn't register the footsteps in the corridor outside.

It was only when the door flung open that she looked up to see Jason's profile; his face tinged moonlight eerie, his lips creased into an evil leer.

"So here you are," he said.

Rachel looked at him and then back at the closet in sheer bewilderment.

"I am fucking freezing," he said, loudly, "my ears are hurting, and my fucking fingers have gone numb, and all because you decided to go for a walk in the woods."

He crossed over to her and yanked her by the hair, out of her daze, and dragged her across the room.

"Ow!" She wailed. "Jay, please no!"

"Too late, you had your chance."

"Please, Jay!" She cried as he dragged her out of the room, and up the corridor.

"No, too late. As much as it's going to be a waste, it has to be done. You're a reject, and there's no way they're going to take you back now, and if I don't deal with it, they won't take me back either."

She was squirming behind him, trying desperately to relieve the strain on the roots of her hair, as her body was dragged over the cold wooden floor. "Jay, p...please...please, please Jay. I promise I won't tell anybody. I promise!"

He shook his head, "No can do, babe. You see, if it's not me, it will be them, and if I don't do it, then they will do the both of us. There really is no other way."

They had reached the banister once more.

Jason paused, giving Rachel the opportunity to struggle against him. He yanked her head forcefully forward and said with a snarl, "Don't piss me off, because I am likely to throw you off this fucking balcony right now and that, believe me, will hurt."

Her eyes welled with tears. She was in excruciating pain, both emotionally and physically, and the man who had purported to love her was casually talking about killing her, about ending her life. How was that even possible? Could all this really be happening?

He is going to kill you like he killed Keri.

"What is it with me and these fucking rejects," he asked himself, as he struggled with her to the top of the stairs, while considering his next move.

Then he stopped abruptly.

"What the fuck…."

Rachel followed his gaze down the corridor, to the window, where, against the moonlit backdrop, they saw what looked like the silhouette of a man.

It stood perfectly still, watching them.

"HELP ME!" was Rachel's instinctive reaction. "PLEASE! He wants to kill me!"

Nothing.

"This is between me and her," Jason growled.

"Please…help me," Rachel begged through sobs, but the figure did not react.

Just watched.

Jason gave it a few seconds and then smiled.

"Wise move."

He then turned back to the stairs and recoiled in shock when he saw that the shadow had moved, and was now standing before him; pale face and blue eyes, shimmering in the darkness.

Rachel pulled herself free and watched with bemusement; Jason appeared to be terrified of the empty space in front of him.

She seized the opportunity, and tried to rush around him, but failed to evade his outstretched arm.

He grabbed her and yanked her back.

"Where the fuck do you think you're going?" he hissed

Rachel lashed out by scraping her nails down his cheek causing him to shriek, but his grip remained firm.

"Not this time, you bitch!"

He turned, caught her by the throat, and began choking the life from her, as she desperately tried to prize open the vice-like hold.

He was enraged, and through gritted teeth, seethed, "I've just about had enough of you…"

He squeezed hard, transferring his rage into his grasp, slowly starving her brain of oxygen and enjoying every moment of it.

Her head pulsed, veins throbbed, and the pressure built as her legs began to buckle.

Jason, still grinning maniacally, enjoying the release of his frustrations. This bitch had humiliated him, and it was time she disappeared.

He began to tremble from the intoxicating deliciousness of her finally being disabled, finally submitting to his will.

Okay, so the light was faint, and he couldn't see every nuance of her dying expression, but his brain filled in the gaps as he felt her body sag over the wooden balcony railing.

It creaked in protestation at the combined weight that was being pressed against it and began to bow under the strain.

Creak...

...Rachel's arms gave up the fight and slowly slipped to her sides.

Creak...

Her eyes bulged, her spluttering slowed.

Snap!

They were falling.

Jason's expression changed from homicidal strain to incredulous wonder, as they waltzed in mid-air for a few seconds, before crashing onto, and collapsing the wooden telephone desk beneath them.

There was a loud, sickening *smack* as Jason's head smashed against the marble floor and, like an eggshell, cracked open, spilling it contents.

The bodies lay motionless; Jason's back arched over the debris of the wooden table and Rachel's body, slumped over him.

The house became deathly quiet once more, with just the occasional creak from the trees outside, as they swayed in a breeze that blew open the front door, and caressed Rachel's hair as a grieving mother would her dead child.

75 RESURRECTION

The sound of someone calling her name was so sharp and so loud it made her bolt upward, screaming.

Eyes wide open, she searched the room, not recognising where she was. Then, slowly, the memories returned and she became aware of her sticky hands.

She looked down and realised that she was lying on someone, she was lying on Jason and the stickiness in her hands was his blood!

She fell backwards, and became aware of a pain in her neck and the small of her back.

She cried out, and lay still for few seconds before, slowly, crawling to her feet.

Eventually, after steadying her sway, she looked down at the outline of Jason's unmoving body. She could just about see that his eyes were still open, and that blood had dribbled from his mouth to pool with that leaked from his head and was now oozing towards the open door.

She straightened her back and grimaced. She was cold, numb, and in pain, but she was alive.

Somehow she had managed to land on Jason. He had broken her fall, and now he was dead.

She noticed, on the floor nearby, the gleaming metal innards of the telephone that had been smashed in the fall.

She followed the wire to the receiver and shuddered when it led her under Jason's arm.

Looking away from him, and with a quivering grimace, she pulled out what was left of the receiver and gingerly placed it to her ear. She wasn't surprised to find that there was no dial tone.

Despondently, she let the telephone's hacked-off limb slip from her hands and clatter loudly to the floor.

She looked down; Jason's dead eyes stared back at her, prompting her to back away as bile slid up her throat.

She ran out into the fresh air, where she vomited, for the second time that evening, into the virgin white snow.

After a few minutes, her head began to clear but she felt awful. Her mind was a frozen lake. Underneath it was an ecosystem of thoughts as surreal as they had been terrifying.

What happened to me?

She looked at her blood-stained hands, crouched down and vacantly wash them in the snow, leaving behind dark inky smudges.

As she did this, a breeze blew up out of nowhere and shook the snow from the surrounding trees. It whistled through branches and brought with it a sound, a whisper…

"…r a c h el….."

She looked up as the branches rustled off each other.

"…r a c h el….."

She looked at the front door. For a terrifying moment, she thought Jason had survived the fall.

"…r a c h el….."

She looked around, the sound seemed to be coming from everywhere; the sky, the driveway, the forest, but there was nobody there.

"…r a c h el….."

She looked at the house. Only this time, her attention was drawn to the hedge that led to the rear of the building. That's when she noticed them; footprints.

They led from the front door to the rear of the house. They were faint, partially filled in by freshly fallen snow, but they were distinctive.

Somebody else was, or had been, here.

Inexplicably, she carefully followed the trail to the back of the building, where the moon continued to shine brightly. It gleamed on the snow, almost turning night into day.

She passed a frozen pond, a dusted white hedge, and beyond that, a frozen lake, surrounded by a snow clad forest.

The footprints led her to a mound of dirt covered with a thin layer of snow. All around it was a crisscross pattern of muddy footprints and a shovel.

Something was buried here.

She hesitated a few moments; looked at the shovel, at the mud and then at the shovel again.

Is this where Jason buried Keri?

Was this her grave? Or was this the grave of somebody else? Maybe another of Jason's victims.

Without thinking, she picked up the shovel and started digging, as deep and as fast as her energy reserves would allow.

It took some effort, as the earth had frozen over, but eventually, she hit something solid, which sent shivers through her.

She tapped the surface a few more times and realised that it was a plank of wood.

She hesitated, afraid of what she might find beneath, and then promptly dropped the spade and to her knees.

She tugged at the wood and yelped, when a deathly white face appeared to her.

She jolted, slipped and fell backward.

"Oh my God," she uttered, as she sat in the snow, while the freeze grew through her veins, like roots from a tree.

She was exhausted. Paralysed by the horrors of the evening, and this was the last straw.

Rachel broke down and sobbed.

She remained that way for a few minutes, until the breeze returned. This time, it blew snow dust across the frozen lake towards her.

"....r a c h e l...."

She looked up as the chill played with her hair, but she knew she was alone. There was nobody else out here in this Godforsaken winter hell. Nobody, but she and the corpse in the hideous makeshift grave.

She turned to it once more, and that is when she noticed the long hair; it was a woman.

She scrambled to her feet to take a closer look. So close that she set off a landslide of soil that fell onto the body's pallid face, and that's when she recognised her, "Oh no!" She cried, "It can't be!"

She fell to her knees once more, and leant over the grave. She clasped the lapels of the woman's coat, and pulled her up with whatever strength she could muster.

After several weary attempts, she half lifted, half dragged the body out of its burial place, and onto her knees.

There, with clumsy, numb fingers, she released the bound hands and laid the head back, using her legs as a pillow.

"Oh no, oh no, oh no," she chanted, as she settled on the mud pile, and cleaned the freshly dug earth from Ashley's grey face.

"Oh my God, Ashley! Ashley!" she screamed as if she could wake her. "Ashley!" she cried, as fresh tears found their way to her eyes. "What did he do to you? Oh no, oh no," she chanted, stopping only to put her ear to her friend's mouth; nothing.

"Ashley!" She felt her friend's blood-drained face, not knowing what to do.

"NO!" she whined. "Oh no. please, no!"

She put fingers to Ashley's throat, searching for a pulse, but she knew that this was futile because her hands were so cold, numb.

Tears welled in her eyes as she looked around, and then up at the star-spangled sky.

It was hopeless.

They were alone.

"HELP US! Somebody, please HELP US!" Her voice echoed around her, but there was no reply.

She pulled Ashley's limp body close, subconsciously trying to keep her warm as she sobbed, helplessly.

That's when she noticed them.

They emerged from the woods like dancing fireflies; flashlights, about a dozen of them, were walking towards her.

At first, she thought she was hallucinating, but as they drew nearer, the stillness of the night amplified their voices.

She started laughing, such was her joy.

"We're saved, Ashley. We're saved," she said, caressing her friend's face. Then she yelled out, "Over here! Over here! We're over here!"

Flashlight beams homed in on them, dazzling her eyes.

She started laughing, excitedly, but paused when she heard Ashley murmur something.

"Oh, thank you! Thank you, God!" She said, while fixing Ashley's hair around her face, as if the woman was going to come to and complain that she looked a mess.

Their saviours were only a several feet away now, a whole crowd of them. No less than ten, maybe fifteen, police officers had been sent to save them.

She squinted into the bobbing lights, grinning like a deranged person.

They were close now, talking animatedly, and glad that they had found them.

"Thank God," she said to the first of the men who arrived by her side.

She squinted, and held up a hand to fend off the glare of the lights as the chatter grew louder.

Then, the group parted, and out of them a single light appeared. Rachel was suddenly overwhelmed with dread because, despite her state, there was no mistaking him. There was no mistaking his towering seven-foot frame.

He loomed over her, silhouetted against the moonlit sky.

"No, no, no!" She cried.

"We meet again, Rachel," he said, in an unmistakable cultivated voice that snatched Rachel's hopes and drowned them under the ice of the lake.

It wasn't the police or the rescue services that had found them, but the sect. Jason's comrades had set out to ensure that he had accomplished his mission, and that he had not failed them.

Turns out that he had, but this was no comfort to Rachel, who knew that where Jason had failed, they would not. With that in mind, she pulled Ashley close and apologised to her friend, as she surrendered them to their fate.

She was exhausted and way outnumbered.

But, that's when she heard it.

The beat was so faint, Rachel thought she had imagined it, but she hadn't.

The sound echoed around the lake and it caused the group to stir.

Suddenly, someone yelled and pointed at a powerful spotlight that slashed across the night sky like a laser beam.

The murmuring of the congregation shifted in pitch.

Lurch said, "Calm down everybody, calm down."

"It's coming this way!" somebody cried.

"Remain calm," Lurch insisted.

Somebody wailed and Rachel looked up to see a flashlight

scarper back towards the forest, this was closely followed by another and then another.

The searchlight, less than a mile away now, skimmed the tree tops and eventually found the house behind her, while the loud whistling engine and beating blades scared the rest of the group off, into the night.

The only person to linger was Lurch. He stared, in stupefied fear, at the sky, as the helicopter's powerful beam licked across the pond, the lake, and then over them.

Lurch's eyes darted from the flying machine to the nearby shovel and, for a terrifying moment, Rachel thought he was going to have the last word. However, when their eyes met, she saw in them the same resignation she had experienced moments before.

It was over, and Lurch knew it.

He turned and followed the rest of his cohorts into the night.

The Jet Ranger helicopter was carrying four passengers: the pilot, Rupert Harrison, D.S. Mark Warner and one of his officers. Its engines were reassuringly loud as it landed in a blizzard of snow that sparkled like glitter.

As if sensing Rupert's arrival, Ashley finally opened her eyes to see her future husband, her friend and a sky full of twinkling stars.

76 POWERLESS

It was with a lump in his throat that Rupert fell to his knees, took his fiancé in his arms and vowed never to let go.

That was until Mark intervened, insisting that they get Ashley into the helicopter and to hospital as soon as possible.

Rupert removed his jacket, and wrapped it around his fiancé before carrying her over to the chopper, and strapping her into a seat.

The officer, known as Bass, did the same for Rachel.

"Okay, Rupert," Mark shouted over the drone of the helicopter's engine, "Bass and I will wait here. You go with the girls."

Rupert climbed inside as the two men backed away from the rotating blades, and waited as the engine sound increased and the chopper began to climb, resurrecting another snow blizzard.

However, the machine had only lifted a few feet before it landed once again with a thud.

Bemused, the pilot flicked switches and tapped the glass of the gauges; they were all falling, the engine sound decreasing, the rotors slowing.

"What the hell..?"

The power down continued until the engine suddenly cut out, restoring silence to the land once more.

"What the hell's going on?" Mark demanded, walking back up to the chopper.

"I don't know," the pilot said, checking and rechecking the instrument panel, "it looks like the alternator isn't putting out any power."

"Bloody hell," Mark mumbled, looking back at Rupert who was clutching onto a semi-conscious Ashley and a frightened Rachel. "Don't worry," he said, "we'll get you out of here."

But the pilot didn't agree since, no matter how much he tried, he could not get the engine to restart. The clicking sound was unmistakable; there was no power. The helicopter wasn't going anywhere.

Mark shook his head, angrily. The temperature was below freezing, and he had a hypothermic woman who needed treatment.

"Okay," he said decisively, and turned to the pilot, "get on the radio, call base, and tell them to get a medical chopper out here right now."

The pilot complied by picking up a mobile phone and dialling numbers.

Mark looked at the house and then at Rupert. "I'm sorry. We're going to have to take shelter inside, until we can get the helicopter restarted or another one out here."

"No!" Rachel said, abruptly.

All eyes turned to her.

"We... we... can't... go back in there," she stated, eyes filled with fear, "Jason's in there, he.... He... tried to kill me. I think he's dead," she garbled through shivers.

Mark exchanged looks with Bass, not sure exactly what to make of the statement, but reluctant to get into it right now.

"Okay, well, either way, we need to get you both inside."

He rummaged under one of the seats and retrieved a flashlight. "Rupert?"

Rupert took his cue; he unbuckled Ashley, and helped her out of the craft. Bass followed suit with Rachel, who panicked when he tried to disengage her seatbelt.

"It's okay," the officer soothed. "We're with you now, and we won't let anything happen to you."

Rachel wasn't convinced. She didn't want to go back into that house, not after what had happened there, but she had no choice. Bass was already helping her out of the helicopter, and leading her towards the front door.

77 THE RECKONING

Mark swore when the pilot informed him that emergency services would not be able to reach them for at least a couple of hours. Apparently, the heavy snowfall and icy conditions meant that they were already working to capacity.

Worse, he discovered that the power was out at Kenning Hall. Rupert explained that this was normal in bad weather, and promptly retrieved a collection of vintage lanterns, kept specifically for such an eventuality.

Therefore, it was by lantern light that Rupert escorted Ashley to the master bedroom, stripped her down to her underwear, wrapped her in several warm blankets, and put her to bed.

Then, he lit a mobile gas heater, drew the curtains, and sat with her until Mark arrived with some warm tomato soup.

"How are you feeling?" Mark asked.

"Co..cold," Ashley said, through shivers.

"Drink this," Mark said, handing Rupert the mug and spoon.

She shook her head.

"Ah now, Miss Marshall, I didn't say it was optional. You need to eat something warm."

"Ash...Ashley, I told you, my name is Ashley," she stuttered, looking at Rupert, and then the mug, as if contained poison.

Mark smiled, "Yeah, sorry, I forgot. Makes you feel like a school teacher, right? You're going to be okay," he said, warmly, and then added as a stern parent, "as long as you drink that soup."

He exchanged glances with Rupert, who nodded.

"I'll be downstairs if you need me. Stay warm," he added and left.

Ashley looked up at Rupert, "I...I must look awful," she said.

He smiled, lovingly, "Trust you. You've just been resurrected from a shallow grave, and you're worried about how you look."

Ashley frowned, suddenly, and tears pricked her eyes, as frozen memories melted back into her consciousness.

"Hey, hey now, come on," Rupert said, softly. "You're going to start me off."

"I...I... thought I was going to die down there," she said, through shivers.

"I know, I know," he cooed, feeding her more soup.

She spluttered a few times and then said, "Adam..."

"...Shhh, he can't hurt you anymore. Nobody will ever hurt you ever again," he added with conviction, as he leaned down to kiss her forehead, tenderly.

Rupert's heart ached as he remembered the news articles he had read in the car.

They chronicled the story of a little girl who had lost her mother at the tender age of nine, and had been betrayed by her abusive father; the man Rupert visited in the care home.

Andrew Skelton had taught his daughter how to assume the role of his wife. How to cook, clean and please him, as only a lover should.

This abuse had continued until the girl awoke one day to find her father having sex with his new girlfriend.

In a jealous rage, the girl had lashed out with a knife, wounding the woman and disabling her father.

As a result, he was sent to a secure hospital and she to a juvenile detention centre.

Eventually, the young girl was released and placed with a wealthy family, who committed to raise her as their own.

However, one day, whilst her foster parents were holidaying in Barbados, their two teenage sons took advantage of the young girl; one held her down while the other violated her.

By the time the foster parents returned, the two boys had brain washed the girl into believing that if she told, nobody would believe. Because she was already *damaged goods*.

She already had a history. Who did she think their parents would believe?

She'd be sent away again without a home, a family, nothing.

Eventually, the young lady left to attend the best education money could buy. Whilst there, she studied English, among many subjects, including psychology, where she learned that the first step to making amends with the past was to confront it.

She did, as well as her foster parents, who refused to believe the despicable things she accused their beautiful sons of.

They disowned her.

She left, and assumed the identity of the one person she believed had the perfect life, but not before sharing her story with a local paper.

It was this story that Rupert had read, and it was the memory of this story that brought tears to his eyes.

"I thought you told me not to get all emotional," Ashley said, weakly.

Rupert sniffed, "Yeah well, I said you would get me started

didn't I?" He forced a smile. "I love you so much," he said.

"You sure?" She asked, wearily.

"I'm sure," he said, and pulled the covers up around her. "I'll always take care of you," he whispered.

She replied with a murmur.

He waited a few minutes until she was asleep, and then he left the room, closing the door as quietly as he could behind him.

Downstairs, in the study...

Mark asked, "How is she?" before handing Rupert a coffee.

"Sleeping."

"Yeah, well, that's to be expected after what she's been through. The best thing you can do for her now is make sure she stays warm, and rests, until we can get out of here."

Rupert nodded. "Thanks Mark."

"Don't sweat it. It's all part of the service," he replied. "She's been asking after you both," Mark added, nodding toward Rachel, who was curled up on the couch, in front of a roaring open fire.

Rupert walked over and sat next to her.

"How are you doing?" He asked.

She nodded, "Better."

But Rupert noticed that she was still shaking, and put a comforting arm around her.

Their eyes met.

"Thank you," he said with a voice brimming with emotion; Rachel had saved Ashley and he would be forever indebted to her.

She smiled at him and held his arm.

Mark sat opposite them. "We've called back, Rachel. I told them about the place you talked about, but with the exception of this Trevor bloke who attacked you, I doubt there's much we're going to be able to pin on any of them."

Rachel didn't reply, she watched the fire, vacantly, as it crackled and snapped, and then she suddenly whispered, "I think they killed Keri Paxton."

"What did you say?" Mark asked, but not because he hadn't heard her, but because he thought he had misunderstood.

"I think Jason killed Keri."

"How do you know this?"

"He told me that they wanted rid of her because she became pregnant by one of them, and they didn't want a scandal."

She drank from the mug she was nestling in her hands.

"He said the same about me. He said that if he didn't deal with me, they would deal with us both…" her voice faltered as hideous memories pushed their way back. "I thought he loved me," she added, her voice a quiver.

Rupert pulled her to him and comforted her.

He looked around the room. "It's turned really cold in here," he said, as she trembled in his arms.

"It's freezing," the pilot, who was sitting at the desk, agreed. "Are you sure someone didn't just turn the electricity off at the mains before you left?"

"Good point," Bass, who was sitting in one of the armchairs, agreed.

"It's possible," Rupert said.

"Well, why don't we go and take a look?"

"I'll go and check," Rupert said, getting up, but Rachel clung to him.

"It's okay. I'll go. Just tell me where the main switch is," the pilot said.

"It's in the cellar. There's a trapdoor in the kitchen."

"Seriously?" the pilot forced a smile, looking at the others.

Rupert nodded with a knowing look.

"Take the flashlight," Mark grinned, handing it to him.

"Do you want me to come and hold your hand?" Bass asked in a mocking tone.

The pilot pulled a face, "I think I'll survive."

When he finally found the trapdoor hidden under the rug, he secretly wished he hadn't volunteered for the mission.

Yes, he was a grown man, but this house gave him the creeps.

It had, ever since he walked through the front door.

The dead body in the hallway didn't help.

He pushed the thought from his mind, pulled the trapdoor open and trained the light inside.

It did little to push back the darkness, but it did reveal the upper rungs of a ladder which, reluctantly, the pilot began to descend.

Back in the study...

"Rachel, are you going to be okay? I just want to go and check on Ashley," Rupert said, after finishing his coffee.

Before Rachel had a chance to reply, Bass stood up and said, "It's okay, I'll sit with you, if you like."

"Do you need me to come with you?" Mark offered.

"It's okay," Rupert said. "I'll let you know if anything's changed, but you can put the kettle on the gas if you like."

Mark nodded.

The cold seemed much more intense in the entrance hall, made worse by a gale that had blown up out of nowhere, and was now howling around the building.

Rupert held the lantern high in front of him, scaring away the shadows. He tried hard not to glance at the body in the hallway.

It had been hastily covered with a white tablecloth that seemed to move as the light danced across it.

The icy cold wind moaned under doors, as it scurried down the hall and the stairs until it met Rupert, pulled his hair, and then attempted to extinguish the lantern's flame.

He paused at the top of the stairs, and looked down the gloomy corridor, as if expecting to see somebody standing there, but it was empty.

He couldn't quite explain it, but something felt off about his childhood home.

He no longer felt welcome.

That's when he felt it. Another puff of cold air. It blew directly into his face, as if spitting at him, and that's when he realised; the door to the master bedroom was wide open, yet he distinctly remembered closing it when he left earlier.

As he drew near to the doorway, the lantern's flame began to dance wildly, as if trying to flee from its metal enclosure.

Rupert could see into the bedroom now.

The lantern he'd left on bedside table had been

extinguished. The room had been plunged into darkness, but for the flame of the gas fire and the moonlight streaming in through open balcony doors.

He also noticed, to his dismay, that the covers had been pushed back and that bed was empty!

He rushed forward, but yelped when the door slammed shut in his face, propelling him backwards and sending him teetering over the edge of the broken railing.

The lantern slipped from his hands, as he struggled to keep his balance, and smashed loudly to the floor below.

It took a few seconds but, eventually, and with immense relief, Rupert managed to regain his footing on the right side of the drop.

As soon as he did, he launched himself at the door, but it would not budge.

Instinctively, he banged on it with his fist.

"Ashley! ASH! Open the door!"

His face contorted with exertion as he turned the handle and pushed his shoulder into the door, until it finally gave way and he fell, heavily, into the room.

A gale hissed at him, through the fluttering curtains of the open balcony, as he jumped to his feet.

He looked over to bed, and saw that Ashley was lying in a foetal position on the floor, next to it.

"Ash!"

"Rupert!"

He heard footsteps running up the stairs. It was Mark.

"I'm in here..." Rupert shouted back.

"Is everything okay, we heard...?"

...Mark's words were cut short as, once again, the door slammed shut.

Then, much to Rupert's incredulous horror, a dresser scraped its way across the floor and stopped in front of it.

The action instantly cut the turbulence, the curtains fell still and the room quiet.

Rupert stood, unmoving.

All was still.

He could see no one but Ashley, yet he felt a presence nearby. Someone was watching him from the other side of the room.

He could hear them breathing!

The breaths were slow, deep, and had a guttural rattle, like that of an animal.

It was in the corner, between light and shadows, and it was waiting.

"Rupert!" Came Mark's voice from beyond the door as he banged on it.

The sudden sound startled Rupert.

"I'm alright," he said, hastily, as if not wanting to disturb the moment.

"Are you sure?" came the muffled reply.

"Yes."

Rupert slowly took in the room, as his breath fogged in front him.

He could hear Ashley's shallow breathing. She was shivering, and he wanted to go to her, but he didn't dare move.

Then, he looked up and around, as the scent of moss filled the air.

He sniffed, instinctively.

The scent was strong, familiar, and it instantly transported him back to his childhood.

Ben?

The world was still. Silence reigned.

Mark had gone quiet. Ashley had stopped breathing. Rupert's heart had stopped pounding.

All that existed was the silence, and the smell...

...and then...

The blow hit Rupert with such force, it launched him backward, through the air, smashing him into the mirrored door of the wardrobe. He, and hundreds of tinkling pieces of glass slid to the floor and lay, motionless.

The dankness of the cellar made the pilot gag.

Thankfully, the blue spy light of the gas burner was a beacon in the blackness.

He carefully made his way towards it, as his flashlight made creepy, moving shadows of boxes and wine racks.

It was only when he reached the burner that he realised; the thing was already on, which meant that the heating upstairs should be working, but it wasn't.

He peered closer at the blue flame, as if not trusting his own eyes, and leapt when something slammed loudly behind him.

He whirled around, pointing the flashlight in the direction of the sound, and saw that the trapdoor had shut, sealing him down there.

He rolled his eyes. "Oh yeah, that's right. Very funny. Now open up!"

Silence.

"Come on, Bass, stop pissing around!"

The quiet continued, until something scuttled on the floor next to him. He turned, quickly, to see a rat's tail disappear behind a wooden box.

He breathed, taking a few seconds, in an attempt to control the anxiety that was beginning to smother him, like the dark down there.

He made his way over to the ladder, where he quickly climbed the rungs and pushed on the trap door, but grunted with the effort when it did not move.

He was starting to lose his patience now. He didn't like it down there, and Bass was making the whole thing worse.

"Come on, open up!" he said, banging on the wood. "Bass? Come on!"

Something else scampered, in the far corner of the room. He turned and aimed the flashlight, like a weapon, in that direction, but saw nothing.

"Jesus Christ! Bass open the bloody door!" he yelled, banging on the wood above him.

Nothing.

"BASS! ANYONE!"

Still nothing.

Frustrated, he turned and froze.

Was he hallucinating?

It seemed that there were now three blue pilot lights across the room; the burner flame, and two more next to it. Only these were almond shaped and seemed to shimmer.

They looked like…eyes!

Shit!

He lifted the flashlight but it flickered and went out.

He slapped it, instinctively.

"Come on!"

He jumped off the ladder, and attempted to point the light once more, but each time he lifted it, the beam faded.

"Fucking thing!" He said, angrily, slapping it a few times, before lifting it again.

This time it worked, albeit with a scary strobe effect, that yielded a series of terrifying snapshots that planted a daggers of terror into the pilot's heart.

The first flash revealed a shape.

The second, an outline.

The third illuminated the profile of a man, who was standing in the corner of the room, watching.

Then, the light gave up once more, plunging the room into pitch black.

"Shit!" He staggered back.

The eyes were moved towards him, glowering in the dark.

He backed further.

"No…"

Faster…

"No!"

Faster…

"NO!"

He tripped, and fell to the floor.

The eyes drifted over him.

Instinctively, he lifted his torch in defence, just as the beam flickered, temporarily revealing a presence, dressed in black.

"JESUS!"

The pilot scrambled backward, and then flipped onto all fours. He rushed forward and slammed, head first, into one of the large wine racks.

He looked back; the eyes were right behind him!

In a blind panic, he tried to climb the rack, as if it were the ladder to his salvation.

It jangled, clinked, creaked and moaned.

"NOOO!" he screamed, heaving himself upward, clinging for dear life, but he didn't get far.

The rack gave way under his weight, and then, he was falling backwards until...

SLAM!

...he hit the back of his head against the cold stone floor.

Seconds later, thick glass smashed into his face, drowning him in wine. Then, a weight, as heavy as the world itself, landed on him, pinning him to floor.

It pressed and squeezed the air out of his lungs, to a cacophony of smashing glass and glugging bottles.

Blood frothed and oozed out of the pilot's lips, dribbled down his cheeks, and mixed with some of the finest vintages money could buy.

Back in the study...

Bass tried hard to ignore Mark's urgent calls, but the natural investigative instinct in him made him stand up.

"Where are you going?" Rachel asked, panicked.

"It's okay. I'm just going to see what the commotion is all about. Make sure the DS is okay."

"No, please, don't go!" Rachel said, eyes wide with apprehension.

"I'm just gonna' be in the hallway," he said, reassuringly.

Rachel looked over, the door was open, and she could imagine Jason's body lying, motionless, beyond the threshold.

"Oh please," she said through trembling lips, "Please don't leave me, please don't go out there. He might get you."

"Who's going to get me?"

"That man."

"What man?"

"The man I saw earlier, up on the landing."

"Rachel, there's nobody else here besides us..."

"...There is!" she said in a loud whisper, clutching onto his arm, like some kind of a crazy person, "I saw him."

"Well, that's even more reason for me to see if the Detective's okay. You'll be alright here, I promise. I'll be right back."

"No," She complained, but Bass had already picked her hands off him, and was making his way to the door.

Rachel shrunk back into the sofa.

With only the firelight for company, she felt vulnerable and afraid.

She scanned the room. It was watching her. Hundreds of eyes scrutinising her shivering body, as she tried to disappear beneath her blanket.

She jumped when the fire crackled, loudly, summoning a legion of demonic shadows that danced wildly off the books and walls.

She looked back at the door, just in time to see Bass disappear into the hallway.

"No," she squeaked, but it was too late, he had gone, swallowed up by the darkness.

Upstairs, in the bedroom…

"Rupert? Mr Harrison?" someone was calling.

Rupert opened his eyes to see Bass peering down at him.

It took him a few seconds to get his bearings. His cheek was stinging, and he instinctively touched it.

It had swollen.

"What happened here?" Bass asked.

"Where's Ashley?" Was Rupert's response, as it stood up to quickly and swayed.

The policeman caught him.

"Easy does it. Looks like a pretty nasty blow," Bass said, holding onto him, and nodding at the welt on his cheek.

"Ashley?" Rupert looked at the bed, but it was empty. He rushed over to it, as if disbelieving his own eyes, as Mark came out of the bathroom.

"Where is she?" he asked.

"What happened here, Rupert?" Mark asked.

"Where's Ashley?" Rupert continued.

Mark caught him arm and asked, seriously, "We were hoping you could tell us."

Downstairs, in the study…

To Rachel, it felt as if Bass had been gone for hours when, in reality, it was only minutes. She didn't want to be here, certainly not with the ever-present thought of Jason's body in the hallway.

She had to wrestle, once again, with the urge to look at the open door; her terrified mind telling her that he was out there, watching her with that death stare.

The fire shifted suddenly. The flames darted to and fro, as if a giant was blowing on them.

Then she heard it, distant at first. It blew around the building, rattled the glass in the window and made the door creak.

It was looking for her; it growled down the corridor, howled down the stairs and exploded into the lounge, where it blasted her in the face with a gust of freezing air.

She squealed, and retreated further under her blanket as the gale swept around the room, rocking the chandelier, knocking down ornaments, and tugging at paintings.

Eventually, it found the fire. It violently shook the flames, as if choking them to death, until they were snuffed out, plunging the room into darkness, but for the glow of hot embers.

Rachel's heart hammered as she remained still, frozen to her seat with terror.

The room had fallen silent. The only thing that could be heard was the squeaking of the chandelier, as it rocked above her.

Rachel's trembling breaths were like a foghorn in the quiet of the space that that turned as frozen as the world outside.

Her whole body, that was just normalising from her earlier ordeal was, once again, shaking uncontrollably.

She shrank back, as far as she could, into the safety of the couch, and then peeked out from behind her blanket, as the silence continued.

She felt alone, but she knew she wasn't.

She sensed she wasn't.

Somebody else was in the room with her. The same person

she'd seen upstairs.

Slowly, tearfully, she turned her head and looked across the moonlit skeletons of furniture, to the wide open door.

There was nobody there.

She was alone.

"R a c h e l!" the whisper was sharp in her right ear, just as it had been earlier when she was trapped in the closet. She leapt to the opposite side of the sofa.

She opened her mouth to scream but, like a nightmare, it emerged as a whimper.

Now she could see - right where she had been sitting just moments before - Jason, wrapped like a Madonna, in the shimmering white, blood stained, table cloth. His eyes were closed and he was mouthing something.

Rachel's heart thumped like a runaway train as she pushed back into the sofa, the arm digging into her, like a giant claw.

She tried to scream but nothing came out.

Then, Jason's eyelids opened, but instead of beautiful eyes, there was just two black cavities.

"NOOOOOOO!" the scream finally emerged.

She leapt out of the sofa, fell to the floor and twisted onto her haunches to see that Jason, the apparition, had gone; the sofa was empty.

She stared, eyes brimming with terror, as her convulsive shivering continued.

She was in the middle of the room now, with no furniture around her for protection.

Like a performer on stage, she was alone, spot lit by the moon that was streaming in through the large window.

Silence reigned.

Then, it returned, this time much stronger. The gale ripped around the room, tearing paintings from walls and launching ornaments into the air.

Rachel screamed and ducked, scrunching herself into a protective ball, as the projectiles flew overhead.

Silence again.

She didn't dare move; she was numb with terror, paralysed by fear.

Seconds ticked by. The only sound was the chinking of

chandelier crystals.

She was afraid to open her eyes, afraid of what she might see but, eventually, she found the courage. Slowly, she raised her eyelids to reveal a room littered with debris; shattered ornaments, broken paintings.

She looked at the open doorway and considered making a run for it; she could be out of there in seconds.

But just as she was summoning the strength, just as her mind was willing her body to stand, a loud ear-shattering screech sawed through her nerves and the wall to her right exploded in a cloud of dust, as if an invisible truck had just slammed into it, generating fracture cracks that reached all the way up to the ceiling.

There was another screech; the same happened to the opposite wall, and Rachel was showered with splintered wood and mortar.

She was screaming, hysterically, now.

"Rachel?"

She looked up; Bass was standing at the door. His face a mask of bewilderment.

"Bass!" she cried out. Instantly, the door slammed shut, locking him out.

Then, there was a whooshing sound, and invisible hands picked up every piece of furniture and flipped it onto its side.

The desk, the chairs, the couch, all somersaulted and then fell loudly to the floor once more.

Rachel covered her ears and cowered into the rug as dust filled the air around her.

Seconds passed.

"Rachel!" Bass was calling to her as he punched the door.

She looked up, as invisible hands clawed books from the shelves, launching them into the air and to opposite sides of the room.

They rained down on her in a hail of pages.

The destruction continued until most of the shelves were empty.

Then, silence once more, but for the hammering and splintering of the door, until it burst open and Bass appeared.

He ran, and threw himself over her, in a protective gesture, just as the window imploded and showered them in a hail of tiny glass particles, that fell to the floor in a dissonant symphony of tinkles and jangles.

Nobody moved, as the fresh scent of the night rushed into the room and brought with it the sweet scent of freedom.

Upstairs, in the bedroom…

"Rupert, calm down and tell us what happened in here," Mark said, as he watched Rupert pace the room, like a madman.

"I don't know what happened. I came in here and…" he broke off when realisation dawned. He looked at the open balcony doors, "Oh my God."

In that moment, a loud crashing sound travelled to them from downstairs.

The two policemen looked at each other, and then raced out of the room, but Rupert didn't follow. Instead, he stepped out, onto the balcony and surveyed the polar landscape.

Below him, crosswinds created a blizzard of the snow-covered lawn, where a trail of footprints led to Ashley, draped in a blanket.

She was walking towards the lake.

"ASHLEY!" Rupert shouted. His voice echoing around the nearby forest, but she didn't respond.

"ASH!"

Nothing.

He looked over the balustrade; the ground was about twenty feet below him.

There was only one way that Ashley could have left the room, and it was the same way he had used with his twin brother countless times before.

He climbed onto the balustrade, and grabbed the frozen trellis, which he used as a ladder to the ground.

He chased the footprints to the side of the lake, where he skidded to a halt.

Ashley was standing on the ice, motionless. She had her back to him.

A gale howled around them.

"Ashley?" he called, his voice suppressed, as if his mere presence would cause the ice to crack beneath her. "Baby, please come off there, please," he said, trying to mask the panic in his voice, for he was suddenly overwhelmed by the memory of what had happened right here, years before.

"Please Ash," he said, and waited.

Suddenly, the wind calmed, the trees stopped swaying, Ashley's matted hair fell still about her shoulders, and Rupert could hear himself panting.

He waited.

And then, very slowly, she turned around.

Rupert gasped when he saw how, under the moonlight, her beautiful body had turned pallid blue. He wanted to rush over to her, he wanted to take her in his arms and warm her body with his. He wanted to take care of her.

"Rupert?" she uttered in bewilderment.

"Oh yes, baby," he said with a big smile. Relief at her recognition spread through him. "Come off the ice, baby, please, come off the ice."

"Where am I?" she asked, suddenly afraid.

Rupert reached out to her, "Just come off the ice, and come to me."

But Ashley looked confused. Her face contorted into an expression of total incomprehension. She didn't recognise where she was, nor knew what she was doing there.

Rupert, his whole body taught with tension, spoke calmly, "Walk over to me, baby."

"...I don't understand..."

"Just walk over to me, now!" he said more, forcefully.

Ashley looked down at her bare feet, her body, and then she looked at his outstretched arms.

She hesitated, but, slowly, began to move towards him.

"Oh yes, that's my girl, reach out for me, come on baby."

She kept her eyes on her bare feet, as she shuffled forward on the ice.

"That's my girl," he said, his voice coaxing, hiding the trepidation he felt.

She was moving painfully slow.

But inched closer…

…closer

And then it happened, just as it had many years before. He scanned the ice, but could see nothing.

Ashley was still shuffling towards him.

Had he imagined it?

No, the cracking sound was unmistakable. It was an awful, unforgettable, splitting sound that had haunted many of his dreams.

Oh sweet lord, please, no.

It seemed that Ashley too had heard the sound, for she had stopped and was looking around herself, in a panic.

"NO! Keep moving!" Rupert screamed. His eyes were wide with terror, for he could see it; like a giant arachnid, unfolding its legs, the cracks were actually appearing in front and reaching towards her.

"NO! ASHLEY! RUN! NOW!"

She followed his gaze, and saw the cracks snaking to her. She leapt away from them, towards Rupert, but he was still at least thirty feet away.

She reached out to him.

He reached out to her, "RUN!"

Fifteen feet…the lake was opening up like a wide mouth with jagged teeth.

"ASHLEY!"

But, it was too late.

Rupert's faced drained of all colour, and his heart stopped when, suddenly, just like his brother many years before, she disappeared in front of him.

"NOOO!"

He didn't think, he ran and jumped straight into the water after her, and instantly lost his breath.

It took him a few seconds to make out his surroundings; it was dark beneath the water, the moonlight struggling to pierce the surface.

But then he saw her.

Ashley was near.

She was looking up at him. Her face, distorted with panic in the filtered moonlight.

He struggled, in the freezing water, to reach out to her. His muscles were seizing, his vision blurring, and the more he fought, the further she appeared to drift from him.

Deeper and deeper until...

...he felt something close around his hand, it was hers.

He pulled, but nothing seemed to be happening, yet her face was drifting closer, closer until it was level with his.

Their eyes met in the dreamy white washed world, where light beams danced in the water around them.

Then, she was moving, her body floating gracefully past him, until he could see her feet, and then nothing, but two blue lights.

They drifted towards him, like headlamps in the night; closer and closer, until they took the form of eyes, piercing blue eyes that slowly metamorphosed into a face, one that he recognised, his own.

The End.

EPILOGUE

…Rupert plunges his hands into the freezing lake water, yearning to make contact with any part of his brother's body.

He stretches further and deeper. Further and deeper.

Just a few inches…

…closer…

…closer…

YES!

Contact.

He clutches his brother's outstretched fingers, and then pulls, with all the strength he can muster.

Ben's head emerges from the frigid water, a mass of shudders and splutters.

Rupert moves to heave him out of the icy well, but hesitates. Instead, he looks around. Nobody appears to have heard the commotion. Nobody appears to have heard their screams.

They are alone.

He turns to his brother, who is paralysed by the freeze, barely breathing.

"I'm sorry," he says, and releases his grip, allowing his brother to slip beneath the surface once more.

Rupert watches, as Ben's boyish face contorts into an expression of horrified bewilderment. Slowly, it dissolves into a white blur, until all that remains are his eyes, his beautiful blue eyes that are now, lifelessly, watching him from the watery gloom.

"NOOOOOOO!

Ashley Marshall awoke from her nightmare to a bedroom filled with sunshine.

A year had passed since Rupert Harrison's death, and the same dream had stalked her sleep, periodically, ever since.

She thought about her fiancé as she stepped into the shower, and wondered what their life would have been like, had she not lost him that night to the lake.

It had been very difficult for Ashley to come to terms with the fact that Rupert had given his life for hers.

Detective Sergeant Mark Warner had risked his to free

Rupert from the clutch of the weed that had anchored him beneath the water, but to no avail.

She missed Rupert.

She desperately missed the one man who had truly loved her, the one who had given her more than his money ever could.

Rupert Harrison had made a will, and apart from a trust fund for the upkeep of Kenning Hall, and some donations to friends and a few distant relatives, Ashley had inherited everything.

And she deserved it.

During the past year, she had worked tirelessly to ensure that Harrison Publishing remained one of the biggest, and most successful, publishing houses in the world.

She continued in her vein of publishing highly controversial fiction and non-fiction, and a sensation-hungry public had rewarded her for it.

Not even the over-dramatised hour long special about the Harrison dynasty, which won an award for Abigail Palmer, dented hers or the company's popularity. If anything, it enhanced it; bringing to the world the plight of a woman who had come from a background of pitiless tragedy, and had made good.

Ashley was busy rinsing her hair, so she didn't notice the bathroom door creak open, but she did feel the cold breeze shift the steam around the room.

Her eyes snapped open, and she stiffened as a shadow appeared behind the opaque glass of the cubicle door.

"Ash, I bought us some croissants from the bakery, and I've made tea."

"I'll be right there," she called.

Rachel Harper had moved in with Ashley shortly after the events at Kenning Hall.

The subject of what actually took place that night was often thought of, but never discussed, along with the happenings at Heron Heights, which had ceased as suddenly as they had begun.

The ladies concluded that they were good for each other, because they each empathised with how the other was feeling, albeit for different reasons.

It was a fitting arrangement. One they both knew wouldn't last forever but, for now, it worked.

An hour later, they were sharing cake and hot chocolate outside a café, off Oxford Street.

The air was winter crisp, and the sun was shining brightly in a pale blue sky.

They reminisced about the past year, consciously selecting topics they knew would make them laugh, for they had decided that today would be a happy day.

They often did this, and it had helped them through some of the more difficult times. They covered a variety of subjects, including Harrison Publishing, where Rachel now worked as an IT manager.

Then, as had also become customary, Rachel teased Ashley about Detective Sergeant Mark Warner, with whom Ashley had remained close. Which in turn, prompted Ashley to mention police officer Bass, and tease Rachel about how relationships born of stressful situations seldom worked.

"Who said I'm interested in him for his relationship potential," Rachel said, winking.

"You're so bad."

They chatted happily for most of the day, but paused when they walked by a bookshop window display.

A cardboard stand, sporting the Harrison logo, stood amongst a sea of hardback books, bound in blue.

The author's name, Jackie Harris, stood out in gold lettering upon the faded emblem of the London Metropolitan Police. Underneath it, the title read, *'INSIDE THE MET - A true story.'*

Like the events that it chronicled, the book attracted a lot of media attention, and this helped push it onto the bestseller list.

It was printed from the manuscript that Jackie Harris had entrusted to her lawyer, to be released to Ashley Marshall in the event of her death.

Rachel and Ashley hugged each other.

It was an emotional moment for both of them. The book was a milestone on the road to the rest of their lives, and it would probably be a bumpy one, but together they knew they were going to make it.

***

In a hotel room, on a small island, thousands of miles away, angry eyes read the Financial Times' article about the new Chief Executive Officer of the Harrison Group.

Then, the reader promptly flung the tablet across the room. It bounced off the dresser, and landed on the floor, face up, with a smiling photo of Ashley Marshall.

The lawyer swore.

Adam Lewis had failed.

He had risked everything for this plan. A plan that he had meticulously constructed many years before, and that imbecile had failed!

Now, he had nothing.

But this wasn't over.

Harrison Publishing, the company to which he had devoted the best part of his life, would be his one day, along with the entire Harrison Group.

It was only a matter of time.

Until then, he needed money, but nobody from the consortium that he had assembled, the very men and women who had profited greedily from events that he had orchestrated, were returning his calls.

They were distancing themselves from him. He knew the drill.

James Howard was alone for now, but that would change soon.

Very soon.

Acknowledgements

"As we express our gratitude, we must never forget that the highest appreciation is not to utter words, but to live by them." - John F Kennedy

I'm so very grateful to everyone at a Different Angle, who have supported me throughout this book's journey, from manuscript to print. In particular, I'd like to thank those who have actively contributed to its realisation.

UNSPEAKABLE FOCUS/READER'S GROUP
My heartfelt thanks to all members of the Unspeakable reader's group, for giving so generously of their time and opinions!

(In no particular order)
Francesca Marturano-Pratt, Anna Pratt, Tamanda Flynn, Calvin Everdell, Matthew Ainslie, Slavka Salajova, Karen Harber, Renee Owens and Jane Ransom.

Special thanks goes to Anna Pratt, as always, for being my conscience.

YOU, THE READER
If you're reading this book, there's a good chance you bought it. I'm obviously very grateful for that. Thank you!
On the other hand, if you borrowed this book from somebody else. Even better! It means they thought it was good enough to pass on.

Thank you so much for taking the time.
Without you, my words would be but meaningless letters, arranged on a page.

If you enjoyed Unspeakable, please be sure to leave a glowing review on Amazon, so that others may enjoy it also. If you didn't enjoy it, there are other books to choose from.

Take a look on the following pages…

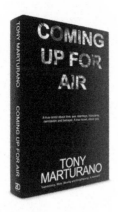

Made in the USA
Coppell, TX
29 March 2022

75695037R00267